How Stephen became Stephanie

and other transgender tales

Kate Lesley

woodlord

www.woodlord.net
www.ebooks-uk.com
www.ebooks-america.com
www.tgfiction.co.uk
www.tvfiction.com

Woodlord Publishing, P.O. Box 36, Chesterfield S40 3YY, UK.

First published by eBooks-UK July 2011
Kindle eBook digital edition
First paperback edition published by Woodlord July 2011
Second paperback edition September 2011

A CIP catalogue record for this book
is available from the British Library

Designed and typeset by Kate Lesley
for eBooks-UK/Woodlord Publishing
Chesterfield, Derbyshire, U.K.

Cover images Mayer George Vladimirovich/Shutterstock.com
Cover design Copyright © Kate Lesley 2011

WOODLORD PUBLISHING
an imprint of eBooks-UK Ltd.

P.O. Box 36, Chesterfield S40 3YY, Derbyshire, UK

ISBN-978-1-906602-15-4

To Rose-Marie, with all my love
and in gratitude for all your help and support

CONTENTS

I was Aunt Mary's Sissy

'You must do as you are told - now put these things on, and no more arguing.'

'But why, Aunt Mary?'

'It's for your own good.'

'But they're girls' clothes.'

'If you want any supper, just put them on.'

There was no arguing with Aunt Mary. After she had stormed out of the room, I stripped off my clothes and lay them on the bed. I stood naked for a few moments, looking at the white nylon bra and panties, honey coloured tights, pale blue blouse, navy pleated skirt and navy lamb's wool cardigan laid out on the candlewick bedspread. I began to shiver - I didn't know whether from the cold, damp atmosphere of the old house, or from fear, anxiety and humiliation at what my aunt had unexpectedly commanded me to do. My mother had warned me that Aunt Mary was eccentric, but I hadn't expected anything like this.

I hurriedly put on the girls' clothes and tip-toed downstairs in my stockinged feet.

'There's a pair of shoes for you,' said Aunt Mary, pointing to a pair of black patent leather sandals at the bottom of the stairs.

'Now put this wig on, girl, until your own hair gets longer,' said Aunt Mary, carefully fitting a blonde curly wig on my head, 'and slip these into your bra-cups.' She handed me two soft conical shapes of foam rubber, covered in white nylon. I undid a couple of buttons of my blouse and slipped them in. Aunt Mary took a wire brush from a shelf of the Welsh dresser and teased out the curls of the wig until they cascaded in soft tresses to just above my shoulders. Then she took a pair of tweezers and plucked my eyebrows into fine arching lines. Finally, she applied some eye-shadow, brushed mascara onto my lashes, and made up my lips with lipstick.

5

'There,' she said, 'now just turn round (she made a twirling motion in the air with her index finger) and let's have a look at you. Hmmn. Not bad. You'll do.'

'But Aunt, I'm not a girl,' I pointed out to her.

'Well you soon will be,' she replied. 'I don't like boys, and I don't know anything about them. If you're going to stay with me, you'll have to be a girl, and that's all there is to it. It's a good job you take after your mother, and not that great hulking brute she married.'

Aunt Mary looked suddenly embarrassed, recalling at that moment that the two people to whom she had just referred - my parents - were recently deceased.

'I'm sorry about your parents, Liam.'

I looked down, not knowing what to say. I felt close to tears - but I was determined not to cry - particularly not in the ridiculous outfit my aunt had forced me to wear. After an embarrassing silence which seemed to go on for ever, punctuated only by the ticking of an ancient clock on the mantle shelf, Aunt Mary said, no doubt in an effort to change the subject:

'Liam. Hmm. We can't call you that. How does Liz sound - or Laura?'

I shrugged my shoulders.

'Come on now, we must call you something.'

'My name is Liam.'

'*Was* Liam. That won't do now. Which is it to be? Liz or Laura?'

'Liz,' I replied sullenly, as it was obvious that she was going to persist, and I had no choice but to reply. I realized as soon as I had said it that I had passed some sort of watershed - by selecting a girl's name for myself I had become complicit in my aunt's scheme to turn me into a girl. My aunt also realized the implication of this small success in getting her way. She tried not to look smug as she said:

'Liz it is, then.'

And that was that. At the age of eleven, my life as a boy had ended. I would never again wear boy's clothes. Under my aunt's tutelage, my transformation into a girl had begun.

Looking back now, I wonder why I didn't protest more; but then I suppose I must still have been in shock and off balance with grief at my parents' sudden death in the car crash, which had happened only a week before. God knows why they saw fit to make Aunt Mary my legal guardian, in the event of their deaths. Perhaps they never seriously considered the possibility that they would both die at once, and that I would be left in her care. Of course that knew that Aunt Mary, my father's spinster sister, had plenty of money - left to her by grandfather Ted, as he knew she would never marry. My father had already started the business by then, and so grandfather left him nothing, assuming that he would be able to fend for myself.

My mother's relatives were poor but at least normal - uncle Fred was a bus driver at that time, I think; it was later he went into the insurance trade, though he never made much money at it. Too honest, Auntie Dot always said. I'm sure things would have been much more normal if I'd gone to live with Uncle Fred and Auntie Dot.

Everyone knew Aunt Mary was - strange. And what she did to me was certainly not normal. She claimed to have special intuitive powers, the 'second sight' as she called it. She believed she sensed something about me: 'a dark feminine stream in your subconscious,' she called it. I don't know where she got all the Freudian stuff from - perhaps she had psychoanalysis during her stay at Walthorpe Hospital. No one in the family liked to mention that she'd been in a mental hospital for several months when she was a young woman. Mother told me once it was after a young officer in the RAF had promised to marry her and then was found to have got another girl into trouble, whom he had to marry instead. Aunt Mary never got over it - and carried a grudge against all the male sex from then on. Perhaps that was why she did what she did to me - she couldn't bear the thought of having a male around.

She claimed it was for my own good, of course - something she sensed that I really wanted myself, though I might not know it. And before I had time to recover from the shock of my parents' deaths and realize what was happening, she had put her plans for me in motion. I was very vulnerable; still stricken with grief, I was beyond the point of caring. I went through the next months like a sleep-walker in a dream, unable to resist my Aunt's scheme to turn me into a girl. It was as if I knew what was happening but was detached from myself; I watched from without, like a disembodied soul, as my transformation went on. I observed but somehow felt uninvolved; perhaps it was the grief and shock working their way through, which made me so submissive to her will. Or perhaps she was right about me - and there was something in me, some impulse towards the feminine, which made the whole thing inevitable. At any rate, by the time I came to fully appreciate what had been done to me, it was already too late - the process had gone too far to turn back. Everyone who knew me thought of me as a girl - I cannot deny that I had come to think of myself as one. I had got used to wearing girls' clothes, to being referred to as 'she', 'her', etc. I was Liz, the young niece who had come to live with her Aunt Mary after the tragic death of her parents. All the locals in the village and on the farms around Aunt Mary's cottage knew me as Liz. How could it suddenly be revealed to them that I was actually a boy?

The process by which Aunt Mary feminized me was inexorable, a carefully thought-out campaign which I had no resources to resist. Having got me into girls' clothes that first night, she made it clear that there was no question of me ever resuming my life as a boy. I was Liz, her niece - and that was that. All my male clothes and the few boy's toys I had brought with me were disposed of - burned or put in the dustbin. I was given no respite from her relentless crusade to feminize me.

At night, I was expected to wear a nightie. She had given me several pink and cream silk nighties with lace around the collars and hems. When my own hair was long enough, she would tie it in bunches with pink ribbons, or pull it back in a pony tail. When it was longer still, she would make me kneel before her in front of the fire and brush out the tangles until my hair cascaded in soft curls about my shoulders and down my back; then sometimes she would plait it or dress it in a French braid.

'You are lucky to have such beautiful hair,' she would murmur dreamily to me, as she slowly brushed it; 'it was wasted on a boy - how much better you are as a girl, don't you agree?'

At first I didn't reply to these sort of comments, which she made frequently. Noticing my lack of response, she would then brush my hair more vigorously, pulling it with such force that it made my eyes water and I wanted to cry out. I quickly learnt that it would be less painful for me if I agreed with her that I was better off as a girl.

My education was a matter to which Aunt Mary had apparently already given consideration. She announced to me one morning that of course it would not be possible for me to attend the local state comprehensive school, and she had therefore contracted the services of a private tutor for me - a Miss Wimpole.

Miss Wimpole turned out to be a severe-looking spinster in her late thirties, her prematurely greying hair scraped back in a bun. Miss Wimpole was thin to the point of being scrawny; she wore dark, drab clothes and had absolutely no sense of humour. I can never remember having seen her laugh, although I do recall one time when a grim smile broke out on her thin lips, cracking her characteristically pained expression - the occasion was when Aunt Mary's revolting wheezy pug-dog was made to run for its life across the lawns, hotly pursued by a black and tan sheep-dog from the neighbouring farm.

'My poor Dodo!' wailed Aunt Mary, seeing the wretched animal come snuffling in at the back door of the kitchen; 'did that horrid common farm dog chase my little diddy Doddy?'

Aunt Mary was apparently besotted with the animal,

an enthusiasm which Miss Wimpole did not share, having fallen over the pug more than once due to its habit of sleeping, spread out like a bolster, in the middle of the study floor.

Miss Wimpole gave me instruction not just in the normal school subjects but also in all activities most girlish and feminine. I was taught by her to sew and embroider; to paint dainty watercolour landscapes; to dance, taking the female part. My aunt instructed me in the culinary and domestic arts, and soon expected me to do my share of cooking, washing, ironing and cleaning. My aunt had at first employed a help daily, but when I had become proficient enough at domestic chores, she dispensed with the woman's services two days a week, and on these days I was expected to do all the cooking and household work. My aunt had bought a maid's uniform for me to wear at such times - a little black silk dress with a white apron edged with frills and lace, and underneath, a stiff white frilly petticoat which made the dress stick out a little and just showed beneath the hem, black seamed stockings, and suspender belt. Very high-heeled black court shoes which I found painful to walk very far in until I got used to them, completed the outfit. My hair was pulled back in a pony tail tied with a black silk ribbon. My aunt delighted to see me in my maid's outfit, performing menial tasks. It was as if in humiliating me in this way, she has scored some victory over the whole male sex.

You make a good little maid and will make someone a good wife one day,' my aunt commented on more than one occasion, a twinkle in her eye. I sincerely hoped that this was her idea of a joke, although I began to wonder if this wasn't more in the nature of a prediction.

When it looked as if I was beginning to reach puberty, Aunt Mary took me to the local doctor, an elderly man who had treated me from time to time for the normal childhood ailments. Doctor Stringer, having had no need during these minor bouts of illness to look in my knickers, had naturally assumed that I was a girl, and was flabbergasted to discover my true sex. He made an appointment for me to see a specialist in gender identity problems at a London clinic, who quickly diagnosed me as transsexual, my aunt having informed the specialist that I had begged to dress as a girl from the first day that I had come to stay with her, and that although she had misgivings about it, she had finally gone along with my wishes, as it was so obviously what I wanted. This hardly represented the truth as I recalled it, but as by this time I had been living as a girl for several years, there didn't seem much point in setting the record straight.

The specialist put me on female hormones immediately, which blocked any beard growth, and prevented my voice from breaking. Over the next few months, I noticed too that I was starting to grow breasts and that my hips were broadening. Aunt Mary rejoiced to see these changes in me:

'You're blossoming into a shapely young woman, and no mistake,' she said to me, grinning like the cat that had got the cream.

As soon as I turned eighteen the specialist put me forward for gender reassignment surgery. There was no need for me to prove that I could live in the female role, as I had been living as a girl for seven years by then. I had the operation, which was both traumatic and painful, and after the normal period of recuperation in hospital, and examinations by the surgeons to check that my new female genitals were working properly, I was pronounced fit to return home to Aunt Mary.

I was now undeniably and forever her niece. Aunt Mary was overjoyed. As for me, I have accepted my fate. I am a girl, I accept what Aunt Mary has done to me. At least now that I have had the operation, I can wear a bikini and go swimming if I want to.

Last summer I went on holiday to Spain with Aunt Mary; she loved to see me in my bikini, sunbathing on the beach.

'I expect you feel so much better, now you've got

11

rid of all that rubbish between your legs,' she said. I smiled, looking down at my broad hips, flat tummy, and the feminine curve between my legs. And yes, I have to admit it, I enjoy being a girl.

© *Kate Lesley 1994*

I turned my husband into a girl

It's true, I turned my husband into a girl. Why did I do it? How did I do it?

As to why I did it - I suppose it has a lot to do with my own preferences. I didn't realise what I wanted, for a long time. I knew things weren't right as they were before; neither of us was very happy. Whereas now - I have my career, and a partner who really suits me - and I think she's happy too. I say 'she' quite naturally, because my partner is a girl, now - though she wasn't always.

But let me start at the beginning. I met - John, as he was then - at university. We were the same age, but he was in his first year at university - a 'fresher' - and I was a second year student. He had taken a year off after his 'A' levels to travel and see a bit of the world. He had spent some time in Australia, and there was something of the 'wild colonial boy' about him when we first met. He was quite small but sturdily built - he said it was all the 'T'-bone steaks and Aussie beer - and there was a slight Australian twang to his accent. His hair was long, curly and fair - bleached blonder by the Australian sun. He struck me at once as the 'rugged individualist' type - he had his own views on things, and was quite prepared to argue his point - but he was also fair-minded, and had a gentle side. He had an anarchic and irreverent sense of humour, which often made his hazel eyes sparkle - his whole face lit up with mirth, at times. I liked him at once - he was just such good fun to be with.

That's what John was like, what originally attracted me to *him*. And what is *she* like now - the person whom John became? *Joanne* is an attractive blonde with a stunning 38-26-36 figure; she is very feminine and enjoys being a girl very much. I look at Joanne, sunning herself in her bikini on the patio, or 'done up to the nines' in her favourite little black cocktail dress and high heels, waiting for the taxi to take us out - two girls together - for a night on the town, and I marvel at the transformation, even though I know how it happened, and indeed was instrumental in bringing it about. And it seems so - *right* - for her, for both of us.

I first saw John in the student History Society common room - a bit of a 'dive' in the basement of the History block, where you could get coffee and sit around on battered sofas chatting between lectures. John was immersed in conversation with a dark-haired girl wearing an Afghan jacket. This was the early Seventies, the tail end of hippydom - flaired jeans, 'peace' and 'love', and all that. I wandered casually over to where John and the dark-haired girl were sitting, and stood near them, trying to eavesdrop on their conversation. John was talking about Australia - about some youth hostel he had stayed at near Cairns, where all the people were permanently stoned, having done the 'trans-Asia' hippy trail via Kathmandu. It sounded very exciting and exotic, and I wanted to but in and ask all sorts of questions. I was frankly jealous of the dark-haired girl, another first-year student, who was doing the same course as John.

Just then a stream of students started pouring into the common room - a lecture must have just ended - and one of them nudged me in the back as he was trying to ease his way through the throng to the coffee machine. I overbalanced (I was wearing platform-soled clogs at the time) and tipped my coffee in John's lap (it was an accident, I swear!). He jumped up in surprise, although fortunately the coffee wasn't too hot by that time - and before I knew it, I was trying to wipe down his lap with some tissues from my bag, spluttering my apologies. In doing this, I was suddenly aware that I was rubbing his crotch, which was standing out rather prominently, in the tight brushed-denim flares he was wearing. I blushed - we both did - and I was impressed by his presence of mind and gallantry when he said:

'Look, let me get you another coffee. I was just going for one, anyway.' He looked at the dark-haired girl and asked: 'Do you want another coffee, Helen?'

I caught a furious glance directed towards me from the dark-haired girl, who then shook her head and got up, mumbling sulkily that she had to go and do some work in the library.

And that was how we met. We hit it off straight away, and were virtually inseparable. John was in a hall of residence, as it was his first year; I had a flat down Horewood Road, which I shared with two other girls. We had a Welsh landlady who was pretty tolerant, given her 'chapel' background, but she drew the line at boys staying all night. John left about midnight most evenings, starting his old motor bike with a fearful clatter and roar - when it chose to fire up; sometimes he had to push it back to his hall.

After going to a rock concert or a film, we would occasionally spend the night together in his hall room. More than once, the hall cleaning lady had a shock when she found us squashed like sardines in his narrow bed, in the morning!

I was surprised to discover, on the first night that we spent together, that John was still a virgin. However, he soon became an enthusiastic but sensitive lover; he knew just how to please me, and was so tender and delicate in his loving - there was something almost girlish about him even then.

When the Easter holidays came John and I drove up to the Lake District in my little Renault. He'd got a tent and other camping gear which he'd brought back from Australia. We spent a lovely couple of weeks walking around the Langdale Pikes, before returning to the city. It was still a week before the new term was due to start, and I suggested while we were driving back that as my two flat mates were still away and wouldn't be back for a few days, John could come and stay in Horewood Road.

'What about Miss Jones - won't she object?' asked

John.

'She's away as well - she's gone back to Wales to visit some of her relatives,' I replied.

'What about the neighbours?'

I stared through the windscreen of the Renault, watching the tail lights of the lorry ahead. Then I said:

'I've got an idea.'

'What?'

'Well, with boys having long hair, and everyone wearing jeans and all, it's quite difficult to tell whether someone's a boy or a girl - particularly if it's dark, and you're wearing a long coat.'

'Are you suggesting what I think you're suggesting,' asked John, 'you're going to try to pass me off as a girl when we go into the flat?' John's looked doubtful - but I noticed a twinkle in his eyes which meant thast he might be persuaded, if I could convince him it would be fun.

'The thing is, John, the neighbours around here are such prying, meddlesome types that they will probably tell Miss Jones if they think there's been a boy staying all night; on the other hand, they couldn't say anything if they just saw a girl coming in with me. They might even mistake you for Sarah - one of my flat mates - you're about the same height, and you're both blond.'

So we stopped in a deserted lay-by and I tied John's long blond hair back in a ponytail, which is how Sarah usually has her hair, and clipped a pair of dangly ear-rings on him. He slipped on my long black raincoat, and as a finishing touch, I made up his eyes with eye-shadow and a little mascara.

'You look great - your own mother wouldn't know you,' I announced, surveying my handiwork.

John looked abashed, but his eyes were gleaming with merriment.

'I wonder what my father would say, if he could see me now,' he said.

That night, in bed in Horewood Road, our love-making

was more intense and energetic than ever. John seemed especially randy.

'I think pretending to be a girl turns you on,' I said to him. I had put John's head between my legs, and was enjoying the feeling of him lapping me and nuzzling me with his nose. I stroked his long blond hair and massaged his neck, then ran my fingers over his shoulders and back. His skin felt soft and smooth - he didn't seem to have much body hair or muscle development for a boy. I was glad - I have always hated 'he-men', hairy macho types who think they are God's gift to women. I once had a boyfriend with a hairy back; I was disgusted when I first saw him without his shirt on - he reminded me of a gorilla.

John had fine blond hairs on his arms and legs, which didn't notice very much; and very little hair on his chest. I found myself very attracted to him, to his smell, his soft warm body - and some indefinable, almost feminine quality about him, which I had never found in a man before.

He rolled over on his back and I got on top of him, giving him my tit to suck, guiding it to his lips with my fingers. He nibbled and sucked at my nipple until I felt as if it would burst in his mouth. I pulled gently away, moving my hand down until I found his cock, hot and hard as iron; I gripped hold of it and guided it towards the wetness between my legs. I couldn't wait to feel him inside me again, rubbing and massaging and moving on the places which turned me on. I wanted to possess him entirely, to swallow him utterly, to get him so far up inside me that we would be one.

Afterwards, when we were laying back on the pillows, he said:

'Do you know how an angel is made? An angel is made when two people who love each other come together so completely and finally that they fuse and make one new being - a being made entirely of love. Do you think we will make an angel, one day?'

I turned my head to look into his hazel eyes, and

noticed for the first time how small his face was, and how delicate his features. I ran my finger over his finely arched brows, and then slowly down the line of his small, slightly retroussé nose, to his full, feminine lips. He kissed the end of my finger as I said:

'You are so beautiful, I think you must be an angel already. You are far too beautiful to be a boy.'

It was that night that I began to fall in love with him.

In the cold light of morning, we began to consider for the first time some practicalities of our position.

'What are the neighbours going to think,' asked John, as we were eating toast together at the little pine table in the kitchen, 'if they saw what they thought was a girl going in with you last night, and a boy comes out with you this morning?'

'Mmm. They may not have been watching last night,' I replied, 'but they most certainly will see you this morning, in daylight.'

'Is it that serious?'

'Well, they probably *will* tell Miss Jones, if they see you - and it will be fairly obvious that you spent the night here. And what about the rest of the week? I was hoping we could spend the whole week together. Miss Jones is a fairly harmless old dear - if it was just up to her, she probably wouldn't mind. But she obviously has to keep up appearances with the neighbours, and she is a chapel-goer. She can't leave herself open to charges that anything immoral has gone on in her house. The lease comes up for renewal at the end of next term, and I was hoping to keep the flat for another year. She might not allow me to renew it, if she thinks I've been having boys sleeping overnight.'

'What can we do then?'

'There is something we *could* try, but I don't know whether you'll agree to it.'

'Try me.'

'Well, we could try passing you off as a girl, for the whole week.'

'It would never work.'

'Why not? You've got long enough hair already. You're not very big - I reckon some of Sarah's clothes and shoes might fit you.'

'Good God - you're serious, aren't you?'

'Well why not give it a try? What do we have to lose? If we succeed - we shall manage to spend the week together in perfect safety, and I won't have to worry about losing the lease. If we don't pull it off - I'm no worse off than I would be if they found out you were a bloke from the start - I can only lose the lease once.

'Anyway, I think you'll be quite convincing. The first thing we have to do is make it quite clear that you're a girl when you leave the house this morning. The best thing is for you to wear a skirt. That'll leave people in no doubt. Although the hairs on your legs are quite fine and fair, I think you'd better begin by shaving them. Sarah tends to favour short skirts, and you'll probably have to wear one of hers. You'd also better shave your face as close as you can. I'll go and see what Sarah's got in her wardrobe that might fit you, while you get on with that.'

While John was shaving his face and legs, I found a pink panty and bra set, edged with lace, and a pair of honey coloured tights from my own underwear drawer, which I left on the bed, while I went into Sarah's room to look through her skirts and blouses. I shouted to John through the bathroom door:

'I've left some things on the bed for you to put on, when you've finished shaving.'

I wanted to see if he would put on the bra and panties without further prompting from me.

When I came back, carrying several skirts and blouses over my arm, I was pleased to see John sitting on the bed wearing the bra and panties, and struggling to put the tights on.

'Here, let me show you how to do that,' I said, going over and sitting on the bed next to him. I demonstrated how to start off the tights by rolling them over one toe at a time. When they were up as far as his knees, I said to him:

19

'Now stand up, and carefully roll them up the rest of the way, and make sure you pull them up firmly round the gusset.'

When John had done this I could see a little bulge between his legs, which seemed to be growing.

'I think you're enjoying this!' I exclaimed.

John blushed and looked embarrassed, but didn't say anything.

'We can't have you going out with a bulge like that,' I pointed out ' - it might show beneath you mini-skirt. Can't you do anything about it? Try pushing your bits down between your legs more, and then pulling on the panties and tights a bit tighter.'

John tried this, but it didn't seem to work. Then I had another idea. Naomi, the other girl I shared the flat with, was rather plump. She might have a bigger size of knickers or some other underwear which would help. I went into Naomi's room and searched through her underwear drawers. I was in luck - I found a black elasticated garment - a sort of panty-corset - which looked as if it might do the trick.

'Take off what you're wearing, try to push your bits down as hard as you can and pull them between your legs, and then put this on,' I said, handing him the panty-corset, 'pull it up as high as you can.'

John did as he was told, without demur. I looked at the black corset and pink bra he was wearing. I went round behind him and unhooked the bra. I put it back in the drawer and found a black lacy bra that matched the corset better. I helped him on with it and said:

'Now put the tights back on.'

He rolled on the tights as I had shown him and pulled them up. I looked at the now smooth, rounded contours between his legs, nodding with approval. There was no sign of any tell-tale male bump - he looked exactly like a girl there. I got some tissues and made two little rounded wads, which I inserted in his bra so they filled out the cups but could not be seen above the lace.

Then I told him to sit at the chair by the dressing table.

I picked up a pair of tweezers and said:

'This could hurt a bit.'

I began working on his eyebrows. They were by no means bushy, but I plucked them into fine arcs. I looked at his face, which was already beginning to look distinctly feminine, and wondered whether I'd gone too far. I swivelled the chair round so that he couldn't see himself in the mirror. I found some foundation on the dressing table and began to apply it to his face, smoothing it onto his upper lip, around his jaw and neck, and over his cheeks. John's beard was very light, and hardly showed normally; with the foundation, any sign of it was gone, and his face looked even more smooth and girlish. I powder-puffed his face to fix the foundation, then added a little highlight each side just below the line of the cheek bone. Then I got to work on his eyes, using several shades of shadow, a darker shade on the outer part of his lids and crease line, toning to a lighter shade on the brow bone, under the eyebrows. I was grateful that I had worked the previous summer holiday in my Aunt Sue's beauty parlour, as it had given me some valuable insights into how to use make-up to help plain middle-aged women look attractive - a pretty young boy like John was no challenge at all by comparison. I put two coats of waterproof mascara on John's lashes, and a soft cherry shade of lipstick on his full lips, which I outlined with a fine lip-pencil in a darker shade. Finally, I painted his fingernails in a cherry colour which matched the lipstick. The whole time, John just sat there and let me do it, without saying a word. He seemed to be in a sort of trance state.

I gave him a short nylon mini-slip, which he put on. Then I helped him try on various combinations of skirts and blouses until we found something which suited him and was a good fit. We settled for an emerald green corduroy mini-skirt with a wide black belt of tooled leather, and a white silk blouse with a soft collar trimmed with lace. I took him into Sarah's room to try on some of her shoes, but although they were about the right size,

21

they proved to be too narrow for his foot. We next went into Naomi's room, and I found a pair of medium-heeled black leather court shoes in the bottom of her wardrobe. John slipped them on - and they proved to be a good fit.

'You must have very small feet for a man,' I said.

'I take a six and a half,' he replied.

We went back into my room, and I sat him down on the bed. I went to work on his long, wavy hair, trimming up the uneven ends and brushing it into a feminine style, with a centre parting.

I led him over to my wardrobe and opened it so that he could see himself in the full-length mirror attached to the inside of the door. He gasped at the sight he saw in the mirror - a beautiful blonde girl with long slender legs, a slim waist, and a very pretty face. I saw his eyes open wide in amazement. I think something happened to him in that moment - the birth of Joanne, perhaps. He swung himself slowly first to one side, then to the other, before slowly twirling all the way round, his eyes all the time transfixed by the reflection in the mirror. Even in that first movement, there was the beginning of something feminine and graceful.

Finally, he said in a quiet voice:

'I just don't believe it.'

'I know, I can hardly believe it myself; but it's you, all right. You make a stunning girl. You are really wasted as a boy.'

And so that was the start of it. We found a handbag and coat for him, and we went out shopping. John was from the start very convincing as a girl, but it wouldn't be true to say that he didn't get anyone staring at him. He certainly did - he looked such a pretty girl, that he caught the eye of quite a few lads while we were out, and even got one or two wolf whistles. At first he didn't know how to deal with this - then, when he realised that he was attracting attention as an attractive *girl*, he began not to worry. He didn't quite dare smile back yet at any lad who was eyeing him, but I began to notice the beginnings of little feminine movements that I can only describe as flirtatious - a slight swaying of the hips, or the way he crossed his legs, when we were sitting in a coffee bar. He was discovering what all attractive young girls discover, the power of feminine allure to attract the male of the species. You could see him enjoying this new power. I could hardly believe what I was seeing! This boy with whom I had made passionate love the night before was turning into a coquettish young girl before my eyes!

At first I didn't know what to think. I was glad that our plan was working out so well - clearly there would be no problem fooling the neighbours in Horewood Road - but I began to realise that something fairly drastic had happened. I had lost John, and in his place there was this totally new person - this *girl*.

'I can't call you John while you're dressed like that,' I whispered to him, as we were sitting next to each other in the coffee bar. 'We'll have to think of a girl's name. What about - *Joanne*?'

John looked confused for a moment, as if he hadn't considered this, then smiled and nodded.

'Welcome to the wonderful world of being a girl, Joanne!' I teased him.

John, or rather - *Joanne* - didn't dare to speak out loud while we were out the first day, for fear that her voice would give her away. We communicated in whispers or by non-verbal signals; I would ask Joanne a question, and she would nod or shake her head in reply, or indicate that she was ready to go by picking up her handbag and glancing towards the door.

When we got home to Horewood road that night, I said to her:

'We can't carry on like this, Joanne; you're going to have to learn to speak like a girl, so that when we're out we can talk normally.'

I suggested that she shouldn't try to put on a falsetto, but just lighten and soften the tone of her natural voice. She practised doing this, and with some more coaching from me, had managed by bedtime to modify her voice to sound very passably like that of a young woman. It had a slightly husky quality that I always think sounds rather sexy in a woman, but Joanne had been able to capture and imitate with comparative ease those modulations of speech which instantly establish the feminine gender of a person - even on the telephone.

I notice that I am already referring to Joanne as *she* and *her*; I am unable to think of her, even at this early stage, as anything other than a girl. It was remarkable! John had allowed me to transform him into *Joanne* without offering any objection or even showing hesitation; and the transformation had been accomplished with such ease! I couldn't quite believe what I had done already, and I wondered how much further I could go with him.

I put a cream baby-doll nightie and matching frilly panties on the bed, and told him to undress and put them on. And would you believe it? - *he just did it!*

Our love-making that night was more marvellous than ever, though I noticed that he seemed particularly to enjoy being underneath me, with his legs open, while I rode down on top of him.

John spent the rest of the week as Joanne, wearing various outfits which we put together from the clothes in Sarah's and Naomi's wardrobes. On the Saturday, Joanne had to make do with jeans and a tee shirt of mine, while we washed and dried the clothes at the launderette, then ironed them together before putting them away. Joanne was so natural in the feminine role by now that I was finding it hard to remember that she was really a boy, and would have to go back to being John next week. We decided to give Joanne one final outing - a sort of grand finale to her week as a girl. We'd been invited to a party by some student nurses, in one of the big houses that fringed Princess Park, where they each had a flat. The whole house - all three floors of it - was going to be opened up for the party, which had been advertised on the notice board in the students' union. The nurses were expecting the numbers to go into three figures. It was going to be a 'bring your own booze, do your own thing' typical student bash.

I found a ruby velour mini-dress of my own which Joanne could just get into, and a pair of very high-heeled black stilletto shoes of Naomi's which I thought went well with the dress. I suggested that as it would probably get hot at the party, Joanne might prefer to wear stockings and a suspender-belt, so that she could at least stay cool between the legs and around the thighs. I had slipped out from the launderette while we were there earlier in the day, telling Joanne I was just going to get some more change for the drier from the tobacconist on the corner, but in fact I had gone across the road to a lingerie shop and bought a lacy black suspender-belt and some sheer black stockings, which I was dying to see Joanne wearing. I don't know why - the thought of Joanne in suspender-belt and stockings just turned me on. Perhaps it was knowing 'she' was really a *boy*, or perhaps it was the start of - *other feelings* - which I became more aware of in the years ahead.

Anyway, I helped Joanne on with the stockings and suspender belt, showing her how to hitch the stockings; then I really did a good job on her make-up and hair, pinning up her blonde locks with slides and combs into a sophisticated 'evening' style. We doused ourselves with some rather expensive French perfume my brother had given me, which I only used on special occasions, and then we were ready - two attractive girls stepping out with an evening of fun ahead of them!

And what a night we had! The party was really wild, going on to about four in the morning. Joanne and I both got fairly well plastered, and we both had to fend off numerous attempts by young drunken males at the party to pick us up! I saw more than one roving hand on Joanne's thigh or bottom during the course of the evening - but somehow she managed to stop any of the boys from going too far - not that I think that any of them would

25

have been able to discover her true sex, which was pretty well concealed by the panty-corset.

It seemed obvious that Joanne was having a good time at the party, and wasn't at all fazed by playing the role of a *her*, rather than a *him*.

The next morning, John had to go back to his room in hall, ready for the start of term. He left Horewood Road for the last time as Joanne, in jeans, pony tail and duffle-coat; we drove to a lay-by and I wiped off the few traces of make-up he was still wearing and took the elastic bobble out of his hair. I surveyed him critically; his eyebrows still looked pretty plucked, but I scuffed my fingers through his hair and pulled a hank down partly to conceal his brows. He would pass as a boy - just! I felt sad; he looked so plain and boring and colourless as a boy. I felt such a pang of tenderness - for this person whom I had got to know so well, during the last week. But for which person? It was the company of *Joanne* that I had enjoyed - I realised that I wanted to see *her* again. How could I bring this about?

John and I carried on going out together, for the rest of out time at university. I finished my course a year before him, and took a clerical job in the city works department while he finished his degree. Then we moved down to London and set up flat together in Clapham. John got an administrative job with the G.L.C., and I managed to get into a publishing firm in Covent Garden, where I began to work my way up the career ladder.

Neither of us ever mentioned that strange week in Horewood Road, yet I couldn't help remembering it - and how close we'd been. After a couple of years living in Clapham we got married and bought a small terrace house in Norwood. I hoped that getting married would bring us closer together, but if anything, within a few months, we seemed to be drifting farther apart. Neither of us was happy - although my career was going well; I'd been promoted to Assistant Editor in the fiction department and was beginning to handle some quite important writers.

John's career seemed to be going nowhere - he was stuck amid the complex structure of grades in local government, on which there was sometimes no promotion for years, and there was the first talk of the G.L.C. being disbanded. He was growing to hate the daily drudge of commuting to London, to a job which no longer held any interest for him.

His company, I have to admit, was becoming rather boring to me, and I began to make excuses not to go straight home after work, preferring to go out for a drink or a meal with colleagues from the publishing house - or occasionally with a writer, who had come up to London to discuss some editorial point.

Conscious of the dangers of a 'romance at work', and not wishing to be unfaithful to John, I avoided going out with male colleagues - particularly if they were young and attractive - but could see no harm in dining with a female writer who was on my list, or having a 'girls night out' with one or two of the other female editors. I would explain to John that I had to work late, and he always accepted this without complaint.

After I had been at the publishing house for five years, I was offered a very good job by a rival house; they 'head-hunted' me to take over as chief editor of their feminist authors. I accepted, as it meant a lot more money. John meanwhile had resigned in disgust from his job at the G.L.C. when he had failed to get even one step up to the next grade at his annual review; he was now out of work, and feeling pretty depressed. What made it all the worse was that it was obvious that my career was going so well; he didn't begrudge me my success, but I could tell that it hurt his male pride that he hadn't done better himself.

One of the writers on my list in the new job was a radical feminist, who wanted to meet with me to discuss some revisions she was making to the final draft of her latest book   Alyson Jedburgh her name was - she's not very well-known now, but she was up there with Germaine Greer in the halcyon days of women's lib. I rang Alyson up and asked her if she would like to go for a meal at a new Chinese restaurant which had recently opened in Soho, and was supposed to do authentic Szechwanese food.

'Yes, let's go for it - I love Chinese food,' replied Alyson, 'and I know one or two clubs in the area we could try afterwards, if you like.'

'Great, I'll meet you at the restaurant then, at eight o'clock.'

I hung up.

The meal proved to be delicious - we had Chinese dumplings with spicy fillings, and various noodle and rice dishes, which we shared.

After the meal, we walked to one of the clubs which Alyson suggested, which proved to be - interesting. It was called 'Lips', and was a gay club which catered mainly for lesbians, although there were one or two transvestites in there as well. I looked at one of them, a gorgeous long-legged creature in a black leather mini-skirt and stillettos, her black hair in a spiky punk-cut. Her face was whitened with pan-stick and her arched brows were pencilled in black; her lids had matt black shadow on them. Her lips were like a crimson gash in her white face. She was wearing a red silk top under her leather jacket that revealed a cleavage which looked real. Alyson saw me staring.

'Hormones,' she whispered. 'She's a trannie all right, or more likely transsexual. Calls herself 'Angel' - she's a regular in here.'

'It's hard to believe she's not a real girl, with a figure and face like that,' I commented. And that set me thinking about John, and remembering that strange week in Horewood Road, when we were students. I began to get an idea.

I found I rather enjoyed the rest of my evening at 'Lips'; the clientele were interesting not just to look at, but to talk to. Alyson and I got into conversation with one or two of her lesbian friends, and one of them asked me to dance. After we'd danced, she took me to the bar and bought me a drink, a double Southern Comfort, I think. I was beginning to feel a bit light-headed, as we had already had some wine in the Chinese restaurant. The girl I had just danced with, a rather 'butch' young woman with short red hair, wearing Levi 501's and a white tee shirt, asked me my name.

'Debbie,' I replied.

'You know, you're very pretty, Debbie,' she whispered, and she leant across and kissed me full on the lips. I was taken aback, but didn't find the sensation unpleasant. I looked at the red-headed girl, screwing up my eyes to try and focus on her face.

'What's your name?' I asked.

'Roz,' she replied.

'Funny name,' I said. I giggled. Alyson was watching what was going on with amusement.

'Come on,' said Alyson, 'time to get you out of here. You can come back to my place for a coffee, if you like - to sober you up a bit before you go home.'

I nodded.

Alyson had an attic flat ('pent-house', she called it) in a large bay-fronted Victorian house in Wimbledon. There were overgrown pot-plants on the window sills, pre-Raphaelite prints on the white-washed walls, and Moroccan rugs on the stripped-oak floor boards; on the back of the living room door was a print of Angela Davis with an Afro hairstyle, doing a clenched fist black-militant salute.

I sat down on the sofa, and Alyson brought in a mug of coffee for us both and put them down on a low glass table. She switched on the hifi, selected a cassette of Joan Armatrading singing 'Love and Affection', and sat down beside me on the sofa.

Neither of us spoke. The air seemed charged with

electricity.

Alyson moved closer to me on the sofa, and put her arm round me. Gently, she began stroking one of my breasts. I didn't stop her. She kissed me, and then asked:

'Do you want to spend the night?'

I thought of poor, boring John, but couldn't muster much enthusiasm to rush back to him. What was happening here with Alyson was interesting - and dangerous.

'I'm expected back,' I said.

'Why not 'phone and say you've missed the last train, and I'm putting you up for the night?' said Alyson.

I made the call.

That was how I discovered that I liked women - sexually. I saw Alyson - and slept with her - several more times over the next few weeks, and she showed me some of the ways that women have of giving pleasure to each other. Eventually, after the editing work on Alyson's book was finished and it was ready for publication, we drifted apart. Alyson had introduced me to a whole new world of lesbian sexual experience, for which I was grateful, but what was I to do now?

I was stuck with John. What could I do?

Seeing the punk transsexual at the night club had already given me the germ of an idea; the discovery of my lesbian tendencies made me think that perhaps the idea was worth trying. What was there to lose? I didn't think my marriage to John was likely to last much longer, if things carried on as they were; we were drifting further and further apart.

So I decided to try it. The very next day I went shopping for clothes in my lunch hour, and again after work.

When I got home that night, I found a note from John saying he had gone to visit an old school friend in Islington and didn't expect to be home until late in the evening. This gave me a chance to empty his clothes drawers of male underwear and socks; I put them all in dustbin liners together with his shirts, suits, and jumpers, and took the sacks to the Oxfam shop round the corner.

When I got back I went upstairs and layed out the clothes I'd bought on the bed:

I'd got six 'firm control' black bodyshapers from Marks and Spencer, in strong elesticated material, with lace on the side panels and around the legs. They were in several sizes, the largest for waist 27-28 inches, and hips 38-40 inches; the smallest for waist 24-25 inches and hips 34-36 inches. My plan was to put him in the largest size first, and then gradually get him into the smaller sizes over the next few weeks, as he got used to the feeling of constriction. They were intended for ladies who were fighting 'flab' on the tummy and hips, but the elasticated material was strong enough to smooth away any tell-tale male bits and give him a lovely flat female contour between the legs. I had first visited a specialist shop for transvestites and drag queens off Tottenham Court Road, where they sold an item called a 'cache-sex', a little pink rubberized sling similar to a jock-strap which was intended to pull back the male genitals - but it looked rather unattractive and clinical to me. I figured the bodyshapers would do the job just as well, and were much more pleasingly feminine. I wanted to get him used to real female underwear as soon as possible, so that it would be clear that he wasn't 'playing' at being a girl, but was to think of himself, right from the outset, as a real girl. The drag shop did provide a couple of useful items, however, which I couldn't get anywhere else - a pair of very life-like silicon breast prostheses, which the assistant assured me had a realistic feel, weight and bounce, and could be worn with or without a bra. Even with a low-cut evening dress or a swimming costume, they were guaranteed to provide a realistic cleavage.

For the rest of John's new wardrobe, I shopped at high street stores like Dorothy Perkins, Etam, and Miss Selfridge, buying a variety of skirts, dresses, blouses, tops and jackets, in sizes 12-14. He had not been eating properly for some months, probably as a result of his depression, and had lost quite a lot of weight; I guessed that he was already somewhere around a size 14, and I had hopes of getting him down to a 12, or perhaps even a 10, in time.

I chose several pairs of shoes for him, including low-heeled court shoes, strappy sandals, and two pairs of spiky high-heels. I got plenty of underwear - packets of tights in differents shades, suspender belts and stockings, lacy bras, full and half-length slips - and some very feminine nighties, edged with lace and ribbon. I'd also bought two wigs, a blonde wavy one in about the same shade as his own hair, and a shoulder-length bobbed style; these would do until his own hair had grown longer.

I put most of the clothes away in the drawers and wardrobe, leaving out on the bed a pair of the bodyshaper panties, a matching Marks and Spencer bra, a pair of black 10 denier tights, a silky blouse and lycra mini-skirt, also in black. I left the low-heeled court shoes on the rug at the foot of the bed and combed out the blonde curly wig, placing it on a stand which the assistant at the wig store had provided free of charge, as I had bought two wigs.

On the dressing table I put a new pair of tweezers and a selection of cosmetics.

I surveyed the room with satisfaction: everything was ready. I felt a flutter of excitement and anticipation; now all I had to do was wait for John's return. I went downstairs, took a chilled bottle of Muscadet from the fridge, and poured myself a glass, to settle my nerves. How would John react? It might mean the end of our relationship......or the beginning of something new.

John arrived home at about 10:45, looking tired and dispirited. I asked him if he'd had a good evening with his friend, Shaun.

'Shaun's done well for himself,' John replied; 'he runs his own computer business. Built it up from scratch. You should see the size of his house - one of those three-storey Edwardian places in Islington. Beautifully decorated - they had professional interior designers to do it. And of course he had to take me for a spin in his BMW - this year's model, a soft-top.'

John looked thoroughly down-cast at his friend's good fortune. I sat down beside him on the sofa, put my arm round him, and kissed him on the cheek.

'Never mind, love,' I said; 'maybe we can do something about changing your luck. You're not enjoying life much at the moment, are you?'

'You can say that again,' John replied.

'Look, I've had an idea. Do you remember years ago, when we were students - that week when we dressed you up as a girl?'

'You mean when we stayed in your old digs in Horewood Road?'

'Yes, we called you 'Joanne' - and you passed amazingly well as a girl.'

'What of it?'

'I remember that as a very happy time for both of us - we were so close. Look, I'm going to suggest something, and I want you to just go and do it, without saying anything.'

John shrugged.

'It might cheer us both up - and be a bit of fun. I'm going to run you a hot bubble bath. While you're in the bath, I'd like you to have a really close shave - do your arm pits, chest and legs, as well, then I'll see you in the bedroom. I've got a surprise for you.'

John raised his eyebrows in query. I put a finger to his lips and said:

'Wait and see.' I went off and ran the bath. When it was ready, he went up to the bathroom without further comment.

'When you've bathed and shaved,' I called out, 'go into the bedroom and put on what you find on the bed.'

I realised that what happened next would be a crucial turning point. I poured myself another glass of Muscadet and sat down to wait. I began leafing through a copy of 'Cosmopolitan', though I couldn't settle to read any of the articles. After what seemed like hours, I crept upstairs

33

and saw that John was out of the bathroom. I knocked softly on the bedroom door and asked:

'Can I come in?'

Without waiting for a reply, I took a deep breath and went into the bedroom; and there was John, sitting on the bed, wearing the whole outfit - the blouse and mini-skirt, even the tights and shoes. My heart leapt with joy! I rushed over, gave him a big hug and exclaimed:

'You look lovely! How I've longed to see Joanne again!' I took his hand and led him over to the dressing table stool.

'Now sit here', I said, 'while I just finish you off.' First I got to work with the tweezers, plucking his eyebrows; then I smoothed on foundation, fixed it with loose powder, and made up his eyes and lips. I sensed that he seemed to enjoy being 'taken in hand' by me; he didn't say a word the whole time, but just let me do whatever I wanted to him. I clipped on some dangly earings, enamelled with tiny flowers, and found a matching bracelet and necklace. I carefully fitted the blond wig and fluffed it out with a brush, then got the silicon breast forms out of a drawer, undid the top buttons of his blouse, and slipped them into his bra-cups. John looked down at his new breasts in amazement but didn't say anything. Finally, I took him by the hand and led him over to the wardrobe so that he could see himself in the full-length mirror on the door. I say 'himself' but really *herself* would be more appropriate - for there was Joanne, the lovely young woman whom I had known for a week once before, and who had now come to life again!

'What do you think?' I asked.

'I - I don't know. It's quite a change....' replied Joanne.

'You can say that again. I think you look great. I love you as Joanne - it's like having an old friend back. Let's go out to a nightclub to celebrate.'

I felt it was best to keep the initiative - to keep the ball rolling now, so that Joanne would scarcely have time to think. I wanted Joanne to enjoy herself straight away, so that she would associate being Joanne with having a good time.

I ordered a taxi and we were soon in the West End, two girls together, determined to have a great night out.

I noted with approval how quickly Joanne was remembering and resuming her former feminine role - her movements and mannerisms, her voice, everything about her - was becoming more girlish by the moment. I began to feel confident that my hunch was correct - John was actually *happier* as Joanne. John obviously had a very strong feminine side to his personality - he was one of those rare boys who would actually have been happier as a girl. I felt as if I was liberating him, or rather *her - the girl she was meant to be.*

I kept glancing at Joanne as a couple of attractive guys in their late twenties bought us drinks and set about chatting us up. She was loving it! Any doubts about whether I had done the right thing evaporated as I watched Joanne get up and move onto the dance floor with one of the guys. She was so animated, so alive - and so different from poor John. John was no more - *long live Joanne!*

Over the next weeks and months, I took steps to ensure that John's transformation to Joanne would be permanent. I had already got rid of all of John's clothes, so she had no alternative but to continue to dress as a girl. When her hair had grown long enough, I made an appointment for Joanne at my hairdressers, where her hair was trimmed into a feminine style, so that it would gradually grow out into a shoulder-length wavy bob. She also had her ears pierced and began electrolysis treatment on her facial hair, so that in time she wouldn't need to wear foundation.

I persuaded Joanne to visit our GP to get herself referred to the Charing Cross gender clinic, but as there proved to be a long delay in referrals on the National Health Service, I payed for her to have a private consultation with Dr. Ruskin Reidmann, so that she could begin taking female hormones as soon as possible. Although the silicon breast prostheses looked very convincing, I was longing to see her with real female breasts.

There was one Saturday morning, about six months after she had begun the hormone treatment, when I was standing behind Joanne in the bathroom while she was making up her face in the mirror, and I couldn't resist placing my hands over her chest to see if I could feel anything. I felt her nipples go hard and she gasped and sighed softly, then turned and kissed me full on the lips. I gently palpated the soft tissue around her nipples as she kissed me, and rejoiced at what I could feel - unmistakably, she had budding female breasts! Her nipples were also obviously very sensitive, and I gently placed each one in turn in my mouth, and sucked it. She moaned softly and moved her hand down to my crotch, rubbing gently between my legs with her fingers, until I grew wet there. I led her through to the bedroom, lay her down on the bed and pulled down her panties. I began to kiss and massage her cock; it began to stiffen, and I placed it in my mouth for a few seconds and worked on it until it was fully erect, then I got on top of her and came down on her, guiding her penis into me with my fingers. It was the most incredible love-making I have ever experienced, for I could enjoy at one and the same time her manhood hard between my legs, and her delicate budding breasts and burgeoning feminine sensuality. It is given to few to experience the best of both worlds in one individual, as I could at that moment in my dear, lovely Joanne, fast becoming woman but still partly man!

Of course it couldn't last, and I knew I'd have to make a choice: should I leave Joanne as she was, this marvellous androgynous creature, or encourage her to pursue the course upon which she had embarked to its logical end - to become wholly woman?

As the months passed, her transformation to complete femininity seemed more and more inevitable. As the hormones took hold of her body, her hips had broadened and her breasts had enlarged (though they were not as big as I would have liked - she could still barely fill an A-cup). She was also growing plumper and more female-looking around the thighs. Her hair grew fuller and more glossy, and her skin became softer, particularly on her face, where the hormone treatment seemed to round off her features, making them appear more feminine. *John* had grown so thin that he had begun to look rather gaunt; *Joanne* had started eating properly, and this had coincided with her going on female hormones; I guessed that as she had begun to regain weight, the hormones had caused the fat distribution to be laid down in the feminine pattern.

I was careful not to let Joanne put on too much weight; she was now a comfortable size 12, which I guessed was her natural size as a female. I had put her into a 'waspie' style corset, which I insisted she wore during the day, to reduce her waist. At first she complained a little that it was too tight and that she could hardly breathe, but she soon got used to my lacing her into it first thing in the morning, before I went to work. I would check the corset when I got home. There was no way she could take it off during the day and get it on again, pulled in as tightly as I insisted, without help, so it was easy for me to tell whether she had tampered with it. After checking for a few days, it was clear to me that she was not trying to loosen off the laces and had got accustomed to wearing it.

The combination of the corset and the smallest size of bodyshaper panties gave her a lovely curvy female shape, narrow at the waist, broad at the hips, and of course, lovely and smooth and flat between her legs. The top edge of the waspie also forced up her budding breasts, giving her the beginnings of a cleavage and making her bust look more prominent.

I couldn't resist taking her out and showing her off like this. Her figure looked absolutely divine in a clingy black evening dress I had bought for her. I insisted she wore high spiky heels with the dress, which had a short, tight skirt and showed off her long shapely legs to maximum effect.

I took her to 'Lips' and several other gay pubs and clubs, where I introduced her as my lesbian partner. It gave me not a little secret amusement to know that this luscious curvy blonde beside me was - none other than my husband! And Joanne was amazing - she just seemed to take it all in her stride, accepting her new feminine status without reservation. We didn't talk about what had happened to her - there was an unspoken agreement between us not to discuss her change to the female role. I had decided early on that it was best to be matter-of-fact about it, treating it as both 'normal' and inevitable that it should happen. Joanne took her cue from me, just carrying on as if nothing unusual had happened. This was certainly the easiest way of dealing with it for both of us.

We did talk about most other things, though; we grew closer and became very good company for each other. We had so much more in common, as two girls; we went shopping for clothes together, and sometimes Joanne would come up to town and meet me after work, and we would go to the theatre or for a meal. We were good friends, but what was the long term future of our relationship, sexually?

The day came when it was no longer possible for us to make love as man and woman. Joanne had been on the hormones for more than a year, by this time, and could no longer even begin to get an erection, no matter how much I massaged and stimulated her. Her male parts were now pretty useless to her (and to me). Her shrivelled penis and testicles hung between her legs on her otherwise feminine body, looking pathetic and incongruous. I couldn't bear the sight of them any longer, and decided it was time for her to take the final step.

One morning, as Joanne was getting out of bed, I pointed to her crotch and said:

'Why don't you get yourself tidied up down there?'

'What do you have in mind?'

'Well, you can't possibly have any use for those male bits you've still got there, what's left of them - why don't you join womankind properly, and get yourself a fanny? Of course it would mean you'd have to pee sitting down for the rest of your life.' (I felt that I should at least point out this consequence to her).

Joanne frowned slightly, and said:

'It would be very final - is it what *you* want? You married a man, after all.'

'Oh I don't care about that - we could probably have *more* fun if we were both girls. I'd certainly be prepared to give it a try.' (I didn't think this would be a good point to mention that I already had some experience of the ways girls can pleasure each other; Joanne had no idea of my affair with Alyson.)

Joanne sat back on the bed and made no further reply for some seconds. I looked out of the window, at the fine spring day, and listened to the morning chorus of the birds which were fluttering around the leaves and blossoms outside. Spring - new beginnings, new growth. I believe in change and growth in human lives, too. *John* had been reborn as *Joanne* - her outward appearance was now that of a lovely girl; would she decide to finish her journey to full womanhood?

At length, Joanne asked:

'You think you could still love me - if I was *fully* a woman? You wouldn't want us to split up? Because I don't think I could bear that - I've been so happy lately with you, as we are now....' Her voice trailed off, sounding small.

I took her hand, looking down at her delicate fingers and varnished nails. I gave her fingers a little squeeze, leant over and kissed her softly on the forehead.

'No my love - I think it would be the right thing for you - for us.'

Joanne turned and looked long into my eyes, then kissed me on the lips, and nodded.

'Okay, I'll go for the operation - I don't think I could ever go back now anyway, to how I was before. I feel as

39

if this is the real me, now and forever.'

There were tears in her eyes, and I could feel my own eyes moistening. She suddenly giggled and said:

'So I'll just have to get used to peeing sitting down, won't I? I'll just be like any other girl.'

And so it was decided. I didn't want Joanne to have to wait too long for the operation, so I booked her into Dr. Ruskin Reidmann's clinic as a private patient. She had the sex-change operation that autumn - the full operation, creating a proper vagina with which it would be possible for her to make love as a woman, and hopefully even experience female orgasm, although there seems to be some doubt about how far post-operative transsexuals are able to achieve this.

While at the clinic she also had a minor operation to remove all trace of her adam's apple, and I persuaded her to have silicon implants in her breasts, so that she would be able to fill a 38 B-cup.

When I went to see her in hospital after the operations, she looked pale and a little frightened; she was propped up in bed in a private room in the clinic. She was looking at some flowers in a vase on the bedside table.

'Are they from you?' she asked, as I sat down.

'Yes, my love. How are you feeling?'

'Sore - it hurts like hell between my legs, now the anaesthetic has worn off, and my breasts are very tender, too.'

I looked at her newly augmented bust and cleavage with approval, and said:

'Well I think it was worth it, and the worst is over now; all you have to do is recover your strength and get back to normal as quickly as you can.' I stroked a towelled blonde lock of her hair away from her eyes, and took her hand in mine. She looked into my eyes intently for a moment and asked:

'Do you think I've done the right thing?'

'Of course you have. Welcome to the wonderful world

40

of being a girl - forever! You've got your whole life as a girl in front of you. You're really going to have a good time, and I'm going to take good care of you.'

Joanne frowned a little and said:

'But I'm no longer your husband.'

'No, but actually, we're still legally married, aren't we? I guess you could think of yourself as - as my *wife*, now, if you like.'

Joanne smiled at this.

When she came out of hospital, I gave her plenty of time to recuperate, taking two weeks off work myself so that I could take care of her. After the dressings had come off, she had to wear a sanitary pad for a while, which we both found rather amusing.

'Now you really know what we girls have to put up with,' I said,

'- you'll be telling me next you're having a period!'

About four months after the operation, we were cuddled up together in bed one night, when I asked her if she would mind if I touched her between the legs. I was very curious to explore her down there, but I had waited patiently until she was well and truly healed and no longer tender.

She took my hand and put it on her belly, then guided my fingers slowly down, until I could feel the soft hair of her bush, and then on down over the wonderful smooth new femaleness of her, until I could feel the lips of her vagina. We both gave little gasps at once, she perhaps because her new fanny was still a little sensitive; me, because - well because I simply couldn't believe what I was feeling, it was so completely perfect and *female*.

I put my head down between her legs and gently kissed her fanny; then she did the same to me. Finally, she penetrated me with her finger, and brought me to a climax.

The next day I called at a sex shop and bought vibrators and a selection of dildos, including a strap-on one which

Joanne loves me to wear. She likes to play the passive role, lying beneath me with her legs open, as I penetrate her. Our sex-life is wonderful; she is more tender and gentle than ever, and truly I believe she does climax to an orgasm, when I excite her enough.

What more can I say? Joanne is the perfect wife for me, what every career woman needs. She cooks, cleans and keeps house for me as if born to it. I have bought her a couple of sexy little maid's outfits - black taffeta dresses, white frou-frou petticoats, black seamed stockings and suspender belts - the works. She loves wearing one of her maid's outfits while she is doing her housework, rejoicing in her role of subservience. I take good care that she feels safe and well looked after, my little wife who always has a smile and kiss for me when I come in.

She prepares romantic candle-lit dinners for us, and sometimes I bring her home chocolates or flowers, or take her out and wine and dine her, spoil her and indulge her, as any woman loves.

We are very happy together, although I suppose our ménage must seem strange to some people. *John's* family will have nothing to do with us - his father and mother were disgusted when they found out what I'd done to John. My family are more tolerant, and have accepted us as we are and wish to be, as they can see that it suits us and works for us.

But Joanne is not only the perfect wife - she is also a good mother to our child. No, she didn't have the baby herself; medical science hasn't achieved that yet. Before John started taking the hormones, I persuaded him to deposit some sperm in a private sperm bank. I had myself artificially inseminated with the sperm, and gave birth to our lovely baby girl - Rebecca. I naturally went back to work as soon as I could, and Joanne looks after Becky. She loves pushing Becky's pram to the park and chatting with the other young mothers about nappies and bottle-feeding and all that baby stuff that I would have found boring. Joanne's only regret is that she hasn't been able to breast-feed Becky, although once or twice I have found Joanne in Becky's room in the middle of the night, letting the baby have a quiet suck of her nipple, to comfort her when she is fractious from teething.

We look forward to the future with confidence, and are happier together than many more traditional families, secure in our love for each other and in the knowledge that we have each found our true role in life. Yes, I turned my husband into a girl, the girl she was always meant to be; and that girl is now my beautiful wife, and the mother of my child.

© *Kate Lesley 1994*

A Walk on the Wild Side

'Holly came from Miami, FLA,
Hitch-hiked her way across the U.S.A.;
Plucked her eye-brows on the way,
Shaved her legs -
Then he was a she,
She said, "hey babe, take a walk on the wild side,"
She said, "hey honey, take a walk on the wild side....."'

- Lou Reed

My name is Michelle LaBelle. That's the name I chose for myself. I am also sometimes called Michael. Welcome to my world.

I am sitting in a bar called Michelangelo's, in the Village. The Village is an oasis of gay bars and clubs near Manchester city centre, a beautiful area of red-brick warehouses, bisected by the canal. Find Sackville street, and you will not be far off. A beautiful area, and beautiful people are out tonight, for today is Wednesday and tonight is TV night in the Village. TV means trannie - transvestite or crossdresser - like me. Wednesday is our night for stepping out - the gay bars expect us, the police accept us. It is a glorious thing to come out of a club at one in the morning on to the wet shiny pavements in your high heels, and feel the cold air wafting up your skirt and around your nylon-clad legs - and behold the white police van across the road, and know that Manchester's boys in blue know who you are and what you are - and are not going to arrest you. They may even give you a friendly wave.

'Fucking hell, not another one!' a charming young policeman said to my friend Karla the other night -

'They thought I was a woman from the back, and then I turned round,' explained Karla, 'and that was what he said - but his mate just asked, 'Is everything all right - sir?' and I said 'Yes, fine thanks.'

44

The policeman continued, 'You know where you are and where you're going?'

Karla replied, 'Yes, I've just been to a club and now I'm going on to a party,' and the policeman said, 'Have a good evening then, sir,' and they went off.

Karla says they patrol the area regularly and are here to protect us and the women of the streets and the gays. It's nice to know the police are not going to break your arm because you like to wear a frock.

My friend Karla is a big girl. I feel safe enough when I'm with her - I think she can take care of herself. She used to be in the Forces - Royal Artillery.

Karla has a hundred and fifty pairs of shoes - 'You're as bad as Imelda Marcos,' I told her.

She also has four motor bikes. One is a Yamaha eleven hundred cc., on which she's claims she's done a hundred and fifty miles an hour. 'Where?' I asked.

'On the motorway,' she said.

'But the speed limit's seventy miles an hour,' I pointed out.

Karla grinned at me shyly.

Karla can't shave her arms because the young lads she teaches to ride are macho types - leather-clad bikies.

'They might think it was a bit funny if they noticed, because I'm supposed to be macho too,' she says. Karla is wearing a white satin pleated mini-skirt, very high-heeled court shoes, a canary yellow top buttoned over her ample falsies, and a white plastic rain coat.

I have on an Indian batik skirt and blouse - beautiful flowing colours - the hem of the skirt is fringed with tassles, and the blouse has a sort of false waistcoat in the same material - pink and purple and black and green. I like to look a bit hippyish - that is my style. I was a teenager in the late Sixties and early Seventies, and I like to think that I dress as a woman in the sort of clothes I would choose if I really was a woman. My tastes as a woman and as a man are coming together. My wife suggested perhaps this is like an integration of my personality, of my feminine and masculine parts. Even for work, I now

45

sometimes wear shirts in soft colourful fabrics which are very similar to the blouses I wear.

The irony is, if I was a real woman, I would probably wear jeans a lot of the time - perhaps I would be a feminist.

Of course, as a TV, I like to wear skirts - what would be the point of wearing trousers? I have to wear them for long enough, as it is. I love the feel and look of my legs in pantyhose and a skirt - and usually I wear a lacy slip. I am wearing low heeled patent leather black shoes from Marks and Spencer, this evening, as I shall be dressed (we say 'dressed' meaning dressed as a woman) until the early hours of the morning, and I don't fancy crippling my feet in anything higher or more pointy-toed.

I feel sorry for 'straight' men - they don't know what they're missing. I love being a TV and I wouldn't be any other way. Well, I suppose if I could have chosen, I would have chosen to have been born as a real girl. But being a TV is the next best thing......

The Lady of the Lake

Thirteen hundred years ago, most of England was covered in thick primeval forest: the original native greenwoods of this country. The Romans had long since departed, taking the comforts and certitudes of classical civilisation with them. The people of Britain were slowly returning to the ways of an earlier time, a time of hill-forts, barrows and standing stones, of ancient superstitions and mysteries.

Carthule was a young hunter who had heard that Anmal, Lord of Minan Hru was offering a reward to any man who would go into the enchanted forest and discover its secret. Carthule arrived at the gates of the castle and demanded admittance. The lord's men stripped him of his weaponry and thrust him into Anmal's exalted presence in the great hall. Lord Anmal, a huge man with a wiry black beard and mane of shaggy hair, was picking his teeth with a dagger, surrounded by his drinking cronies, who were roaring and guffawing on cue at Anmal's jokes. Bones from the meal were scattered among the upturned goblets and smashed amphora on the oaken table; the air was thick with smoke and the smell of burnt fat and unwashed men.

'Why do you disturb my meal?' Lord Anmal gruffly demanded of Carthule, when he saw the young hunter bowing gravely before him.

'I am come, Lord Anmal, to ask permission to enter the enchanted forest.'

'Why do you want to go in there, are you a fool?' replied Anmal; 'don't you know I have lost twenty of my best men in that infernal place?'

'Nevertheless, I seek your permission to go, and if I

return with its secret, I claim your reward.'

'What is your name, boy?'

'I am Carthule of Vinan Scree; I am a hunter.'

'Well Carthule of Vinan Scree, you have courage if not sense. Go then with my blessing; if you discover the mystery of the enchanted forest you shall have a thousand pieces of gold and the hand in marriage of my fair daughter, Princess Leisha.'

And so Carthule left the lord's castle, watched by Princess Leisha from her high tower above the western ramparts, and journeyed across brooding heather-capped moorland, through dark woods and over many steep and craggy mountains, until he came to the borders of the enchanted forest.

Carthule pulled his sturdy sword from its hilt, and thrust himself into the forest, hewing a path through the thicket by slashing this side and that with his sword. After some time Carthule came to a clearing in the woods in which there was a dark lake, its edges overhung with willows. He bent down to the still water and touched it; a ripple spread out across the surface from his fingers, and he heard a soft wind moaning like a sigh through the branches of the trees. Cupping his hands, he scooped up some of the water and sipped it - it was cold and sweet. He gazed into the inky depths of the lake but could see nothing; 'perhaps it is bottomless,' he thought.

A sudden weariness overcame him, and Carthule lay down where he was beside the lake, and resting his head on a bank of soft moss, fell into a deep sleep. He was dreaming a strange dream in which Lord Anmal was holding the head of a wolf, and was trying to wrest his sword from him, when he felt a gentle tugging at the sleeve of his tunic. Carthule opened his eyes and saw that a beautiful young woman dressed in a gown of ruby velvet was bending over him; he felt her long raven-black silken hair gently brushing his face as she peered earnestly down at him.

'Are you all right?' she asked; her voice was soft and

refined, but had a sadness to it which reminded him of the sound of the wind sighing in the trees.

'Yes, I was sleeping; that is all. What is this place?'

'This is the Lake of Dreams,' said the lady.

'I am seeking the men from the land of Lord Anmal who came into this forest and have not returned. Can you tell me what has happened to them?'

'I can show you,' said the lady, 'come with me.'

She took Carthule by the hand and began to wade out into the lake.

'No!' shouted Carthule, 'I will drown.'

'You will not drown if you have faith and follow me,' replied the lady, but Carthule tore away from her and splashed back to the bank. When he looked again towards the lake, the lady was gone. Only a soft sighing could be heard in the trees.

Carthule camped by the lake for many days and nights, waiting for the lady to return. He caught small silver fish from the lake, which he roasted with nuts and berries and wild mushrooms gathered from the forest.

Still the lady did not return, and Carthule was tortured with a sense of nameless loss, for the lady had been gentle and beautiful. Carthule thought of how her hair had carressed his face when she had bent over him, and he wept bitter, lonely tears.

Finally, he could bear it no longer, and taking off his sword, he waded into the lake. Deeper and deeper he went, until the icy water was up to his chest.....then up to his neck; at last, the water closed over his head, and he knew that he didn't care, for he did not wish to live any longer if he could not see the lady again.

As the cold blackness closed around him, he suddenly felt a small hand in his, pulling him, pulling him; opening his eyes, he saw that it was the lady of the lake, her raven hair floating like gossamer around her face. She was smiling at him and pointing downwards towards a cleft in the rocky bottom of the lake. They swam towards it and she gently pulled him into the dark opening, then

49

urged him along a water-filled tunnel which seemed to be hewn from the living rock, until they emerged into a gigantic chamber of stone. Carthule gasped for breath as he looked around him. The water from which they had come appeared to be an underground river - it rushed in a torrent out of the blackness of the tunnel, spreading out into a channel which had cut deep into the floor of the vast cavern.

'This is my domain,' said the lady; 'come, you must meet my friends.'

'What shall I call you?' asked Carthule.

'My name is Sarah.'

Sarah led Carthule through a short passage cut from the rock into another cavern, in which there were a number of men and women, dressed alike in beautiful gowns of velvet and silk, spinning and weaving the finest fabrics - silk, satin, damask, velvet, cloth-of-gold - in colours that shimmered in the glow of a thousand candles.

'Are these Anmal's men?' asked Carthule.

'They come from his lands, but they are his no longer,' replied Sarah; 'they are free men who choose to stay here. They have given up the ways of the warrior and hunter. All live here in peace and love.'

'Who are the others?'

'They are the women and men of the forest and lake, who have always lived here, since long before the Romans came.'

Carthule was taken into other caves, where women and men, all dressed in the same way, were engaged in every conceivable art and craft: there were manuscript writers and illuminators, book binders, embroiderers, weavers, tailors, painters, sculptors, stone masons, jewellers - all working on pieces of the highest quality.

'Our aim is to keep alive the flame of civilization in these dark times,' explained Sarah.

'Why are the women and men dressed similarly?' asked Carthule. 'As the men are clean-shaven and both men and women wear their hair long, tied and adorned in the same way, it is difficult to tell them apart.'

'Here we make no distinction,' replied the lady; 'we dress in the same clothes, we do the same work. Why should there be a difference?'

Carthule stared at her in amazement.

'But who protects you? Who leads you? Where are your soldiers?'

'We have no soldiers. We need no protection - no one can enter our realm without being shown the way; those who are shown the way - like yourself - have always chosen to stay with us. We have no lords or rulers; we decide what to do by voting, as in ancient Athens.'

'What about food?'

'There is plenty for all. We have fish from the lakes and streams - the lake you saw is the smallest of seven - we have berries, nuts and mushrooms from the forest; we have also made clearings deeper in the forest, where we have planted orchards and we grow corn and oats.'

'I haven't seen any children.'

'All our children, both girls and boys, go to special places of instruction, where they learn the arts and crafts you have seen.'

'I have heard there were such places long ago, during the time of the Romans.'

'In time, you will understand more of our ways. Now I will show you where you will sleep, and tomorrow you can see our domains in the forest.'

Carthule was at first overjoyed to find himself in this lost paradise. He had expected that Sarah, his lady of the lake, would now be his wench, but although she came to his bed sometimes, she refused to pledge herself to him and relinquish her independence.

'You cannot possess me, Carthule,' she told him; 'it is not our way. I had my own life before you came, and I will not give it up.'

As the weeks turned into months, Carthule grew tired of the people of the enchanted forest and began to yearn for freedom, for the excitement of hunting wild boar and deer in the lands of Lord Anmal, and for the companionship of the ale house and the camp fire; for honest soldiering and sword-fighting and wenching.

Finally he determined to leave, taking Sarah with him. He waited until dead of night, when everyone was asleep. He knew no guards were ever posted in this strange land, as the people had no fear of enemies. With the stealth of the hunter, he crept to Sarah's cave carrying a neck cloth of silk and some leather cords he had stolen from a book-binder; roughly shaking her awake, he gagged her mouth with the silk cloth and bound her with the cords, then carried her to the cavern in which the water tunnel emerged from the lake. Diving into the icy water, he swam into the black entrance of the tunnel, dragging Sarah with him. During her struggles to get free, Sarah cracked her head on the roof of the tunnel and lost consciousness. When she came to, she found she had been carried by Carthule to the edge of the enchanted forest. It was nearly dawn.

News of Carthule's return to the lands of Lord Anmal spread quickly; soon Carthule and Sarah had an entourage of beggars, cut-throats and n'er-do-wells who gambolled and cavorted along beside them as they made their way towards Anmal's castle.

Carthule had managed to procure a horse on the credit of the reward he would receive from Lord Anmal; he rode on the horse like some princeling, his ragged retinue trailing behind him. Sarah was wretchedly walking along beside Carthule's nag, her hands tied before her to a lead which was attached to the saddle, so that she couldn't escape. One or other member of the beggarly entourage prodded her from time to time, cackling:

'So this is the lady of the enchanted forest, is it?' Or -

'Now let's see you work your magic!' or other words of scorn.

Carthule's party finally arrived at the castle, and he and Sarah were ushered into Anmal's presence.

'Well, the long lost adventurer returns at last!' exclaimed Anmal. 'And who have we here?' Anmal picked a piece of meat from his teeth with his dagger and thrust the blade in the direction of Sarah.

'I said I would bring you the secret of the enchanted forest. This is the witch of the forest, who has been enchanting your men.'

'Hah! She looks enchanting, certainly. Let's see if she can enchant her way out of that.' Anmal pointed to an iron cage in a corner of the great hall. Two soldiers roughly bundled the struggling girl into the cage, and slammed the bars shut.

'Now I suppose you will be wanting your reward?' asked Anmal, looking malignantly towards Carthule.

'Yes Lord,' replied Carthule.

'Here's your money, damn you,' shouted Anmal, 'and now let's get rid of my daugther. Bring the girl in.'

A fat, stupid-looking young woman who had obviously been listening at the door was hurriedly ushered in by two serving women.

'This is your daughter?' asked Carthule in disbelief.

'Correct, replied Anmal, 'This is my delightful daughter Leisha; I believe that part of your reward was that you marry her?'

The girl leered stupidly at Carthule, who by now was wishing that he had stayed in the domain of the enchanted forest.

And so the marriage between Carthule and Princess Leisha took place, amid much pomp and panoply, but very little rejoicing, at least on Carthule's part.

Although rich, Carthule was miserable. In time, he grew as fat as his wife, and was killed one day in a hunting accident. Few mourned him.

Sarah, the lady of the enchanted wood, meanwhile languished in the cage in Anmal's great hall, fed on scraps from his banquets and tormented by his loutish henchmen.

Lord Anmal also had a son, younger than Leisha, as unlike her as a song bird is unlike a sow. He was a boy of refined sensibilities, intelligent and sensitive by nature, who was constantly flogged on the slightest pretext by his brutish father, and belittled by his debased henchmen. The boy looked nothing at all like his swarthy and hirsute father, having the fair skin and blond hair of his mother, a gentlewoman from a neighbouring land who had long since died, unable to stand the coarseness of her husband and his cronies. The boy, like his mother, was musical, and could sing sweetly and accompany himself on the lyre, a talent for which he was more likely to be abused than praised at the court of Minan Hru.

The boy had a favourite toy, a golden ball, with which he would amuse himself for hours. One day, when he was eight years old, he was playing with the golden ball in the great hall, rolling it backwards and forwards across the stone slabs that made up the floor. In one part of the floor was a broken slab, its edge raised above the level of the others; the ball struck this slab and glanced off towards the iron cage in the corner. Before the boy could stop it, the golden ball had rolled through the bars of the cage. The ragged creature who had once been the beautiful maiden, Sarah, picked up the ball and peered at it, her head on one side, like a sparrow surveying a seed it was about to peck.

The boy approached the cage cautiously, for he had heard that the woman who was kept in it was a powerful witch.

'May I have my ball back, please?' asked the boy.

Sarah looked through the bars, her tired eyes straining to see the owner of the voice in the smoky gloom of the great hall.

'What do they call you?' she asked the boy.

'I am Sianna, son of Anmal; will you give me my golden ball?

'Come closer, so I can see you better.'

54

Sianna took a tentative step forward. Sarah beheld the face of the young boy, and saw at once that although he was Anmal's son, he was no son of Anmal's.

'I will make a bargain with you boy; come to me tonight, when everyone is asleep, and I will give you your ball back if you open the cage.'

Sianna was frightened by the woman's words, and even more by her appearance - her ragged clothes; her long black fingernails and tangled mane of raven hair; her hollow cheeks, flushed and hectic with suppressed excitement; and her staring eyes, wild with urgency. Sianna remembered what he had been told about her being a witch; he stood irresolute and trembling a moment longer, then he turned and ran off, without even answering.

Seven years passed, and Sianna grew into a comely youth. But still he could not forget his golden ball, and so he went again to the wild woman's cage and asked for it back.

'I will give it back to you if you let me out of the cage,' the woman replied. Sianna shook his head and walked sadly away.

Another seven years went by; Anmal was by now a grizzled and degenerate old tub of lard, addled with the pox, his face bloated and veined with drink. Merely to behold his son, now in the first full strength of his manhood, was an affront and torment worse than the plague for him. Sianna was cursed and reviled by the old man whenever he saw him, for more and more the boy had come to ressemble his mother - in his blond hair and fair skin; in the regularity and refinement of his features; in the suppleness and grace of his movements; and worst of all, as far as the old man was concerned - in his sensibility and kindheartedness to others.

One evening, after Anmal and his lackeys had retired to their chambers, Sianna was alone in the great hall, playing his lyre and singing softly a tune taught to him long ago by his mother. The wild woman, whose hair by now was streaked with grey, heard his sweet song and called out to him:

'Sianna! Sianna! I will return your golden ball if you let me out of my cage.'

'I care nothing for my golden ball,' replied the young man, 'I would let you out of your cage if I could, but I don't know where the key is.'

'The key is under your father's pillow.'

Sianna crept into his father's bed chamber, stole the key, and returning to the great hall, brought it to the wild woman's cage and opened the lock. The wild woman leapt out of the cage and was already disappearing into the shadows when Sianna called out to her:

'Wait! If I stay here my father will have me killed for releasing you!'

'You'd better come with me then to the enchanted forest,' Sarah replied. 'We must disguise ourselves or your father's men will recognize us as we escape from his lands. Can you show me where in the castle the servants sleep?'

Sianna and Sarah crept to the servants' quarters and found an oaken chest used to store the spare clothing of the serving women.

'I cannot wear these fripperies!' exclaimed Sianna, as Sarah measured petticoats and gowns against him for size.

'Ssssh! hissed Sarah. Do you want to wake up the whole castle? Quickly, take your clothes off and get into these things - it will prove the best disguise.'

The young man reluctantly did as he was told.

Sarah meanwhile dressed herself in men's clothing and cut off most of her hair with a kitchen knife, then blackened her face with charcoal around the jowls to look like whiskers. Posing as a married couple who were journeying from the castle to pay a visit on their relatives in a distant village, they made their escape from Minan Hru and by morning had travelled several leagues from the hated fortress.

Onward they journeyed, their way taking them across moorland bogs, through dismal woods and over precipitous moutains, until they came to the borders of the enchanted forest. Sarah led the way now, along secret paths long remembered which she thought never to see again. At last they reached the willow-fringed lake, and tearing off their clothes, plunged into the cool sweet waters. The trees around them whispered with the murmur of the wind.

As the water closed over their heads, Sianna saw Sarah smiling at him and pointing downwards towards a cleft in the rocky bottom of the lake. They swam towards it and she gently pulled him into the dark opening.

* * *

(The idea for this story comes from a fairy-tale first set down by the Brothers Grimm about 1820; however, the story itself could be thousands of years old. The original 'Iron John' or 'Iron Hans' story is an allegory about a wild man who represents a notion of masculinity dating back to a pre-industrial, hunter-gatherer past - an intuitive, emotional, instinctive human being who is in tune with nature and aware of the rhythms of his body.

The story is about an archetypal concept of lost masculinity, in which, despite the aspects of 'wildman hairiness', there is something of the feminine. 'The Lady of the Lake' appears at first sight to stand the 'Iron John' tale on its head, but in a sense it has the same theme: the recovery of lost parts of ourselves.)

How Stephen became Stephanie

The story of a young supermarket trainee manager who is changed into a check-out girl and part-time maid

Chapter One

It all started that night, after we'd been to the film together. I'd been admiring Sarah for some months, and had finally plucked up the courage to ask her out. I was working as a trainee manager for a large supermarket chain - at that time I was based in one of their superstores in a suburb of Sheffingham. I'd done a degree in marketing and business management at Sheffingham University, and started with the company straight after graduating, having passed their management selection procedures. I lived in landlady accommodation arranged by the company, near to where I worked.

Sarah was a stunning girl in her mid-twenties - glossy light brown hair cut in a bobbed style to reveal her fine neck. She had startling blue eyes and long, slender legs. As the branch's personnel manager, she had to look smart at all times, and wore beautifully tailored business suits - jackets sculpted to accentuate her slim waist and short skirts which showed off her legs. She was a real 'power dresser', and had quite a commanding manner to match her appearance, a self-confidence which underscored her responsible position within the store.

It was with some trepidation, therefore, that I asked her whether she would like to go to see a film with me. I was elated when she agreed, and even more pleased when she invited me back to her flat for a drink, after the film. I remember the film was 'Fatal Attraction'. I can still recall how she held on to me tightly during some of the violent, climactic scenes in the film, her small fingers clutching at my hand, her long nails pressing into my palm.

Her flat occupied the first floor of a large, bay-windowed Victorian house. It was well decorated in a simple style - whitewashed walls, panelled doors stripped to the bare wood, a large, intricately patterned Moroccan rug on the floor.

'Make yourself comfortable,' Sarah said, indicating a cream coloured leather sofa. She went into the kitchen, returning with a bottle of red wine and two wine glasses. She poured the wine, handed me a glass, and put an 'Enya' album on the CD player. I sunk back into the soft leather of the sofa, allowing the wistful music to wash over me. I felt very relaxed, as if I had known Sarah for years, but at the same time I was conscious of a sense of anticipation; part of me was waiting for something to happen, something inevitable. We chatted in a desultory way, and discovered that we had much in common; our tastes in music, books, and films closely coincided.

We listened to several more CD's - Bruce Springsteen, Dire Straits - and then some Tina Turner; by this time we'd finished the wine and were drinking Scotch on the rocks. Sarah had kicked off her high heels and was curled up on the sofa next to me. I felt her nuzzling into my side and turned towards her; she looked up into my face with her ravishing blue eyes, slipped her slim arm round my neck and drew my lips down onto hers. My eyes closed as I drank in her nectar in that first long kiss, and inhaled her sweet aroma; at length, to my disappointment she gently broke away from me and stood up, but still holding my hand. The next thing I knew, she was leading me through to the bedroom.

'You can't drive home now, you've had too much to drink and it's too late anyway,' she whispered to me; 'you're welcome to stay if you want (she raised her eyebrows archly and gave me a wicked grin as she said this, leaving me in no doubt as to her meaning) - but there's just one little thing I'd like you to do for me. I really can't stand to have hairy skin next to mine. It's a bit of a phobia, I suppose. Would you mind terribly going into the bathroom and shaving the hair off your legs and chest?'

59

I was a little surprised at the request, but I think if at that moment had she asked me to walk with bare feet across a bed of hot coals, I would not have refused. I was more than a little drunk, and very much in the mood for spending the night with Sarah.

'Okay,' I shrugged, and she presented me with a Bic disposable razor in one hand and a Ladyshave electric razor in the other:

'Take your pick,' she said. I took them both and put them on the end of the bed. She walked into the bathroom, calling back over her shoulder:

'I'll run a bath for you - that'll soften your skin up and make it easier.'

I sunk into the hot perfumed bubbles, and began to dream of Sarah's soft skin and slim waist, and the way her hair smelled clean and swung when she turned her head to give a tantalizing glimpse of her finely shaped ear-lobes.

After soaking in the bath for a few minutes, I shaved off the hair on my legs and chest, as she had asked. I looked at the hair sprouting in tufts from my arm-pits; somehow it looked unsightly now, and I decided to take this off as well.

'Here, you can wear this,' she said, passing me her silk dressing gown as I emerged from the bathroom, wearing only a towel.

I leave you to imagine the bliss of her embraces, the sweet tenderness of her young body, the feel of her soft skin on mine, as she gave herself in love to me..........

The following morning I awoke before Sarah, and decided to make a cup of coffee - to tell the truth I had a bit of a hangover, and was suffering from the usual dry mouth and raging thirst. I couldn't find my clothes anywhere, and so slipped into Sarah's dressing gown again, while I padded through to the kitchen to put on the percolator. I found croissants in a bread bin and heated them up under the grill until they were brown and crispy. I put the coffee jug, cups and hot croissants on a tray and carried it back to the bedroom. Sarah was already awake, propped up on pillows, with the duvet pulled modestly over her. She pushed the hair out of her eyes as I came in, a movement which caused the duvet to slip down, uncovering her small, firm breasts, on which the nipples were rosily standing out. She noticed that I was staring at them and blushed, then giggled mischievously:

'Ah, maid service! You know, you don't look at all bad in that dressing gown. You've got nice legs.'

I glanced at myself in the mirror door of the wardrobe, and was momentarily taken aback by what I saw - the nakedness of my shaved legs, the shape of me in a woman's bath robe.

After we'd had the croissants and coffee, she said to me:

'You know, as it's Sunday, we could spend the day together if you like. You needn't hurry back to your landlady, unless you prefer her company to mine.......'

Of course, I did not demur; I was grateful for the opportunity to spend more time with this ravishing young woman.

'Well then, seeing you in my dressing gown like that has given me an idea. Are you game for a bit of fun?'

I raised my eyebrows and asked her what she had in mind.

'Your legs look so nice and shapely in their shaven state, let's see how they'd look with these on ' - she tossed me a pair of charcoal-coloured tights from a drawer.

'And perhaps you'd better put these on first,' she said, handing me a pair of lace-edged panties, 'you can hardly wear your striped boxer shorts under tights.'

I slipped into the panties and began pulling the tights over my feet.

'No, not like that,' she said, 'let me show you.' Having first put on a pair of black silk panties, Sarah chose a pair of diaphanous black tights from the drawer, sat on the edge of the bed, and carefully gathered them up, rolling the nylon hose gently up one leg at a time until over her knees, then stood up and with a deft movement pulled the tights on over her thighs and buttocks until the gusset was neatly in position under the crotch of her panties. The sheer fabric of the tights stretched smoothly between her legs, emphasizing the rounded femaleness of what lay beneath.......

'Come on then, get on with it!' she exclaimed, and I realized where I had been staring for some moments. I sat down and rolled on the tights as she had shown me, thinking of nothing at all, carried along by the sensuality of the situation and my carnal longing for her. I suppose the situation was a little strange, but I continued to do as she asked, as if my will had leaked away and I was under her express command.

'Look, why stop now?' she asked, 'let's go a bit further.' The next thing I knew she was fastening a bra onto my chest, and passing me a waist-slip to put on. I stepped into the slip and noticed that it had a lace-edged slit opening from the bottom hem, an inverted V which revealed my nylon clad legs above the knee. She slipped silk handkerchiefs, gathered into conical shapes, in each bra-cup.

I used to be quite a bit plumper than I am now,' she said, ' and I've kept some of my old clothes in case I put on weight again. I think this skirt and top should fit you, if you'd like to put them on.' She passed me a green cotton skirt with a tiny blue flower motif, and a matching jacket-style tailored top with the waist gathered in by a bow at the back.

'Now shoes. My flat mate is quite tall - I suspect her feet are about the same size as yours.' Sarah went into an adjoining room and returned with a pair of high-heeled court shoes in navy calf. 'She's away this weekend; I'm sure she won't mind if we borrow these.' She put them down on the carpet in front of me and I slipped into them - they were a perfect fit.

'Now sit down here,' she commanded, indicating a fluffy-topped bedroom stool in front of the dressing table. As I sat down she swung the dressing table mirror up and over so that its back was towards me. 'I don't want you to see how you look until I've finished. I'm going to have to do something with your eyebrows, to begin with,' she announced.

'Hang on a second,' I replied, but before I could object further, she was busy plucking away at my eyebrows with tweezers.

'Ouch! That hurts,' I protested.

'Beauty was never achieved without a little suffering!' she replied chirpily. When she had finished my eyebrows she ordered me back into the bathroom, telling me to give my face a close shave. I tottered into the bathroom, unfamiliar with walking in high heels. The feel of the skirt on my legs, the way the tights moved against the silky slip underneath the skirt, the constraint of the bra - all felt so strange, and yet not unpleasant.

I peered at myself in the mirror of the bathroom cabinet; Sarah had apparently forgotten that I would see myself in this mirror - she need not have bothered to turn round the mirror in the bedroom. What a strange sight I was - my face still recognizably my own, a slight shadow of whiskers on my cheeks and chin, but my eyebrows completely feminized - plucked and raked into fine arches. Surely it would be noticed when I was back at work on Monday? What was Sarah doing to me? Why was I allowing her? I seemed to have no will left. I got on with shaving, and observed when I had finished that my face no longer looked so strange. With now smooth skin and shaped eyebrows, my face looked distinctly feminine - I was rather taken aback to see how feminine. My features are small and my beard, as I am fair-haired and fair-skinned, has always been light - after a close shave it did not notice at all.

Even my hair looked androgynous; in these days when cropped or even shaven hair, in the style of Sinead O'Connor, is not unknown for women - my hair, which was of moderate length and naturally wavy - could easily pass muster as a feminine style. But why was I thinking like this? On some impulse I had taken a brush from the shelf and was fluffing up my hair a little, before I realized what I was doing. I put the brush down, feeling confused by what was happening to me, and returned to the bedroom.

Sarah told me to sit down again on the dressing table stool. She lightly touched her fingers against my face, and whispered:

'Hmm. You have lovely soft skin; your complexion is just like a girl's.'

She began smoothing on some foundation: 'Fortunately we won't need too much of this; we can go for a more natural look.' Sarah next applied a little blusher, some creamy eyeshadow, and a touch of mascara to my upper lashes.

'Some girls would die for lashes as long as yours,' she announced. She completed my make-up by outlining my lips with a lipliner pencil and filling them in with a dark burgundy shade of lipstick. Then she put a blonde wig on my head, styled in the same straight bob as her own hair, and brushed and teased it out until she was satisfied. Finally, she clipped two small imitation gold and pearl ear-rings to my ear lobes, and ordered me to stand and take a twirl before the mirror doors of the wardrobe. I twirled and stared in amazement at the attractive blonde girl I saw in the mirror! Could this really be me? I looked at my trim legs and slender ankles in the tights and high heels. I looked at the way the green flowered jacket was tailored so that it nipped in at my waist, and how the padded-out bra underneath created the effect of a gently swelling bosom. I appeared to have feminine curves in all the right places. I sat down again on the stool; Sarah turned round the dressing table mirror and I gazed in astonishment at my face - the face of a well made-up young woman.

'Yes, you're certainly wasted as a male,' announced Sarah, 'you make a lovely girl - very pretty - better even than I expected. How do you feel?'

'I - I don't know,' I stammered in reply; ' I can hardly recognize myself.'

Sarah gave me no time to think about it.

'I insist you stay like this for the rest of the day, Stephen. Hmm - I can't call you that now, can I? I'll call you Stephanie. How does that sound?'

I shrugged. Obviously I was not going to be given any choice. I didn't seem to have any control over the situation; Sarah was in command, that was all there was to it. My role was to do as I was told.

'You look so convincing,' Sarah continued, that I'm going to take you out dressed like that to a pub I know, that does a really good Sunday lunch.'

So I spent my first day as Stephanie. No one in the pub suspected that I was anything other than the attractive blonde girl I appeared. Sarah did most of the talking, although she said the tone and pitch of my voice would sound quite acceptably girlish, if I practised a little:

'It's just a case of speaking in a slightly softer tone. Your voice is naturally quite high, Stephanie. Speak with confidence as a girl, and no one will notice anything unusual.'

We went back to Sarah's flat after lunch, and I helped her make the bed, hoover and tidy up.

'You'd make a lovely little maid,' she laughed.

Finally, it was time for me to go home. She gave me some make-up removing gel, cotton wool balls, and a jar of eye make-up cleansing pads, for removing mascara.

'Not a mention of this to anyone,' she whispered, as she returned my clothes to me, 'I think we might both find it embarrassing if word got out.'

Chapter Two

I was relieved to find, when I was back at work, that people are much more unobservant than one might suppose - no one noticed my plucked eyebrows, which I had mussed up to disguise the attention they had received. I imagined for the first couple of days that I was being stared at, but this just wasn't the case. Who really looks at anyone else's face? Everyone was much too busy getting on with their own lives, preoccupied with their own concerns, to take notice of slight changes in a colleague whose features had long been familiar to them.

I was somewhat puzzled by Sarah's behaviour at work. She remained aloof, playing her personnel manager role for all it was worth. She said no more than the occasional curt good morning to me, and avoided eye-contact. This went on for some weeks, and I began to think that I had dreamt that Sunday with Sarah, when she had turned me so skilfully into 'Stephanie'.

One or two odd things started to occur at my landlady's at about this time. Of course, I thought it was just coincidence. I only began to see the pattern later.

My landlady, Mrs. Clarridge, has a daughter called Claire, a couple of years younger than me. Claire was away most of the time, doing a Business Studies course at the London School of Economics, which is part of the University of London. Mrs. Clarridge was very proud of Claire's academic accomplishments, and anticipated a golden future for her.

Mrs. Clarridge was a motherly, plump lady in her late forties, with a fluffy permed hair-style. She was a good cook, but tended to over-feed me; she was mortified if I did not eat up the huge meals she set before me. She had kindly offered to do my laundry for me, although this was not part of the usual arrangement negotiated by the company.

'It's no trouble dear, just to put your few things in the machine when I do a load,' she had informed me, the day after I had moved in. She ironed my shirts for me, leaving them for me to collect as needed from the airing cupboard, carefully hung on wire coat hangers.

I found that she also put away my clean underwear, in the top drawer of the chest of drawers in my bedroom.

It was when I came to look in this drawer one morning that I got rather a surprise. In among my underpants and boxer shorts were two pairs of silky knickers, a slip and a bra. I got them out and brought them downstairs.

'I found these in my drawer,' I said to Mrs. Clarridge, who was pottering about in the kitchen, getting breakfast.

'Oh they must be Claire's,' she replied, 'they must have got in with your clothes by mistake.'

Nothing more was said, but I was puzzled by this 'mistake'; Claire hadn't been home for several weeks, so how had our washing got muddled up?

The next incident occurred on my birthday. Mrs. Clarridge gave me a surprise birthday present - I hadn't told her the date, but she said my date of birth and other details were on the accommodation payment form from the company (my rent was deducted direct from my salary). I opened the flowery wrapping paper and took out what appeared to be three pairs of white panties.

'No, they're not knickers,' she said, when I looked at her quizzically. 'They're called mini-briefs: men wear them these days, and I'm sure they'll be a lot more comfortable than those awful boxer shorts of yours.'

'But I thought boxer shorts were fashionable again,' I protested.

'Oh no, dear, you try those,' she insisted.

I thought I'd better start wearing them to please her. If I didn't put them out for a wash occasionally, she'd know I hadn't been wearing them.

A couple of weeks later, I was rummaging in my underwear drawer for some socks when I came upon a pair of the briefs, which had looked like panties to me, though I hadn't wanted to hurt Mrs. Clarridge's feelings by telling her so. Unaccountably, the briefs had turned a shade of pink. I looked for the other pairs - they also were pink.

I took a pair of them downstairs and showed them to Mrs. Clarridge.

'Oh yes, I'm sorry about that, dear,' she chirped, 'I'm afraid I accidentally put them in the wash with a red jumper of mine, and some of the colour must have run. I hope you'll still be able to wear them.'

'I suppose so,' I replied doubtfully.

'Of course you will, dear - who's going to know you're wearing pink underwear?' she asked. Was there a mischievous glint in her eye? Or had I imagined it?

Bras, slips and even pairs of tights 'unaccountably' found their way into my clothing drawers on several other occasions. Each time, I returned the female clothing to Mrs. Clarridge, who invariably protested her ignorance of how these dainty items came to be misplaced.

Something else which I now recognize was part of a carefully planned campaign, was Mrs. Clarridge's insistence that I should wear a full-length floral apron, edged with frills, everytime I helped with the washing-up:

'You mustn't spoil your clothes dear,' she pointed out. One time, when the apron was unavailable, she even made me wear her nylon housecoat, doing it up so that I looked like a proper Mrs. Mop!

One Saturday morning in early November - it would be five years ago now - things came to a head, and the situation was suddenly radically altered. It started when I went to my underwear drawer one Saturday morning and could find none of my normal underwear at all - not a single pair of the socks or underpants which I had brought with me. There were just the three pairs of pink mini-briefs which Mrs. Clarridge had given me for my birthday. I put on a pair of these, and looked in the wardrobe for a clean pair of jeans. I couldn't find any. I put on my dressing gown and went downstairs to find Mr. Clarridge.

I'm ever so sorry, dear,' she chirped, 'but what with it being such wet weather at the moment I've not been able to get anything dry.'

'But I thought you had an electric clothes drier,' I pointed out.

'Yes, but it's broken down, and it would be very expensive to call out Mr. Jones, the man who normally fixes things for me. He says he'd have to charge double time for labour, if he comes out over the weekend. If I wait until next Wednesday, he can drop in and have a look at it then, as he's got to make another call out this way - and it won't cost me anything like so much.'

'But what am I going to wear?' I asked, 'I haven't got any trousers. My company blue suit is in my locker at work, you took my other suit to the dry cleaner's, two pairs of my jeans are in the wash, and the only other pair I have with me here have a broken zip, which you said you were going to mend for me....'

'Oh, I'm sorry dear, I haven't had time to do that.'

'Well then, I haven't got any trousers to wear.'

'Perhaps if I looked in Claire's wardrobe, she might have a pair of jeans you could borrow.'

Unfortunately none of Claire's jeans would fit: thanks to Mrs. Clarridge's enormous meals, my waistline was several inches larger than Claire's.

'Well, I don't know what we're going to do,' sighed Mrs. Clarridge at last.

'I can't stay in my dressing gown all weekend,' I pointed out.

We looked at each other in silence for a few moments. We were still standing in Claire's room, in front of the open wardrobe. There were rows of dresses and skirts on the hangers. Mrs. Clarridge looked at them, and then back at me. Finally, she asked:

'Look, dear, I don't suppose you fancy wearing a dress,

do you?' One or two of the looser-fitting styles would probably fit you.'

There was a long, embarrassing silence, which ended suddenly when we both broke out laughing.

'Go on dear, who's to know but me? Do it for a laugh, eh?'

Before I could reply, Mrs. Clarridge had one of the dresses off the rail, and was measuring it up against me.

'This'll do, just pop back into your bedroom and slip it on.'

I took the dress and did as she asked - to this day I don't know why exactly, but it turned out to be a final, irrevocable step, part of a pattern which had begun on that Sunday at Sarah's flat.

I came out wearing the dress, a loose apricot coloured shift with a tulip neck and front buttons down to the waist. The shoulders were puffed and the skirt was mid-length and quite full. Underneath I was wearing only the pink briefs, which, incidentally, I had noticed carried a 'Miss Selfridge' label. I mentioned this to Mrs. Clarridge, pointing out that she really couldn't deny this time that she had given me girl's panties as a birthday present.

'No dear, I assure you I didn't intend to - I must have got your briefs muddled up with some knickers I bought for Claire - they look so similar.'

'Oh really?' I replied, trying to imply by my tone that I was starting to doubt Mrs. Clarridge's innocent intentions. Here I was, standing in front of my landlady wearing nothing but a pair of panties and a dress. How had this happened to me?

'Look dear, I think it's time I owned up. I've been dying to put you into a skirt and knickers for months. I just miss my daughter so much; it's the first time she's been away from home, you see. I just thought if I could get you to dress as a girl, it would make me feel as if I'd still got a daughter about the house, and I wouldn't miss Claire so much and feel so lonely.' She looked quite desolate and pathetic as she said this, and I couldn't help feeling sorry for her. I didn't know what to say. Before I had a chance to think further about what was happening and to formulate an appropriate response, Mrs. Clarridge continued:

'As we've started now dear, perhaps you could humour me just this once. We really haven't got anything else for you to wear, anyway. Look, your legs will get cold dear, best put a pair of tights on.'

I did as I was bid.

'You seem to know what you're doing, dear; if I didn't know better, I'd almost say you must have put tights on before....'

I blushed, but didn't reply. I thought of my Sunday with Sarah. Was all this just coincidence?

'You've got very shapely legs - and they look almost as if you've shaved them - of course, that isn't possible, is it? Now, we need to do something about your figure. Just slip off the dress for a moment, will you?'

While I was taking off the dress, Mrs. Clarridge went into her own bedroom and came out with a full-length corset and a pair of black high-heeled court shoes. She helped me on with the garment and laced me in vigorously, until my waist was pulled in tightly and the fleshy skin on my chest was pushed into the bra-cups, so that it looked as if I had breasts. She padded out each cup a bit more with a handkerchief folded into a circular pad, placed behind a foam rubber bra-filler of the type sometimes used by young girls to give their budding breasts more shape.

'Claire used these when she first started wearing a bra, because she didn't have much of a bust, to begin with,' she explained as she tucked in the bra-fillers; 'now just slip the dress back on and put on the shoes.....Hmmn, not bad; fortunately you've had a shave this morning, so we just need to make you up.'

Foundation, lipstick, eye-shadow and mascara were soon expertly applied, and Mrs. Clarridge took a hair brush and fluffed my hair up, which had grown quite long - I had been intending to get a hair-cut that very weekend.

71

'Yes, it's a good job your hair's so thick and naturally curly,' she said as she brushed and teased it out. 'Now you let it carry on growing. Don't you dare get it cut without me saying so!'

Of course, when I did eventually get my hair done, she took me to the hairdressers herself and gave the stylist explicit instructions - by that time my transformation was almost complete. But I am running ahead.

The rest of that weekend at my landlady's I spent dressed as a girl. Mrs. Clarridge even insisted that I wore a nightie when I went to bed.

Chapter Three

Things returned to normal in time for me to go to work on Monday morning. Mrs. Clarridge had decided to teach me how to replace the zip in my jeans myself. We sat on the sofa on Sunday night, and she showed me how to unpick the stitches on the old zip. I think she took some secret pleasure from the fact that I was dressed as a girl while doing needlework with her. I was wearing a beige corduroy skirt, a white blouse with lace-edged collar, honey coloured tights, and light brown low-heeled espadrilles. I found the clothes quite comfortable and by this time had become accustomed to sitting in a skirt; Mrs. Clarridge had given me a few broad hints about keeping my legs together and not 'showing off my underwear'.

After taking out the old zip, Mrs. Clarridge took me over to her Singer sewing machine which she had set up on a small table in the bay window of her sitting room, and showed me how to use it to sew in the new zip.

'We'll make a seamstress of you yet,' she laughed.

I thus had a pair of jeans to wear to work on Monday morning, and changed into the company suit I kept in my locker once I was there.

I noticed that Sarah seemed to be more friendly towards me - several times I caught her smiling at me in a knowing sort of way. But what did she know? Could she possibly have found out what had happened at my landlady's? Was there some sort of conspiracy between them? I later discovered that my suspicions in this respect were not unfounded.

At Mrs. Clarridge's, more and more of my male clothes continued to disappear, to be replaced by female attire. Soon, my underwear drawer contained nothing but panties, tights and bras, which Mrs. Clarridge insisted that I should wear underneath my male clothes at work. At weekends and in the evenings, she kept me completely in skirts. My hair continued to grow, and even though

I slicked it down at work, some of the other employees were starting to notice and make remarks. I heard two of the warehouse lads refer to me as 'Stephanie'- if only they knew how appropriate their jibes were!

I seemed to have turned into a complete sissy! No, it had got beyond that - I was allowing my landlady to turn me into a girl. Why did I submit to her will and go along with what she was doing to me, without complaint? I had never been considered - or thought of myself - as effeminate, in the past, and yet I was now willingly wearing female clothes all the time, either under my work clothes, or completely dressed as a girl during my spare time.

I had even started going out dressed as a girl with Mrs. Clarridge; sometimes I helped her with the shopping at the local supermarket (not the company I work for - that would have been too great a risk.) She introduced me as her niece, to any acquaintances of hers whom we might meet. On several occasions we went to play bridge or whist at the Women's Institute. We attended talks on cookery, flower arranging, and fashion (though the fashions on display were a little too much for the 'older woman' for my taste); we also went out for evening meals and to the theatre a couple of times. I found that I gained in confidence with these excursions, and had no difficulty in passing and being completed accepted as a girl.

Mrs Clarridge said it was like having another daughter, and that she really enjoyed my company when I was 'Stephanie'. She too had decided to call me by this name and chose to refer to me as Stephanie even when I was wearing my male work clothes on a week day morning, as if my male persona was the masquerade and we both knew that I was really a girl.

I felt ashamed - surely my behaviour wasn't very 'manly'? - and at the same time excited and exhilarated by what was happening to me, as if an important part of my personality was finally being drawn out, and some deeper need attended to. I could no longer deny my urge to become more feminine, an urge which was growing stronger each day.

Most inexplicable of all, I began to notice changes in my body. At first I thought it was just my imagination, and that I was putting on weight because of all Mrs. Clarridge's good home-cooked food. But it was *where* I was putting on weight that disconcerted me. After a few more months I was no longer in any doubt. My waist was of course much smaller, because Mrs. Clarridge insisted that I wore a corset at all times about the house, and she continued to lace me in tightly. By this time she had taken several inches off my waist, and in fact had fitted me into a smaller corset, a white garment of strong elasticated material, with laces at the back, little frills around the bra-cups, and a silk bow with a flower motif at the centre of the cleavage. This garment she referred to as my 'little mistress' - 'Don't forget to put on your little mistress,' she would remind me as soon as I arrived home from work, and then she would come into my room when I had got it on and lace me up firmly at the back. By this means she had managed to reduce my waist to about 26 inches, a not unreasonable waist measurement for a girl, as she regularly pointed out. I had to agree with her that the outfits she made me wear, the dresses, skirts and blouses she had 'found' for me (I suspected she was buying them) - always looked better with the slim, feminine waist she had been able to give me by insisting I wore the corset.

But the change was not just in my waist size; I noticed that my hips were broadening out and becoming more rounded, and even more surprising - I was definitely developing breasts. By this time I could already fill an A-cup bra without resort to any padding. How could this be? It was scarcely possible, but the cleavage of my swelling bosom, which the corset forced up and made more pronounced, was now all my own! Soon, it would be impossible for me to conceal the changes in my body under the male clothes I wore for work - and what would happen then?

Chapter Four

The answer came suddenly, when Sarah called me into her office one morning.

'Sit down,' she ordered, imperiously. 'I am speaking to you now as your Personnel Manager, not as your friend or former lover; you've forfeited those roles for ever by what you have allowed us to do you. When I say 'us' I mean myself and Mrs. Clarridge, who has been following my instructions throughout. Yes, Stephanie (that will be your name permanently from now on - I have the deed-poll papers here for you to sign, so that it becomes legal), Mrs. Clarridge and I worked hard at your transformation, which has been accomplished for your own good. I sensed that it was right for you, that weekend you came to my flat - you loved me making a girl of you. A normal man just doesn't put up with those things. So I could see what was inevitable for you - what you wanted, though you didn't know it yourself, then. I put my plans for you into motion, and now we have come to the moment that I am sure you have been longing for, and you must understand that there can be no turning back, Stephanie. When you leave here, you will return home to Mrs. Clarridge's, where you will put on female clothing - I gather you dress as a girl there all the time now, anyway. Mrs. Clarridge will dispose of your remaining male things - although I don't suppose there's much left, from what she tells me. You will then be taken to the hairdresser's, after which you must make your way to your new lodgings in Donthorpe. It's about forty miles, and you'll have to go by public transport, dressed as a girl, of course, but that shouldn't present any difficulties to you, given the advanced training in femininity you've received. We've chosen to relocate you in Donthorpe because it's far enough away to make it unlikely that anyone there will have known you in your former life. You will live as a girl and work as a female cashier at the supermarket near your new lodgings - I've spoken already to the Personnel Manager about you. You have forfeited your management status as well as your male gender. You must now be satisfied with your new role in life, as a girl. I am sure you will soon get used to it - you know it's for the best.'

I sat there, unable to reply, trying to grasp what was happening to me, wondering if I should protest, and feeling as if I might burst into tears at any moment - though whether they would be tears of shame or joy, I couldn't say. As I watched Sarah go to a cupboard and get out two female cashier's uniforms, I sighed inwardly in resignation, accepting my destiny. This was what I had come to - the reality of my new future. I had been moving for months, as if in a dream, towards this point, amazed at myself - a little disgusted, perhaps, at how easily I had been relinquishing my manhood -   and yet at the same time yearning for this. Now there was no turning back.

'Here are your uniforms,' Sarah said, 'which you can take with you.' She handed me two neatly folded blue pinafore dresses, two white blouses, and a lapel badge with 'Stephanie Donaldson, Cashier' printed on it. 'Remember you must wear navy or plain light tan coloured tights, and only a little make-up is permitted. I have booked you into a private clinic in Donthorpe for a course of electrolysis treatment, to remove your remaining facial hair; until this is completed you may have to wear a little foundation - although looking at you now, your complexion already looks positively girlish. You obviously never had much facial hair in the first place. Just as well you have decided to give up trying to be a man - it just wasn't right for you and you were never going to make much of one. It's so obvious that you should be a girl.' I did not comment.

'A couple of other points we have to make to female employees: ear-rings are against company regulations - only sleepers may be worn. Your shoes should be black or navy blue pumps with low heels. This is practical anyway, as you may be on your feet shelf-filling some days, and that's pretty tiring in high heels. Only clear or pearl nail varnish may be worn - no crimson nails at work, please. Well, I think that's everything. Now just sign this, to authorize your change of name (she passed me the deed-poll document to sign). Have you anything you want to say, Stephanie - or any questions?'

I shook my head. Everything seemed to have been decided for me - my fate was sealed.

'Oh yes,' concluded Sarah, 'there is one final thing. Once a month, on a Sunday, I should like you to make your way over to my flat so that I can see how you're progressing. We'll start from this Sunday. Come promptly at 9.00 a.m.'

And with that, I was dismissed.

Chapter Five

I went home to Mrs. Clarridge's, who told me to strip down to my bra and panties, which as always now, I was wearing under my male work clothes. She gave me a lacy waist slip and a new pair of tights to put on, and then helped me into a skirt and blouse.

'You don't need the corset any more, dear; your figure's come on a treat. You have a lovely little girlish waist and your hips have broadened out nicely. As for your bust, it's nothing short of a miracle - how have you managed it?' Mrs. Clarridge plumped one of my breasts lightly with her finger-tips.

'I don't know,' I replied truthfully, looking down at my cleavage.

'Now dear, I know all about you're going to live in Donthorpe, but before you make your way over there, I've booked you an appointment at the beauty salon. You're going to have your hair done, and one or two other treatments. As you'll have to strip off again to your bra and knickers, you'd better just pop into the bathroom and put this on under your panties. Pull it on as tight as possible.' She handed me a little flesh-coloured garment of strong elastic material, which looked like a cross between a jock-strap and a G-string. 'It's called a 'cache-sex',' she explained; 'it's to pull in what you've got between your legs so that your panties look as flat as they should if you're a girl.'

I went into the bathroom, took off my tights and panties, and put on the elastic garment. It flattened down my genitals, pulling them in as far back between my legs as possible, so that, sure enough, when I put my panties back on and rolled up my tights, my crotch looked exactly like a girl's. I marvelled at the smooth roundness between my legs; all signs of my maleness had disappeared. I rolled the slip back down over my thighs, eased down my skirt and straightened it, making sure that the lace hem of the slip didn't show. The skirt was quite tight and fairly short, tailored with a vent on the back hem, and of a black silky material which stretched smoothly across my hips. Mrs. Clarridge had left a pair of black leather court shoes on the landing for me, which I slipped on. The stiletto heels were at least four inches, slightly higher than I was used to; Mrs. Clarridge laughed as I swayed down the stairs in them.

'Aren't they a bit high?' I asked her.

'Not at all,' she replied, 'you're a girl all the time now, so you'll have to get used to suffering a little pain for the sake of beauty. They really show your legs off - you've got lovely slender ankles, dear. By the way, there's a matching leather handbag in the hall to go with the shoes. I've put a purse with some change in for you, and a few items of make-up. That tailored jacket in the hall is also for you - it matches the skirt, so you'll look very smart for the journey. It's size 14 - that's your size now, isn't it?'

I nodded. I went down the hall, slipped the jacket off the hanger and tried it on. It was quite close-fitting, shaped in so that it emphasized the smallness of the waist and accentuated the bustline and curve of the hips.

'Well your figure certainly does that outfit justice,' said Mrs. Clarridge. 'I've got a couple of little going-away presents for you,' she continued, producing two small gift-wrapped packages from a drawer of the sideboard in the hall. We went into the kitchen and I sat on the edge of a stool, balancing precariously in my tight skirt and high heels as I opened the presents. One was a ladies' digital watch - 'It was all I could afford dear, but you can't very well wear that great heavy man's watch any more, and you'll need to know the time to get your connection for Donthorpe - you need to change trains at Leicester.' I thanked her and opened the other package, which proved to be a delicate necklace and matching bracelet, two simple silver chains with a matching enamel flower suspended on each. The flowers had blue petals and golden stamens. 'They're very rare flowers,' she said, 'called 'Jacob's Ladder' - they grow in a Derbyshire dale out beyond Bakewell.' She undid the clasp of the necklace and fastened it round my neck. 'I found this jewellery in a craft shop in Bakewell - it's made locally - and I thought of you straight away.'

'Why?' I asked, slipping the bracelet on my wrist.

'Because you're a rare flower, dear, and it matches the blue of your eyes.'

'Oh Mrs. Clarridge,' I said, giving her a hug and planting a kiss on her cheek.

'Call me Alice, dear.'

'Thank you, Alice, it was a very kind thought.' I could feel tears starting into my eyes.

Now then, dear, we want none of that - you'll make your mascara run. Come on, let's get off to the hairdresser's. Your appointment's for 11.30, so we've just got time to walk there, if we leave now.'

'Walk there?'

'Of course, dear, why not?'

'It's just walking any distance in these heels.....'

'You'll be wearing high heels quite a lot from now on, so you may as well get to walking in them.' I thought ruefully of the state my feet would be in by the end of the day. Up to now I had only worn high heels for a few hours, when we'd gone out in the evenings, and my toes had ached enough then.

'Just a little sacrifice you have to make,' she added, 'for the sake of showing off a well-turned ankle!'

When we got to the hairdresser's, the girls in the salon greeted me cheerfully by name, as they knew me quite well by now. Mrs. Clarridge had insisted that I let my hair grow during the preceding months, and had only let me get it cut with her permission, on two occasions, provided I went to this salon. She had given instructions to the stylist to leave it as long as possible, each time, tidying it so that I could get away with it at work (just) if I plastered it down. The stylist had allowed the length of my hair to grow out evenly, so that it was now thick enough and long enough on top to give me a fashionable bob cut, with a wedge-shape at the back of my neck and just above my ear-lobes. The girl had put conditioner on while washing it, so that after blow-drying, my hair swung loosely in long, soft tresses when I moved my head from side to side - a delicious sensation which confirmed that my hair was now cut in an unmistakably feminine style.

I next went through to another room, which constituted the 'beauty parlour' part of the establishment, where my eyebrows were plucked and re-shaped professionally. Then my ear-lobes were pierced and gold sleepers put in them. My face was cleaned of existing make-up, my skin toned and freshened, and I was expertly made-up again, the girl explaining what she was doing and giving advice to me at each stage. Finally, I was asked to strip down to my bra, panties and slip. At this point I was glad that Mrs. Clarridge had given me the little elastic garment to wear - the cache sex - before we came out. As I was wearing this under my panties and waist slip, and my breasts by this time were quite pronounced, the beautician saw nothing unusual in the appearance of the young woman before her. I was already in the habit of shaving under my arms (at the insistence of Mrs. Clarridge), and of removing any other body hair which in the normal way of things would be considered unfeminine; the beautician now gave my legs, arms and 'bikini line' the full waxing treatment, after which she rubbed moisturising creams and oils into my skin, so that it ended up feeling softer and smoother than ever before. I got dressed again and walked back to the hair-dressing salon, where Mrs. Clarridge was sitting under the drier, reading a magazine.

'Wow!' she gasped, as I entered. I grinned back at her, not knowing what to say.

You're going to turn a few heads, and no mistake,' she laughed.

Chapter Six

In the well-groomed young woman who emerged from the salon, no trace could be discerned of the male trainee supermarket manager who had come to stay at Mrs. Clarridge's so many months before. I saw my reflection in a shop window, as we made our way up the street. There was no doubt of it - I was a girl, and quite an attractive girl at that. Mrs. Clarridge caught me smiling at my reflection, and smiled back at me:

'You're one of us now, dear, and you look lovely,' she laughed.

'There's one thing that's been puzzling me,' I said, but before I could continue, a wolf whistle came from the top of some scaffolding across the street. Mrs. Clarridge nodded towards a couple of loutish lads who were working up the scaffolding on a half-finished building.

'I think that was directed at you, dear,' she said, looking askance at the two workmen, who were still leering at us. 'You'll have to get used to that sort of thing. To all appearances you're a very attractive female. Welcome to the wonderful world of being a girl, and getting ogled at all the time.'

I thought about this for a few moments, and then remembered what I had been about to ask her, before:

What I'd like to know is - how did the changes in my body happen - my breasts?'

'Ah well, I've got a little confession to make, dear. I've been slipping something into your food for some months past - female hormones. They were actually prescribed for me, because of my time of life. It's called hormone replacement therapy - it's supposed to stop me having hot flushes and all that, because of the menopause. I started taking them, but they didn't seem to make me feel any better, so I gave them to you, as an experiment. I never expected the results to be so dramatic, but as your figure was filling out so beautifully, I carried on collecting the prescriptions and giving the pills to you, in your food and drink. What is your bust size now, by the way? I should think you must be at least a 34A.'

'36A, actually,' I replied, blushing.

I made my way over to my new lodgings in Donthorpe carrying only my handbag and an overnight bag containing my nightie, one of my new cashier's uniforms, some underwear, and make-up; Mrs. Clarridge said she would arrange to have my other things sent on in a trunk. (When the trunk arrived, it proved to contain my favourite sling-back high heeled sandals, the light brown espadrilles, a pair of comfortable low-heeled pumps, and the dresses, skirts, blouses, tights and slips, etc. I had worn while staying with Mrs. Clarridge - there were none of my remaining male things, which Mrs. Clarridge had obviously disposed of, as she said she would.)

No one gave me a second glance on the train, except one young man in a business suit who sat opposite me, and whose motives for staring at my legs, I suspected, were less than pure. So this was what girls had to put up with!

I soon settled into my new life as a girl cashier at the supermarket. The other employees both male and female accepted me as Stephanie without reservation, having no reason to think that I was anything other than the young woman I appeared to be. The trolley boys tried to flirt with me, as with the other girls, although I certainly did not give them any encouragement. After a while I hit upon the idea of making it known that I already had a steady boyfriend, and this meant that I was generally left in peace by the more wolfish males in the store.

Once a month, on a Sunday, I went to pay my visit to Sarah, my one-time lover and Personnel Manager of my old branch, who it would seem had been in large part responsible for my transformation.

On my first visit to her flat since moving to Donthorpe, I had no sooner arrived than she had whisked me into the bedroom and ordered me to put on the clothes which were spread out on the bed. It was a complete maid's outfit: a black satin dress with white lace around the collar and cuffs; a white lace-edged apron and cap; a white petticoat hemmed with several layers of frills; black seamed tights and black high-heeled leather pumps. When I'd got the dress on, the skirt proved to be rather short - well above knee-length - and the frothy petticoat made it stick out so that (as I soon discovered), it was hard to bend down without giving a glimpse of my frilly underwear. I felt embarrassed and humiliated in this costume, which was apparently Sarah's intention.

'Because of what I have done for you, which you know is what you wanted, you will repay me by spending the day, once a month, as my maid. If you refuse, I will let them know at your new branch that you used to be a boy, and what you have let us do to you. While you are here you will address me as 'Miss'. You will clean the flat, do my washing, and prepare a meal for me and my guests, when I request it. Is that clear?'

'Yes Miss,' I answered, blushing with the shame of my position. I had once been a man, a manager - in time, I would have been an executive; I had thrown it all away to become what I was now - a female servant, a part-time skivvy and check-out girl.

Chapter Seven

One Sunday she had a guest, an elegant young woman who stayed for dinner. Sarah introduced her:

'This is Miss Claire. She is your ex-landlady's daughter. You may be interested to know that she has finished her course at the university and is now working as a trainee manager at your previous place of work - she has your old job, in fact.'

Claire looked fondly at Sarah, and whispered, 'It was so clever of you to arrange it all.'

Sarah gave her hand a little squeeze in return.

The truth was beginning to dawn on me. I served dinner to them, answering their every beck and call. As the evening progressed, I couldn't help but notice the soft looks they exchanged and the little starts of pleasure when they touched each other. Every subtle, sensuous movement between them gave further evidence of what I had guessed - they were lovers!

Had they been lovers all along? Was this why I had been turned into a check-out girl and part-time maid - so that I could be got rid of at work to make way for Sarah's protege and lover? Claire had got my old job - that was a fact. Had they conspired against me - Mrs. Clarridge, Sarah - to achieve this end all along? And I had permitted them to do this to me - I had been a willing victim, submitting to their wills as if in a dream. I had been a sleepwalker, colluding in my transformation to a girl and embracing my degradation to my present lowly status. What had they done to me? What had I done to myself? Tears started into my eyes.

What are you snivelling for, girl?' demanded Sarah; 'serve me another coffee, and then you may go back to your hovel in Donthorpe.'

And so I was dismissed, until I went back a month later, to do my duty as a maid again. I dreaded these Sundays; Sarah and Claire seemed to delight in humiliating me. They loved to make me bend down to pick or sweep things up - I suspected that they dropped things on purpose, so that they would get a glimpse of my frilly undies when I bent down in my short maid's dress and high heels. They liked to make fun of me on these occasions, saying things like:

'Look at all that lace - the little minx just loves the frou-frou of her petticoats, you know,' or

'Look, she's showing her knickers, the naughty girl,' or

'Her seams aren't quite straight, the little slut.'

I blushed with shame at their taunts, but remained silent and submissive in my demeanour, as was expected of me.

One evening while I was serving dinner, I got another insight into their motivations. As I was going out of the door to fetch the next course from the kitchen, I heard Sarah say quietly:

'You must agree Claire, she makes a lovely girl, does our little Stephanie. I'm glad for what we've done to her.'

I stopped behind the door and listened as Sarah continued:

'She never would have made much of a man anyway, so it's just as well she's given up trying, and taken so readily to wearing skirts. Deep down, I sensed there was something feminine and girlish about her; all we've done is help release that side of her personality, which has now taken her over completely.'

Claire replied:

'Well, it's one less man in the world, and that can't be a bad thing. Here's to womankind, and a plague on all men!' I heard the chink of their wine glasses, as they drank a toast to this.

Had these women, I wondered, reduced me to my present state partly out of some misguided impulse to get back at the male sex? Or had it been a sort of game for them - an experiment in petticoat training, with me as the guiless victim? Or was the motive more practical - to get me out of my job so there would be a management vacancy for Claire at Sarah's branch of the superstore? Most likely all these factors played some part; I would never know for sure, and did it matter, anyway? Here I was - transformed into a girl - a female cashier and part-time maid. Was this then to be my life, my future?

Chapter Eight

One day I got a letter from Sarah:

'Dear Stephanie,

You have adapted so well to your new life that I have decided to reward you by releasing you from your duty to attend on me as my maid, once a month. However, there is one condition: there must be no question of you ever resuming your former gender role and existence. You are living as a girl now, and you must give me your solemn promise that you will continue to do so in the future.

If you agree to this, I am prepared to arrange for the Company to reinstate your management status - you will recommence the Company's programme for trainee retail managers from next September, at another store, the location of which will be determined later. You will, of course, dress as a female trainee manager, and will be issued with two management suits appropriate to your gender - you will be familiar with the blue tailored skirt and jacket worn by our female junior managers. You should make an effort to see that you are always well-groomed and maintain the high standards of dress we expect from our young female executives. I have every confidence in you in this respect; you make a very attractive girl, and I am sure you will be a credit to the Company.

Best wishes for your future career,

Yours sincerely,

Sarah Downes,
Personnel Manager,
Sheffingham Branch,
Freshways Superstores'

What could I do? What would you have done? I accepted my fate.

The events I have recorded, my transformation from male trainee manager to check-out girl and part-time maid, and finally to female trainee manager, happened several years ago.

I have progressed rapidly in the Company; I believe my change to the female role has given me more confidence, releasing my energies and potential to pursue my career and use my skills and talents to the full. As a man, I do not think I would have achieved so much. I think that I must always have had a strong feminine side to my personality; had I remained as a man, the conflict between the feminine and masculine within me would have diverted a lot of my energy. Paradoxically, I believe that by giving full expression to my feminine self, I have been able to channel what masculine characteristics I possess into my business and management roles. At times I have been required to show a degree of aggression and ruthlessness which I don't think I could have found within myself before my change of gender. I was, in fact, rather a wimpish young man; I have become, instead, an assertive and successful woman, who enjoys life to the full.

Thus I now manage my own superstore. I have an executive car (a Mercedes), a pleasant detached house in large grounds, on a wooded hill-side, and plenty of money to spend on clothes. For work, I like to be a bit of a 'power-dresser'; I wear immaculately cut skirts and jackets, creamy silk blouses, and hand-made leather court shoes with medium heels. My jewellery is restrained but classy, usually a simple necklace or broach in solid silver. I can afford the best designer lingerie, beautiful lacy slips, panties and bras.

I have continued with the hormone treatment, and have recently had some minor cosmetic surgery to further enhance my appearance; this included the removal from my throat of all traces of my adam's apple, the remodelling of my nose to make it smaller and more feminine, and the augmentation of my breasts by moderate-sized silicon inserts, so that I can now fill a 36B cup. I have not had to shave for some years, thanks to the hormone treatment and the course of electrolysis I had while I was still working as a female cashier. This means that I do not have to wear any foundation, and in fact sometimes I don't wear any make-up at all. I prefer a 'natural' look when I do use make-up, usually restricting myself to eye-shadow, a little mascara, and a subtle shade of lipstick.

I cannot deny that I derive great pleasure from my feminine body shape. I enjoy the feel of my breasts when I walk, the slight bouncing movement and the way the soft elastic fabric of my bra gently restrains them. On holiday in southern France recently, I was able to sunbathe on the beach in a bikini, concealing the male appendages between my legs with a cleverly designed front pad which I obtained from a specialist supplier, who caters for the needs of drag artists. It flattens me and holds me in so that my bikini panties fit me very snugly.

I look down at my body and marvel, recalling what I once was, and seeing what I am now - an attractive curvaceous blonde in her late twenties, at least to all outward appearances. I look at the soft roundness of my bosoms, which amply fill out my bra cups; I look at my slim waist and broad hips, at the way my panties stretch flat over my lower abdomen and curve smoothly down between my legs, my shape perfectly feminine, with all signs of maleness gone.

Of course, I have had to learn new skills, like the art of getting out of a car wearing a short skirt, without providing any randy males watching with a full display of my lacy underwear. I slide out my nylon-clad legs, placing my high heels firmly on the ground and retrieving my handbag from the passenger seat, before deftly completing my exit from the Mercedes.

After living as a girl for so long, I still enjoy the sensation of my panty-hose slipping silkily under my skirt and slip, and the soft rasping of the nylon on my inner thighs. I have found that male senior managers who come on inspections of the superstore can be quite easily distracted, if I sit them down in my office where they will get a good view of my long legs, and then periodically move my thighs or cross my legs to produce this whispering of my panty-hose and lingerie. Combine this with a sweet smile, and a slightly lower-cut blouse, which reveals a glimpse of my cleavage, and most male executives forget whatever criticisms of my store they may have been about to make. Thus have I discovered the power of feminine charms!

Although my appearance is that of an attractive woman, and men regularly ask me out on dates, I usually decline their invitations, as I am not attracted sexually to men. I have had to learn to play the feminine role at social functions and of course when partnering men for dances, but I try to make it clear at the outset with men that I am not interested in a sexual relationship. Some of them find this hard to understand, and I have been accused of having lesbian tendencies more than once! I have a couple of male friends who accept my reluctance to get involved, and are happy to partner me when I need a male escort for social occasions. These I regard as genuine friends, who value me for my company. How difficult it is to find such men - as I am sure every pretty woman knows!

I confess I have flirted once or twice with men, but for obvious reasons I didn't allow this to get beyond kissing. One date did get fresh and try to fondle my breasts a little, for which he got a slap round the face. I haven't enjoyed these episodes, and in spite of my feminine gender role and life-style, I realized some time ago that I am still male in one important respect.

But how on earth could I expect to have a relationship with a woman now? What woman - other than a lesbian - would be interested in me? And a true lesbian would be quickly turned off by what I still have between my legs, which I have no intention of getting rid of.

Chapter Nine

I was beginning to feel as if, outwardly successful young woman as I am to all appearances, my sexual and emotional needs were doomed to be frustrated, when my secretary unexpectedly went off back-packing to Australia with her boyfriend.

My new secretary is a tall, rather mannish eighteen year-old called Tracey, who has a thick mane of raven-black hair. When not at work, Tracey likes to wear denim jeans torn across the knees, and tee-shirts with 'MegaDeath' or the name of some other heavy metal band emblazoned across them. I know this because by chance I came across Tracey one evening in a night-club in the town centre which I visit sometimes, and this was exactly how she was dressed. As she had just started working for me it would have been churlish not to speak to her, and we struck up a conversation about the cabaret at the club, which that night happened to be a drag act. I was surprised by her frankness, but she is the sort of girl who holds nothing back, and enjoys the thought that her unorthodox views and lifestyle may shock:

'What do you think of the act?' I asked her.

'I think it's great,' she replied; 'I'm really turned on by men in dresses. I hate all that macho shit - my father was a real he-man type - watched sport on TV every evening, drinking six-packs of beer and never lifting a finger to help my mother. He used to shout at her and knock her about when he got drunk. He was a fat, ignorant, arrogant pig - but he thought he was a real man. Give me a she-man, the more sissy the better, every time.'

I thought about her words, and eventually decided to put her to the test. I told her I'd got a lot of company correspondence to catch up with, and asked her if she'd like to earn some overtime pay and come over to my place at the weekend to help me with it. She agreed.

Well, after doing some work we got talking, and I led the conversation round to what she'd said at the night-club. Was she serious about her taste in men - or perhaps she didn't like men at all?

'Hey, I know I dress a bit dykey, but I don't think I'm a lesbian,' she replied.

'Neither am I,' I said.

'Oh, only I've heard rumours at the store that you're a lesbian - they say you won't let men near you.'

'It's true I won't let men near me, but there's a reason for that......'

And so I launched into my story, the story you have just read. Tracey was amazed by what I told her, and just would not accept that I had once been a man - and still had one part of my male anatomy to prove it. By this time we had had quite a bit to drink, and we were both giggling like a couple of school girls, and she said there was only one way I could convince her I was a man. Before I knew what she was doing she had started to undress me, and I began to undress her. We finally got to the panties; when she gently pealed down mine it was very obvious by what my male member was doing that I was attracted to her. We ended up in bed, and our loving-making was very tender and wonderful, like a new awakening for both of us.

'Maybe I do have lesbian tendencies,' she said, 'I certainly get horny when I look at your body. I get the best of both worlds with you. Soft skin, shapely breasts, supple thighs, slim waist - and you're as gentle and sensitive as a woman in your love-making. I find out what it's like to be a lesbian, without the guilt that I'm doing anything unnatural - and believe me, what you've got between your legs is better than any dildo or vibrator - it's the real McCoy all right.' I kissed her on each nipple, then on the soft velvet triangle between her legs. She nuzzled up to me, fondling my breast gently with one hand, and with the other holding firmly on to my member, which was still aroused. We made love again.

This then, is the end of my story, the story of how Stephen became Stephanie.

Tracey recently moved in with me - though of course this is kept secret from everyone at work. Tracey has a strong masculine side to her personality - what she calls her 'dykey' side. Although I am her boss at the office, the roles are reversed at home; she likes ordering me about and treating me as the 'little woman', and as there is part of me which enjoys the submissive role (otherwise I would never have submitted to the humiliations imposed on me by Sarah and Mrs. Clarridge), we suit each other very well. Do I have any regrets? No! I am indeed a very lucky girl. Je ne regret rien!

New Girl on the Ward

The story of a boy's transformation into a female nurse

I had always had a 'thing' about nurses. Yes, it's partly the uniform - can there be a male in existence who isn't turned on by what nurses wear? The black stockings; the blue dress with crisp white collar; the waist-cinching belt; the little cap with the hair pinned back under it; the sensible low-heeled shoes.....But it's not just what nurses wear, it's how they carry themselves and what they represent. That air of brisk, no-nonsense efficiency, combined with the caring, compassionate manner - there is something in the nature of nurses which reverberates deeply in the unconscious fantasies of all males. Nurses represent female power - the caring, cosseting power of the mother figure, who knows what is best for us, and will take a firm line with us when necessary. When we go into hospital, we hand over daily control of ourselves to nurses; they do all the things for us which our mothers did when we were young children - they feed us, comfort us, make our beds, plump our pillows - even wash us and attend to our bodily functions. Although there are certainly plenty of middle-aged nurses, over-weight nurses, nurses with big noses, nurses with bad complexions and greasy hair and little moustaches - in our fantasies at least, nurses are attractive young women with slim waists, bright smiles and gentle hands. Nurses, in short are angels - but sexually unattainable. Beneath those crisp blue uniforms we know that there are firm female bodies, but we can only lay in our sick beds and dream about them.

This is how I used to think of nurses, never dreaming that one day I would be wearing that blue uniform myself, feeling the eyes of male patients on me, admiring my black nylon-clad legs, trying to look up my skirt when I bend over to make a bed. I know what women have to put up with now, how men try to undress you with their eyes.

I know this because today I am Nicola Hopkins, S.R.N.; but I haven't always been called Nicola. This is my story:

I was born Nicholas Hopkins, the second child and first son of my parents. My sister, Pamela, is two years older than me. I still see Pamela occasionally, but I never see my parents, now. They wanted nothing to do with me, after I became Nicola.

I had a fairly normal childhood, I suppose. I was brought up in one of those amorphous suburbs of south-east London, one of those non-places which came into existence during the 1930's, consisting of streets of semi-detached houses, a parade of shops and a station. I attended the local primary school uneventfully, and scraped through the eleven-plus to get to a mediocre grammar school, at which I passed some 'O' levels and a couple of 'A' levels - enough to get me into a polytechnic in a northern city to study engineering. It was while I was in digs during my second year, sharing a big old red-brick Victorian house with some student nurses, that events began to unfold which brought me to my present situation.

I had a bed-sit on the second floor of the house, an attic room with a gable window which looked out over the slate roofs and smoking chimneys of the city. I was lonely. At night I would lay on my bed, listening to the street sounds below, the drunken voices when the pubs closed, the car doors slamming and engines revving; and the sad, distant lowing, like lost souls, of the fog-horns on the great river.

I attended the lectures and tutorials in the day, returning to my attic room at night, to listen again to the sounds of life going on around me. I wasn't enjoying my course, and I didn't much care for the other students, among whom I had not managed to make any friends.

The landlord, Mr. Tuttle, had warned me that the other

97

two floors of the house were occupied by student nurses, explaining that the house often acted as an overflow for St. Bride's, the hospital about a quarter of a mile away, on the main road. The nurses' residential wing next to the hospital was not big enough to accommodate all the student nurses employed at the hospital.

I didn't mind at all sharing the house with nurses, although I was the only male in a house of four women. Sometimes it was hard to find a bathroom free - but this was the only drawback, as far as I could see.

My co-tenants were Laura, Tracey, Eleni and Melissa. These girls had plenty of boyfriends, got stuck into the booze at every opportunity, smoked marijuana as well as cigarettes, dressed casually, fashionably, or in a tarty or wacky way to suit themselves, and generally believed in having a good time when they weren't at work. Although I'm sure they were good, caring nurses at work, they didn't take the academic part of their nursing studies too seriously, left doing essays and assignments as late as possible, missed lectures when they had hangovers, and copied each other's notes shamelessly.

I listened to the sounds of these young women getting on with their lives - sometimes giggling and shrieking; often quarrelling; occasionally, quietly weeping, when one of them had been let down by a boyfriend. I envied their matter-of-fact lust for life particularly; the way they just got on with living, loving, losing and winning; I envied too the cheerful female companionship they all shared.

I lay on my narrow bed, looking at the peeling flock wallpaper and the cobwebs in the corner of the room, trying to read some engineering text book, but really listening to the sounds of their lives, thinking how empty and dull and grey and lonely was my own existence.

I felt as if I was still waiting for my life to begin.

I didn't dare ask any of them out for a date, for fear of being ridiculed; they seemed to accept my presence among them without taking any cognisance of my gender. They took a casual, sisterly interest in me, but there seemed to be an unwritten rule that anything of a romantic or sexual nature was out of the question. It was partly a matter of age. Most of their male friends were several years older than me; I was viewed as little more than a half-grown boy. Their romantic interests were definitely directed towards what they considered to be 'real men'. I apparently didn't qualify as a 'real man', not just because of my youth, but also, I suspected, because of my puny physique. I was five feet five inches tall, small-boned and slight, with wavy dark brown hair and not much in the way of beard growth. Two of the girls were actually bigger than me; one of them - the black-haired and hirsute Greek girl called Eleni - even had more of a moustache than I could have produced.

So there I was sharing a big old house with four student nurses, a house awash with girlish laughter and bitchiness and femininity. There were tights and stockings and bras and panties and lacy slips drying on every rail and radiator around the house.

Now, you will be expecting at this point that I'm going to begin to tell you about some innocent pretext arising which caused these four lovelies to force me to dress up as a girl - a fancy dress party, perhaps. Then, if this followed the normal pattern of transvestite stories, I would comment: 'And that is how it all began...', and before you could say panty girdle, I would be launched on the inevitable path towards girldom.....

But I am sure you are not so unsophisticated as to believe such fantasies. As this is a true story, dear reader, I'm going to tell you what really happened:

One lonely evening, with nothing better to do, I crept

out on to the landing and borrowed a pair of tights which had been draped over a radiator to dry. The girls had all gone down to the pub, and I was alone in the house. I took the tights back to my room and stripped off my jeans; then I sat on the bed and rolled them on, one foot at a time, as I had seen Tracey doing through the open door of her room one morning. I had been waiting to get into the bathroom (which was occupied as usual); her room was nearly opposite, on the other side of the landing, and her door was open far enough for me to be able to observe her without being seen myself. Tracey was one of the more extrovert of the nurses, a chestnut-haired beauty with a bubbly, infectious laugh. I'm sure Tracey hadn't realised I was able to see her getting dressed, but I doubt whether it would have bothered her even if she had known. The girls were quite unembarrassed about appearing in front of me half-clothed, on their way to the bathroom or whatever; it was almost as if they looked on me as one of them, as 'one of the girls', even then.

Having carefully rolled on the tights one foot at a time, I gently eased them up the rest of the way until they were snug over my crotch. They were black tights, as worn by nurses at work. I went over to to the mirror on my wardrobe door and surveyed the effect. My legs looked surprisingly slim and shapely, but I was not impressed by the appearance of my Y-fronts underneath the the panty part of the tights.

Listening to make sure no one had come home, I crept back out onto the landing and found on another radiator a pair of lacy black panties - and for good measure - a matching bra. I began to wonder what was happening to me - what on earth was I doing? I had never had the inclination to try on girls' clothes in the past, but I seemed to be governed now by some sort of strange compulsion. I could hardly breathe, and I could feel my heart thudding in my chest. I felt I was doing something that was taboo and deeply wrong, something that might well prove to be dangerous and destructive to my peace of mind - and yet I couldn't help myself. If you are a true transvestite, you will have experienced these feelings.

I returned to my room and stripped naked. With shaking hands, I pulled on the panties and struggled with the bra until I had got the clasp done up; then I rolled the tights on again. I surveyed myself in the mirror, and gasped in ecstasy to see how feminine my body looked, turning to look at myself from one side, then the other. Of course my hips were too narrow and my chest was too flat; I couldn't do much about my hips, but I could at least try the effect of padding out the bra cups. I tried a sock in each, which looked decidedly false, and eventually found that a more natural contour could be achieved by making a conical shape from a wad of tissues, although I had to make sure that the tissues didn't show above the line of the black lace edging the bra cup. I was surveying my handiwork again when I heard the lock of the front door go, and the next instant, the clatter of high heels on the floor tiles below and the sounds of tipsy girlish giggling. I realised there was no time to strip off and replace the underwear I'd borrowed, so I leapt into bed, praying that the girls wouldn't notice what was missing from the radiators. Of course they didn't notice - they were too drunk to do any more than get to their rooms and fall into bed; so I was able to replace the undies I'd borrowed without anyone knowing.

From that night onwards I was hooked. It was as if something had snapped in my personality; or perhaps it was more like something falling into place. I just couldn't help myself. Whenever the girls had gone out and I was alone in the house, I would search round the radiators and drying rails until I had found some suitable female clothing to put on. It had started with underwear - panties, bras and tights - but soon I was progressing to slips, skirts and blouses. I wanted to make my feminine image ever more realistic - to go just a bit further each time, and see the effect in the mirror. I let my hair grow and tried the effect of washing it and fluffing it up with a brush in different styles. As it was thick and wavy, I was soon able to produce a style which looked quite feminine.

None of us locked our doors in the old house; some of the doors were unlockable, and we trusted each other anyway. I was dying to try on a pair of girl's shoes, and eventually the temptation to go into one of the girls' rooms and borrow a pair was too great for me. Melissa's room was on the same landing as mine. I passed her door numerous times every day. Melissa was a big-boned, friendly girl with light brown hair which she wore in a bob; she was an inch or two taller than me, but I guessed that we had feet of about the same size.

One Saturday night, when all the girls were either on duty at the hospital or out socializing, I crept into Melissa's room and selected a pair of medium-heeled navy-blue court shoes from the bottom of her wardrobe. I carefully noted their exact position before I took them, so that I could replace them without Melissa noticing that they had been moved. I was about to close the wardrobe door when I noticed the row of dresses, skirts and blouses hanging on the rail. I couldn't resist having a closer look at what was on the rail. I put the shoes down for a moment and flicked through the clothes hanging there until I came to a gorgeous clingy velour dress in a navy-blue which seemed to match the shoes. I undid the zip at the back enough to slip it off its hanger, put it over my arm, and picking up the shoes, returned to my own room. My heart was pounding fit to burst!

By this time I had taken to wearing female underwear under my male clothes during the day. I had bought myself several bra and panties sets from Marks & Spencer and Debenhams, together with packets of tights in different shades. I quickly took off my jeans and shirt and slipped on the velour dress over the black panties, tights and bra I was already wearing. I put a spare pair of tights folded into something resembling a boob shape into each bra cup, then zipped up the dress at the back. It fitted me well, although it was a little tight under the arms. I slipped my feet into the court shoes, fluffed up my hair and scuttled to the full-length wardrobe mirror to view the effect. I was disappointed. My figure looked quite good and I was pleased with how feminine the shoes made my legs and feet look - but there was something wrong with my face. Of course - how silly of me! I needed some make-up!

I took off the dress, had a very close shave, doing my arms and arm pits as well, and then went back into Melissa's room. I looked at the scatter of cosmetics all over her dressing table, wondering what I needed. I saw a tube which said 'No. 7 foundation base, honey tone, for natural cover.' I removed the top, squeezed a little onto my finger, then smoothed it onto my cheek, studying the effect in the dressing table mirror as I did so. Yes, this seemed to be what I needed; I worked the creamy substance over my face and neck, noting the results with approval. What should I do next?

On Melissa's bed was an issue of *Cosmopolitan*. I picked it up and leafed through its contents until I came to the 'beauty' pages, which gave make-up tips. After carefully reading these, I realised that I needed a powder to 'fix' the foundation. I looked around the dressing table until I found a blue powder compact; I took out the pad and gently patted powder onto my nose and around my cheeks and neck. Finally, I put on some eye-shadow, mascara and lipstick, trying to follow the tips I had read in the women's magazine. I fluffed my hair up again, found some pear-drop clip-on earrings, and hurried back to my room. I slipped the dress back on and went again to stand in front of the mirror.

And this time - oh yes! I was delighted with the results. For what I saw in the mirror was a young brunette girl in a navy-blue dress - I could hardly believe that it was me. I swayed from side to side, minced a little, pouted, and so did the girl in the mirror. Oh what bliss - *I was the girl in the mirror!*

I was so enraptured and enthralled by my feminine

appearance that I didn't hear the soft click of the front door latch below. By the time I heard the footsteps on the stairs it was too late! The next moment my bedroom door opened and in walked Tracey and Melissa. When they saw me, they looked embarrassed and Tracey said:

'Oh sorry, we were looking for Nicholas.' They hadn't recognised me!

Melissa added:

'He's a bit of a dark horse is our Nicholas - he kept you quiet; we never even knew he had a girl friend.' Then I suppose the penny dropped, as Melissa must have recognised what I was wearing; the next moment she said:

'Good lord, that's my dress - and it can't be - I do believe that's Nicholas wearing it.!'

Just then there was the noise of the other two girls arriving home downstairs. The next moment Eleni and Laura burst into the room.

'Oh here you are,' said Laura.

'Who's this?' asked Eleni.

'This,' said Melissa, 'is our little house-boy, Nicholas, and he, or perhaps I should say *she,* is wearing my dress and shoes.'

'Good heavens!' exclaimed Laura, 'why ever is he doing that?'

They all looked at me expectantly. I had no idea what to say. I could feel my face flushing crimson under the foundation.

'Perhaps he's not so much a house-boy as a sissy-boy,' suggested Eleni.

'A she-boy,' added Laura.

Suddenly I could bear it no longer. I sat down on the bed and burst into tears. Melissa sat down beside me, put her arm round my shoulder, and said:

'Come on Nicholas, we're only joking; we're just a bit surprised, that's all. I don't even mind you wearing my dress and shoes, though it would have been nice if you'd asked me first. Why don't you tell us what all this is about?'

Tracey pulled up the only chair in the room, swayed a little, and sat down; Laura knelt down on the floor, patted my lap and said: 'It's alright love, tell us in your own time.'

Eleni said: 'Hang on, before you start, I'll go and make some of my special coffee.'

When we were all sipping Eleni's strong, sweet, Greek coffee, Melissa asked gently:

'Do you want to be a girl, then; is that it?'

'I don't know,' I replied.

'It's okay to say,' said Laura, 'we're all girls here - and you're among friends, you know.'

I thought about Melissa's question. Did I, in fact, want to be a girl? An inner voice in me answered at once: Yes - oh yes! I felt my whole soul and heart and being crying out in affirmation.

'Yes,' I said out loud, 'I want to be a girl - at least I know I'd like to dress and live as a girl, if I could.'

'Well, that's not the end of the world. We could help you do something about it, if you like,' said Melissa.

'Yes - please,' I replied.

'There might be some practical problems,' pointed out Tracey. 'What about his engineering course at the polytechnic?' Wouldn't the lecturers and other students think it a bit funny if he suddenly turned up dressed as a girl?'

'Oh I don't care about my course a bit - I'd rather pack it in, actually,' I said.

'What would you do, then?' asked Tracey, pushing her blonde hair out of her eyes.

'I think I'd like to be a nurse, like you lot.'

'What - empty bed-pans and change dressings? It's not very glamorous, you know,' said Melissa.

'Why do *we* do it then?' asked Eleni.

'Because we're so saintly,' suggested Melissa.

'Mugs, more like,' said Tracey. 'It's a pretty drastic step, Nicholas; don't you think you'd better think about it a bit more?'

I nodded. 'I suppose I ought to,' I said.

'Why don't you have a try-out at being a girl, Nicholas - see if you like it first, before you commit yourself? asked Melissa.

Before I had a chance to respond to the idea, Laura said:

'Oh yes! It could be fun. Let's take him out with us at the weekend - for a girls' night out!'

'Why not?' giggled Laura. 'What do you say, Nicholas? Or perhaps we ought to call you - Nicola....'

'Okay,' I nodded.

'That's settled, then,' said Melissa.

I couldn't wait until the weekend! Friday finally came. Laura and Melissa were at home all day; the other girls would be in after tea, when they had finished their shifts.

I was in the kitchen making myself a piece of toast, at midday, when Melissa came in and said:

'Oh, would you make me a piece as well - Nicola?' I looked up quickly, to see if she was taking the mickey. She was smiling, but her expression was friendly and reassuring.

'No, we've not forgotten, love; and you might as well get used to being called Nicola. As soon as you've had that toast, you'd better have a long soak in the bath to soften your skin, and then shave closely all over. Actually, I think you've got less need to shave than some of us.' I thought of Eleni and nodded. 'When you've bathed and shaved, come to my room,' said Melissa.

After my bath, I tip-toed along the landing in my dressing gown and knocked gently on Melissa's door. My heart was pounding.

I heard someone giggle and then Melissa said:

'Come in, Nicola.' I opened the door and saw Melissa and Laura standing expectantly by a pile of girl's clothes on the bed. Laura picked up a black girdle in a strong elasticated material and passed it to me, saying:

'Pop back to the bathroom and put this on.'

I stood on the bath mat, looking at the label of the foundation garment I had been given; it said 'Firm control girdle, 24-25" waist, 35-36" hips'. I pushed my male bits down as hard as I could bear, holding them between my legs while I eased the girdle on with difficulty, finding it a very tight fit. When it had covered my crotch area, I pulled it up hard, so that my penis and balls were held back firmly between my legs. I stared down and gasped with pleasure at the flattened, feminine curve of my crotch - no tell-tale bump now - I looked exactly like a girl there! I padded back along the corridor to Melissa's room.

The girls nodded approvingly at my hairless body, running a finger here and there to feel my smooth skin; then Laura noticed my flattened waves, and put a tortoise-shell comb into each side to hold back the tresses at the front. Finally my nails were painted, and the girls went off to the kitchen to make coffee while I waited for the nail varnish to dry. While they were away I stood up and wobbled over to look at myself in the full-length mirror on the wardrobe door. I gasped at what I saw! A beautiful girl looked back at me! I looked at her shapely legs in the mini-skirt and high-heels, at her narrow waist, at the curve of her bust and hips, and at her brunette hair falling in soft waves nearly to her shoulders (had I really allowed my hair to grow so long?). I gazed finally at her girlish, pretty face - and the eyes looked back at me, and I knew, oh joy of joys, that they were my eyes, and that *I was this pretty girl.* I smiled then, and thought that I would swoon with the glory of it. And I knew in that instant that this was how I wanted to be, for ever more. I would give anything, if only I could stay as the girl in the mirror.

I heard Laura and Melissa coming along the corridor, and sat down on the bed, lest they should catch me looking at myself in the mirror and think me vain. Laura was carrying a coffee mug in each hand and pushed open the door with her foot; then she turned towards me, and as if seeing me for the first time, said:

'Wow! You really look the business! I think we're

107

a bit surprised ourselves at how far we've succeeded. You really do make a very pretty girl, Nicola. I should definitely give up any idea of being a boy, ever again. What a waste of your natural assets! You were meant to be a girl, no doubt about it.' I smiled like the cat that had got the cream at her words, but before I could reply Laura said:

'You need some accessories just to finish off your outfit.' She handed me a burgundy tailored jacket which had been hanging behind the door, which I slipped on, then pointed to a black handbag by the bed. She then fastened a necklace of black beads round my neck, clipped enamelled pendant earrings to my ear-lobes and slipped a black bead bracelet on my wrist.

'There, now you're ready. Let's go for a drink at the Sadler's Arms while we're waiting for the others to get home.' And so, before I had time to think further, I was launched on my first expedition in the outside world - as a girl!

We went into the lounge bar of the Sadler's Arms, and I didn't dare look around - I was convinced that everyone was staring at me. I sat down on one of the upholstered bench seats that ran along the side of the room; Laura sat down with me and Melissa asked us what we wanted to drink.

'Half a shandy,' I whispered.

'Very lady-like,' commented Laura; 'I'll have a pint of lager and a packet of pork scratchings.'

'Depraved as ever,' commented Melissa, digging in her handbag for her purse as she turned to make her way to the bar.

'Well, so far, so good,' said Laura, when we were alone. 'How do you feel?'

I shrugged; 'Okay,' I said, 'but I'm a bit worried my voice will give me away.'

'You sound quite all right to me,' said Laura; 'just remember to talk a bit softer than you used to. You haven't got a very deep voice, and I think you sound quite like a girl already.'

We knocked back our drinks (the speed at which Laura could sink a pint was something to behold) and then Melissa looked at her watch and said:
'We'd better be getting back - Eleni and Tracey will be home for tea soon.'

We were sitting at the kitchen table when Eleni and Tracey came in, looking tired and hungry after their shifts at the hospital.
'God, that old man on Male Surgical tried to put his hand on my bottom again when I was changing his catheter,' announced Tracey; 'hello, who's this elegant young lady? (she nodded towards me) - don't tell me it's our Nicola?'
'The very same,' replied Melissa.
'Well, she looks gorgeous; we'll have to keep an eye on her tonight, or she'll be pulling all the best-looking boys.'
After tea, Eleni and Tracey showered and got on their glad rags and make-up, while we washed-up and cleared away; and then we were off - five lovely lasses hell-bent on a good night out on the town! And I was one of them - I was one of the girls!

It seems so long ago now, that first night out as Nicola - but I remember it as the best night of my life. What can I tell you about it? I drank, I danced, I giggled, I clattered up wet streets in my high-heels to dark night-clubs which smelt of perfume and sweat and stale cigarette smoke, where I drank and danced some more.....Sometimes, while we girls were bopping together under the flash of the strobe lighting, sloshing our drinks on the sticky floor and screeching at the tops of our voices to make ourselves heard over the thundering beat of the sound system, a boy would sidle up and dance with us and try to chat us up; and maybe one of us would go off and dance with him. It happened to me, more than once - I would find myself dancing with some clammy-handed, sozzle-eyed lad who reeked of *Brut* and beer - who would try to gyrate himself close enough to rub against me or get his hand on my thigh.....

And it surprised me that I took all this without batting an eye-lid, as if I was just another one of the girls - as if I had been born to it. It seemed *natural*, that I was treated as a girl, and I vowed that I would *be* a girl, and never again go back to being a boy.

I kept my promise to myself - I never again put on boy's clothes. The next morning, I got up and put on the mini-skirt and blouse I had been wearing the night before, although they stunk of spilt beer and cigarette smoke; I got a large black plastic bin-liner, gathered up all my male clothes - underwear, trousers, shirts, ties, everything - and dumped the bin-liner next to the dustbins. Then I caught a bus into town, went to the bank, and drew out all of what remained of my grant money from the cash machine. I met Tracey and Eleni, who had a day off and knew what I was planning to do, and together we went trawling round Dorothy Perkins, Etam, Miss Selfridge and every other girl's fashion shop in the centre of town until I had spent all my grant money on my new wardrobe of female clothing. I had my hair cut and styled properly at a hairdresser's, and my ears pierced by the beautician.

The next week, dressed as Nicola, I went to see my tutor at college, and explained that I was leaving the course and that I would be living henceforth as a girl. He tried to dissuade me from what he saw as a very drastic step - obviously believing that I was completely unhinged and having some sort of breakdown. I declined to see the college counsellor, saying that I didn't need counselling or advice as I knew what I was doing and my mind was made up.

I decided that my best long-term career option, as I

had no interest whatever in continuing with engineering, was to explore seriously the possibility of becoming a nurse. I knew that I had sufficient qualifications to apply for admission to a course for student S.R.N. nurses, but of course I needed to be able to enroll as a female nurse.

The girls in the house advised me to go and talk to Dr. Jones, the female G.P. who was doctor-in-residence at the nursing college. Dr. Jones proved to be a sensible, sympathetic woman in her mid-thirties, who at first didn't appreciate what my problem was:

'Now you tell me you have the qualifications dear, and you are serious about wanting to be a nurse, so I really can't see what's stopping you.'

'I want to enroll on the course as a *female* nurse.'

'That seems logical, dear, seeing as you're a girl.'

'But that's just it - I'm *not*.'

'Not what?'

'Not a female - not yet, anyway.'

I watched the penny drop as Dr. Jones at last grasped what I was saying, and her face took on an expression of stunned surprise. She quickly became aware that she was gawping incredulously at me, as if I was a fair-ground freak; she flicked a switch somewhere inside, putting herself back into "concerned professional" mode.

'You're *not* a girl? You're telling me that you're a *boy*, then? It's hard to believe. Would you mind stripping down to your bra and panties?'

I got the impression that she half-suspected that I was a girl under the powerful grip of a *delusion* that I was a boy! If only it had been true! I did as she had asked, stripping off so that she was able to confirm that I did indeed have the equipment between my legs normally associated with the male of the species.

She told me to put my skirt and blouse back on.

'All right, Miss - er - Mr.- er -'

'Just call me Nicola.'

'All right, Nicola, I'm convinced. I suppose you've

111

always been a boy? Well of course you have, silly question. But you dress as a girl, and you make a very convincing one, I must say. *I* certainly had no idea that you were - er, anything other than you appear to be. Have you been dressing like this for long?'

'Quite a while,' I lied, 'and I've made the decision that this is how I want to be. My mind's made up.'

'I see.'

Dr. Jones put her hand on her chin, rested her elbow on her desk, and gazed out of the window, as if seeking inspiration from the morning sunshine. After a few moments, she sighed and said:

'I've heard about this sort of thing, but you're the first case I've come across personally. According to one of my medical journals it's becoming more common, but no one knows why. Perhaps it's chemicals that have got into the water supply - I've heard some of these fertilisers act on the body like female hormone. Perhaps it's just the strain of being male these days. I can't imagine it's a very appetising prospect, but I'm a woman, so I would think that, wouldn't I?'

I nodded, hoping that there was some point to all this. She continued:

'I gather there is quite a lot that can be done these days, to help people like you - hormones, to begin with, and then - '

She left the sentence hanging - not wanting to say - what? The chop? The sex-change operation? Was this what I was moving towards, my ultimate fate? I wasn't sure how I felt about the operation, which of course I'd heard of. I knew I wanted to live as a girl, to take on the female role full-time, but did this mean I was destined for such a drastic step, ultimately?

'I'll make an appointment for you to see a specialist in London,' she said. 'I'll ring up the clinic this morning. You should hear from them in a few days - they'll want you to go and see them. I think it's a Dr. Lambert who deals with this sort of thing initially. If everything is okay, they'll probably put you on a course of hormones. Once the clinic's given the go-ahead, you can get the hormones on prescription from your G.P. If you do get onto the nursing course, that will be me.

'Regardless of your gender, you'll have to get accepted onto the course in the normal way. If your qualifications are up to scratch and you get accepted for next September, I'll do what I can to ensure that your - er - medical problem - remains confidential. You won't be able to live in the nurses' quarters at St. Brides, which is usual for first year student nurses, as some of the facilities are communal. Where are you staying at present?'

I explained where I was living.

'Oh, that address is on our approved accommodation list - I think there are some student nurses already living in your house.' I nodded, explaining to Dr. Jones that I was friendly with the girls from St. Brides who lived there.

'Well that's ideal then. If you get onto the course, you can just carry on living there.'

A few days later, I had my appointment with Dr. Lambert at the Charing Cross Hospital gender reassignment clinic. Dr. Lambert was a cheerful Scotsman with a large nose and masses of wiry gingerish hair which stood up on his head like a brush. He bore a rather strong resemblance to Tin Tin. I found myself staring at his ginger nostril hairs while he informed me that it seemed very likely that I was a transsexual, and that he would be putting me on a course of hormone treatment, which would assist breast and hip development and begin to soften and reduce beard growth.

'How does that sound?' he asked, smiling at me encouragingly. I tore my gaze away from his nostril hairs and replied that this sounded like a good idea.

'Mind you, you don't seem to have much difficulty passing as a girl already,' he concluded, rising and shaking my hand vigorously with his large, freckled paw before he showed me to the door.

I wrote to my school examining board enclosing a letter from Dr. Lambert explaining that I was undergoing gender reassignment treatment, and got new copies of my GCE 'O' and 'A' level certificates, made out in the name of 'Nicola Hopkins'. I then applied to St. Brides, and after interview was accepted onto the S.R.N. course for the following September.

As it was then April, I realised that I would have to get myself a job to pay the rent until I could start the course. I had noticed that the Sadler's Arms was advertising for staff, and got myself taken on as a bar maid and waitress. The money was lousy and the hours were long, but I managed to stay solvent and I was at least living and working as a girl. Occasionally I had to fend off the amorous advances of drunken male customers; I soon learnt the necessary female skill of doing this without causing offence - talk about grace under fire!

The girls in the house were very supportive about my change of gender, treating me as as one of them and including me whenever possible in anything they did.

Soon it was Summer - the scorching Summer of '76, and the Sadler's Arms was packed out night after night with folk slaking their thirsts. One weekend in August we even ran out of lager. The trade was up so much that the landlord asked me to work quite a bit of overtime, and I was exhausted by the end of most evenings. The landlord, a burly Irishman from Dingle, liked his barmaids to look 'attractive' - he said it brought in more custom; his idea of 'attractive' was black mini-skirts, four inch high-heels, low-cut white blouses, and little lacy aprons. I began to realise wearing high-heels was a mixed blessing - I was walking about or standing up for long hours, and my feet were often killing me by the time I got home.

I was not sorry when I noticed the first autumnal chill in the air, walking back one night from the Sadler's Arms

- a change of weather which heralded the approach of September, and the start of my nursing course.

*　*　*

On a bright, crisp morning in the second week of September, I found myself sitting in a large lecture hall at St. Brides, along with twenty-five or so other young women and three young men - that year's intake onto the SRN training course. I watched the dust motes floating in a shaft of sunlight above my head, as the Dean of the Nursing School welcomed us to St. Brides, and then a succession of lecturers and tutors went through the procedure for registration, gave us our timetables for lectures and initial ward practice, and finally told us where to go to get our uniforms.

We had to wait for what seemed like hours on a long, dingy corridor outside the stores annexe, while an elderly nursing Sister asked each of us in turn for our bust and waist size, then presented us with two complete sets of student nurse's outfits, each consisting of a light blue cotton shift, a navy blue webbing belt with steel buckle bearing the emblem of St. Brides, and a white starched cap. When we were all equipped, the Sister led us to the locker room and told us to sit down on the benches and be quiet while she went through the regulations about the uniform:

'No make-up is to be worn, *ever*, while you are on the premises of St. Brides. Only clear or light pearl nail varnish may be worn; tights or stockings are to be black, 20 denier or more. I'll allocate your lockers in a moment, and you are all to change into your uniforms. Any questions?'

This Sister was an unsmiling, thin-lipped old bird with iron-grey hair pulled sharply back into a bun; as she reeled off the regulations, she pointed her claw-like finger at us for emphasis. I shuddered at her whining voice and was just vowing to myself that I would try hard not to fall foul of her when I realised that she was speaking to *me* :

'We haven't got quite enough lockers in here for all of you - one of you will have to use a locker elsewhere - *you* nurse, you'll do - come with me.'

I followed her into the corridor. When we were out of earshot of the others, she turned to me and said:

'Hopkins, isn't it? I chose you for a reason. I already know about you; Dr. Jones felt one of the senior nursing staff should be made aware of your particular - ah - medical condition; she felt that you would have special needs, for which I would be able to make provision quietly, without anyone else in the nursing school needing to be involved. Obviously you can't share a locker room with the other girls at present, not until your - medical situation is altered, finally. I have a spare locker in my quarters - you can use that.'

She led me through a door into a small, bare room, in which there were two steel-framed beds pushed against the walls opposite each other; through a curtain there was another small room, where there was a linen basket and two battered wardrobes. Behind another curtain - this one of plastic - there was a shower cubicle.

'You can use that wardrobe on the right as your locker. Do you know the difference between night shift and night standby duty?' I shook my head.

'Night shift means you're working on the ward all night. When it's your turn on night standby, you have to sleep here, although you're not actually on duty unless there's an emergency. The bed with the pink blanket is yours, when you're on night-standby.' She pointed back through the curtain.

'Sharing these quarters with me, Nurse Hopkins, was the best we could come up with. I know all about *you* , don't worry.' She curled her lip in a sneer, as she said this.

'You're nothing but a *sissy* -*boy* , in my opinion. My brothers would have known how to deal with you. But times have changed, for the worse, in my view. Now people like you are pandered to. So you think you want

116

to be a girl, eh?'

By this time I was blushing crimson, and close to tears.

'What's this, Miss - crying? A cry-baby as well! You really should be a girl - for you certainly wouldn't have made much of a man. So you want to be a girl - and a nurse? Hmmph! We'll see how well you like it, once you're on the wards! Get into your uniform and report to me on Willoughby Ward B, in fifteen minutes.'

She looked me up and down once more, and without uttering another word, turned on her heel, whipped back the curtain, and swept out of the room.

This personage was the redoubtable Sister Gwynneth Briggs, nicknamed 'the Dragon' -and the terror of St. Brides. Even the doctors were afraid of her. And I was sharing her quarters!

Sister Briggs made it clear from the outset that she was going to make me suffer. Whenever I was on duty with her, she gave me the dirtiest, rottenest jobs she could find - emptying bed-pans, changing incontinent patients, and so on. One of her favourite jobs to give me was changing the catheter on the senile old man on Male Surgical, who invariably tried to touch-up, molest, and sexually harass any nurses who came near him. At such times she would watch behind a screen as he tried to pinch my bottom or stroke my thigh, cackling to herself like an old crone and whispering to me:

'There, still think it's so wonderful being a girl, do you?'

There was nothing I could do about the way she treated me. On one occasion, I nearly rebelled; I could stand it no more and began to say to her:

Sister Briggs, you're very unfair to me; I'll complain to the Director of Nursing Studies......'

'Oh you will, will you, Miss?' Well, you might just find your little secret gets out, and becomes the chief topic of conversation in St. Brides - everyone talking about you, knowing what you *are*. And we all know what you are, don't we? A little *she-* boy who wants to be a girl. Why, I should think it would get into the Sunday papers - that we've got a little pervert like you running around St. Brides. *I* could make sure it does get into the Sunday papers. How would you like that?

'Now, you were saying something about the Director of Nursing Studies, who by the way happens to be a friend of mine, and would no doubt think that you are an ungrateful little slut, after all I've done for you, sharing my quarters with you and all.'

I didn't know how much of this was bluff, but I decided that it was not in my interests to find out. She was virtually blackmailing me, and there was nothing I could do about it.

After my little show of spirit, matters improved somewhat. It is often the case with bullies, that if you try to stand up to them, they start to behave more reasonably.

On one occasion, she was almost human. She had come in while I was undressing; I was standing there without a bra on; I was just wearing panties, suspender-belt and stockings (many of us chose to wear stockings rather than tights, as these were cooler on the hospital wards, which were invariably over-heated and stuffy.) I could feel her eyes on me, and was embarrassed about the tiny bump in my panties. Normally I wore a panty-girdle which smoothed me out completely between the legs, but it had been so hot on the wards recently (it was even worse than usual because the central heating had gone wrong), that I had taken to wearing plain cotton panties to stay cool. I expected her to say something sneering about my being a sissy-boy, but instead she looked approvingly at my budding breasts and said:

'Your figure is filling out nicely Nurse Hopkins, since you've been taking the hormones. We'll make a girl of you yet.'

Unaccustomed to a kind word from her, I didn't know what to say.

I put on my bra and blurted out:

'I hope I'm doing the right thing....'

Why on earth had I said that? I could have kicked myself! I had not, up to then, had any doubts about my change of gender; it was almost as if, by sounding unsure of myself, I was seeking her approval. What did I expect her to say? Of course you're doing the right thing - you're meant to be a girl....Is this what I wanted to hear her say? Maybe I did want her approval, her acceptance of me as a girl and not as a sort of she-boy.

All she said was:

'It's too late to turn back now, Nicola.' I turned towards her and she continued: 'You'll feel better once you've got rid of that thing - ' She nodded towards my crotch, indicating my masculine bump. But she had called me Nicola for the first time!

Sister Briggs was a spinster, and in living memory, no one had ever heard of her going out with a man. It was rumoured that she was a lesbian. As the months passed and my body became more feminine, I began to wonder whether her change of attitude towards me was due to the fact that she was beginning to find me attractive - as a woman. My breasts had developed further, my hips had broadened and my waist had become slimmer. The uniform certainly fitted me better, now that I had curves in the right places....

One day, in my second year at St.Brides, my uncertainty about Sister Briggs's feelings towards me was ended, and I was left in no doubt that she was beginning to find me sexually appealing. A patient had been sick all over me, and I was going to take a shower before changing into a clean uniform. I was naked and about to go into the cubicle, when I heard a voice behind me saying:

'You've still got your cap on.'

119

It was Sister Briggs. I glanced round and caught her licking her lips, her eyes fixed longingly on my buttocks!

Sister Briggs began to ask me when I was going to have the operation. She seemed to take an almost unhealthy interest in this. I had been leaving this final, irrevocable step in my gender change in the indefinite future - if I was going through with it at all. Did I need to go any further? I felt confident that even under the closest scrutiny, I could pass muster as a young woman. Regular electrolysis sessions and the effect of the hormones had eradicated what little beard growth I had, and my facial skin was as soft and smooth as any girl's. My hair was cut and styled to take advantage of the natural curl in it, and seemed to be thicker and glossier than ever before. My figure, which had always been slight, was rounding out into feminine curves. My outward appearance was now completely female, and there could obviously be no going back, so it seemed logical to go forward to the sex-change.

Yet....there was something holding me back. And I knew what it was: it was the question of sexuality. I had put off dealing with it, but could do so no longer. The truth of the matter was that I had never felt attracted towards men, and still couldn't imagine having a sexual relationship with a man. I doubted whether I would feel any different after the operation. I knew that I was sexually attracted towards women, and had to confront the possibility - the likelihood - that this would always be the case, even after the operation. Here was a paradox indeed; I was apparently a heterosexual male, fast turning into a woman! I had taken on the female gender role, was happy in it, and could not imagine living any other way; and yet I still had between my legs the paraphernalia required to give pleasure to a woman. True, it was a bit shrivelled and not in proper working order, sexually, due to the female hormones I had been taking; I had not had an erection for many months. But should I part with it?

Although it had never been stated explicitly, the hospital authorities clearly expected me to go ahead with the sex-change operation, and had given me a place on the SRN course on the basis that my anomalous gender status would be 'normalised' as soon as possible. Hovever, the attitude of authority has never in itself been sufficient to resolve any course of action for me.

As sometimes happens in life, my decision was facilitated in a way which I couldn't have predicted. I met Debbie.

Debbie was a student nurse a year ahead of me on the SRN course. How can I describe Debbie? *Determined* would be a good word for her. She knew what she wanted and was single-minded in getting it. I can see her as she was the first time I met her, standing in silhouette by the swing doors on Nightingale, one of the the female surgical wards, arguing with Sister Jenkins. There was a quiet resolution and defiance about the way she stood up to the Welsh Witch, as we called Sister Jenkins. Debbie's arms were folded across her chest, one toe tapping in irritation on the floor, as she shook her head slowly in response to Sister Jenkins's words. Finally Debbie shrugged her shoulders and turned from Sister Jenkins, walking purposively away from her towards the nurses' station, where we were watching what had been going on.

'What was all that about?' asked Melissa, who was on duty with me. Melissa was now a qualified staff nurse. She had been one of the student nurses sharing the old house in Mossbrook where my transformation into a girl had begun. I had been grateful for her early kindness and encouragement, and we were now good friends.

'The Witch was saying I couldn't have tomorrow night off because of Claire Dawkins being sick,' replied Debbie. 'I told her it was my night off, and I was taking it whether she liked it or not. They'll have to get an agency nurse in to cover.' Debbie tucked a stray curl of her blonde hair under her nurses's cap and glared back towards the end of the ward where Sister Jenkins was still standing, hands on hips. The Welsh Witch finally turned and flounced out of the ward, angrily pushing the swing doors aside as she passed through them, and narrowly missing the tea trolley at that moment being wheeled into the ward by Delbert, the Jamaican orderly.

'Good for you,' said Melissa. 'Sister Jenkins never considers how unfair these last minute rota changes are - and it's all to save money. What *are* you doing tomorrow night, by the way?'

'Well, I haven't got anything planned, actually, but it's the principle of the thing.'

I'm off tomorrow night - and so's Nicola, so why don't we gang up and do something?' Debbie looked towards me and said:

'Hi, Nicola. I don't think I've run into you before. This your first duty on Nightingale Ward?'

I nodded.

'If you have any bother with Sister Jenkins, let me know. I'm not frightened of that old bag.'

'Nicola doesn't seem to have a lot of luck with our illustrious Sisters - the poor girl's been sharing sleep-over quarters with the dreaded Briggs,' said Melissa.

'Oh God, not that old dyke!' exclaimed Debbie. 'Hubble bubble, toil and trouble, Briggs and Jenkins' cauldrons bubble!' Talk about the Weird Sisters!'

I giggled.

'Is she really a dyke?' asked Melissa.

'You bet,' replied Debbie.

'How do you know?'

'Takes one to know one, I guess,' said Debbie, eyeing Melissa belligerently.

'Oh,' said Melissa, looking embarrassed.

'Oh what?' asked Debbie, determined not to let the subject drop yet.

'Well - nothing. I didn't know, that's all,' said Melissa, giving a little shrug of her shoulders.

'It's not the sort of thing I go around advertising, but I'm not ashamed of how I am.'

'Of course not.' Melissa was now looking as if the she

was hoping the floor would open and swallow her up.

'So do you still want to come out tomorrow night?' asked Debbie.

'Well - er...'

'Okay, say no more. I'm sorry if I've embarrassed you.'

'I'd still like to go out....' I said.

'Would you now,' replied Debbie, turning to me and looking me over properly for the first time.

I nodded.

And that was how we got started. I admit it, I was attracted to Debbie from the start, and fortunately, it turned out that she was attracted to me.

That Saturday night, Debbie and I got fairly drunk doing the rounds of several city centre pubs, before fetching up at a black metal door on a quiet side street. On the door was a single word in bright pink capitals: HOLLY'S. Debbie knocked hard on the door, and the next moment it was opened half-way by a huge bald man wearing a black tuxedo and gold lurex bow tie. He peered at Debbie for a moment, nodded, and then glanced at me.

'My guest,' said Debbie. The bald man nodded again, and ushered us in. The interior was dark and smoky. I stood waiting for my eyes to adjust to the dim lighting, listening to the strains of a tenor saxophone playing a mournful blues number, coming from behind a heavy red velvet curtain a few feet in front of us. We made for the red drapes and pushed our way through them, entering a large, low-ceilinged room with a marble-topped bar and some stools along one wall, and a few tables and chairs around the edges of a small dance floor. At the far end of the room was a low stage on which a five-piece jazz band was playing, the saxophonist carressing the silky notes from his instrument. The place was half empty, but several couples were dancing slowly to the music, entwined smoochingly about each other. On looking

123

more closely at the couples, I realised that they consisted of men dancing with men, and women dancing with women.

We went over to the bar, and Debbie bought me a drink.

'What do you think?' she asked.

'Interesting,' I replied, surveying the clientele. I meant it.

After a few more drinks, Debbie and I were dancing together too. And I told her about myself - everything. She said it didn't matter.

'But - I'm a man,' I pointed out, feeling like the Jack Lemmon character at the end of *Some Like it Hot*.

'Of course you're not,' she said. 'I can tell. I'm not attracted to men, but I fancy you like crazy, so you must really be a girl. You have the soul of a girl, take my word for it. You've just got one or two extra bits you need to get rid of.'

And so I did get rid of them - eighteen months later. My appointment for the operation at Charing Cross hospital came through, and I went ahead with it, without any second thoughts. I have never regretted it. Debbie and I have been together now for almost sixteen years. We both still work at the hospital. I am a senior staff nurse and Debbie is a Sister. We keep our private life to ourselves, although most people know about us and accept us for who we are and what we are.

In the early days of our relationship - *romance*, I'm tempted to call it, there were times when we couldn't keep our hands off each other, even at work. Of course, we were discreet, stealing kisses where we could, in a lab or linen room, perhaps, or in some other dark corner of the old hospital when there was no one around. We were very much in love. We still are. Who can ask for more?

Thus ends my story, dear reader, the story of how

I became Nicola Hopkins SRN. If you are ever in hospital, look closely at the staff nurse who is taking you temperature or tucking you into bed; if she has brown curly hair and a pleasant but inscrutible smile, it may be me. If she winks at you, you'll know for sure........

Mother's New Daughter

I'd always wanted a daughter, you see. I believe every mother does. So I suppose it was only a matter of time; sooner or later it was bound to happen. And he was such a sweet looking boy - a very pretty boy, really. Fair hair, lovely long lashes that a lot of girls would kill for. He was slightly built, with small hands and long tapering fingers and almond-shaped nails. His face was already feminine-looking - high cheek bones, a gently rounded chin, delicate brow bones, a small nose with finely-shaped nostrils. He was more than pretty - he was beautiful.

Unfortunately he'd been born a boy.

When Lucien was very young, little more than a baby, I had let his fair hair grow long. I dressed him in boy's clothes most of the time, I had to while Roger was around. Roger was so masculine, he wouldn't have put up with me making a sissy out of his son. But when Roger was away on business, I couldn't resist dressing him up sometimes. I'd bought one or two little dresses, with frilly petticoats and matching lacy knickers. I'd get him dressed up and tie his hair back in ribbons, then sit him on my knee and pretend he was my little daughter. I even gave him a little rag doll to play with. I'd keep him dressed as a girl for the whole weekend if Roger was away. I'd take him out in his pram to the shops or the Saturday market in the square, and I how I loved it if one of the market traders or shop keepers bent over 'her' and said: 'What a pretty little girl!' or 'Isn't she gorgeous?' or some such cooing nonsense which people say when they see a baby girl.

Of course I stopped once he was a toddler and old enough to remember - and perhaps blurt out something to his father. But I remembered what a lovely little girl he had made, and thought of what might have been.

Lucien had just turned sixteen when Roger died. It was a motorway pile-up; the police said Roger must have fallen asleep behind the wheel. He was coming back from a sales conference - they always exhausted him - and his Sierra has slewed across from the middle lane into the path of an articulated lorry. They said at least Roger wouldn't have known anything about it.

After Lucien's birth, which had been difficult, I hadn't been able to have any more children. Roger was away so much, Lucien and I had grown very close. After Roger's death we grew closer still. He always liked to please me. Perhaps he sensed something - some disappointment in me, though I tried to hide it. Finally, I decided to take matters in hand. Perhaps I was being selfish, but I had always wanted a daughter so much.

At this time, Lucien was nearing the end of his first year in the sixth form at school. In spite of Roger's death, he had done well in his G.C.S.E.'s the previous year, passing nine, all with good grades; I suspected he had taken refuge in his studies as a way of handling his grief. He seemed to have a natural flair for languages, and was now taking French, German and Italian 'A' levels.

Lucien was planning to go on a camping and walking holiday in the Lake District with two school friends during the Summer holiday. This would be our first holiday apart. I had not got away at all the previous year, following Roger's death, as there seemed to be so much to do to sort out our affairs, and somehow I just couldn't face a holiday without Roger. But this year, as Lucien was obviously wanting to be independent, I had decided to take up the offer from a cousin of mine to stay with her in a quiet villa in Tuscany. The villa was a sort of retreat house in the beautiful grounds of an ancient nunnery. The nuns were of a strict religious order and would only hire out their accommodation to all-female parties. The situation sounded ideal; I could spend the weeks of the summer vacation in quiet rest and reflection, perhaps do a bit of painting, and maybe begin to make sense of my life, what had happened to me, and what the future might hold. It suited me to be only among women. I didn't feel ready yet for male company; even to look at another man seemed like a betrayal of Roger's memory. I felt cheated by life; I had been deprived of a daughter, and now I had no husband. I could do nothing to bring back poor Roger; but was there, just possibly, a way in which I could have a daughter?

While Lucien was at school during the last week of the summer term, I began to put phase one of my plan into action. I went on a shopping spree, buying a variety of skirts, dresses and blouses which I guessed would be in Lucien's size, together with several pairs of girl's shoes, some lacy bras, panties and slips in different colours, and plenty of pairs of tights. I also got a long, wavy, blonde wig and an auburn wig in a page-boy style.

I wasn't sure what I could do about creating a realistic female figure for him. Eventually, I purchased several 'body-former' panty girdles from a shop which specialised in foundation garments; these were made of strong elasticated material, which I thought would do to conceal the tell-tale masculine bump between his legs. Just along from the corsetry shop I found a surgical suppliers, where I was able to buy a pair of silicon breast forms which were intended for women who had had mastectomies. The woman in the shop looked at me pityingly and assured me that they created a realistic bust-line. Little could she guess that they were intended not for me, but for my son, who as yet had no bust at all, poor dear! My shopping came to rather a lot of money, but fortunately Roger had been well-insured, so I had received a windfall of quite a few thousand pounds after his death.

Having got all these girlish things for Lucien, I couldn't wait for him to break up from school so that I could begin my plan to feminise him and turn him into the daughter I had always wanted. I decided to begin the first Saturday of the holiday. Lucien had been out with his friends John and Robert the night before; they had been on a pub crawl and had had far too much to drink. They were supposed to be planning their trip to the Lake District, but I guess they were also celebrating breaking up for the holidays.

Lucien was not used to drinking and was rather ill when he came in; I put him to bed and soon he was sleeping heavily.

I crept into his room and collected up all his male clothes; I piled everything into plastic bin-liners, which I put out for the dustman. I then filled his wardrobe and drawers with all the girl's clothes I had bought.

The next morning, while Lucien was still sleeping, I telephoned John and Robert and told them that Lucien had decided to come on holiday with me, rather than going to the Lake District. Both boys were naturally surprised and disappointed, but I explained that we were still getting over his father's death and that Lucien felt that he didn't want to leave me on my own. John and Robert were understanding and said that they would go ahead with the camping holiday without him. I next telephoned my cousin Rachael, who had booked the holiday in Tuscany, and asked if there would be room for one more in the villa.

'Yes darling, there's plenty of room,' replied Rachael, 'the villa sleeps up to six, but only women are allowed, you know.'

'The person I'm bringing will be a girl - sort of.'

'What on earth can you mean, darling?'

'I'm going to tell you now something which might sound very strange, but I know you're broad-minded, dear.'

'Oh I don't bat an eye-lid at most things, Samantha; you know me. Go on.'

'It's about Lucien.'

'Your gorgeous son?'

'Yes; you'd never believe it, he's told me he wants to dress as a girl - *be* a girl, in fact. It all came out after Roger died.'

'Good Lord! You read about these things in the papers. What do they call them? Trans- something or other.'

'Transvestites. Or if they actually want to change sex - transsexuals.'

'And Lucien's one?'

129

'So it would seem. I've said to him that if he comes on holiday with us, dresses and lives as a girl, and manages to convince everyone, I'll take him seriously.'

'Will he pull it off? Although I suppose the idea is not so much to pull it off as have it cut off, eventually.'

'Really, Rachael, it's no laughing matter.'

'No, of course not - sorry. Well, if you're okay about it, and it's what Lucien wants to do, I don't have any objections. It might be rather a hoot, actually.'

'Then it's settled. We'll see you at the Al Italia desk at Heathrow tomorrow morning. Bye for now.'

'See you soon darling, bye.'

As I hung up, I could hear Lucien moving about upstairs. The next moment he appeared at the bottom of the stairs, looking very confused and embarrassed, and more than a little hung-over. He was wearing only a pair of cotton panties.

'Mother, something really weird has happened,' he said, 'all my clothes are gone and there's just girl's clothes in my cupboards and drawers.'

'I've got to have a serious talk with you about things, Lucien,' I replied, 'go and put on the dressing gown hanging behind your door, and then come back down and we'll talk.'

Lucien reappeared a few seconds later looking sheepish in a woman's burgundy dressing gown decorated with floral motifs and edged with lace at the collar and cuffs.

'I feel ridiculous in this,' he said.

'I'm afraid you're going to have to start gettting used to wearing girl's clothes,' I replied, trying to give my voice a matter-of-fact tone. 'Here's a cup of coffee; now sit down at the table and let me explain.' Lucien slumped down on the kitchen chair, looking sullen and puzzled.

'About two weeks ago,' I began, 'I got a letter which surprised and shocked me. It was from the Finance Director at your father's old company. The letter said that they had found certain financial irregularities in their accounts, that in fact a very large sum of money was missing from a particular account for which your father and two or three other executives had shared responsibility. After a long and thorough investigation, the other executives had been cleared of any impropriety. The company has passed on its findings to the Fraud Squad, who will be getting in touch with us to investigate Roger's affairs further.'

Lucien sipped the last dregs of his coffee and let out a long sigh.

'Are you saying Dad may have been involved in something illegal? I don't believe it.'

'I couldn't believe it anymore than you; so I went through all of your father's papers a few days ago. I found details of an account in Italy - at a bank in Florence. There seemed to be a huge amount of money in the account, even allowing for the rate of exchange in Italian Lire. I'm talking about several hundred thousand pounds, Lucien. The account is in your father's name, and I knew nothing about it. I have no idea where the money came from. Apparently the interest from the money in this account has been payed regularly into a joint current account which I held with Roger. I had thought the money was coming from life insurance and pension policies which matured on Roger's death; when I 'phoned up the insurance companies I found we had no such policies.

'Then, yesterday, I had a 'phone call from a Chief Superintendent Bilson of the Fraud Squad; he has made an appointment to come here first thing on Monday morning with his team to start going through all of Roger's papers.'

'My God!' exclaimed Lucien. He had gone as white as a sheet. 'But I still don't see where the girl's clothes fit in.'

'I'm coming to that,' I said. I took a deep breath. Would Lucien believe me? He seemed to have swallowed what I'd said up to now, although it had all been a complete fabrication.

'It's really serious, Lucien. I thought we'd been left comfortably off by your father, but now it looks as if we could be ruined - left without a penny. They might even take the house away from me.'

'We could manage, I could work,' replied Lucien bravely; 'perhaps even *you* could get a job, Mother.'

'Lucien, what could I do? I haven't worked for twenty years. And it would be such a shame if you didn't go to university.'

'I wouldn't mind.'

'But *I* would. You've worked so hard at your studies, you should have the chance of getting a degree. It will make all the difference to the sort of job you can get.' I felt as if I was beginning to lose control of the conversation. This wasn't how I had intended it to go at all.

'Anyway,' I continued, it's not as simple as that. The interest from the money is being paid into our *joint* account. I may be implicated in other ways. Your father's out of it now, but *I* may be prosecuted - perhaps even have to go to prison.'

'But you said you knew nothing about it.'

'Yes, but can I prove it to the satisfaction of a court? Probably not. I can't afford to take the risk.'

'So what are you suggesting?'

'I've booked us on a flight to Italy tomorrow. I propose to remove the money from the bank in Florence, and deposit it elsewhere, perhaps in Switzerland, before the Fraud Squad can freeze the account. Then we'll lie low for a few weeks, try to stay somewhere incognito, while we decide what to do next. I need some time to think and plan for the future.'

'I still don't see where the girl's clothes come in.'

'Well, you know that I'd already agreed to spend the summer in Tuscany with Rachael, while you were walking in the Lake District. At this short notice I felt it was best to go ahead with that plan - you can see how urgent it is that we get out of the country. The trouble is that the villa which she booked is only available to parties of women; it's in the grounds of a nunnery, and they simply won't allow men anywhere near it. You can see the problem. I'm sorry, Lucien, but you'll simply have to come disguised as a girl. It would be a good idea anyway, because we can both stay at the villa under assumed names and identities. The accommodation is booked in Rachael's name. If the police start looking for us and find out we've left the country, they'll put out a request for information as to the whereabouts of a woman and a young *man;* they'll never trace us if you can manage to pose successfully as my *daughter.'*

'What about the passports?' asked Lucien. 'We'll have to go through customs and passport control at the airport.'

'You can wear a pair of jeans and a tee-shirt and go through under your own name. Then we get a hire car as soon as we land in Italy, and you can change on the road, once we're out in the country.'

'What about Rachael? Does she know all about this?'

'Not about the fraud case, no. I reckon the fewer people who know, the better.'

'So how are you going to explain when I start dressing as a girl? Won't she think that's a bit odd?'

'I had to tell her that you *want* to dress as a girl, that you want to *be* a girl, actually.'

'Oh great.'

'I'm sorry Lucien, but you'll have to convince her that it's true.'

Lucien shook his head. 'We'll never make her believe it,' he said.

'Yes we will darling, You'll see. We'll make a start right now - get you used to your new role.

'The first thing you must do is to shave all over - arms, legs - and under your arms. It's lucky you haven't got any chest hair yet, and that your beard growth is so slight. Give your face a really close shave anyway; you should be able to get away with only a light foundation.' Lucien frowned out me.

'You're serious about this, aren't you?'

'It's deadly serious, darling, if you don't want me left penniless, or ending up in jail.'

Lucien shrugged, and gave out a huge sigh.

'Okay,' he said, 'it doesn't look as if I've got much choice.'

After he'd bathed and shaved, Lucien came through to his bedroom, where I was laying out some clothes on the bed. I handed him a panty-girdle and said:

'Put this on. You might find it a tight fit, but you'll soon get used to wearing one. It'll conceal - what needs concealing; we don't want any tell-tale male bits and bumps giving the game away.' Lucien turned his back and pulled on the garment under his dressing gown, giving a little groan as he did so.

'Just slip this off, now,' I said, helping him off with the dressing gown. I took a bra from the bed and fastened it on to his chest, then slipped a silicon breast prosthesis into each bra cup.

'What's this?' he asked, looking down at his new bust.

'It's to give you the right shape,' I replied.

'You really have thought of everything, haven't you mother?'

'Why not call me - mummy? I think that that would sound more appropriate and rather sweet, coming from my daughter. You've got to start thinking - and sounding - like a girl.'

'Yes, mummy, of course mummy, three bags full, mummy.'

'Now, now, Lucy.'

''So I'm to be Lucy, am I?'

'Of course, darling. You're Lucy from now on. You must get used to your new name.'

I gave Lucien - or Lucy, as I shall now call her - a pair of black tights and explained how to roll them on one toe at a time. I next passed her a silky waist slip edged with lace and then helped her into a flouncy dress with a fitted waist, full skirt and puffed half sleeves. I pointed to a pair of medium-heeled navy court shoes which coordinated well with the blue floral design of the dress fabric.

'Just slip those on,' I said, 'and then come through to

my room and sit down at the dressing table.'

I soon got to work on her eye-brows, plucking them into fine, feminine arcs. I was determined that having once got her into skirts, there would be no going back. I wanted to keep my new daughter! I next applied a light coat of foundation, and decided not to bother with powder or blusher, as her skin was so clear. I made up her eyes with care, using just a little shadow and mascara, and applied a subtle, natural tone of lipstick to her lips. It was obvious to me that the less make-up we used the better; Lucy was supposed to be a young girl of seventeen, and girls of that age tend not to wear much make-up unless they're going out on the town for a night of boy-watching! (Would Lucy be interested in boys, I wondered? Then I shook myself for my silly dreaming - she was hardly used to being a girl, yet.)

Having finished making up her face, I found the long, blonde wig I had bought and fitted it on her head. I combed out the waves and let them fall to her shoulders. Not bad, but maybe not quite right for day-time. I tried the hair back in a pony-tail, with tortoise-shell combs on either side, and some wispy tresses falling down in front of the ears. Perfect! It had just that slightly dishevelled look so beloved of teenage girls, and looked really natural. I brought Lucy over to the full-length mirror on the wardrobe door and watched her expression as she surveyed herself properly for the first time. Her eyes widened in disbelief as she exclaimed:

'Good God. I look just like a girl!'

'Of course, darling; that's what you're supposed to look like. You must think of yourself as a girl from now on.'

'Don't you think that's going a bit far?'

'Not at all. The more you think of yourself as a girl, the easier it will become for you. Try and walk, talk and sit like a girl. Keep your knees closed when you sit down in a skirt; soften your voice; make your movements more feminine and fluid.'

Lucy sat down on the bed, stared at me intensely for a moment, and said:

135

'If I didn't know better, I'd begin to suspect this was all a plot of yours to turn me into a girl.'

'You know that's ridiculous darling; I've explained why you must do this for me,' I answered. Could she detect the tremor in my voice? Was I blushing? To change the subject I said:

'Come on, we've got no time to lose. We must start packing immediately if we're going to be ready to get that flight from Heathrow tomorrow.'

And so *that* was the beginning, and perhaps the most difficult part of turning my son into a daughter. Having created the pretext and got him into skirts, the rest was comparatively easy.

Well, we got the flight, and of course Lucy had to go as Lucien, to get through passport control and customs etc. Fortunately they didn't open our cases. Rachael looked at Lucien as if she was dying to say something, when we first met at Heathrow; but she just exchanged the normal polite conversational pleasantries with us until we were in our seats on the plane. Then, scarcely able to contain herself any longer, she turned to me and whispered:

'I can't believe what you told me about Lucien. He looks perfectly normal to me.'

'You'll see,' I replied.

As soon as we'd landed in Italy and gone throught the formalities, we found the hire car desk and were directed towards a white turbo-diesel Fiat Punto parked in the compound outside. Soon we were bowling through the foothills of the Apennines, amid olive plantations and rows of gnarled vines; the hot summer sun of Tuscany beat down on us, and we threw open all the windows of the car to try and keep cool.

'I could use a cold drink,' announced Rachael, 'let's stop soon and find a cafe.'

The next village was a settlement of white, pantile-roofed buildings piled onto the hill-side around an ancient domed church and central square lined with olive trees. A couple of teenage boys were revving and racing their mopeds up and down one side of the square, raising clouds of dust off the surface of the road. On the other side of the square was a small ristorante and bar, shaded by trees, with rickety tables and chairs outside under coloured parasols.

'That'll do,' said Rachael. We pulled up outside the ristorante and got out of the car. Rachael was about to sit at one of the tables outside when I called across:

'No - let's sit inside.' I took a holdall out of the boot and led the way to a Formica-topped table in a dim corner of the bar. The place seemed deserted; there were no other customers and no one had yet appeared to serve us from the room behind the counter.

'Perfect,' I announced. I took Lucien by the hand and led him quickly through to the ladies' toilet. Fortunately it was a clean, fairly large room with a lockable door, a chipped sink, a chair and a foot-print WC.

'What on earth's that?' asked Lucien, pointing with distaste at the footprint loo.

'Never mind about that,' I replied; 'get into these things as quickly as you can.' I produced from the holdall the underwear, floral dress, and shoes which Lucien had tried on the day before; he was already wearing the panty-girdle, which I had instructed him to put on under his jeans first thing in the morning, before we left home to catch the flight. I had put a portable electric razor in the holdall, but was pleased to find that we didn't need it; the skin of his face was still smooth and hairless from his previous shave. I fished the blonde wig out of the holdall and fitted it to his head, pinning back the hair in a pony-tail, as before. Then I quickly applied the make-up, and as a finishing touch, added pendant clip-on earrings.

'We'll have to get those ears pierced,' I whispered; 'but you'll do for now.'

We left the toilet and made our way back to where Rachael was sitting; she was sipping a cup of cappuccino coffee and studying a map spread out on the table before her. She looked up as we approached and exclaimed, with a mischievous glint in her eye:

'Good Lord! Whose this?'

'This,' I announced, 'is Lucy.'

'Hello Lucy; do come and sit down and drink your coffee before it gets cold,' said Rachael. If she had any questions, she had obviously decided to postpone asking them until later. I could have hugged her! And so, I think, could Lucy.

We arrived at the convent in the cool of the early evening, and were shown to our villa by a smiling old nun who needed no English to make us feel welcome. It was a beautiful white-walled farm-house amid the semi-tropical foliage of the convent grounds. There was a spring of tinkling, crystal water issuing from the rocks behind an outhouse, and a patio shaded by ancient vines at the front of the house.

'I think we've found paradise!' said Rachael.

The days merged into weeks at the Villa della Etruria, a blissful time for us all, I think - delicious meals under the vines, of sweet tomatoes and peppers, fresh pasta, sardines and olive oil, washed down with the robust red wine of the region; a little reading or painting; relaxing walks in the grounds. Sometimes we would go for drives in the hills, to visit a quaint little chapel or the castle of some medieval count or prince of the Renaissance.

We also made longer, more tiring trips into Florence, unable to resist such a treasurehouse nearby - we saw the gothic splendour of the Cathedral of Santa Maria del Fiore and the campanile begun by Giotto; we stood in the Piazza della Signoria, gazing up at the sturdy Vechio palace with its crenellated bell tower; we spent a whole day in the Uffizi Gallery, gorging ourselves visually on its unsurpassed collection of Italian and Flemish masters. We walked across the fourteenth century Ponte Vecchio, lined with goldsmiths' and jewellers' shops; and of course we had to visit the Medici chapel, and the beautiful Franciscan church of Santa Croce, housing the tombs of

Michelangelo and Machiavelli. We really pigged out on the Renaissance culture of central Italy, until we felt as if we couldn't look at another palace or painting!

And how did Lucy get on? The first time she ventured out from the villa she was a little unsure of herself, but as it became clear that everyone took her for what she appeared to be - an attractive young English girl - she relaxed into her new role. I was delighted to note the subtle changes in her behaviour - gradually her mannerisms were becoming more feminine, the way she walked and held herself, the way she smiled and even the way she ate and drank.

One evening, while we were sitting on the terrace, sipping iced drinks and enjoying the cool and fragrant night air after a hot, dusty day in Florence, Rachael had asked Lucy:

'You certainly make a very convincing girl. I'm sure no one had the least idea of - well, your true sex - while we were in Florence today. No one gave you a second glance - no, that isn't true; I caught quite a number of young Italian males leering in our direction in obvious appreciation, and I don't think it was too old boilers like your mother and I that they were looking at.'

'Speak for yourself!' I replied; 'mature English ladies are very attractive to Italian men.' Rachael ignored my comment and continued:

'So how does it feel, to know that you can pass as a girl, and that boys find you attractive?'

Lucy shrugged. 'It's okay,' she replied, not knowing what to say.

'Only okay? I gathered from your mother that you have always longed to dress as a girl; you must be delighted to find that you can pull it off so successfully. Or is this just a game for you - a masquerade?'

I gave Lucy a warning look. She nodded slightly, to show me that she knew what she must say.

'No, it's not a game; I want to be a girl.'

'You mean you want to live as a girl - for the rest of

your life?' persisted Rachael. Lucy nodded.

'Yes, I've always wanted to be a girl.' Rachael looked at her intently for a few more seconds, then breathed out audibly through her nostrils. She seemed satisfied at last, and from that moment Rachael was a great help to Lucy in her transformation from male to female, taking it upon herself to school Lucy in small ways on things feminine, to offer gentle advice and encouragement. Rachael had been to drama school in her youth, and she was able to recall some of the voice control techniques she had learnt to coach Lucy in developing a feminine voice. I'd also brought a course of Italian language audio tapes which Lucy was working her way through, and as the tutor on the tapes was a woman, it became natural for Lucy to imitate the tone and inflection of her voice. In short, Lucy's Italian sounded particularly feminine - the slight huskiness in her voice sounded exactly right and rather sexy! As long as she spoke Italian she could convince anyone of her femininity!

How far did I take things? *All the way,* of course! I now have a lovely daughter, who will always be a girl, for the rest of her life, because she has no choice. Yes, all those nasty male bits are gone from between her legs. She's got the right parts for a girl, now. She looks lovely in a bikini, with her 38 inch bust, 26 inch waist and 36 inch hips - and when we sun ourselves on the beach on the Italian Riviera, she turns more than a few male heads. You know what Italian men are like - she positively has to fight them off; they are constantly wanting to get to know the beautiful English signorina. But I'm running ahead - so how did I accomplish the final transformation of son into daughter?

A few days before it was time for Rachael to return to England, I told her we had decided to stay on in Italy.

'I'm going to Port'Ercole today,' I announced on the last morning over breakfast, 'to look at a beautiful little cottage I've seen advertised. If it's suitable, we're going to rent it

140

for a whole year. Lucy can't go back to her old school in England, anyway, so I'm going to see about enrolling her in a language school here; her Italian is improving daily and she also has good French and German.'

Rachael nodded and said, 'I'll be sorry to leave the Villa della Etruria, but I'm due back at work next week. I'll be thinking of you enjoying a gentle Tuscan Autumn, while I'm freezing back in England.'

We took Rachael to the airport in the white Punto and then set off for Port'Ercole. We fell in love with the cottage at once; it was an ancient, sun-drenched little villa with a low roof of pink pantiles and a veranda which gave on to the beach, near the very spot where Caravaggio died of a fever. The cottage had a large cellar which would be ideal for storing wine; I imagined it lit in a chiaroscuro tableau of light and dark, like a Caravaggio painting. The cottage turned out to be for rent or sale and I bought it on the spot.

I had explained to Lucy that it would be safer for us to remain in Italy, as the English police might still be looking for us. Fortunately, she never found out that I had made up the whole story. She went off meekly to language school, believing that she had no choice, that to do anything else might land her mother in penury and prison. She gradually became reconciled to her new role in life as a girl - as my lovely daughter, the daughter I had always wanted. I persuaded her to start taking hormones, and in time, I booked her into a private clinic in Milan, where the operation was performed.

Lucy did well at the language school and went on to university in Florence - by this time she was fluent in Italian. After graduating, she got a well-paid job as an interpreter with the European Commission, and is currently based in Strasbourg. I am still living in Port'Ercole, where I've opened a little gallery in which I display my own paintings and those of other local artists. Lucy comes to stay with me regularly, and seems very contented with her life as a successful career-woman.

'Mummy,' she said to me recently, 'I have to admit it - I

141

like my life as it is now. I enjoy being a girl so much.'

'Lucy,' I replied, 'no mother could hope for a better, more talented or more beautiful daughter than you.'

Virtual Reality Woman

It was a crisp October morning when I parked my ancient Citroen for the first time outside the new Post-Modernist block on the UCET campus which housed VIRED. I paused for a moment before getting out of the car, peering through the windscreen beyond the low, rustic-brick wall of the car park; the thin sunshine was sparkling on the roiling waters of the polluted river, making its surface glint like the back of some huge reptile. I felt butterflies in my stomach - a mixture of excitement, anticipation and a touch of nerves - at the thought that my undergraduate days were now behind me. This was the beginning of the rest of my life. I realised that I had been so grateful to get a place on the post-graduate research programme at UCET, at a time when the alternative was unemployment or even worse - teaching - that I had given little thought to what my work with Dr. Klonek might entail.

As a mere male, I had been surprised to get the job at all; Dr. Klonek's reputation as a feminist academic was formidable. At a time when the proportion of new entrants to university places, both undergraduate and postgraduate, was running at 75 per cent female, I had perhaps been recruited to make up the number of token males, in line with the Department for Education and Employment's Equal Opportunities Programme. Male unemployment had been growing steadily since the turn of the century. The notion originally propagated by an influential group of radical feminists - that males were virtually unemployable, due to their behavioural peculiarities - was gaining common currency.

The Virtual Reality Engineering Department at UCET, the first of its kind in the country, had been up and running for three years when Dr. Klonek had begun to consider the possibilities of using virtual reality as a research tool to investigate the nature of sex and gender. The University of Central England (Trent site) was one of those brash new universities which advertised on television, having arisen from the lowly clay of a polytechnic and two colleges of higher education during the great expansion of higher education in the 1990's. The vice-chancellor of UCET was anxious that the university should prove its pioneering academic credentials, and had gained new money to set up the VRE faculty from OFFCOM, the Office of Computing and Cybernetics, a government quango established during the second Becket premiership. The VRE Department at UCET was exactly the sort of enterprise with which the Becketite 'women in suits' wished to be associated, representing a re-working of the 'white-hot heat of technology' mythos first coined during the Wilson era. Becketism, if it was about anything, was about wresting the technological highground from the countries of the Pacific Rim.

In those early years, the VRE Department at UCET was awash with money, and so Dr. Hannah Klonek had secured sufficient funds to begin modifying two Total Virtual Reality Suits to her own specifications, without anyone asking awkward questions about the ultimate purpose of the modifications.

The VRE Department (or VIRED, to use its acronym) had drawn its staff from a variety of more traditional disciplines. Dr. Klonek's background was in the psychology and sociology of gender. Her doctoral thesis had been supervised by Professor Mary Rose, the professor of Women's Studies at the University of West Mercia, who had been associated with the controversial 'Ascent of Woman' series for Channel 5.

The electric doors closed silently behind me as I passed into the lobby of the VIRED building and made my way to the reception desk. A brisk-looking young woman in a navy-blue tailored suit was sitting behind the desk. She glanced at the list of names on the monitor in front of her, then looked up at me and asked:

'Mr. Thompson, is it?'

'That's right.'

'Dr. Klonek's room is in the West Suite on the 11th

floor.   Take the lift there and when you get to Floor 11 come out of the lift and turn left along the corridor and it's the second door on the right.'

I followed the receptionist's instructions, and a couple of minutes later found myself standing outside a door bearing a stainless steel plaque with the name 'Dr. Hannah Klonek' etched into it in bold black letters. I took a deep breath and knocked lightly. Nothing happened, so I knocked again. The next moment I heard a female voice mutter something that sounded like: 'Oh shit -' and then the the door was flung open, and I found myself being examined by a short, solidly-built woman wearing a purple jogging suit. Her black hair showed one or two streaks of iron grey and was pinned back severely, exposing a broad brow. Having looked me over from head to foot, she stared straight into my eyes and said:

'Yes?'

I held her gaze and replied:

'I'm Andy Thompson.'

'Oh yes; our new postgraduate student. Come in.'

She pulled back the door and ushered me through a small, cluttered office, into a larger room beyond in which there were benches of computers and electronic equipment to one side, and on the other, two large suits suspended from the ceiling by a complicated system of pulleys, cables and wires. Dr. Klonek saw that I was staring at the suits, which looked vaguely reminiscent of the sort of space outfits worn by astronauts in science fiction films of the 1980's.

'Yes,' she said; 'those are our pride and joy - the two Total Virtual Reality Suits that we've been working on. Each suit has over four hundred pads and bands which exchange the sensory input and output information. The pads and bands - we call them sensory exchange units, or SEU's - can contract or enlarge in any sequence programmed by the computers, applying and reducing pressure to different parts of the body, and producing a wide range other sensory experiences. The crotch and nipple areas of the suits are particularly well provided with

SEU's, in view of the nature of our research project.'

Dr. Klonek looked at me keenly as she made this last comment, to see my reaction. I nodded, attempting to keep my expression neutral.

'How much do you know about out work here?'

'I've read some of your papers,' I replied, 'I know you're interested in using virtual reality technology to explore the nature of sex and gender.'

'That's correct, Mr. Thompson. Can I call you Andy?'

'Of course.'

'And you will call me Hannah; we don't stand on formality here. Yes, put simply, we are interested in using the suits to investigate what it means to be a man or woman, psychologically, culturally and physically. We believe that many of the problems there have been in the past in relations between the sexes - the lack of mutual understanding which has produced the historic polarisation of sex-role stereotypes - originates from the inability of each sex to really comprehend what it means to be a member of the other sex. We are using virtual reality technology to create the sensory experiences associated with sex and gender.'

'To what end - what is the purpose of your experiments?'

'You are aware that there are a growing range of social problems associated mainly with young males in our society. Crimes of violence and vandalism, for example, are largely perpetrated by young men - the unemployed male underclass which has been growing for some years. Women, as you know, have adapted well to the needs of the modern state, and now do most of the paid work in society, as well as having the major role in raising the family and running the home. Men on the other hand, at least unreconstructed men of the old type, are just about redundant. There is no heavy industry requiring unskilled manual labour anymore; poorly educated young males have little to contribute to society in the workplace and their outdated attitudes to child-care and domestic chores make them very little use at home. Their chauvinistic attitudes, violence and tribalism make these sort of males not just an anachronism but a positive menace to modern society. Something has to be done about them.

'Put simply, it is the nature of *maleness or masculinity* which we have identified as the biggest problem - the traditional male gender stereotype is what has to be changed. The interpersonal skills of women, and the behavioural traits traditionally associated as feminine - the ability to nurture, cooperate, show empathy, be aware of the feelings of others, are of far more use to modern society than the traditionally male attributes of aggression, competition, and individualism. In short, we need to make boys much more like girls. In the long-time, we can adjust the way we socialise boys and bring them up differently; this won't, however, solve the problem of the several million adult males who are unemployable and useless to society because of their unreconstructed *maleness.*

'Our research is addressing the problem of what to do with these individuals; we can't very well just *cull* them like so many mad cows, as has been suggested by one or two of our more extreme sisters in the Radical Feminist Party. No, we have to find a more humane solution. We are looking into the possibility of *reprogramming* them. The best way I can show you what we are working on is by asking you to put on one of those suits and actually try out the program we are developing.'

Dr. Klonek pointed to a door in the wall behind where the suits were hanging and said:

'You can use that as a changing room. Go in there and remove all your clothes, then we'll get you into one of the suits and run the program on you....'

I went through the door in the wall behind where the suits were hanging, and found myself in a narrow windowless room, little wider than a corridor, lit by a single bare bulb suspended from the ceiling. The room was unfurnished except for a steel-framed chair and a long glass-fronted cupboard used for storing ancient three and a half inch floppy disks of the type used in the last century. I looked at the rows of obsolete disks and wondered why they hadn't transferred the information on them to more modern data storage media, such as the 1010 gigabyte CDS2 mini-disks which were now standard in the computer industry. Maybe it was some sort of historical archive; this was a university, after all. Reflecting on this was stopping me from feeling anxious about what Dr. Klonek had just proposed - 'Remove all your clothes,' she has said, just like that! I hadn't been in the place five minutes and my new boss was ordering me to get my kit off. I wondered whether it was a sort of test. If I refused, would I fail the test or pass it?

A light tap on the door made me jump half out of my skin, then I heard Dr. Klonek's strident voice asking from the other side of the panel:

'Are you undressed yet?'

'No, I'll just be a few seconds,' I replied. I removed my Karrimor fleece jacket, shirt and jeans, and piled them on the chair. I stood in my underpants, shivering slightly, a knot of anxiety tightening in my stomach, then took a deep breath and opened the door into the main laboratory.

I stood in the doorway, looking around until I saw Dr. Klonek working at a computer console nearby. I cleared my throat, and she looked up towards me.

'Ah Andy.'

She walked over to me and pointing to my spectacles, she said, 'You won't be needing these.' She gently removed them and folded them, putting them on the work-top in front of the monitor. Then she came back and looked down at my underpants; taking her slim index finger, she inserted it in th waistband and pinged the elastic:

'And you won't be needing these...'

She looked up at me and grinned - the first time I had seen her smile. Tiny lights seemed to be dancing in her eyes. I raised my eyebrows and smiled back at her. I returned to the little room, removed my underpants and

148

threw them on the top of my pile of clothes, then presented myself again before her, now butt-naked. I wondered if I had passed the test?

She glanced down appraisingly at my genitals, making a sort of 'hmmm' noise with her mouth before saying:

'It's okay honey; I've seen it all before. Anyway, you're not my type - you're not even the right sex - the male of the species doesn't interest me *that* way. You're quite safe. Just call me doctor.'

I raised my eyebrows again, and said:

'Okay doctor, what do I do now?'

Dr. Klonek went over to the nearest of the two suits and began to work on the system of pulleys and cables which suspended it from the ceiling. As I watched her, I compared the two suits and noticed that they were not both the same. One of them was flat across the chest and had an extra protrusion of material between the legs; the other suit was flat between the legs but had two raised mounds on the chest, which looked like breast swellings. Dr. Klonek was working on the suit with breast compartments. After a couple of minutes she had lowered the suit to the floor and undone the Velcro side fastenings.

'You can get into it now,' she said. I sat on the floor next to the suit and eased myself into its legs, then stood while Dr. Klonek helped me pull up the suit over my crotch and buttocks. I shimmied my arms into the sleeves of the suit and the doctor fastened the velco around my neck before checking the main harnesses between my legs and under my arms. She then placed a strange contraption over my head and face which completely shut off my vision; I could still just hear her muffled voice as she said:

'That's the virtual reality headset. It's a prototype - we still have some improvements to make, but everything basically works on it - how does it feel?

'The ear-pieces are pressing in a little too tightly,' I replied.

She made a couple of adjustments, and then moved away. Suddenly I could hear her voice coming crystal

149

clear through the tiny ear-speakers:

'More comfortable now?'

'Yes, thanks.'

'How's the sound quality? Not too loud?'

'No - it seems about right.'

I waited, listening to a very faint background hiss coming from the speakers. Although my eyes were open, I could at first see nothing; then a cascade of lights exploded suddenly onto my retinas, configuring themselves almost at once into the walls of a virtual room bathed in soft blue light coming from a window in the opposite wall. Next to the window was a door.

'I'm just running some test sequences now,' explained Dr. Klonek; 'tell me what you can see.'

I described the room and the window and door.

'You'll be going through that door shortly', said Dr. Klonek, into the brave new virtual world beyond. Before you begin that journey, we just have to run some final tests on the SEU's - the sensory exchange units.'

The suit felt almost alive as gentle pressure modulated through the 400 or so SEU's distributed throughout the suit. I could feel the pads and bands of the sensory exchange units contracting and enlarging in sequences programmed by the computer, applying and reducing pressure to the skin surface of different parts of my body - including the crotch and nipple areas, which were particularly well provided with SEU's. The sensations were not unpleasant. At length, I heard the doctor's voice saying through the ear-phones:

'The preliminary test sequences have all run smoothly - all systems seem to be functioning correctly. How do you feel?'

'A little strange, but okay.'

'Right, let's proceed with the test.'

The next moment, I was aware of some slight pressure in the body harnesses between my legs and around my arms as the suit raised me gently off my feet. I guessed that I was now suspended a few inches above the surface of the floor. I was hanging like an astonaut in zero gravity.

150

I heard the voice of Dr. Klonek again saying:

'I'd like in a moment for you to begin to walk slowly towards the door in the virtual room you can see; open the door and go through it. When you have passed through the door you're on your own and will not hear my voice again until the program is over. If for any reason you are in difficulties and want to terminate the program before the end, we can have a code phrase which will shut down the system. We need to decide on the code phrase now, a form of words which I enter into the program before you start. These words, and these words alone, will arrest the sequence at whatever point you've reached. Saying 'stop', 'help', 'get me out out here', or begging for mercy will have *no* effect. Do you understand?'

'Yes.' I wondered whether I had just misheard my own voice - some effect of the headset. The voice which had just said yes in the earphones had not sounded like my own. The tone had been softer, the pitch more varied.

'Think for a moment, and then give me your emergency code words. They should be something you will remember easily, but not an expression that you are likely to use in the course of normal conversation. Three to five words would be ideal.'

I paused, then said:

'The fat lady is singing.' Again, I noticed that the voice played back to me through my earphones did not sound quite like my own; there was a subtle change in it - it had been distorted in someway to make it sound - *feminine.* Something about the resonance and tone was different. 'The fat lady is singing,' I said again, to see if I could work out the difference. What was it? It wasn't to do with how high or low my voice was; it was more the way the words went up and down - the range between them. The tonality of my voice sounded as if it was going up and down in stair steps - it had almost a sing-song quality about it - and it definitely sounded like a female voice; softer, warmer, more appealing - *sexy*, even. I repeated a third time: 'The fat lady is singing.'

'Yes, I heard you the first time - "the fat lady is singing," those will be your emergency code words. I've just entered them into the program. You can walk through the door now.'

I walked towards the door, actually performing the movements inside the suit. Although I guessed I was still raised off the floor a few inches, the sensory exchange pads in the feet of the suit somehow created the impression that I was walking on firm ground. I reached towards the door handle, and saw a slim arm, with slender, delicate fingers reaching towards the handle. I stopped and held up my left hand, palm upwards, in front of my face. The hand I saw through the tiny visual display units in front of my eyes had exactly matched the movements I had made. I was looking down at a small, delicate hand, palm upwards. I wiggled my fingers inside the suit. The fingers on the hand wiggled. *Incredible!* I thought.

I put the hand down to the knob on the door again, turned it, pushed the door open and went through. I looked around and found that I had entered what appeared to be the room I had just left - I was standing in a very accurate simulation of Dr. Klonek's laboratory. I could see the benches of computers and electronic equipment to one side, and the two virtual reality suits suspended from the ceiling. The quality of the images was stunning; everything looked exactly the same, down to the shadows cast by the eco-lighting in the ceiling panels. Dr. Klonek was standing in front of me in her purple jogging suit.

'Hello Andy. Yes, the virtual reality environment we have created in this test program is as near as we could make it the same as the world you are used to. Instead of creating some ludicrous fantasy world, we have embedded virtual reality in reality - the present reality as perceived by you. There is just one difference. Look down at your body.'

I bent my head down to examine myself - and found that I was looking at the naked body of a *woman*. I could see the mounds of two breasts - they appeared to be *my* breasts. I put my hand to squeeze one of them, and found that the sensory units in the suit applied the same gentle pressure to my own chest tissue. I massaged the nipple on the breast, and noticed that the suit created the sensation of my own nipple being massaged. I looked down again, this time bending my back to peer between my legs. Instead of male genitalia, I saw a bush of dark hair and underneath, the soft curves of a vagina. I touched myself between the legs, and saw my fingers - now slim and feminine - touching the bush of hair and the labia. I felt at the same moment a strange sensation in my groin, as the pressure pads matched the touch of my fingers. I gasped.

'Yes, honey - that's *you* ; at least in virtual reality. Don't you think you'd better get dressed?' Dr. Klonek pointed towards the small room where I'd left my clothes before getting into the suit. I nodded, and walked towards the room. Instead of finding my own clothes piled where I had left them, a cream silk blouse and tan linen skirt were neatly folded over the back of the chair; a black lacy bra and panty set; a suspender belt and a pair of sheer black stockings were resting on the seat, and there was a pair of high-heeled leather court shoes on the floor. Dr. Klonek came up behind me and stood in the doorway.

' Those clothes match your new body. They should be a perfect fit. Sorry about the quaint, antiquated underwear, but we chose ultra-feminine garments deliberately; it's part of the programming. We couldn't have our new girl tatting around in jeans. Put the clothes on as best you can, then come back into the lab.'

I struggled into the panties, suspender belt and bra, fiddling with the clasp at the back of the bra until I had got it secured correctly and the straps untwisted. I looked down at the breasts filling out the bra-cups; I could feel the constriction of the bra around my chest, and somehow the VR suit even conveyed a sense of the weight and movement of the breasts as I bent down to put on the stockings. I had seen enough erotic movies to know how to roll on the stockings and attach the tops to the clasps of the suspender belt.

I put on the blouse, my fingers struggling with the unfamiliarity of doing up the buttons from the other side. I pulled on the linen skirt, which appeared to be lined with a silky fabric, doing up the zip at the back. The skirt was cut narrow and felt quite a tight fit; I could feel the hem of it restricting the movement of my legs as I slipped my toes into the court shoes. I noticed that the fabric of the skirt was pulled fairly tight across my hips, which seemed to be wider, while the cut of the garment accentuated the smallness of my waist. I could feel an unaccustomed tension in the muscles at the back of my legs, caused by the redistribution of my weight in the high-heeled shoes. How could women put up with this sort of footwear all day? I wobbled back into the laboratory.

'Very nice,' said Dr. Hannah, surveying my new virtual self. 'Now, I'd like you to go and see a colleague of mine, Dr. Smedley, who is going to examine you and make sure everything is as it should be. But before that, we need to think of a name for you. We can't very well continue to call you Andy.'

'Oh.' I looked down at myself, taking in first the cleavage of my breasts inside the silk blouse, and then my broad hips and slim, nylon-clad legs in the skirt and high-heeled pumps. This experience was beginning to stir up strange feelings in me. I found my new appearance interesting and attractive - and yet I had never consciously wished to cross-dress in real life. Maybe *unconsciously?* - I could recall one or two strange dreams I'd had in the past, which seemed to involve an element of cross-dressing. I had awoken from these wondering about their meaning, and had been embarrassed to find on one occasion at least that the sheets were sticky from a nocturnal emission. I'd read that all men had a feminine side; perhaps I'd been repressing this part of myself?

'I see what you mean,' I replied, 'do you have a name in mind?

'Well *Andrea* would be an obvious choice. Maybe too obvious. I think you should choose.'

'What about Laura?' I said. I'd had a girl friend called

Laura a few years back, whom I had greatly admired, although we'd lost touch after she'd gone off to college. The name seemed charged with good memories and positive associations.

'Laura it is then.'

At that moment, a large young man in a white doctor's coat came through the door of the lab, and Dr. Klonek said: 'This is Peter Frankel, Dr. Smedley's assistant. He'll show you the way to Dr. Smedley's room. Peter, this is our new postgraduate student, Laura.'

I wondered how Dr. Klonek had managed to introduce the name I had chosen so quickly into the VR program. She couldn't possibly have known the name I'd pick. Was she monitoring the simulation second by second, feeding new information and adjustments into the program as necessary? When I heard her voice, was she actually speaking into the simulation in real time? I'd noticed a small microphone in front of one of the computer systems.

'Follow me,' said Peter Frankel. We left the laboratory and walked down a long corridor. I moved my legs, making the motion of walking; the VR suit allowed a surprising freedom of movement, and the sensory exchange units created the sensation of walking in high-heeled shoes with what I guessed was considerable accuracy, although I'd never worn such shoes in real life. My heels were maintained in a raised position and I began to feel a strain in my calf muscles as I clicked down the corridor. I could hear through the ear-pieces the *click-clack* of the heels as they struck the plastic floor tiles, and the visual display exactly matched my movement; I could see Peter Frankel's back as he walked in front of me, the off-white walls and ceiling of the corridor, the eco-lighting units. We reached the end of the corridor, and I was ushered into what looked like a doctor's consulting room, with a screen, a couch, a desk on which there was a computer, a leather-bound swivel chair in front of the desk, and a steel-framed chair off to the side. The room was empty.

'Take a seat, Laura,' said Peter Frankel; 'Doctor Smedley

will be with you shortly.' I sat down on the steel-framed chair, and was surprised to find that the chair felt solid. I looked down at my legs; the tightness of the skirt obliged me to keep my knees together. After a few seconds a middle-aged man in gold-rimmed spectacles appeared. He was wearing a white doctor's smock and had dark brown curly hair which was thinning at the front. He held out his hand to me and said:

'Hello, Miss Thompson - Laura, is it? May I call you that?' I stood up and shook hands with him, feeling the pressure of the hand-shake in the glove of the suit. I nodded and said:

'You can call me Laura, if you like.'

'Good. Now to get straight down to business, I'm going to run a few tests on you. Would you mind going behind that screen and stripping off to your bra and panties?'

I stepped behind the screen, and undid the buttons of the blouse. The thin fabric of the VR suit covering my fingers seemed to be made of a special flexible material which left me with a fair degree of tactile sensation in my finger tips.

I could feel the buttons quite well and undid them fairly easily, then unzipped my skirt at the back and slipped out of it. I needed to fiddle more with the suspenders before I had released my stocking tops and rolled down my stockings. I stood for a moment, looking in wonder at the breasts - *my breasts* - filling out the bra-cups, and at the smooth, flat curve between my legs. I came out from behind the screen, feeling suddenly vunerable in presenting myself before Dr. Smedley - this *man* who was a stranger. *But wasn't I really a man?* This was all very confusing!

'Good,' said Dr. Smedley. Now would you just lie down on the couch for me, please?' I hesitated, feeling a pang of anxiety.

'It's okay, Laura. Don't worry. You're really doing very well. It must seem very strange to you, adjusting to your new body.'

I nodded and lowered myself onto the couch.

156

Dr. Smedley took out a stethoscope from the drawer of the desk, bent over me and placed the disk of the instrument just above my left bosom. I gasped and shuddered slightly - *I could actually feel the coldness of the disk on my chest!* The sensory exchange units were amazing - I couldn't even guess at the nature of the advanced systems they employed. I had heard that Virtual Reality technology had come on in leaps and bounds in recent years, but I had no idea just how sophisticated it had become.

Dr. Smedley listened to my heart for a few moments, nodded approvingly, then removed the disk from my chest and hung the stethoscope round his neck.

'Nothing wrong there, Laura; you've got a good strong heart.'

He next placed two fingers on the inside of my wrist. I could feel a slight pressure on the veins, as he took my pulse.

'I'd like to inspect your breasts now; would that be alright?' I shrugged, and nodded.

He placed his hand on my right breast and gently plumped it; then did the same with my left breast. Within the VR suit, I felt a gentle upward pressure on each side of my chest, the sensations exactly matching his actions, as far as I could tell.

'Can you feel that?' he asked.

'Yes.'

'Good. You still seem a little anxious, Laura, so I'm going to give you a shot which will help to relax you. Would that be okay?'

'I'm not sure; Dr. Klonek never said anything about injections.'

'You see? You *are* anxious. I assure you it's nothing to worry about.'

Before I could say anything else, Dr. Smedley produced a small hypodermic syringe, held it up and squeezed the plunger a little to force out any air bubbles, then put the needle to my left arm. I felt a sharp pin-prick in my arm, as the needle went in. Had I really been injected with something? How could that be the case? This was supposed to be *virtual* reality only. I was alarmed to find that I was beginning to feel sleepy; I was dropping into unconsciousness, and could do nothing to keep myself awake. The last thing I saw was Dr. Smedley standing over me, smiling benignly down.....

I awoke to find myself hanging face down in a dark, bare room - it looked like some sort of loft or basement, illuminated by a single dim bulb which cast a sickly light over the cob-webbed corners and dusty floor boards.   I was suspended by my ankles and wrists, which were manacled and tied by rope to the rafters above. Now that I was fully conscious, the pain was quickly becoming excruciating; the muscles in my arms and legs ached appallingly from being stretched by the weight of my hanging body, while the steel edges of the manacles were cutting into the flesh of my wrists and ankles, making me feel like screaming.

'Help!' I shouted. 'Will somebody please help me!' I noticed that my voice still sounded female. I looked down at my body, and saw the breasts hanging out of my open blouse. I also seemed to be wearing again the suspender-belt, stockings and high-heels, though no panties or other clothes. What on earth was going on? Where was Dr. Smedley? Where was Dr. Klonek? What were they doing to me?

I called out:

'Dr. Klonek! I've had enough of this! Get me out of here!'

Nothing happened. I hung in the manacles, whimpering to myself, and occasionally yelling out for help, but no one came. The pain in my legs and arms was becoming unbearable.   Then I remembered the emergency code words:

'The fat lady is singing!' I gasped. Then I yelled it at the top of my lungs: 'The fat lady is singing!'

I waited. Nothing happened. I tried a third time: 'The fat lady is singing!'

Then I heard a door creak open in the wall somewhere behind me. A bright shaft of light spread across the boards of the floor; then I heard footsteps clicking towards me and a voice saying:

'You didn't really think that would work, did you?' It was a woman's voice, quite deep and husky, a sexually charged voice, but with an underlying coldness in the tone. The owner of the voice proved to be a tall, slim woman with a long mane of thick black hair. She was wearing a tight leather basque which forced up her ample bosoms into a provocative cleavage. The basque had long suspenders attached, which were holding up fish-net stockings. Her panties were little wider than a thong of black leather between her legs and buttocks. In her hand was a riding crop, which she swished playfully against her thigh. The heels of her black leather stilettos struck the flag-stone floor with metallic clicks, the sound echoing slightly as she came round to stand in front of me, and said:

'If you are going to experience what it means to be a woman, you must experience everything, including sex as a woman. We didn't think you would agree to that voluntarily, so we have devised this little exercise in compulsion. Consider it your baptism of fire, into the most secret rites of womanhood.'

'This is getting ridiculous. You've had your fun, but I want out of here, *now*. Dr. Klonek? You must be able to hear this. I'm sure you're out there somewhere, monitoring what is going on. This is gone far enough. I resign, with immediate effect. Come on, let me down! You can stuff your postgraduate studentship where the sun don't shine!'

My show of bravado had no effect. The woman was still standing in front of me, peering up through her beautiful green eyes, and gently shaking her head in disapproval.

'This attitude doesn't help. Speaking of stuffing, the only thing that's going to get stuffed around here is you, young lady. Resistance is useless. You must calm yourself, resign yourself to what is going to happen. I'm

159

sure you will agree that a submissive posture would be more appropriate now - more in line with your new gender, little girl. Her full red lips pulled into a sneer as she said the word 'girl'. She grinned lewdly at me, revealing her small white teeth.

She reached up and pulled apart my blouse, studied my breasts for a few moments, and then licked her lips and said:

'Okay, let's get on with it.'

She went round to the back of me and swished the leather riding crop close to my buttocks, without actually making contact. She laughed then - a tinkling sound like shards of ice dropping in a crystal glass.

I began to kick and struggle, but found that this just hurt my ankles and wrists more than ever, as the manacles bit more deeply into me. 'Stop kicking girl,' she ordered, cracking the whip hard across my bottom. I shrieked, struggled again, and then hung still, waiting.

'I told you, you must not resist, or I will have to hit you again. You must submit to what is going to happen. I haven't introduced myself, have I? You can call me Madam Cynthia, if you like; or Mistress will do - I expect you'll be screaming that soon enough.'

She manoeuvred herself until she was underneath my breasts, and then put her lipsticked lips to my right breast and sucked at the nipple, tweaking my left breast at the same time with her fingers. The sensations I felt on my chest so closely matched what she was doing, I began to wonder if I was really still wearing the VR suit. I was beginning to find it hard to separate virtual reality from reality. The feeling of a warm, wet mouth closing over my right nipple and sucking, while my left nipple was being squeezed gently and massaged, was unbelievably realistic.

She released my nipples and peered at the triangle of hair between my legs.

'Please, no more....' I whimpered.

'Ah! She even cries like a girl,' hissed Madam Cynthia.

She moved her head underneath me, positioning her face between my legs, and began working with her tongue, licking my sex. I was unable to feel my male genitals within the VR suit, and instead experienced a moistness between the legs; I began to imagine that I could actually feel her tongue inserting itself within the lips of my vagina - but how could this be? I could feel a sort of heat growing in my crotch, and I was definitely getting wet between the legs. I was becoming sexually aroused, and yet not in a way that had ever happened to me before. My breasts still felt sensitive, and my nipples were hard. I moaned softly, as Madam Cynthia continued to work on me with her tongue.

'Hmm. That's good,' she said.

Suddenly I knew what I wanted. I wanted to be penetrated. I was desperate for it. I had never felt like this before, but I couldn't help myself - the longing had leapt into my very soul from nowhere, and burnt like a bright flame in every cell of my body. I wanted to submit, submit to penetration, feel it thrusting up hard inside me.

'Do it to me,' I moaned.

'Do it to me *Mistress*,' Madam Cynthia whispered.

Do it to me, Mistress,' I repeated.

Madam Cynthia produced a pink rubber dildo, contoured with knobbles at one end. She inserted the knobbled end up inside me, and began to gently work it up and down. And *YES!* I could feel it inside me. But how? Perhaps she was using my back passage? And yet it felt as if the dildo was thrusting between my legs - I was sure I could really *feel* the lips of my vagina; I was even aware of a small lump of erectile tissue at the upper end of my opening - my clitoris, surely?

The Mistress thrust the dildo up and down inside me, and the sensation of heat began moving up inside me in waves, until it was pervading my whole body.

'Oh, I beg you, please stop,' I moaned. In spite of my supplications, she continued to work away with the instrument, until I felt as if a volcanic eruption was

161

searing apart my insides. I surrendered to the waves of orgasm, gasping and sighing until it was over.

'You see, Laura, my little girl, you loved what Mistress did for you, didn't you.'

'Yes Mistress, oh yes,' I whimpered.

Finally, she released the manacles on my wrists and ankles, and lowered me down to the ground.

'Now get dressed, you strumpet,' she said to me gruffly, handing back my panties to me and pointing to my skirt, which was thrown in the corner of the cellar. I struggled into my panties and pulled up the skirt. I was still straightening out my clothing when I noticed her looking at me intensely, with something like respect in her eyes.

'Magnificent, little Miss Laura. I never would have dreamed that you'd develop so quickly. Hannah's guess about you was correct. Of course, she selected you with great care......Come on, you have the whole weekend before you.'

'What do you mean, the whole weekend before me? It was Monday morning when I arrived at Dr. Klonek's laboratory.'

'Ah, some time has elapsed since then.' Madam Cynthia paused, looking amused at my confusion.

'How much time have I lost? How long was I out after Dr. Smedley gave me the injection?'

'I'm sorry, I can't tell you that.'

'What are we talking about - hours, days?'

Madam Cynthia shrugged. 'You'll find out, all in good time. It's time to leave here now. Wait here while I change.' Madam Cynthia returned a couple of minutes later carrying a fawn-coloured rain-coat, which she put down on top of a leather shoulder-bag. She was wearing faded blue jeans and a loose denim shirt under which there was a scimpy black V-necked top held up by thin straps, which emphasized the fullness of her breasts. I noticed the top of some sort of tattoo on her left breast, but couldn't make out the design. Her eyes were hidden by dark glasses and her luxuriant mop of black hair was tied back with a broad band of fabric on which there was a jazzy, abstract pattern. Noticing that I was still looking a bit anxious, she laughed and said, 'Don't worry pet, the worst is over. Just relax now and enjoy being a girl. And you can drop all that 'Mistress' and 'Madam Cynthia' stuff - just call me Cindy.'

She picked up the fawn raincoat and handed it to me, saying, 'Here, you'd better slip this on; it'll be cool outside.'

I put on the raincoat, without doing it up, and looked at her expectantly. She gave me an encouraging squeeze and led me to a stone flight of stairs. As we began slowly to ascend them, I heard the click-clack of my high-heels echoing on the steps. At the top of the steps, we passed through a heavy panelled oak door, riddled with the tiny holes of woodworm. The door opened onto a long corridor, brightly lit with electric candelabra; I screwed up my eyes for a moment, to give my pupils time to adjust after the gloom of the cellar and stairway.

'Now I know why you're wearing dark glasses,' I said to Cindy. She ignored my comment and set off hurriedly along the corridor, on the walls of which were hanging framed prints of 18th century hunting scenes. The floor was bare stone-work, the uneven flags worn by the marching of many feet. At the end of the corridor we passed through another oak door and out into open air.

It was night-time; there was a clear sky, with the stars standing out brightly and an almost full moon floating like a dinner plate above the tree tops. It seemed like just a normal night - I couldn't believe what I'd just gone through in the cellar. Had it really happened? Of course not; I reassured myself with the thought that this was all part of the virtual reality simulation inflicted on me by Dr. Hannah Klonek. But what did Cindy mean about the time I'd lost? I looked up again at the shining white orb of the moon, as if I expected to be able to read on it the meaning of what was going on.

I turned round to survey the building we had just left. It appeared to be a large, dilapidated country house built of some yellowish stone, partly obscured by thick coils of ivy. The house had three floors, the top floor windows having mullioned gables. The garden in which we were standing was overgrown with weeds. I shivered, aware of the cold night air. I could feel my nipples standing out hard against the fabric of the thin silk blouse. Incredible! I pulled the raincoat closed, and buttoned it up.

'Come on,' said Cindy, marching off briskly in the direction of a gravelled driveway on which a car was standing. We got into the car, an ancient American model - an olive-green Chevrolet of some sort. Cindy removed her dark glasses and put them in the glove compartment, then fired up the engine and pumped the gas pedal; the car roared off in a spray of gravel.

We sat in silence as Cindy drove fast along the country lanes, the car's soft suspension bouncing and lurching as we took the corners. After about twenty minutes, we stopped.

'This is as far as I go,' said Cindy. We got out of the car, and Cindy took out a handbag and a small case from the trunk and handed them to me, saying, 'These are for you. There's some money and makeup in the handbag, and more clothes in the case.' She pointed to a wide-fronted bungalow, standing on its own amid carefully landscaped lawns and trees. 'That's where you'll be staying. Good bye now. Be good!' Cindy gave me a hug, and then kissed me full on the lips; I stepped back in astonishment. A look of mischievous fun danced in her eyes as she lowered herself into the driver's seat of the Chevrolet. She winked at me in a suggestive way through the car's side window, started the engine, and roared off into the night.

I looked at the bungalow for a few moments, shrugged and began to walk slowly towards its front door. 'This is one hell of a virtual reality program,' I thought to myself. Then I said out loud: 'The fat lady is singing.' Nothing happened.

I banged on the door of the bungalow, which had a

curious black wrought-iron knocker in the shape of a hand holding a ball, hinged so that the ball struck the black stud set into the door.

There was a pause, then I heard footsteps approaching and a bolt being thrown back. The door opened to reveal a middle-aged woman with short blonde hair. She was wearing a knee-length maroon skirt, a burgundy-coloured cotton top and matching woollen jacket.

'Ah, you must be Miss Laura Thompson,' she said, in a rather upper-class, plummy accent. 'Do come in.'

We entered a hallway decorated in post-modern baroque, with gilt framed mirrors on the walls and a brass candelabra on a shelf which ran along one side of the hallway. I caught a glimpse of myself in one of the mirrors, and saw the face of a young woman with short, dark curly hair. The features resembled my own, but were feminine, the chin smaller and more rounded, the cheek bones slightly higher, the lips fuller, the eyes larger, the brows finer and more arched. The expression in the eyes was of mild astonishment.

The blonde woman turned to me and said:

'I'm Julia. Welcome, Laura. Follow me, if you please.'

We passed into a large rectangular room, our heels clicking on the polished parquet floor tiles. The room was furnished with an oak-panelled dresser and chest of drawers, a double wardrobe, an over-stuffed arm chair, a coffee table and a king-sized double bed with oak headboard and thick legs of carved oak.

'This is your room. I hope that you'll find everything that you need here. I'll give you a few minutes to unpack and settle in, then we'll have dinner. I expect you're hungry?'

I nodded, in fact I was feeling ravenous. But how was I going to eat in a VR suit? Once again I was amazed at the authenticity of the experience which had been created within the virtual reality simulation. But was this still virtual reality? Was I still in the suit, or was all this actually happening to me? How could I be sure? When

165

it comes down to it, what can you be sure of? What was it Descartes said? Cogito, ergo sum. I think, therefore I am. Beyond that, I could be sure of nothing.

I put the suitcase up onto the bed, sprung the catches and opened it. Inside there was a selection of female clothing - on top were several panty and bra sets, a couple of suspender belts, some unopened packets of stockings and tights in different deniers and shades; underneath the underwear there were a couple of skirts similar to the one I was wearing, some tops and blouses, a slinky dress in some sort of red silky fabric. At the bottom of the case was a short pink nightdress, frilled around the hem and neckline. There was a toilet bag containing scented soap, hairbrush, toothbrush and tooth paste. I noticed a fluffy cream towel folded over a radiator and a pink dressing gown hanging on a hook behind the door. I hung the fawn raincoat on the hook next to it. I opened the drawers and wardrobe and found more women's clothing, all of which appeared to be new. In the base of the wardrobe there were several pairs of shoes. I took out a pair of low-heeled pumps and tried them on - they fitted perfectly, and gave my feet welcome relief from the high-heels.

I sat down on the arm chair, putting my head back for a moment. Just as my eyes started to close, I heard a dinner gong sounding. I sighed, and walked out of my room, pulling the door closed behind me. I noticed there was no way of locking the door. I made my way down the hallway in the direction from which the sound of the gong had come. I gently pushed open the door and found myself in a dining room containing a long rectangular table which could seat at least ten or twelve people. Only two places were set, one at each end of the table. I sat down at the nearest place, examining the silver tableware and thick linen napkins and table cloth.

Julia entered the room, nodded to me slightly, made her way to the other end of the table, and sat down. She was now dressed for dinner in a long, jade green cocktail frock. We waited in silence for a few moments, and then

166

a young woman entered the room, a tall girl in a black satin maid's dress, complete with white frilly apron. The skirt of the dress was short, revealing long slim legs clad in black seamed nylon. She was wearing black high-heeled patent leather pumps, and a ridiculous little frilled cap on top of her head. Her auburn hair beneath the cap was long, and pinned back into a French plait which hung down to just below the nape of her elegant, slender neck. Her maid's dress was low-cut and decorated with an edge of white lace, in which the cleavage of two well-developed breasts was much in evidence.

'This is Marie, our maid,' announced Julia. She was one of Dr. Hannah's earlier experiments. She used to be a boy. You wouldn't think so to look at her now, would you?'

Marie coloured prettily, then asked shyly:

'Would you like soup or melon for starters, miss?'

'Soup, please,' I replied.

'I'll have soup as well, Marie,' said Julia.

Marie returned with two bowls of vegetable soup, and a basket of rolls.

Julia helped herself to a brown roll, and then passed them to me, saying: 'You probably have a lot of questions about your present situation?'

I nodded, but was too eager to try the experiment of eating to say anything further at that moment, although there were many things I wanted to ask. I took a roll, and breaking a small piece off, popped it into my mouth. I was astonished to find that I could taste it! I chewed the roll and swallowed - yes, I was experiencing all the sensations of eating.

'I'm puzzled as to how it's possible for me to eat - am I still in the Total Virtual Reality Suit? The technology must have gone far beyond anything that I know about. I thought I'd read all the recent scientific papers on VR, but I've never come across any way of creating what I'm experiencing now.'

Julia took a spoonful of soup, sipped it, then looked at me across the expanse of white table cloth and replied:

'Dr. Klonek will be coming after dinner to talk to you; she's asked me to leave the explanations to her.'

The meal proceeded in silence, with the maid Marie decorously serving each course.

At the end of the meal, Julia said:

'We'll have coffee in the drawing room.' She glanced at her watch and added, 'Hannah will be joining us shortly.' Julia showed me through to a spacious room containing elegant reproduction neoclassical chairs with shield-shaped backs and an Empire-style chaise-longue which looked as if it might be a genuine antique. I poured myself a coffee from the glass jug which was standing on a small Regency style table, helping myself to cream. I sniffed the coffee - it gave off a lovely, freshly-ground aroma. Again, I began to doubt that what I was experiencing was just virtual reality. I sat on the end of the chaise-longue and sipped my coffee. Julia served herself with coffee and was just sitting down on one of the delicate shield-backed chairs when a couple of muffled knocks sounded from the end of the hall-way.

'That'll be Dr. Klonek,' said Julia, 'Marie will go.'

A few moments later, Dr. Hannah Klonek bustled into the drawing-room, nodded to Julia, and turned round to look at me. Dr. Klonek was again wearing a jogging suit, this time a royal blue one with an 'Adidas' motif across the chest. She brushed her fingers through her thick black hair, which seemed to have grown longer since the last time I had seen her, and then stepped back and surveyed me from head to foot.

'And how's my new girl doing?' she asked. Julia looked slightly flustered, as if not sure whether the question was addressed to her or to me. Before Julia could reply, I said:

'I'm feeling fine thank you, though I can't say I appreciated the scene in the cellar very much. Was it really necessary to subject me to that? And when am I getting out of this Virtual Reality suit? The code words didn't work.'

'Ah yes, the suit. I have a confession to make about

168

that. You're not actually in the suit, any more.'

'You don't mean this is happening to me - in real life?'

'Calm down, Laura. I'm just going to pour myself a coffee, and then I'll try to explain what's happened to you.' Dr. Klonek served herself with coffee, arranged her squat body on one of the elegant chairs, and began:

'We soon realised the physical limitations of the Total Virtual Reality suits. The VR suit is a dead-end; in can only be used in the early stages of behaviour modification programmes. We decided that we needed to create a virtual reality environment actually inside the mind. I don't know whether you've come across any reference to the 'altered states' experiments conducted at the Essalin Institute?'

'That place where all those trendy humanistic psychologists and Gestalt therapists used to hang out, back in the last century?'

Dr. Klonek nodded vigorously and took a sip of her coffee. 'Yes, it was at Big Sur, California, a very 'cool' place to be, during the late Sixties and early Seventies of the last century. The experiments were very crude - they used LSD, mescalin, total sensory deprivation chambers, that sort of thing. In the mid-Seventies, the research was taken over by the C.I.A and transferred from Big Sur to a secret location up in northern Idaho, in the Panhandle National Forest area near Coeur D'Alene. It was one of the bases the C.I.A. used to de-brief and 'turn' K.G.B. agents and for other psychological warfare activities. They continued with their experiments right through the Seventies and Eighties, until the National Security Council pulled the funding after the collapse of the Soviet Union.

'How do you know all this?' I asked.

'Some of the data has been declassified and is available for public scrutiny under the U.S. Freedom of Information Act - you just have to ask for it. Our own intelligence services had a hand in the work as well - they ran a parallel study at one of their secret establishments in this country, but of course it's much harder to find out anything about that. The C.I.A. and our people shared their results, and even swapped key researchers between the two teams. As it happens, Dr. Smedley worked for the Ministry of Defence some years ago - he was in the exchange programme and was actually employed as medical officer on some of the experiments at Coeur D'Alene. He kept his own copies of the files.'

'And now he's working for you?'

Dr. Klonek nodded, and said smugly:

'There are very few men employed in university departments these days, as you know. It was only his specialist knowledge which got him the job; there were at least half a dozen female applicants who were better qualified, any one of whom would certainly have been appointed otherwise.'

'So where is all this leading?'

'Well, by the mid-Eighties, they'd developed some more sophisticated techniques. One of the biggest challenges facing neuroscientists in the last century was to discover exactly how consciousness is created in the brain. The researchers at Coeur D'Alene managed to identify the cellular mechanisms by which nerve cells in the brain store memories and create both waking consciousness and dream-states. They mapped out the sensory and memory receptors in the brain, and discovered how to tap directly into these areas by artificially stimulating the brain's neurotransmitters - the chemicals that relay impulses between the neurons.

'Outwardly, the subjects appeared to be unconscious, in something akin to a coma, but in fact they were experiencing vivid dream-states. Even in normal dream-states, we do not always know that we are dreaming. The researchers were able to transmit directly into the dream-state by stimulating the appropriate sensory area of the frontal cortex to evoke any sight, sound, taste, smell or feeling that they wanted; and what was experienced by the subjects was so vivid that they couldn't distinguish it from reality. In effect, they had created an inner virtual reality world, so you can understand our interest in this research, when we realised the limitations of the VR suit.'

'How did they know what the subjects were experiencing?'

'That's the cleverest part. Once they realised how the brain's neurotransmitters worked, they adapted a bank of Kray supercomputers to convert the biochemical and electromagnetic activity of the brain into digital code, which could then be uploaded to multi-media visual display units, enabling them to see and hear what the subjects were experiencing. They could monitor the effect of introducing new elements and sensations, and interact with the subjects' dream-states and memories on a second by second basis. They even discovered how to create artificial memories - to give the subjects false memories of things which had never happened to them.'

'Incredible - it must have cost them a fortune to set up a system like that. The Kray computers alone would have cost millions.'

'Yes, but the budget for counter-intelligence at the height of the Cold War was very large.'

'You're funding for VIRED must be a tiny fraction of what they had to spend - surely you're not going to tell me that you have been able to continue this work?'

'Yes, thanks to the new Intel Quantum computer chip, we didn't need a bank of Kray supercomputers. The Quantum chip is relatively cheap, but its molecular bus technology and bio-cybernetic construction make it a thousand times more powerful than the super-computers of the last century. The Quantum chip uses bio-neural pathways and cellular memory caching; it's actually got living, genetically engineered matter inside it which makes it ideal for connecting directly into the human brain. The problem they never succeeded in overcoming fully at Coeur D'Alene was the creation of a viable long-term interface between the supercomputer and the brain of the subject.'

'How was the connection made?'

171

'A system of electrodes had to be surgically introduced through the skull into the appropriate areas of the frontal cortex. The connectors could only be left in for a limited period before the body's immune system began to attack the terminals and chemically degrade them. In some cases the subjects suffered brain-damage when this happened - the researchers were unable to bring them round. They remained in a sort of coma, on life-support; brain activity within the dream-state continued, but could no longer be controlled externally. Some of them were kept alive for years, in a kind of permanent dream-world inhabited by whatever nightmare apparitions might be fetched up from their subconscious minds...'

'My God! That's not what you've done to me, is it?'

'No, because we don't have to rely on the ancient computer technology they used at Couer D'Alene. The bio-cybernetic architecture of the Quantum chip is ideal for connecting into the neural pathways of the cortex, and the chip itself is small enough to implant directly into the brain. We don't need any external connections, as the chip carries a miniturised digital transmitter which transfers the data automatically to our monitoring equipment.'

'And you've fitted one of these Quantum chips in my brain, which is creating what I'm experiencing now?'

'Yes, that's exactly your current situation.'

'Where is my body?'

'You're lying on a trolley in our medical facility. We took you out of the Virtual Reality suit straight after Dr. Smedley had given you the injection, as soon as you were unconscious. We have a separate medical unit within VIRED which you did not see - it's on the next floor up from the Virtual Reality laboratory...'

' - Which is basically just a front for what you are really doing, which is messing about with people's minds?'

Dr. Klonek frowned. 'I wouldn't put it like that.'

'Where are you at this moment?'

'I'm in front of the monitoring equipment, interacting directly with your dream-state. That's how I'm able to talk to you.'

172

'How are you creating your movements and facial expressions?'

'By means of a sophisticated computer animation programme which uses the latest video hologram technology to model what I want to do. For example, when I frowned just then, it was picked up by a camera which is focused on my face, and the change of expression was then uploaded into the simulation of me to which you are talking now.'

'And the other characters in this simulation - Julia, Marie - and the forceful Miss Cindy?

'Ah, well they're interacting with you in a slightly different way. The Quantum chip has enabled us to go far beyond what they could achieve at Coeur D'Alene. The subjects there were isolated in their individual dream-states. We have found that we can use the Quantum chip implant to network people together so that they all inhabit the same virtual world and are able to inter-relate just as they would in the real world. It's a bit like several people all playing the same interactive computer game at once, as they used to do on the Internet, back in the 1990's.'

'So Julia, Marie and Cindy are real people, lying on trolleys in your medical facility, like me? And you have networked our dream-worlds together?'

'Yes, but just as Laura is your virtual identity - they too have taken on new virtual personas. Like you, all three are male in the real world. They have been inhabiting their female personas in virtual reality for longer than you, however.'

I looked questioningly over at Julia, who had been sitting listening to our conversation, all this while. She returned my gaze, nodding reassuringly.

'You know about this - it's true?' I asked Julia.

'I have been given the same explanation as you - and yes, I think we have no alternative but to believe it. In real life, I was a middle-aged man called John, an electrician by trade. I was employed on a temporary contract by the University of Central England, to do some re-wiring around the campus. I remember coming to

VIRED to install some new circuit-breakers to safeguard the computer equipment. I was working on a socket which shouldn't have been live, (I'd turned off the mains switch myself), when I got an electric shock. I was still conscious, but feeling a bit shaken. Dr. Klonek fetched Dr. Smedley; she explained that he was a medical doctor and would be able to check me over. He listened to my breathing, felt my pulse, and said that I was still in shock. He offered to give me an injection of a mild sedative. He gave me the injection, and that's the last thing I recall...'

'How long ago was that?'

'A couple of years ago.'

'Years? You've been stuck in this virtual reality dream-state for years?' I looked over at Dr Klonek (or the simulation of her), hoping for an explanation.

'You are wondering how long you were out for, after you were injected by Dr. Smedley? In fact, you were unconscious only for a few hours, while you had the operation to fit the implant. Of course, even using terms like 'unconscious' and 'conscious' is problematic when we are talking about the Quantum virtual reality experience. To the outside world, you appear unconscious now - you are laying on a stainless steel trolley in our medical facility. But your mind is not unconscious. Time and space do not have the same meaning, in the Quantum virtual world.'

I asked Dr. Klonek: 'What is the time now, in the real world, and what day is it?'

'It wouldn't help you now to know the time of day or day of the week in the real world,' she replied.

I looked at the brass carriage clock on the marble mantle-shelf. Its ornate hands showed twenty minutes past nine.

'Yes,' continued Dr. Klonek, 'for you, it is 9.20 on Friday evening. That is all you need to know. Your experience of time has been synchronized with that of the other subjects.'

I looked around at the drawing room and its exquisite furnishings.

'Why all the antique furniture - whose your interior designer in these simulations.'

'Oh, we all have a hand in it. At the moment you're in one of Dr. Smedley's creations - fine furniture is a hobby of his.'

'So how long are you going to keep me like this?'

'That is rather up to you; you know the purpose of our research.'

'You're trying to modify my behaviour - to inculcate female characteristics into my personality?'

'Yes, we're attempting to make you psychologically more feminine.'

'How far are you taking this? I think the business in the cellar was already going too far - I never agreed to anything like that.'

'You'll know when we're finished. I'm sorry we had to put you through that. Our experience with some of our earlier cases has led us to conclude that changing sexuality or sexual orientation is harder in some ways than changing the sex of an individual. Attempts to alter sexual orientation at a later stage of the feminisation process have not always been successful. With you, therefore, we decided to try something at the outset. It was a rather a baptism of fire, I'm afraid, but it seemed to work, judging by your response when Cindy was working on you.'

'I know that you believe the feminisation of males to be a social priority, but why do you need to change male sexual orientation? It's a logical absurdity. If all males are eventually feminised, there won't be any men left, so what's the point in making feminised males fancy men?'

'Did Cindy's activities in the cellar make you fancy men? It wasn't a man who did that to you. What Cindy did to you enabled you to discover in yourself an important element of feminine sexuality - the desire for penetration, to be the passive rather than active partner, in a sexual encounter. It did not determine that the gender of the partner should be male - quite to the contrary, in fact, as in this case the active partner who penetrated you was a woman, or at

175

least the simulation of a woman. This does not preclude you from taking the active role again yourself - what we did for you was merely open up other possibilities. But without at least some knowledge of the passive sexual role, you could never really comprehend what it means to be a woman, nor understand the social and cultural implications of female sexuality. The psychological well-spring of women's social skills - the way women are able to nurture, cooperate, show empathy, be aware of the feelings of others - arises partly from an experience of the passive or submissive role, in the sexual act.'

'That's a bit controversial, isn't it? I'm not sure the women of the Radical Feminist Party would agree with you there.'

'That bunch of dykes? What do they know?' The simulation of Dr. Klonek lept up, almost toppling her chair backwards on its slender legs, and began to pace up and down the drawing room. I watched her for a few moments, and then said:

'I thought you were a lesbian, yourself?'

'And so I am. As such, I have experience of both the passive and active roles - and that was all we were trying to give to you.'

'Why didn't the emergency code words work?'

'Isn't that obvious? You attempted to use the code words to halt the scene in the cellar before it had really got started. If you had stopped at that point, you'd never have made that interesting discovery about yourself.'

'Did you say Cindy is like Julia and myself - she has a male body back in the laboratory, while her consciousness is networked into the same virtual reality world as we are experiencing?'

'Yes, and I'm afraid that was one of her fantasies you experienced. It wasn't exactly what we would have designed ourselves, but it was possibly more effective - it served it's purpose.'

'Do we have any free will, in any of this?'

'Yes, within certain limits, you can do what you like, within Quantum reality.'

'What are the limits?'

'You'll find out, if you reach them.'

'What if I got up now and tried to strangle you?'

'You can try it if you like, but I was leaving anyway.' Dr. Klonek pointed her short, solidly built body towards the door, and walked rapidly from the room, before I had a chance to put my threat into action.

The next moment, the sound of the front door closing with a heavy thud could be heard from the hallway.

I looked at Julia, who was twisting her hands nervously in her lap.

'I'm going out,' I announced; 'I think I'd like to explore the local area.'

Julia glanced up at me and said, 'I don't know how wise it is for a young woman to be walking round the streets alone, this time of night.'

'Pffghh! You'll have me believing I am a young woman, if you carry on like that. I'll see you later.'

And with that, I walked out of the room. In the hallway, I caught my reflection again in the gilt-framed mirror. It was the reflection of a young woman. Julia had a point. Pffghh! I thought again. I went to my room, found the fawn coloured raincoat and put it on. As an afterthought, I grabbed the leather handbag given to me by Cindy, then went out the front door into the cool night air.

I walked up the long, curved drive which bisected the lawns at the front of the bungalow, passed through a gateway with wrought-iron gates still open, and found myself standing on the pavement of a quiet, suburban street. Unsure which way to go, I listened, and thought I could hear the rumble of traffic off to the right. I turned in the direction of the sound, and began to walk. I was grateful that I had exchanged my high-heels for the low-heeled pumps that I'd found in the wardrobe.

After walking up several more quiet streets, I noticed that the housing was becoming more modest in size and style – detached houses built in the Thirties of the last century were gradually giving way to small semi-detached dwellings, and then to rows of red-brick terraced houses, with bay windows and tiny front gardens enclosed by hedges or low brick walls. Where was I? The sound of traffic was growing louder. I was obviously approaching a town or city centre. I could be anywhere – Nottingham, Sheffield, Leeds, Manchester...

The street of late-Victorian and Edwardian villas came to an end; I had reached a wide, busy road. The air was heavy with the stink of diesel and petrol fumes from the cars, buses and taxis; the pavements were bustling with groups of young men and women out for a Friday night on the razzle. In spite of the winter chill in the air, most of the young women seemed to be wearing hardly anything; skimpy dresses or tight-fitting tops with short skirts, tottering precariously along on clumpy, high-heeled shoes; they were laughing and eyeing-up the groups of lads, who were similarly dressed as if for summer, in tee-shirts and chinos. A street-scene in any northern city in England on a Friday or Saturday night.

I began to thread my way through the milling groups, feeling overdressed and middle-aged in my rain-coat, and frumpy in my low-heeled shoes. Walking past a group of young men who were hanging about outside a night-club, I suddenly became aware of my bare legs – bare except for the sheer black stockings which I was wearing. I could sense one or two of the lads eying me up; I could feel the cool air around my legs and up my skirt. I had never felt so vulnerable before – and yet I also felt a tightness in my chest, as if I couldn't breathe – was it something like excitement – or arousal? How could I be aroused by this attention? What was happening to me?

I took off my raincoat, folded it up and draped it across my shoulder-bag. I swished past the group of boys, aware of their eyes still on me, on my legs and on my cleavage, aware that my nipples had gone hard and were showing through the fabric of my bra and thin silk blouse; aware that I was swaying my hips slightly; I could feel the nylon rasp of my inner thighs as I walked, and the silky slip of the lining of my skirt. Sensations were which were very new to me – but not unpleasant.

I noticed that I was passing a Wetherspoons pub – nothing unusual in that, as most pubs were now owned by J.D. Wetherspoon. In my former life as Andy, I had enjoyed a pint of real ale. I went into the pub, passing a couple of tuxedoed bouncers, who growled a 'Good evening, miss,' at me. I threaded my way through to the long bar, and ordered a pint of Director's Bitter.

'Was that *a pint* you wanted, pet?' asked the barman. I nodded. The barman raised his eyebrows and pulled my pint. He put it on the bar to let the head settle, saying, 'I'll top that in a minute. £3.89 please.' I unzipped my shoulder-bag, took out a leather purse, and found a £5 coin. The barman took my money, gave me change and topped my beer until it was overflowing the sides. Then he winked at me, slid the beer across the bar-top, and said: 'There we are, sweetheart; enjoy your beer.'

I took the glass, sipped some beer and froth from the top before it spilt, and gazed around, looking for somewhere to sit. In spite of the crowd in the pub, the air was clear, apart from the mixed fragrances of perfume, aftershave, body spray and deodorant. One positive thing that New Labour had done during their previous administration was ban smoking completely in all pubs, restaurants and other public places, following the Californian model. There had been some last-ditch resistance from nicotine-heads, but since cannabis and heroin and been legalised in pill form, these hardcore tobacco addicts were a dying group (literally).

I found a stool to perch on away from the scrum at the bar, and took a good pull of my ale. I looked at the glass and noticed that I had left a lipstick crescent along the rim. Who had put makeup on me? I realised that this must have been done while I was unconscious – after I'd been given the injection by Dr. Smedley. That seemed like a long time ago. But of course – I was still unconscious – or at least still in some weird altered state, thanks to the Quantum chip which had been implanted in my brain. But could I be sure that even that was true?

I finished my beer and decided that I needed another. I fought my way back to the bar, and this time ordered a pint of the stronger Abbot Ale – how much could you drink in an altered state of consciousness? It might be an interesting experiment to find out.

After my fourth pint of strong ale, I was beginning to feel a little groggy. I was also aware that a middle-aged bald man with problem nostril-hair had been leering at me, and was now trying to touch up against me and feel my bottom. I edged away from him, saying, "Must go and spend a penny...'

Without thinking, I walked into the gents' toilet, which blessedly was empty at that moment. I hitched-up my skirt, pulled down my panties, and stood at the urinal, expecting to relieve myself in the normal way. In spite of a very strong urge to urinate, nothing happened. I looked down. *Nothing there!* A triangle of dark hair, but nothing else. I fumbled about between my legs, but my fingers cupped only a roundness and smooth lips of my - my - God! I had a fanny! Of course – I was a girl now!

I quickly pulled up my panties, re-arranged my skirt, and exited. As I went through the door of the gents', I was passed by a slim, good-looking lad with a Brooklyn Beckham hair-cut; he jumped out of the way and said: 'Pardon me - ' He looked at the sign on the door, looked again at me more closely, and began to say something, but I had disappeared through the door of the ladies', which was on the opposite side of the corridor, before he had got his words out.

I went into a cubicle, pulled down my panties, and sat down. What now? I had no penis, apparently, so... what would happen next? I didn't have long to wait...I relieved myself, without any further thought, in the time-honoured female fashion. I wiped myself between the legs, pulled up my panties, straightened my stockings and skirt, and stepped out of the cubicle.

There was a young girl pouting at her reflection in the mirror over the wash handbasin. 'Got any lippy?' she asked.

I rummaged in my handbag, and produced a lipstick.

'Thanks, duck. Busy tonight, in't it? Here on your own, or is your boyfriend outside?'

'No, I'm on my own tonight.'

'Do you wanta stick with us? There's a few of us, doing the normal circuit. We're about to move on to Prada 5 – it's a really good nightclub.'

'Okay, thanks.'

I checked my own reflection. I saw a young woman, dark curly hair, attractive. I brushed my hair.

'I'm Britney,' said my new companion, passing me back my lipstick. I made a pout with my lips, as Britney had done, and applied some more lipstick to them.

'Here, you need a bit of this as well,' said Britney, giving me her mascara brush. I applied some mascara to my lashes, again copying Britney.

'Thanks. I'm Laura, by the way,' I said.

'I like your top, Laura; where d'you get it?

'New Look,' I replied, naming a fashion shop I had passed that evening on the street outside.

Okay, I think we'll do,' said Britney, leading the way back out to the bar. We approached a group of about five or six other girls, all dressed to the nines for their Friday night out. 'This is Laura – she's on her own so I said she can tag along with us the Prada.'

The other girls smiled at me, eyed me up and down.

We trailed out of the Wetherspoons pub together. I looked up at the pub sign: *The Girl Under Water.* The girl on the pub sign had a sort of dreamy expression; she appeared to be floating... That's how I feel, I thought. Moving under water, in a dream.

The next thing I knew, we were queuing up outside the door of a club; there was a pink neon sign above it: *Prada 5.* Three bouncers outside, submitting the punters to scrutiny, admitting only those they liked the look of. Apparently they liked the look of us; we all got in, paying only £15 each.

We threaded our way through onto the dance floor, found a bit of space. A couple of the girls started dancing.

The music was deafening; Britney shouted at me: 'I think I'll head for the bar. Coming?' I nodded.

'What are you having?' asked Britney.

'What do you recommend?'

I'm having a bottle of Commissar – it's vodka, lemon and something else. I can't remember what – but it's quite refreshing.'

'Okay, I'll try it.'

We took our drinks and walked up the stairs onto a metal gallery which overlooked one of the dance floors. We looked down on the mass of bodies gyrating and bobbing to the heavy throb of the music.

Britney said something to me, but I couldn't hear. She placed her mouth near my ear, and tried again:

'Heaving, isn't it?'

'Yeah. Is it always like this?'

'It's quieter on a week night. Do you live around here, then?'

'Er – no; I'm just visiting.'

'Didn't you have a coat, in the pub? I looked down – my coat was no longer over my shoulder bag.

'Yes, I must have left it somewhere.'

'Want to go back and look for it?'

'No, I doubt whether I'll find it now.'

We watched the dancers for a couple of minutes, then Britney asked:

'Fancy a bop, now?'

I looked at the heaving mass below, and shook my head.

'Okay, maybe later. Let's go and sit over there – on those seats. It'll be a bit quieter.'

We walked into a smaller room off the metal walkway, and sat down on chairs beside a table. There were two spare chairs opposite, and almost at once, a couple of boys approached us and asked if the seats were taken. Britney shook her head, and the lads sat down. They looked to be in their early twenties; Club Ibiza tee-shirts, tight chinos, very short hair, big grins...

'Here we go,' said Britney.

'Can I get you girls a drink?' asked one of the lads.

'We've just got one, thanks,' replied Britney.

'Suit yourself,' said the boy.

'Tell you what,' said Britney, 'let's get out of here.'

'But we've only just come on.'

'Yeah, but I'm fed up with this crowd, already. It's always the same on a Friday night. Like a cattle market. Come on. Let's go.'

'Won't your friends wonder where we've gone?'

'No, we'll just tell Mel we're off – she's over on the gallery.' We walked back onto the metal walkway, where Britney shouted something into the ear of a tall blonde girl. The girl looked round at me for a moment, shrugged her shoulders and nodded. We picked our way back down the stairs, through the vestibule, now crammed with sweating bodies all trying to move in the opposite direction, then out the door into the cold night air. Britney hailed a taxi, and we jumped in. Britney gave the Pakistani driver an address, and we were soon leaving the brightly-lit streets of city centre behind us, as we drove along a dual carriageway towards the outer suburbs.

'Where are we going?' I asked.

You'll see,' replied Britney.

I had drunk too much; I was feeling so tired I could I could hardly keep my eyes open. I noticed Britney had put her arm round my shoulders, and that her hand was gently caressing my left breast. Then I felt her lips, soft and wet, closing over mine. We were kissing, and her hand was now on my leg. I could feel the heat of her hand through the nylon of my stockings, stroking my leg, moving up my thigh...

The taxi lurched to a halt; Britney quickly sat up and found the money for the driver in her handbag. Then we were out of the taxi and going up some steps to the door of a large house.

'My flat's on the top floor,' announced Britney, as a security lamp came on and illuminated the steps. I noticed that Britney's hair was dark-cherry red, and cut in a long bob that swished glossily in the beam of the security light. She hunted in her bag, found her front door key, and let us in.

'Hang on a second,' she whispered, fumbling for a light-switch, finding it, and clicking it on. We were in a well-decorated, broad hallway. Britney led the way up three flights of expensively-carpeted stairs, then unlocked another door.

We were now in her flat, and I was sprawled on the soft cushions of her sofa, having kicked off my shoes. Britney had put on some music – some soft Celtic voices singing to guitars and keyboard.

'Coffee, tea, chocolate – or do your fancy a brandy or malt whisky?' she asked.

'Hot chocolate would be fine. Britney – I suppose your parents like Britney Spears?'

'Yes, embarrassing, isn't it? I hate the name. It's nearly as bad as being called Kylie. Laura's a nice name – quite an old name; like something out of a Daphne Du Maurier novel. Where do you hail from, Laura?'

'Oh from down south, originally. South of the Thames, rather than the Trent.'

'You're a cockney?'

'Not really – just from that great amorphous area known as South London.'

'What are you doing up this way?'

'Oh – I went to university up here.'

'Right. I'll go and make the chocolate. How about a nip of something to go with it?'

Britney returned a few minutes later with two mugs of steaming chocolate, and two tumblers of amber liquid.

'Malt whisky – an Islay malt. Try it.'

'Thank you.' I picked up one of the glasses and sniffed the smoky aroma of the golden liquor. I took a sip.

'It's lovely.'

'Yes, a real taste of the island – sea-weed, and peat-smoke, and the oak sherry barrels it's aged in. Do you want any more?'

'Oh no – I'd better not. I feel a bit strange as it is.'
'Drink your chocolate.'

Britney sat down next to me, as we sipped our chocolate. I listened to the plaintive, Celtic chanting of the music which Britney had put on, thinking of the long empty beaches on the west coast of Ireland, where I'd holidayed a few years ago... I drifted in a relaxed state, vaguely aware that Britney was snuggling next to me, putting her head on my shoulder, caressing my thigh... then we were making love, and Britney was kissing me, undoing my blouse, taking off my bra....I could feel her hand between my legs, her fingers gently rubbing and massaging; then she was undressing, and giving me her nipple to suck...

I know we made love for what seemed like many hours, and Britney licked me around my vagina, searching me with her tongue, and that she penetrated me many times with a succession of dildoes and vibrators; she even used an anal plug on me, taking me in both my openings at the same time... and then I did the same for her, and we kissed and caressed each other's breasts, and rubbed and penetrated each other's most private places until we were coming together, over and over again, our orgasms like huge waves breaking on a beach....

And I knew that I had found what was missing in my life, that I was fulfilled and joyful and replete and complete in a way that I had never been and could never be as a mere male...

...I fell at last into a deep sleep.

When I awoke, I found that I was no longer in Britney's flat. I seemed to be lying in a bed in some sort of medical facility – I had a drip in my arm, and I could feel some sort of bandage or dressing between my legs. I could feel a dull pain in my groin, and in around my chest area, which also seemed to be bandaged.

The door opened, and the next moment Dr. Hannah Klonek had come into the ward and was standing there, beaming down at me.

'Well Laura, how do you feel?'

'Is this still a dream – am I still in some sort of altered state of consciousness?'

'No, this is real life?'

'What have you done to me?'

'I think you know. I think it's what you wanted.'

I lifted the covers, and looked down at my body. My chest was bound in a wide bandage, but I could see that there were two very pronounced swellings under the dressing.

'Yes, we have given you breast implants, to supplement the work of the female hormones, which you have been on for many months now.'

'What about - '

'Yes, we dealt with that, too. All your male parts have been taken away, although a few bits were used in re-constructing you, in giving you a perfect vagina. Part of the penis is actually turned inside out...but you are looking rather faint, so perhaps we won't dwell on the details.'

'Tell me I'm still dreaming – this is still part of the simulation, the virtual reality world – the altered state, or whatever – it is, isn't it?'

'I'm afraid not, Laura. This is the real world, and you are really a girl now – forever. There's no going back. You know how much you loved being a girl, in your dream state. *We know* how much you loved it – we monitored you, the whole time. You can't deny it. You know it's what you want. You are a female – a *she*, not a *he* anymore. You have breasts and a vagina, now; rejoice in them, rejoice that you are a young woman, with the best years of your life as a woman ahead of you; you're one of us, dear – isn't it wonderful?'

But was I still dreaming? The pain in those early days

after the surgery was very real, and left me in little doubt that I had awoken finally from my various states of virtual reality and altered consciousness into what passes for the real world in this life, whatever its ultimate meaning may be. I wasn't going to wake up from this dream – the last layer of unconsciousness or subconsciousness had been peeled away in this reality, this moment in the time-space continuum, in the quantum flux, that we call the twenty-first century on planet Earth.

And I had been re-born, a girl-child, naked and vulnerable in my new state of femininity as any girl-child born of Eve. But like any other female, I had glimpsed now the greatest gift of the universe – the joy of giving oneself, of submission; the joy of the earth as it submits to the plough.

© 1996 – 2007 Kate Lesley

Jackie and Melanie Take Charge

Prologue

(Letter to Dr. Celia Hutton from Professor George Chalmers.)

The Witheys,
Moor View Road,
Mickleover,
Nr. Bakewell,
Derbyshire.

16th October 199-

Dear Celia,
It was good to see you again at the conference last July. I enjoyed what you said about Dr. Hunter's paper on gender dysphoria among the Hlutsu tribe, although I think your comments on his research methods were a little hard. Hunter's basically on our side, you know.

The reason I'm writing to you is because I came across a remarkable case recently - a case which apparently you know about as you are a principal player in it. The young woman in question told me that it was you and your colleague Michelle Caultney whom she met in Bangkok. I met 'Laura' purely by accident, in a bar in Soho, and she told me the whole story. As I couldn't publish anything about it in the psychology journals - obviously this case is your's and Michelle's, if what she told me is true - I decided to write it up in the form of a short story; as you know, I dabble a bit from time to time. It's just a hobby, but I've had one or two things published, and I think secretly it gives me greater satisfaction than all the stuffy psychology papers I write.

You will guess when you read it that 'Dr. Jacqueline Connolly' is you, and 'Melanie Goodhew' is your friend Ms. Caultney.

I hope you will forgive me for one or two literary embellishments of my own, to make the story flow, but I think I basically got the facts straight, at least as told to me by 'Laura'. Did you and Michelle really do this? I knew you both spent most of last year in Thailand, so that part at any rate is true. Do write and let me know if you approve of my version of 'Laura's' story, a copy of which I enclose.

Yours sincerely,

George Chalmers

'I think he'd be perfect; he's just what we're looking for. Broad hips, narrow shoulders, fair skin, blond hair - his body hair hardly shows as it is. He's got nice long legs, but he's not big overall for a man - petite really. With a bit of dieting, hormones, some corset training, we'd get him down to a size 14 - or maybe even a 12.'

'His face is promising, as well - his cheek bones are quite high, his chin's not very pronounced - of course his eyebrows will need plucking, and later we can see about electrolysis. His beard growth is rather light anyway - that's the beauty of catching one young, like this; we avoid that heavy shadow and jowl they get as they grow older. His face still has that soft, unlined look. He's not much more than a baby, really. His whole life still before him - or her, I should say, if things work out.'

'So we go ahead, with this one?'

'Why not? He looks a rather pretty boy anyway, so let's turn him into a pretty girl. We'll be doing him a favour. One less man in the world will be no bad thing. I can't wait to see him in a skirt. So when do we start?'

'No time like the present.'

The two women got up from their loungers beside the pool, from where they had been surreptitiously eyeing the young man in the water before them. They dived together into the pool, startling him as they sliced through the water on either side of him. When they surfaced they knew that the boy would be watching them.

'Wow,' thought the boy, watching the lithe bodies of the two women cut through the water as they swam across the pool. They were both confident, powerful swimmers.

'Thirty-something, both of them,' thought the boy, 'but they've looked after themselves. I wouldn't mind a bit of either.'

'He's noticed us all right,' said the woman in the green bikini, pushing her chestnut hair out of her eyes as she gazed back across the pool.

'He'd have to be blind or gay not to,' replied the other girl, whose blonde hair cascaded in a wet pony tail to the nape of her neck. 'Now we move to phase two.'

'What's phase two?'

'We eat him for dinner.'

The two women entered the pool-side bar, aware of the admiring glances of the men they passed. They sat down at a table next to the one where the boy was sitting, without looking at him. The waiter approached and took their drinks order - a glass of muscadet for the blonde woman, a dry martini for her companion. The boy couldn't help staring at them. They looked expensive - immaculately groomed, well-dressed in discreet but casually stylish clothes. Just the right amount of make-up, hair beautifully cut; both women had a languid confidence which said money.

'Out of my league,' thought the boy, and was turning away when one of them - the blonde one - suddenly looked round and caught his eye.

'Do you know, I was just saying to my friend, you look like someone I knew at university, but of course, you're too young. Perhaps it was your older brother? Do you have an older brother?'

'No I don't,' the boy replied, looking surprised and not a little embarrassed - he had obviously not been expecting either of these women to speak to him.

'May we join you?' asked the chestnut-haired one.

'Er - yes, if you wish.' The boy couldn't believe his luck.

The two women sat down on chairs on either side of the boy - two pincers moving in on their prey.

'Perhaps you have an older sister, then?' asked the blonde woman.

'I do, as a matter of fact,' replied the boy, mystified by this turn in the conversation.

'Perfect!' announced the brunette, looking meaningfully at her companion; 'I'm Jackie by the way, and this is Melanie.'

'I hope we didn't startle you when we dived into the pool earlier,' said Melanie.

'No, not at all,' replied the boy.

'What should we call you?' asked Jackie.

'Kevin,' replied the boy.

'Perfect!' said Jackie again.

Kevin had the distinct feeling that these sophisticated women were playing some game with him - were toying with him to amuse themselves. Well, he had nothing better to do, and no objection to being the 'toyboy' of two such attractive women. He began to fantasize...perhaps he would end up in bed between these two beauties?

'It's a warm night,' said Kevin, for want of something more interesting to say.

'It's always warm in the tropics,' replied Melanie. Our suite is air-conditioned; perhaps you'd like to come back with us for a night-cap, Kevin, and then we could go on to a club, later?'

Kevin couldn't believe his ears. His luck was really in, tonight. He'd heard that Bangkok was sin city, with its hundreds of massage parlours and thousands of good-time girls, willing to pander to any whim for Deutsche-Marks or dollars. He'd wondered about trying a Thai girl, but was worried about catching Aids.

And now these women, European women - English middle-class women, in fact - surely there was no danger here? - had just fallen into his lap. They were propositioning him! What luck!

They took the elevator to the seventeenth floor of the hotel, and led Kevin along the corridor to a teak door with the number 2137 on it in gold lettering. The corridors in this part of the hotel were fitted with plush deep pile grey carpets, and the hum of air conditioning could be heard behind the closed doors. Kevin's room was in the 'economy' section of the hotel - hessian matting on the corridors, the rooms facing inwards to a barren court yard

191

of glazed brick and mud, with a single palm tree beside a fountain which was never turned on. There was no air-conditioning in Kevin's room, and he had found it hard to sleep - the hot, heavy air felt as if it would suffocate him. He had laid in bed the last two nights, the sheets wet with his sweat, listening to the buzz of insects against the glass of his window, and the muffled sounds of a city that never sleeps - taxis honking, shouting of street-hawkers, a police-siren...

Melanie turned the key in the lock and pushed the door open; a wave of delicious chilled air swept over them as they entered the suite of rooms.

'Sit yourself down, Kevin,' said Jackie, indicating a cream leather sofa, 'and tell me what you'd like to drink.'

'Gin and tonic would be fine, with plenty of ice, please.'

Jackie handed him a tall crystal glass containing the clear liquid and several nuggets of ice. Kevin placed the cool glass briefly against his forehead, which felt feverish, then sipped at the drink. The gin predominated - he would have to be careful he didn't get drunk.

'Still hot, Kevin?' asked Jackie. Perhaps you'd like to slip into something more comfortable?' She went through to a door to what Kevin supposed was a bedroom, and returned with a shimmering silk kimono dressing gown. 'Why not get out of those hot sweaty clothes?' You can have a shower if you like, and then slip this on. The shower room is through there - the door off to the left as you go in.' She indicated the room from which she had just come.

'Thanks,' said Kevin, 'I'll do that.' He got up, took another belt of his drink, and went through to the shower room.

Melanie raised her eye-brows questioningly at Jackie at she came into the room.

'He's in the shower,' Jackie replied to the unspoken question.

'God, that didn't take you long.'

'He's going to be like putty in our hands.'

'Goodeee! I'll go and get rid of his clothes then. He won't be needing them again.'

'So tell us about your big sister,' said Melanie, looking up from the marble-topped bar which extended out from one wall of the room. Kevin was sitting on the cream sofa opposite her, while she was mixing him another gin and tonic.

'Well, there's not much to tell; she's thirty-five, an accounts executive with Chase Manhattan. She's based in London, but she's in New York at the moment, on some course or other. She's a high flier - a bit of a yuppie.'

'A real career girl, eh?'

'Yes - why the interest?'

Melanie didn't answer.

'And what do you do?' asked Jackie.

'I've just finished my degree - in Psychology; I'm working for Westminster City Council - it's only a clerical job, but it's keeping me going until I find something better.'

'What do you hope to do?'

'I don't know - I've thought about personnel management.'

'And you live - alone?

'Yes, I'm renting a flat in Tottenham - not far from the football ground. It's just a bed-sit, but I can't afford anything better. I'd like to buy somewhere eventually, but that depends on getting a better job.'

'We might be able to help you, there,' said Melanie.

'Really? How?' asked Kevin.

'We'll come to that later.'

There was a pause in the conversation.

'Another drink, Kevin?' asked Jackie.

'I don't know - I'll be getting squiffy if I drink much more.'

'Go on - you're on holiday. We'll make sure you get back to your room okay.'

'All right, then.'

While Jackie was mixing the drinks, Melanie crossed

the room and sat down next to Kevin on the sofa. She turned to Kevin, gave his knee a little squeeze and asked softly:

'Kevin, did you ever dress up in your sister's clothes?

'What - what did you say?' Kevin thought he had misheard.

'Did you ever dress up in your sister's clothes - when you were a boy? You'd be surprised how common it is. Big sisters sometimes encourage their younger brothers to dress up - for a game. You know what girls are like. Perhaps your big sister - what's her name – '

'Judy.'

' - Perhaps Judy suggested it; she might have wanted a younger sister, rather than a brother. I expect you played together - and looked up to her, wanted to do what she did. What could be more natural? Just a dressing-up game.'

'No, never.' Kevin was beginning to feel uncomfortable about the direction the conversation seemed to be taking.

'Never? Are you sure? It's nothing to be ashamed of.'

Kevin thought for a moment.

'Well - I think there was one occasion. I wasn't very old.'

'Yes?'

Kevin shrugged. He was obviously reluctant to go on.

'So what happened?' prompted Melanie. By this time Jackie had returned to the room and was sitting on a stool by the bar, sipping her drink, apparently unconcerned. In fact, she was listening intently to Kevin's responses.

Kevin continued: 'We were playing in her room. Mum was outside - doing some gardening. We were playing a make-believe game, and Judy said she was a hairdresser, and would I pretend to be the customer. My hair was longish, and before I knew what she was doing, she'd brushed it into a rather girlish style and put a ribbon in it.'

'How did you feel?'

194

'I - don't know. I can't remember.'

'And what happened then?'

'She said: "It'd be more fun if you were a girl - let me dress you up in my clothes." I said no at first, but she persisted, started to whine and wheedle at me until I finally agreed.'

'So what did you put on?' This was from Jackie. Kevin looked round, surprised that she had been listening.

'Oh I can't remember - a dress I think.'

'And knickers?' asked Jackie.

'Yes - I think so.' Kevin was blushing now.

Jackie's eyes met Melanie's; she nodded almost imperceptably.

'I think we've got a live one all right,' whispered Jackie.

'You spotted him, at the pool side; I don't know how you do it.'

'Instinct - and of course I did date a TV once.'

'Who was that?'

'Gerry.'

'Good lord, not Gerry Kazinski? He was built like a tank.'

'Yes - they're not necessarily effeminate, you know, to begin with. It takes its toll eventually though - all that shaving of legs and walking in high heels and wearing girlie underwear and make-up - Gerry could mince with the best of them by the time he'd really got into the scene.'

'Was he a trannie when you met him - or did you help him along?'

'Really, Melanie, you have such a suspicious mind.'

'I know you.'

'Well I did give him a bit of encouragement. He didn't know himself, at first; a lot of them don't, you know. But they give themselves away - little signs.'

'How did you find out with Gerry?'

'I came into the bedroom once and found him sitting on the bed holding my tights. He had a funny look on his face - sort of wistful. He put them down of course, when

195

he realised I was standing there, but he was at a loss for a moment - didn't know what to say. Then he made out he was just tidying up - getting things together to put in the washing basket. As he'd never previously shown any interest in tidying up or organising the washing, we both knew he was lying.

'I just said to him, "Gerry, would you like to put them on?" And that was that. I put him in a skirt that same night - made him shave his legs too. if there's one thing I can't stand it's hairy legs.

'Another drink, Kevin?' Kevin jumped. He'd been listening to this conversation with an expression first of puzzlement, then of amazement; now, as he began to realise his predicament, and what these two women might have in mind for him, he looked embarrassed and alarmed.

'There we go again, startling you,' said Jackie, a mischievous glint in her eye. Kevin felt as if he needed a stiff drink after what he'd just heard, although he knew that he'd already had too much.

'Yes please.' Kevin passed his glass to Jackie, who got up and poured the drink. The two women continued their conversation, apparently in no hurry to direct their attention towards Kevin.

'So what happened to Gerry in the end - what's he doing now?' asked Melanie.

'Well there was no stopping him once he got started. He just loved it - was overjoyed in fact. He dressed every opportunity, and got very convincing.

'His firm moved him to Manchester, and he got into the Manchester trannie scene, started going to the clubs and gay bars where they like to meet.'

'Did he turn out to be gay, then?'

'Oh no, he was hetero all right - most trannies are, you know. That's one of the paradoxes about them. In fact he was one of the best lovers I ever had - wanted to do it all the time. Amazingly virile, but gentle as a woman. I've come to the conclusion that trannies make the best lovers - better than so-called 'real men'; I've found the macho types can be a great disappointment. I'd rather have a trannie any day - it's as if they're part woman themselves, so they know intuitively how to turn a woman on.

'Anyway, Gerry went on a diet and lost about three stone - he's no longer burly, but quite petite. The transformation was amazing. It just shows you gender is one tenth biological and nine tenths what you wear and how you feel about yourself. It's socially constructed - little girls are made - not born.

'Gerry went full-time in the end - calls herself Melissa; she's still in the sales game, but now she's a rep. for a cosmetics company; she's one of their best salespersons. She's clinched many a deal by pointing out that she uses the line of cosmetics herself, to which the response is usually - so what? Then she reveals that she's really a man - which is a real gob-smacker for the client, because you'd never guess; she looks stunning these days. "And if these cosmetics can do this for me," she says, "think what they can do for a real woman..." and they fall at her feet, and place an order.'

'Incredible,' responded Melanie.

Jackie had reached the end of her story about Gerry, and no one seemed to know what to say or do next. The air conditioning hummed, and they listened to the sound of it for perhaps a minute. All of them were aware that the pivotal point in the evening had arrived, and that whatever happened next would shape - not just the rest of the evening - but perhaps the rest of one or more of their lives.

'Well?' said Jackie, raising her eyebrows questioningly to Melanie.

'Yes, I think you've put Kevin in the picture,' replied Melanie.

'So now we put him in a frock?' The two women laughed, then looked at Kevin expectantly.

'But why do you want to do this to me?' Kevin posed the question to them both.

Again there was a silence. At length, Melanie replied: 'You could say it's a hobby of ours. We like to think of ourselves as liberators; we liberate suitable men from the necessity to behave in a certain way, to perform a role that they're obviously not happy in. Gender is all a matter of role-playing. We're conditioned to behave in gender-specific ways. You should know some of this from your psychology course.'

'Yes, I've read a bit about the psychology of gender,' replied Kevin.

'Did you come across anything written by Dr. J. Connolly?'

'The name rings a bell. Isn't she a feminist academic at Keele? Made a name for herself by writing a book about the way boys are brought up: "The Macho Trap" I think it was called. Our professor of psychology wasn't very impressed.'

'Who was that?' asked Jackie.

'Professor Summers.'

'Oh, that old fool.'

'She knows of what she speaks,' said Melanie; 'meet Dr. Jacqueline Connolly.'

Kevin looked at Jackie in amazement:

'You?'

'Why not?'

'Well, you're younger than I would have expected,' replied Kevin.

'I think I like this young man more and more,' said Jackie, grinning across to Melanie; 'and this is my research assistant, Melanie Goodhew, B.A., M.Ed.; she's doing her Ph.D. with me at the moment. Nearly finished it, eh Mel?'

'Yes, thank God, wherever she is,' replied Melanie. I'm planning on submitting it next term.'

'Melanie's thesis is on androgyny theory. She argues, broadly, that girls and boys are brought up at present in a way which is unhealthy for both sexes. Most of the things which we think of as specific to one sex - choice of clothes, interests, different types of behaviour - are conditioned by our upbringing and by social factors. Gender is socially programmed - we acquire our gender from the day we are born, according to how our parents dress us, what they call us, how they treat us - and this process continues with peer-group pressure, media influences, etc. - until we become sexually stereotyped. Much of this stereotyping is arbitrary and pointless; for example it is a convention in our culture at present that men don't wear skirts or dresses - and yet at different times in history and in different cultures this type of garment has been completely acceptable for men. Men in Ancient Greece wore a long tunic; Roman men had the toga; in Renaissance Europe men had long flowing hair, and wore velvet and satin blouses and tunics. The hose worn under the tunic was similar to a pair of tights, or they wore stockings held up by garters. In early eighteenth century France it was quite acceptable for men to wear wigs, beauty spots, rouge and other make-up, and to have the finest lace and embroidery on their collars and cuffs.

'It's true that whilst women can now wear almost anything, from the most feminine frocks, to jeans and a tee-shirt or even a male three-piece suit - can have any length of hair, from shaven-headed to waist length - can wear make-up or go completely without - men do not have this choice, and cannot express their personalities except in a very restricted way. Not all men want to be macho anymore than all women want to be a heroine out of a Barbara Cartland novel. But it is still socially unacceptable for men to express their feminine side. Of course the whole business about what is masculine and feminine is arbitrary - who's to say that a particular psychological attribute belongs more to one sex than the other? If you stereotype people from birth, then of course they will believe it, and act accordingly. But who says, for example, that women should be more gentle or submissive than men? Try telling Margaret Thatcher or Edwina Currie!

'There are biological sexual differences, of course, but apart from our genitalia, what do these amount to? In any group of so-called 'normal' men and women, there is a tremendous variation of size and shape, of hairiness

199

and smoothness, etc. In fact, within each sex, there is a greater variation than between the sexes. There are thin women with narrow hips and practically no bust; there are broad-hipped men with narrow shoulders and fatty chest tissue, who have bigger breasts than some women. There are tall, athletic, muscular women, and small-boned, slender men. Between the races there is more variation than between the sexes - you'll have noticed that Thai men tend to be small and slight compared with Caucasians, for example. The point I'm getting at is if this differentiation exists within each sex, how can we justify stereotyping people by their sex?

'Just as much variation exists in the psychology of men and women - there is no one attribute or characteristic which is entirely restricted to one sex or the other. Women, to some extent, have been liberated from the obligation to act at all times in a stereotypically 'feminine' way, and - at least in the West - a full range of occupations and professions are now open to them.

'It's still not easy for a woman to be aggressive - not that aggression is a particularly desirable trait for either sex. But some of us at least are getting better at being assertive. Men on the other hand have a far harder time at expressing any typically 'feminine' characteristic - gentleness, tenderness, empathy for others are all desirable attributes in any human being, I would have said, and yet a lot of men have a real problem showing this side of themselves.

'God I have been going on; my throat's dry - let's have another drink.'

'Not more booze though,' replied Melanie, we've had enough already. I'll make some coffee. Fancy a coffee, Kevin?'

'I'll make it,' said Jackie. She walked over to the drinks bar and switched on the electric kettle.

Melanie leaned across to Kevin and whispered:

'She does get a bit heavy, sometimes, but she's dead right in what she says. She's a real expert on the psychology of sex and gender. And she's been a good

200

friend to me. She got me on to the research programme after my marriage broke up; I think she did it to help take my mind off the trauma of my divorce - it was pretty messy. I'm afraid it gave me a rather jaundiced view of men for a while, particularly the macho type, like my ex-husband. He was a violent creep.'

Jackie came back with the coffees and sat down again next to Kevin.

'So what I'm saying, in my very long-winded way,' resumed Jackie, 'is that there's nothing wrong in what you did that day, when your sister dressed you up. You shouldn't feel ashamed about it. How did you feel, by the way - you never did say.'

'He didn't get a chance, with you gassing on,' said Melanie.

'Well, I thought it was wrong - I knew that boys weren't supposed to do things like that.'

'Did you do it again, any time? asked Melanie.

'Yes.' Kevin looked sheepish as he said this.

'How many times?' asked Jackie.

'Several times, but it was always my sister's idea.'

'Did your mother find out?'

'No, I don't think so.'

'After you've drunk your coffee, I'd like you to go in the bedroom, Kevin, shave your legs and chest - I've left my Lady shaver on the dressing table - and put on the clothes I've laid out on the bed for you.'

'But – '

'No but's, Kevin; just let Jackie and Melanie take charge. We know what's good for you.'

Kevin was too tired and drunk to argue further. He went into the bedroom and sat on the bed. What should he do? These women seemed to be crazy. True, he had dressed in his sister's clothes, but that was a long time ago, when they were both young children. How had he felt, then? Had he liked it? A little, perhaps - it had not been an unpleasant experience. But surely that didn't make him a transvestite? He had never thought of himself as a transvestite - and there was one way that he could prove he wasn't, to these women - go along with what they wanted him to do, and prove to them that the whole business left him cold. Very well then, that's what he would do.

Kevin took the Lady shaver and shaved the fluff off his legs and chest. Then he put on the lacy panties on the bed, and rolled on a pair of black tights - he had watched a girlfriend do this, one foot at a time. There was a bra and slip set edged with lace, like the panties. He put them on, and then the long patterned cotton skirt and cream silk blouse which were also on the bed. Surprisingly, the blouse and skirt fitted him well. A pair of high-heeled navy leather court shoes finished the outfit; he slipped these on and hobbled unsteadily out of the bedroom.

'There you are, I look ridiculous,' he announced to the women.

'No you don't, you look sweet,' said Melanie; 'just unbutton your blouse, love, so that I can make you a bit more busty.' Kevin unbuttoned the blouse and Melanie slipped a circular piece of foam rubber into each bra cup. Jackie then produced a blonde wig from a box under the coffee table, and carefully positioned it on Kevin's head. She then took foundation, lipstick, eye-shadow, and mascara out of an overnight bag and quickly made up Kevin's face.

'There, have a look at yourself in the full-length mirror in the bedroom.'

Kevin walked back into the bedroom unsteadily, and stood in front of the mirror. Instead of seeing his usual reflection, he saw that of an attractive blonde girl. He stared in amazement - could this really be him? He sat down on the stool in front of the dressing table, feeling slightly faint. When he looked up, he saw in the dressing table mirror - not his own face, but again, the face of a pretty young woman. He was shocked - how could it be that with so little effort these women had been able to turn him into such a convincing girl? What did it mean? Were they right - was this how he was meant to be? He felt strange - rather excited and exhilarated, as if he had just pushed open a door onto the unknown. He could feel his heart fluttering rapidly in his chest, and somehow he couldn't quite get his breath. He closed his eyes for a few moments, then felt a wave of tiredness sweeping over him.

'So tired,' he muttered to himself, and curling up on the bed, dropped almost instantly into a deep sleep.

As Kevin slowly came to the following morning, at first he could not remember where he was. He looked around the room, at the luxurious furniture and fitments. Sitting up in bed, he found that he was wearing a cream silk nightdress. Then some muddled memories of the previous night began to filter into his consciousness - but surely that had all been a dream? Yet here he was in the same room, wearing - a nightie. Who had got him undressed? Where were his own clothes? He remembered the two women - they had obviously been making a fool of him while he was drunk. Well he was sober now - painfully so - he felt his head throbbing - so they could damn well stop this fooling about, give him back his clothes, and then he could go back to his own room for breakfast. Kevin leapt out of bed - ouch! What a hangover! He decided he'd better move a little more slowly. He walked gingerly into the next room, feeling the plush carpet between his toes. The air-conditioning seemed to be roaring this morning. He could smell coffee.

'Want some?' asked Jackie, holding up the coffee jug. 'And how are we feeling this morning?'

'Terrible,' replied Kevin.

'How much do you remember about last night?'

'Enough to know that you made an ass of me.'

'Not an ass - a girl - and a very pretty one you made too.'

'Now don't start that again.'

'Sit down, Kevin; I'm afraid you haven't quite grasped the reality of your situation. Let me explain it to you. We are conducting a little experiment, and you are our raw material. You are not leaving here until we decide you are ready to go. That will not be until we have turned you into a girl.'

'I've never heard anything so ridiculous. You can't keep me here.'

'Why don't you try to leave, if you're so sure of that?'

Kevin got up and went over to the door through which he remembered they had entered the apartment the previous night. He tried the handle. It was locked.

'Where's the key?'

'Come on Kevin; I'm hardly likely to tell you. Anyway, I can't see you getting very far on the streets of Bangkok in that nightie.'

'Where are my clothes?'

'You won't be needing them anymore. We're going to keep you in skirts from now on.'

'What does Melanie think about this - is she as mad as you are?'

'Morning Kevin; did I hear my name being taken in vain?' asked Melanie, who had just walked into the room.

'You know,' added Melanie, 'Kevin has the cutest knees; I can't wait to see him again in a skirt and high heels.

'Well I suppose that answers that question,' said Kevin glumly.

'Please take this pill with your coffee, Kevin,' said Jackie, handing him a small capsule.

'What is it?'

'Just something to make your head feel better - you must have an awful hangover to be so grouchy.'

I'm not grouchy; I just don't like being kidnapped. You can't do things like that - this is a free country.'

'Actually it's not. May I remind you that you're in Thailand now - not England. Two or three Europeans disappear in Bangkok every week - the authorities don't bother much about it. When they investigate, they usually find that the missing person was last scene in the vicinity of a brothel or massage parlour. As the police get kick-backs from these premises, they generally don't bother to take the investigation further, reasoning that the honoured foreign visitor now missing was probably some sleaze-bag who got what he was asking for. Life is cheap in Bangkok. Believe me, no one will bother much about your disappearance.'

'And no one who knew you before will recognise you anyway, once we've finished our work on you,' added Melanie.

'You might as well just accept what's going to happen to you, Kevin - show a bit of Eastern fatalism,' continued Jackie; 'we think it's for your own good, anyway. We can either do this the easy way or the hard way.'

'What's the hard way?'

'Both ways you get turned into a girl; the hard way, instead of us doing it, we hand you over to the Ladyboys - the Thai transvestites. They won't be so gentle with you, and they'll expect you to work in one of the transvestite brothels once you've been changed. European Ladyboys fetch high prices - you'll be much in demand, servicing the needs of Japanese and Taiwanese businessmen - they can play rough, so I hear. And of course you'll never get away from Bangkok - where would you be able to go, once you've been a Katoi girl in Thailand?'

Kevin had gone as white as a sheet.

'And - the alternative?' he asked.

'Cooperate with us, and you'll get back to the U.K.'

'But I'll be a girl?'

'Yes.'

'Completely?'

'That has yet to be decided. You may have some say in that - if you cooperate. According to the theory of androgyny which we have developed, it should be possible to change your gender by psychological re-programming alone. There will be one or two minor cosmetic changes we can make to your face and figure, but these will just make life easier for you in your new role - they certainly don't amount to a sex-change. Melanie will be making detailed notes on your training, and will have some questionnaires and psychological tests for you

205

to complete at various points in the process. Your case will be written up in a research paper; you will be described as a young transvestite who was helped in achieving her ambition to live as a woman. There will of course be no indication that coercion was used, and in fact we don't anticipate that any coercion will be needed, once we get going on the programme. We're convinced that you will end up enjoying what's happening to you. Some trannies would give their eye-teeth for the opportunity we're giving you!

'So what's it to be?' asked Jackie, finally.

'I don't seem to have much choice,' replied Kevin.

'Correct - so you're going to cooperate?'

'I suppose so.'

'Right, from now on you must start thinking of yourself as a girl. You will wear skirts all the time. You will always be referred to by the feminine pronouns - 'she,' 'her', etc., and of course we'll have to give you a girl's name. Any preferences?'

'Not really.'

'How about Laura?'

'Okay.'

'Laura, I'd like you to go and get dressed now - you have a wardrobe of skirts and dresses to choose from in the room in which you slept, which will be your bedroom for the next few days. There are plenty of undies in the drawers. Make sure you wear tights, and we'd like to keep you in high heels for the time being, until walking in them is second nature to you. Try to take smaller steps, swing your hips a little. Remember when you sit down to keep your legs together, particularly if you're wearing a short skirt.

'Try to talk more softly - we have some instruction tapes on speech rhythms which will help to give your voice a more female pitch and inflection.

Until your hair grows longer, you will have to wear a wig. We have arranged for a beauty therapist to visit you on a regular basis - a Thai woman who is very discreet and knows her business - she has helped many Ladyboys achieve their goal of femininity. She will give you electrolysis to remove your beard growth permanently, and will help you with make-up until you become proficient.

'We have booked you into a clinic for a couple of minor operations - breast implants and removal of your Adam's apple. You will find that your body-shape will gradually change and become more feminine over the coming months, as you will be taking a course of female hormones - in fact you've already started - the pill I gave you this morning wasn't really for a headache. The hormone treatment will help broaden your hips, soften your skin and assist breast development, but as I have said, we are not just relying on this - you will have the breast implants as well.

'We may also decide to give your figure some corset training, to reduce your waist size - we'd like to get it down to 26 inches, if possible. Soon your own mother won't recognise you! Just think, she'll be losing a son, but we'll be giving her another lovely daughter. Do you think she'll be pleased?'

'I should think she'd be horrified if she knew what you are doing to me,' replied Kevin. 'What's to stop me from writing and telling her?'

'Well you'll certainly have to write to her,' replied Jackie, 'because she's going to be wondering why you haven't returned from your holiday. When are you due back?'

'I've got another week before my flight back.'

'That gives us plenty of time to decide what you should put in the letter. Something near the truth would probably be best. You could simply say that you have met an eminent research psychologist - '

'Such modesty!' Melanie guffawed.

'- who has invited you to stay on in Bangkok and assist with her research. We'll be moving next week to a flat we've found on the outskirts of Bangkok - it's too expensive to stay on here at the hotel indefinitely. I'll give you the address of the flat, so that your mother can write to you, if she wants.

'Say that you expect to be some months, and could she therefore dispose of your flat in Tottenham. She could store your few possessions until you get back. Of course you won't be needing the clothes again anyway.'

'Suppose I refuse to write to my mother at all? When I don't arrive home she'll soon realise something's wrong; then it's only a matter of time before she contacts the Foreign Office to ask them to start searching for me in Bangkok.'

'Do you really want to put your mother through all that worry?'

'No I wouldn't want to worry her. I will write to her to let her know that I'm staying on in Bangkok. I don't see why I should write what you want me to, though.'

'So what will you tell her? That you've been kidnapped by two women, who are turning you into a woman, as well? Do you think she'll believe that? She'll think you've gone round the twist - and that would worry her as much as not writing at all. No, you must agree your best course is to write as I've suggested - just say you're helping with some research; I expect she'll be quite impressed. Then all you need to do is write a letter resigning from your job at the council, and that will tie up all the loose ends.'

'What about your father?' asked Melanie.

'My parents are divorced; my mother hasn't seem him for years, and neither have I.'

'Okay then,' said Jackie, 'so if you do as we say, no one's going to miss you for a few months, while we get on with your petticoat training.'

'My what?'

'Petticoat training - according to the literature of transvestism, of which I've made something of a study, unruly young boys were sometimes subjected to wearing petticoats as a way of disciplining them. I imagine it was quite effective.'

'Sounds like the plot of a transvestite fantasy,' said Melanie.

'Life does follow art, sometimes, you know,' replied

Jackie.

'As in this case, I suppose?' asked Laura.

'As in this case,' replied Jackie firmly; 'now go and get dressed.'

*   *   *

Epilogue - Laura's story

The story you have been reading is based on events as recounted to me recently by an attractive young woman - I had thought she was a woman - who I met in a pub in Soho. Whilst I am not in the habit of chatting up women in Soho pubs, this particular girl looked so pretty, and had such a pleasant manner and calm intelligence about her, that I found myself wanting to get to know her better. She was polite, but resistant to my charms, however. When I persisted, she finally said to me:

'Look I'm not interested in men. No, it's not what you're thinking - I'm not lesbian. Okay, let me tell you about myself.' And the story you have been reading is what she told me. I have merely used a little artistic license in telling her story up to now in the third person. I will let Laura conclude in her own words: I have transcribed them here directly from the tape I made when I interviewed her again - I asked her to come up to the university so that I could get a full account. This is what she told me:

'As well as obliging me to dress as a woman at all times, Jackie and Melanie organised feminine activities and role-playing situations for me. Ridiculous as it may sound, I received instruction in cooking and dressmaking; I was also taught to knit, crochet and embroider. If I performed my feminine tasks well, I was rewarded with a present - always something which they thought a girl would like - some new lacy underwear, a bottle of exotic perfume, a piece of jewellery. At first I didn't care about these presents - scorned them in fact; but as time went on I found that in spite of myself I was looking forward to

209

these little surprises, and could not help but strive to be more feminine so that I would get the next reward. Any masculine behaviour, on the other hand, was punished by little humiliations which the two women thought up for me. Sometimes, for example, I was forced to dress as a maid - a black cotton mini-dress, white lace collar and cuffs, black tights, high-heeled shoes. I had to pin my hair up and wear a ridiculous little lace cap on the back of my head. I felt really silly and humiliated wearing this get-up, in which they would require me to perform some menial task, such as cleaning the toilet and bathroom, scrubbing the floors, or polishing the furniture. Once or twice they even had me doing this in the flat of a neighbour - an American journalist whom they were friendly with. He unfortunately took a fancy to me, and asked Jackie if he could borrow me again to act as maid for him at a dinner party he was giving for some diplomats. Jackie thought this was a splendid idea - more good practice for me in a female role.

'I got through the evening somehow, and certainly found it an object lesson in how disgusting the male sex can be. When his guests were fairly well-oiled, a couple of them took to trying to pat me on the bottom or touch my thigh while I was serving them; I eventually put a stop to this by tipping a bowl of hot custard into one of their laps.

'My hair had grown a lot longer by this time, and had been given a feminine cut and style. I was encouraged to grow my nails, and Jackie informed me that I should always wear nail varnish. I became quite adept at making up my face, and was relieved when the electrolysis treatment was over, so that I no longer needed to wear any foundation, which used to bring me out in spots. My skin was now completely devoid of beard growth, as soft and smooth as a girl's. My eyebrows had been plucked and shaped, and my ears pierced.

'My figure was becoming more and more feminine - my hips had broadened, and my waist, thanks partly to the corset which the women had laced me into for some weeks, was now as slim as a girl's. The female hormones had brought about some breast growth, which was augmented by the silicon inserts that had been implanted. My bust measurement was now 38B; my waist measured 26 inches, and my hips were 36 inches. My Adam's apple had been removed.

'Under the guidance and instruction of Jackie and Melanie, I had become completely feminine in my way of moving and my mannerisms. At first I had tried to resist their training - but they were insistent and rigorous - they wouldn't give me a moment's peace. And then, when my body started to change - I just lost the will to resist. I began to forget what it had been like before - being a girl began to feel - natural for me, somehow. They told me that my voice had also grown soft and girlish. In short, they reckoned that they had succeeded in turning me into an attractive young woman - and I had only to look in the mirror to see that they had a point.

'Let me give you an idea of what I looked like by the morning Jackie announced, "Our work here is finished." It was about ten months after I'd first arrived in Thailand. I remember quite well what I was wearing that morning - as it was a favourite outfit of mine. I was sitting on the sofa skimming through the pages of a copy of Cosmopolitan while I waiting for my nails to dry. My curly blonde hair was by then nearly shoulder-length, held back by two tortoise shell combs to reveal my Thai silver earrings, which were one of the girls' little presents to me. I was wearing a fairly tight black silk skirt which showed off my slim waist and the curve of my hips; the silicon implants had made my breasts rather pronounced, so that they stood out against the fabric of my jade-coloured Thai silk blouse - it has a mandarin collar and is embroidered across the front and around the cuffs with oriental patterns. My legs, which are quite long, must have looked rather shapely in the very sheer black tights I was wearing; around my right ankle I had one of those delicate silver chains. I was wearing very high-heeled black court shoes - I'd got used to walking in them by then. My nails were painted a shade of red which matched my lipstick; I'd made my eyes up carefully with my favourite eye-shadow - smoky lilac and lagoon tones which blend together beautifully; and I had a touch of mascara on. My skin felt very soft and smooth -

"You glow with a natural feminine efflorescence and vitality!" Melanie said to me, after I'd been taking the female hormones for some months; I'd also finished the electrolysis treatment by then. She was teasing me, but it was true that I no longer needed foundation or powder, which was a relief, because that stuff clogged my skin and tended to give me spots.

'Anyway, that particular morning, Jackie asked:

"Would you like to go back to England soon, Laura?"

"Are you serious?" I replied.

"Of course," she said, "Melanie has finished her research. Thanks to you, she has got all the data she needs to complete her thesis.'

"Is that how you have managed to explain your absence for nearly a year from the university, while you've been keeping me here?" I asked.

"Well, more or less - they knew Melanie was on a research project in Thailand. I just came over here on holiday for a couple of weeks, to visit her; when we found you I was so intrigued I decided to stay on to help Melanie with the programme to change your gender and to see how things turned out. I was owed some leave anyway, and I just extended it in the form of a sabbatical."

I thought about this for a moment, then said to Jackie:

"There's one thing I'd like to know about all this - would you really have given me over to the Ladyboys, if I hadn't cooperated?"

"Good heavens, no - what sort of people do you think we are, Laura? That was an empty threat, I'm afraid. I just said that in the hope that it would convince you to work with us - if you'd called our bluff there was nothing we could have done. You could have walked out that first morning, if you'd insisted. If you'd asked me seriously for the key, I would have given it to you - we couldn't have kept you against your will for long.

"You see, Melanie had originally intended to do her research among the Katoi girls, - the initial plans for her project were quite different, involving a survey of attitudes to gender among the Thai transvestite class. But the Ladyboys were proving uncooperative - they were demanding quite a bit of money even to talk to Melanie. Then you sort of fell into our laps, so to speak, and we saw a way of changing the whole focus of the study and doing something more original; you gave us the opportunity to actually study at first hand the processes by which gender - or in your case, a new gender - are acquired. You're famous, Laura - you are the 'Miss X' of Melanie's final research paper; if her research is accepted, you may well find your case is quoted in the journals of psychology, in the future."

"That's all very well, but how can I go back to England like this, and face anyone who used to know me?"

"We'll help you start a new life, as a girl. Can you honestly say that you are not happier as a girl?"

"I suppose I've got used to it. Given what I look like now, I can't see how I can ever expect to live again as a male. You girls did a pretty good job on me."

Jackie laughed, and said:

"Good. You've adjusted well to your new gender. I'm sure it was right for you. Have you given any thought to sorting out what's between your legs - getting rid of those parts that you can no longer have any possible use for? If you like, I can book you into a private clinic here in Bangkok, so that you can get the operation over with, and make your femininity complete and irreversible - before you return to England. You really don't need those nasty dangly bits anymore, and they will be a problem to conceal when you're wearing a bikini - with your new figure, you'll look stunning in one. At the clinic, they'll remove all that and construct a beautiful vagina for you - then you'll be able to experience making love as a woman."

"I think I'll take a rain check on that, for the time being," I said.

"A pity - you could then have said truthfully that you went abroad and came back a broad."

"Very funny."

"Anyway, I'll do my best to help you get settled in England, in your new life as a girl. I have a friend who is Human Resources Director for ICM; she's always on the lookout for good psychology graduates for their personnel management programme. Would you be interested?"

"Certainly."

"I'll write to her at once. I won't mention your - background. She will just assume that you're a young woman who impressed me. I've recommended people to her before. While I'm getting on with this letter, Melanie, do you think you could phone Cathay Pacific and place reservations for the three of us for a flight to London - shall we say next Saturday?"

"What about Laura's passport photo?" asked Melanie. "It doesn't bear much resemblance to her present appearance."

"Don't worry about that - they'll just assume she's a transvestite; they don't take much notice these days, they see quite a few of them."

"Well girls," Jackie said, grinning at us, "I think a little celebration will be in order tonight, now that our work is finished here. Let's all go out to the Kit Kat club."

"What's that?" I asked.

"It's a transvestite night-club in downtown Bangkok, named after that famous seedy establishment in Berlin during the early Thirties. I'm sure you'll be intrigued to see the beautiful 'girls' there, eh Laura?"

"If it's all the same to you," I replied, "I think I'd better stay in and write to my mother. She's going to get a shock when she sees me, unless I give her some warning."

'That night, while Jackie and Melanie were out on the town, I racked my brains trying to think how I could let my mother know what had happened to me. In the end I decided to leave detailed explanations to when I saw her;

214

I wrote a short letter in which I said simply:

"I need to warn you that I've changed - you may be surprised by my appearance when you see me; I hope the shock won't be too great for you."

'My mother was waiting at Heathrow when our flight came in. We went through customs and immigration, and there she was - the other side of the barrier, looking worried and flustered as she scanned the faces of the people who had arrived on our flight.

Of course she didn't recognise me - I had to go up to her, tap her gently on the arm and say:

"Mum, it's me."

'She looked up, startled, still not knowing me, and then recognition and disbelief swept over her features in rapid succession.

"Kevin? Is it you? But you're a girl!'

"Er - yes Mum; I'm called Laura now. Look, I will explain, but it's going to take a bit of time. Perhaps we could go somewhere for a coffee?"

"I think I need something a little stronger, Kevin - sorry, Laura, I mean."

"Mum, this is Jacqueline Connolly - Dr. Connolly - and her assistant, Melanie."

"How are you Mrs. Donelly? You have a fine - daughter, who has been a great help to us in our research. Let me buy you a drink; there's a bar over there."

"Yes, I think I need to sit down," said my poor mother.

'Well, after several rounds of gin and tonic we all began to feel a bit more relaxed, and my mother came round to accepting the situation. I remember one thing she said to me which still makes me laugh when I think of it.

"Laura," she said, "when I got that funny letter from you, the one about needing to warn me that you'd changed, and that I'd be surprised when I saw you, all I could think was that you'd got into some sort of trouble with drugs or something - you hear such awful tales about things that happen to young people in the Far East. I thought perhaps you'd really been in prison all these months, and were going to come back to me looking all hollow-eyed and emaciated, like a junkie."

"So you're not - too horrified?" I asked her.

"Well surprised, rather than horrified, dear, but at least you look healthy enough. It obviously agrees with you; you make a very nice-looking girl, I must say." She grinned at me and gave me a hug.

I think that was the best hug I ever had.'

©Kate Lesley 1992

School for Sissies

The true nature of the school - the particular and unusual training it offered, has always been a closely guarded secret, known only to the staff, the children who attended the establishment, and of course - their parents. If what went on at the school had not been approved of by the parents, it would never have kept going.

Of course it was the parents, or to be more precise - the *mothers* - who most ardently supported the activities of the school, ever clamouring for the staff to press the treatment to its furthest extremes...

No one could have predicted how far things would go, all those years ago, when my mother first conceived the possibility of such a school. Nor could anyone have dreamed that it would be possible to keep the secret for so long. Now however that the whole business is finally out and known to the public, through the recent sensational exposé of the school in the popular press, I think the time has come for a true account of events to be presented; and who better to write the 'official' history of St. Clare's Academy than myself? As the daughter of Madam Lydia Quesney, the founder, proprietor, and first headmistress of the school, as well as a pupil at the school for thirteen years, I was certainly in a good position to observe what really went on. I propose to hold nothing back from my description of the history and development of the school, so I shall leave you, the reader, to judge how far the lurid accounts in the press were accurate in depicting the unusual education and training offered by the institution as debauched, shameless and decadent.

To trace the origins of it all, I will need to tell you more about my mother, Lydia. My mother's family originally came from Strasbourg. My mother's grandfather, Paul Fischer, had made a fortune in Strasbourg as a manufacturer of pâté de foie gras in the early years of the century.

His son, my grandfather Gustave, carried on the family business and made it even more successful. Grandfather Gustave hoped also to have a son to whom he could pass on the business, but instead had only a daughter, my mother Lydia, who was born in 1936. Gustave's wife, Rachel, was from a prominent Jewish banking family; concerned at the rising tide of anti-semitism in Germany and fearing that Hitler might at any time re-annex Alsace, he sent his young wife and the baby Lydia to Switzerland for safety. From 1937 to 1946 they stayed with relatives of Rachel's in Lausanne, in a fine villa on the banks of Lake Geneva.

Rachel's relatives in Lausanne were two wealthy maiden aunts who were thrilled to have their niece and her baby daughter staying with them. It was an exclusively feminine household in which my mother was raised for the first nine years of her life, and I think this had a great influence on her. As well as my mother and the aunts, there was a nanny, and as soon as Lydia was old enough, a governess was appointed to educate her privately at the villa.

This governess was a woman of old-fashioned but decided views, and among these was a predilection for corset discipline. I recently found a letter from the governess among my mother's papers, which I have translated from the German, as it illustrates so well this lady's views on 'figure-training':

'I have long thought that what is called 'Figure Training' may be utilised in a direction little known in this country, though perfectly understood in France and Austria. I am sure that under proper supervision, and in the hands of reasonable people, no harm of a physical nature can result from this most efficacious method of dealing with the 'bumptiousness' of modern youth.

'When we speak of discipline, we must remember that tightness is a question of measurement and degree. At first sight it might appear unaccountable that moral good could be obtained by

eccentricity of costume, but on further enquiry I find that the method pursued has some advantages, not only for girls, but also for boys who have evinced an overbearing and intractable disposition.

'Of course the mere wearing of stays is only one element of the system pursued, but it is properly made the basis of all. For it is found that this restriction renders it easier for ladies to take the government of children into their own hands, without the assistance of masters.

'To the wearing of corsets we should add the other indispensable elements of long, tightly-buttoned kid gloves and boots laced high in the ankles, extremely tight and pointed, and with very high heels.

'Obedience, respectfulness, and a habit of deferring to the judgement of older persons can thus be fully established. In this way, boys as well as girls get the right kind of start in life, and are in almost every respect, better situated as regards their own future, whilst the homes which their misconduct has disgraced and degraded may become again examples of punctuality, politeness and orderly Christian behaviour.'

In the beautiful house in Lausanne, with its balconies looking south-west across the lustrous waters of Lake Geneva, the maiden aunts, the nanny and grandmother Rachel all pampered and doted on the young child Lydia - and soon she was thoroughly spoilt. The Austrian governess, Fräu Mürz, saw it as her duty to take the child in hand and curb her waywardness. Lydia was put into corsets, which she had to wear continually during the day, though she was not expected to sleep in them.

Her outerwear appears to have been very elaborate, if archaic. They clearly made something of a 'doll' of Lydia, dressing her in clothes that were many years out of date, and so fancy and precious as to limit her movements and opportunities for getting into mischief.

My mother recounted to me with pride that at this period of her life her dresses were hand-sewn by a fashionable Geneva couturier, the designs based on patterns dating back to the middle years of the last century. She never suggested that there was anything strange about the way she was treated. Obviously she could not have

219

been dressed in this manner without the approval of her mother; and no doubt the money of the rich aunts helped to pay the couturier's bills.

From photographs of her at eight or nine years old, her outfits often seem to have consisted of a close-fitting, square-cut jacket bodice with short, puffed sleeves and a basque standing out over a wide flounced skirt which was just above knee length. Hanging from under the skirt can be seen her lace-edged pantalettes. Cotton or silk stockings, high-heeled patent leather shoes and white six-buttoned kid gloves completed the ensemble.

Lydia quickly came to accept the restrictions of the clothing, as being dressed so prettily provoked such universal admiration in that feminine household; the maiden aunts and her mother would not have admired her nearly so much in the plain flannel shift and black cotton stockings which would have been more normal for a young girl in the 1940's.

Throughout her life, my mother never paid much attention to what was 'normal', and in psychological terms, no doubt the seeds of her later eccentricity were sown during this period of her childhood.

Following the ending of the war, Grandmother Rachel and Lydia moved back to Strasbourg in 1946. The following year, at the age of eleven, Lydia was sent to an exclusive girls' boarding school in Paris, where she was educated until she was eighteen. She proved to have considerable academic ability, and was accepted at the Sorbonne to study fine arts. She specialised in costume design and spent a year in England, splitting her time between the Courtauld Institute in London and the Bodleian Library in Oxford.

While staying in Oxford she was introduced to another French student, Pierre Quesnay, who was also from the Sorbonne, studying at Oxford on an exchange scheme. Pierre was several years older than my mother, working on a doctorate in chemistry. They found they had much in common and soon became romantically involved.

Pierre Quesnay and my mother were married in Paris in 1957, but they did not stay in France for long, as Pierre's work took him back to Oxford, where my mother was able to accompany him after completing her degree at the Sorbonne.

By this time, Pierre had finished his doctorate and been appointed as a temporary lecturer at Christ Church College, Oxford, though he still held permanent tenure at the Sorbonne. My mother told me that I was conceived one Sunday morning, to the ringing of Great Tom, the 7-ton bell housed in the gateway at Christ Church College.

I was born in Oxford in 1959, and thus have dual British and French citizenship. I was christened François, after a distant ancestor of my father's, François Quesnay, the noted 18th century economist.

Yes, I was born a *boy*. How I come now to be a *girl*, Françoise Quesnay, will become apparent as my story unfolds.

The first event which, looking back now, had a bearing on what later happened to me, was the death of my father, who was unfortunately blown up when some gases ignited in his laboratory, during a chemical experiment. There was a great fuss at the time, not least because the authorities at the Sorbonne insisted on mounting their own investigation, and sent over a prominent professor of chemistry, who had a public row with the vice-chancellor of Oxford University. The French professor published a damning report blaming my father's death on the university's inadequate health and safety procedures; the vice-chancellor countered this by claiming that my father's experiments had been unorthodox and he had some responsibility himself for what had happened.

Whatever the truth of the matter, I was left fatherless at the age of one, and my mother was without a husband. My mother was not, at least, short of money, as she inherited a considerable sum from Pierre's estate, which included property on the outskirts of Paris. Her own father, Gustave, was also becoming very wealthy by this time, having diversified from pâté de foie gras into general groceries; he founded a company that would become the huge *Trans-Marché* supermarket chain. Gustave became one of the leading figures in France's post-war economic re-construction.

Lydia could have gone anywhere in the world and lived a life of luxury and leisure; instead, sensing the excitement in the air as post-war austerity was beginning to give way to the 'Beat Generation' and the 'Swinging Sixties', she chose to divide her time between London and Paris, moving among the bohemian groups of Soho and the Left Bank.

No doubt in an effort to forget Pierre, she threw herself headlong into a succession of relationships with would-be artists, poets and jazz musicians, both male and female. It was during this period that she met Linda Blakely and Julia St. John-Smythe, who became long-term friends and supported her later educational initiatives.

After my father's death, Lydia had to vacate the rooms in Christ Church College and so rented a small white-washed cottage outside Oxford, where we both lived until my mother began her 'bohemian' phase. I was then left in the charge of a nanny - a plump, homely girl of twenty-two called Dorothy - while mother flitted between Paris and London for the next couple of years.

Finally she grew tired of this superficial and futile phase of her life, and decided that she needed to occupy her time more usefully. Never a woman to do things by halves, she determined to put herself through a teacher's training course at a college near Oxford.

Her final teaching practice was at a primary school amid car manufacturing plants and terraced council housing on the outskirts of Oxford; she was horrified by the poverty and cultural deprivation of the children's families and knew at once that though she felt pity for the children, she was too squeamish about head-lice and hygiene to be able to teach within the English state education system.

222

On leaving college at the end of the summer term, my mother therefore applied for a job at a girl's private preparatory school near Buxton, in Derbyshire. As she now had English teaching qualifications and a degree from the Sorbonne, she was somewhat over-qualified for the position. The fact that she could also speak fluent French and could offer this as a teaching subject meant that she was snapped up without hesitation by the school's headmistress, who couldn't believe her luck in acquiring such a prestigious new member of staff.

By this time I was nearly five years old, and my mother decided she would like to have me with her at the school, so that she could spend more time with me; feeling guilty, perhaps, that she had neglected her maternal duties during her gadding about years in London and Paris. She conceived of the idea of actually *enrolling* me at the school, commencing from September, when she would take up her appointment.

One obvious problem presented itself - I was a *boy*, and the preparatory school in question was a *girls'* school. My mother was undaunted by mere details such as this, always having considered my maleness as a sort of unfortunate disability.

On several occasions in the past she had taken a pleasure in dressing me in girl's clothes, bringing back fashionable little outfits from her excursions to Paris. Although only a toddler, I knew enough about what was normal for little boys and girls to wear to feel a sense of outrage at being forced to submit to parading about in some frilly concoction purchased by my mother. Nanny Dorothy - or *Dotty*, as I called her, put up no opposition to these sartorial affronts to my dignity; on the contrary, she positively whooped with delight and clapped her hands to see me in petticoats. For I was forced to be dressed completely as a girl on such occasions, in frilly knickers, a lace petticoat, a little flounced frock, white silk stockings, and girl's court shoes. My light brown hair - which was longish and curly - was brushed and coifed into a girl's style, and I was made to stay so dressed for the day. I was introduced as *Françoise* to any of mother's friends who called, and I can remember both Linda Blakely and Julia St. John-Smythe, mother's two best friends from London, visiting our little cottage outside Oxford on such occasions. They would coo and simper at me, examining the lace of my petticoats, admiring the way I was dressed, and referring to me as *she*, as if I were really a girl.

After securing the job at the girls' preparatory school, my mother came home to Oxford and the next morning we motored to Vidal Sassoon's hair salon in London, where the stylist was instructed to cut my hair in a 'Twiggy'-style; my hair had been allowed to grow into a 'Beatles' mop (as this was 1964), which was just the right length to be re-cut into the latest girls' bobbed style. Then we took a taxi to Biba's in Kensington High Street, where I was fitted out with a little mini-skirt and floral blouse, white patterned tights and a pair of lime-green girls' sandals. We went to fashionable boutiques on the King's Road, in Chelsea, and then to Carnaby Street and the West End, where mother spent a fortune buying the latest fashions for herself, and more skirts, blouses, dresses and girls' shoes for me.

Mother explained that she was proposing to spend the six-week summer holiday at the Quesnay's summer villa in Provence, a beautiful house overlooking the Rhône river near Arles, in which she had inherited a half-share after my father's death. Pierre's sister, Giselle, also had a half share in the villa, but we had the run of the place to ourselves until mid-August, when Giselle would be coming down from Paris with her two children.

'You will be *Françoise*, my *daughter*, while we are staying in Provence; is that clear?' she shouted to me over the noise of the wind and the roar made by the engine of her little red MG sports car, as we were driving back along the lanes to Oxford, from our London shopping trip.

'That's why I've bought you the girls' clothes. It will be good practice for you, as I've enrolled you as a girl at the school where I've been appointed as a teacher,

224

from September. There's no other way I can have you with me at the school; they wouldn't allow a boy on the premises, and anyhow I've told the headmistress that I have daughter.'

I was incredulous at my mother's news, and didn't see how it could possibly work, but what could I say? I was just five years old, with no father and no other relatives even in the country. My mother had complete control of our destinies, and the money and determination to do whatever she wanted.

The house in Provence proved to be an ancient edifice with a pantiled roof and thick stone walls which kept the interior of the house cool. Creepers and vines grew all over the white-washed walls. There was a paved terrace, on one side of which a spring of clear water issued from the mouth of a stone lion, and poured in a crystal stream to the surface of a wide shady pool, partly covered by water lilies. The spring carried on flowing all summer long, and I whiled away many hours lying beside the pool, dipping my fingers in the cool water and watching the water boatmen and pond skaters, and occasionally catching glimpses of several venerable carp floating ghost-like below the surface.

My mother insisted on keeping me in skirts; I generally wore white cotton frocks edged with lace, or print skirts with loose blouses decorated with smocking. I had a wide-brimmed straw hat to keep the fierce Provençal sun off my face. The two local staff at the villa, a housekeeper and her husband, who was the gardener, naturally assumed I was a girl, and my mother forbade me to play any rough games which might have thrown into question their assumption about my gender. The housekeeper, Madam Fleury, was a jovial woman in late middle-age with a nut-brown face and a network of laughter lines radiating from two twinkling brown eyes. She liked to sit on the terrace in the evenings under the shade of an ancient vine-tree and work at a local form of embroidery, making bags and purses which she would sell at the market in Arles. After watching for a couple of nights, my mother asked Madam Fleury if she would show me how to embroider; hoping, I think, that this would head off any incipient tendency on my part to rampage in boyish fashion round the garden, after we had dined.

I was thus being turned rapidly into the very model and pattern of a young girl, when, in mid-August, my aunt Giselle arrived with her two young children, who proved to be *boys* aged four and six.

'And who is this pretty young lady?' asked Aunt Giselle, when I entered the drawing room to be introduced, after their arrival.

'This is my daughter, Françoise,' replied Lydia.

Aunt Giselle looked puzzled.

'But I was sure I'd heard that you had a *boy*, Lydia?'

My mother smiled slyly.

'I did, but I've got no time for boys - horrid things! I swapped him for *Françoise*, as you see before you. Or to be more accurate, I'm changing *François* into *Françoise*, so that *she* can accompany to me to my new school in September.

Aunt Giselle looked dumbfounded. She nodded towards me and said:

'You mean this is your *son* - this is *François?*'

'Yes, *was* Francois; now I call *her Françoise.*'

'But you can't do things like that! It's not right!' Aunt Giselle was shaking her head in disbelief.

'Why can't I? Who's to stop me? I never wanted a son anyway. Françoise is happy enough - ask her.'

I could feel my face getting redder and redder, and my eyes starting to prickle, as both Aunt Giselle and my mother looked towards me. I shrugged, not knowing what to say. My mother took this as confirmation for her point of view.

'There you are, he - *she* - doesn't mind.'

'Well - I'm amazed. It's certainly not normal.'

No more was said on the matter, as at that moment my two young cousins crashed into the room, and chased each other around the furniture until one of them jumped on a

Louis XV rococo chaise-longue and the other attempted to get him off by lifting up one of the delicate ormolu legs.

'My God, that chaise-longue is priceless!' screamed my mother, 'make them stop!'

'Get off there at once!' shouted Aunt Giselle, cuffing the larger boy hard around the back of the head and dragging the smaller boy to his feet. 'Now stand still and say hello to your Aunt Lydia and your cousin - er - *Françoise*.

The two little boys stood still for just long enough to mumble 'Hello', then turned tail and chased each other out of the room.

'They can be rather a handful,' said Aunt Giselle apologetically; 'sometimes I just don't know what to do with them.'

'Well I have an idea which I recall my old nanny, Fräu Mürz, saying always works with rough, disobedient boys. I'm sure we could discipline your two boys in no time, if you would agree to it; it's a little unorthodox, but very effective, I understand.'

'Go on.'

'I think it would be best if we discuss it in private. Françoise, go and play with your cousins while I talk to your aunt.' And so I was dismissed, but not caring to play with my cousins, who I didn't think would have much time for me in my current girlish role, I stayed behind the door and listened:

'What I have in mind,' began my mother, is *corset-training*. They went in for it a good deal in the last century. I know a corset maker in Paris who could make up the corsets, if we gave her a rough idea of the sizes. Then we would need 'Fauntleroy' velvet suits with lace collars - we could get those run up in Paris, as well. Your boys would soon find their freedom for rampaging round much curtailed if we dressed them like that.'

'Oh no, I wouldn't hear of it,' replied Aunt Giselle. But two days later, after the boys had broken a Louis XV clock and smashed a leg off a Second Empire coffee table, my mother was despatched to Paris for a couple of days to buy the requisite clothing. Meanwhile I was left to the tender mercies of my unreformed cousins Claude and Jamie, who quickly made it clear that they didn't want to play with a soppy girl (for so they assumed me to be.) However, within two weeks the tables were turned, and the Louis XV furniture was no longer at risk from their boyish predations, which had been brought rapidly and completely to an end.

After my mother's return from Paris, the boys were soon put into the corsets, which were laced fairly tightly from the outset. Of course they resisted at first and tried to run away, but my mother and Giselle worked together, first catching Claude, and holding him firmly while the corset was put on and laced up, then helping him into the high-waisted, tight-fitting, royal blue velvet coat of the Fauntleroy suit, with its wide frilled collar; and finally compelling him, after a further struggle, to put on the velvet knickerbockers, silk stockings and black leather court shoes with big silver buckles. The ensemble was completed with a wide sash of scarlet ribbon, tide in a bow around the waist. Claude was thoroughly disgusted with his appearance and exclaimed tearfully:

'But I look like a sissy.'

'Nonsense' replied Lydia, 'and if we have any more complaints we'll put you into a skirt like the one your cousin Françoise is wearing, and then you *will* look like a sissy. You don't see Françoise complaining, do you?'

'But she is a *girl*, so she doesn't mind,' said Claude.

My mother looked meaningfully at Aunt Giselle, and began to say something; but Aunt Giselle, glancing at me and seeing my face reddening with embarrassment, shook her head at Lydia to silence her.

'Now let's find Jamie,' suggested Lydia.

Jamie, the older brother, had disappeared from the house immediately on seeing what had befallen his brother, and was eventually located hiding amid the abundant sub-tropical foliage at the bottom of the garden. Jamie had to be dragged back to the house, and put up more of a fight than his brother; finally, however, the determined efforts of my mother and Aunt Giselle prevailed, and he too was laced into his corset and compelled to put on the Fauntleroy suit.

The boys were very quiet and subdued when they appeared at dinner that night in their velvet suits; my mother and Aunt Giselle exchanged meaningful glances, obviously convinced that the new discipline regime had wrought the change in the boys which they desired. After a few days, however, it was clear that the women had merely won a battle, but not the war; the boys' initial sense of shame at their sissified clothes had worn off, and they were becoming as exuberant and bumptious as they were before.

'I fear we may need to take further steps with regard to disciplining Claude and Jamie, if we are to curtail their rough play once and for all and safeguard the Louis XV furniture,' announced my mother over her croissants one morning. We were all listening to the muffled thumps and shrieks coming from the bedroom above, as Claude and Jamie were engaged in their customary early morning trampoline practice on the beds. Looking up at the crystal chandelier shaking and tinkling, Aunt Giselle replied balefully:

'By all means take what ever steps you think necessary, Lydia.'

My mother decided that another shopping trip was in order, but this time it would not be necessary to go as far as Paris:

'We should be able to get what we need in Arles,' she announced; 'I think I'll take Françoise with me. Can I borrow your Mercedes, Giselle?'

'Put on your straw hat, dear,' said my mother; 'we don't want your peaches and cream complexion being ruined by the sun; it burns quickly, this time of year, in Provence.' We were driving along in my aunt's white Mercedes convertible; the roof was folded back so that we could smell the soft, sweet fragrances of the flowers in the hedgerows. In the fields beyond were the rows of vines, their gnarled trunks holding up the ripening fruit that would soon be harvested to make the rough red wine of the region.

I reluctantly placed the straw hat over my bob of brown hair, securing the elastic under my chin so that the hat wouldn't blow off. The warm wind blew in our faces as we hit the occasional rut in the country road, which even the refined suspension of the Mercedes could not disguise. I trailed my arm out of the side of the car, feeling the fronds and leaves of the luxuriant vegetation whipping softly against my outstretched hand. Soon it would be uncomfortably hot under the Provençal midday sun; I actually felt glad to be wearing a cool print dress and sandals, my shoulders and arms bare and my legs unconfined by trousers. Being a girl has *some* advantages, I thought.

We parked in a square near the centre of Arles, and made our way to a department store which had a floor given over entirely to ladies' and girls' fashions.

My mother began by choosing a selection of frilly, silk and satin underwear; occasionally she would hold up a little lace vest or petticoat, and try it against me for size.

'I'm glad I brought you,' she said, 'as I can get a good idea of the sizes to buy for Claude and Jamie. What fits you would be fine for Claude, and we perhaps need just one size bigger for Jamie.'

When she had chosen enough underwear, my mother went to the rails where the girls' dresses, skirts and blouses were hanging, and picked out a number of flouncy, frilled and be-ribboned garments. One or two of these she insisted I tried on: 'Just to see how they hang,' she explained.

My mother had deposited all the girls' clothes she had chosen on one of the counters, and the shop assistant was adding up the bill, when suddenly I heard a little shriek of delight issue from my mother's lips; looking up into her face, I saw that she was staring across the shop to where three little child-sized mannequins were standing on a raised platform, wearing the most elaborate, diaphanous creations of silk and lace.

'Oh yes,' said the shop assistant, glancing up and noticing where my mother was looking, 'they're delightful, aren't they? They are costumes from the outdoor ballet which was put on at the amphitheatre, during last year's Summer Festival. They were worn by the little five year old girls who were in the chorus. Would you like to have a closer look at them? The workmanship is outstanding.'

'Yes, I'd like that,' replied my mother.

The shop assistant called to one of her colleagues: 'Marie, can you finish ringing these up for me?' I'm going to show Madame the ballet costumes.' A young blonde girl took over the totalling and packing of my mother's purchases, while the other shop assistant, a plump middle-aged woman, took us over to see the ballet dresses.

'This one is in cream shot-silk,' said the shop assistant; 'as you can see, the bodice is beautifully decorated with lace and flowers, and the petticoats of the skirt are made of tulle broché and pink gauze silk, covered with more fine lace, which is locally produced. White silk tights and white satin slippers complete the outfit.'

My mother gazed rapturously at the luxurious garment. 'And this one?' she asked.

'Oh this one has even more petticoats,' said the shop assistant, caressing the layers of apricot gauze silk lovingly, 'isn't it adorable?'

My mother nodded. 'Are they for sale?' she asked.

'Well, they're really for display purposes only,' replied the shop assistant, 'but I could go and ask the manager of our department, and see what she thinks. Would you like me to do that?'

My mother nodded again. The plump shop assistant went off, and returned shortly with a smartly dressed young woman. The young woman gave my mother a delicate little handshake of introduction, and said, 'Good morning madam. I am Mademoiselle Dupont, the

231

daughter of the proprietor. I understand you are interested in buying the ballet costumes?'

'Yes, I think they will do very well for my daughter and her young cousins.'

M'selle Dupont smiled down at me and then looked at my mother and said, 'We could sell them to you, Madam, but they will be very expensive.'

'The price is of no concern,' replied my mother, her voice carrying a slight edge of indignation.

M'selle Dupont smiled understandingly and named a figure for just one of the ballet dresses. Even taking account of the fact that it was in French Francs, it sounded astronomical to me.

'I'll take them.'

'All three?'

'Yes please; just wrap them up with my other things.' Mother indicated with a nod of the head towards the counter where the blonde girl was waiting patiently behind a large pile of parcels, wrapped in floral paper.

We got back to the villa just in time for lunch. Mother sat at one end of the long dining room table, Aunt Giselle at the other end; Claude and Jamie sat half way down the table, opposite each other across the expanse of the white table cloth, giggling and making silly noises. I was sitting next to Jamie, trying my best to ignore their antics, when suddenly I felt a hard kick on my shin.

'Ouch! That hurt!' I shrieked.

Mother looked up from her soup and asked: 'What's going on, Françoise?'

'Someone just kicked me,' I said.

'That'll be one of my little horrors,' commented Aunt Giselle. Claude and Jamie were still giggling, and were now exchanging a flurry of kicks under the table. Claude had half disappeared under the tablecloth in his efforts to kick Jamie's shins. I edged away from Jamie, towards the end where my mother was sitting.

'Stop it at once!' screeched Aunt Giselle, in her ineffective, high-pitched wail.

The boys took no notice.

I watched my mother to see what she would do next. Her knuckles were white as she slowly placed her soupspoon down beside her soup bowl and looked menacingly towards the boys.

'Well boys,' she said, in a very controlled voice, her lips drawn back and her eyes boring into them, in their Fauntleroy suits, 'you have succeeded in ruining my lunch. I shall probably suffer with indigestion all afternoon, now. I think the time has come for me to show you what we do with little boys who don't know how to behave.'

She got up from the table, walked round to where Jamie was sitting, and slowly indicated with a curl of her finger that he show get down and follow. She held his hand, squeezing his fingers hard enough to produce a little yelp from his lips, and then went round to the other side of the table and collected Claude in the same way.

My mother exited rapidly from the dining room, pulling the boys behind her; a moment later we heard the sound of their feet scuffling on the steps of the broad oak staircase beyond. The maid brought the main course and Aunt Giselle and I continued with our meal, every now and then hearing a muffled bump or squeal from upstairs.

We had had our coffee and gone through to the drawing room, when my mother finally reappeared. Her face was flushed and she looked hot and slightly dishevelled, but with an expression of triumph she announced:

'May I present to you the M'selles Claudia and Jeannette...?' And in walked Claude, looking very embarrassed and slightly tearful in the ballet dress of cream shot-silk, with petticoats of tulle broché and pink gauze, complete with white tights and white satin slippers. When Jamie did not follow, my mother went out of the room again, and we heard Jamie begging her from behind the door: 'No, please Aunt Lydia, don't make me go in dressed like this....' The next moment Jamie appeared at the entrance of the door, wearing the dress

233

with apricot gauze petticoats, and my mother gave him a little shove into the room, and said with obvious glee:

'And this young lady is M'selle Jeannette. She is a little reluctant to show you her lovely dress at present, but I'm sure she will feel at ease when you tell her how pretty she looks.'

Aunt Giselle clapped her hands with joy and exclaimed:

'Oh you look lovely - and so does your - *sister*. How on earth did you manage it, Lydia?'

'Brute force and determination,' replied my mother. 'I had to pull in the lacing in their corsets, which of course they are still wearing underneath, as the bodices of the dresses are very tight-fitting. They will soon get used to the tighter lacing - and I think you'll agree it does wonders for their figures. I bought some other outfits for them as well, and I suggest we keep them in skirts for the rest of the holiday.'

'Do you really think that will be necessary?' asked Aunt Giselle.

'I'm sure of it,' replied Lydia. 'This is your last chance to discipline your boys and get them properly under control. With corset training and petticoat punishment, we might yet make something of them. If you don't stand firm now, all will be lost, and you will have too unruly louts on your hands for ever more.'

'I suppose you are right,' said Giselle.

'Of course I am.' Lydia fixed the boys with her sternest gaze and said to them: 'You will address each other henceforth by your new names of Claudia and Jeannette. If I hear you calling yourselves by any other name, there will be more punishment. I am quite prepared to cut a switch of birch from the tree in the garden and use it on your bottoms. You will conduct yourselves at all times like young ladies, and we will have no more rough play, fighting, running about or rudeness. Is that clear?'

The boys - or perhaps I should now say *girls* - nodded.

'I'm still not quite satisfied with their appearances,' continued Lydia. 'I think it's the short hair - they look rather ridiculous, in such pretty frocks, with those boyish crops.'

'I think I might be able to do something about that,' replied Giselle. 'Pierre and I used to come with our parents to spend our Christmas holidays here, when we were children. It became a tradition for us to perform some amateur dramatics for our parents and their friends. Over the years, we got together a collection of costumes, and some other props - including wigs, if I remember correctly. They're probably still here - somewhere in the attic or in one of the spare rooms. I'll have a hunt round and see what I can find.'

Giselle appeared again in the drawing room just before teatime, her clothes besmirched with dust and cobwebs, waving several ladies' wigs triumphantly in the hair. After tea, Lydia helped Giselle wash the wigs, and they were hung out to dry in the warm, scented night air.

Just before bedtime, Lydia produced two little lacy nightdresses in pink satin, which the boys were ordered to put on after their baths. They initially demurred, but seeing that they had no choice, and recognizing my mother by this time as something akin to an irresistible force of nature, they reluctantly did as they were told, and reappeared downstairs, ready for their bedtime chocolate drink, wearing the nightdresses.

The following morning, the boys were again forced to put on the ballet dresses, and then my mother and Aunt Giselle made them sit still while they tried the wigs on the boys' heads. Of course they were rather too large for them and looked ridiculous, so Aunt Giselle called one of the maids, who had worked previously at a ladies' hairdressing salon in Arles. She set to with scissors and comb, and had soon cut and styled two of the wigs so that they fitted the boys. Claude's wig was light brown, with a fringe, and curled down over the shoulders of his satin ballet dress. Jamie's wig was blonde, and Julie had tied it back in a ponytail with a broad pink ribbon that complimented his apricot dress.

'Well done Julie,' said Lydia to the maid; 'now we really do have two pretty young mademoiselles, ready to play dolls with their young cousin. Could you look out some dolls and other girls' playthings from the attic, do you think?'

'Yes Madame,' replied Julie.

'And Julie,' continued my mother, 'please tell the cook and gardener that from now on, for the rest of their stay, these two are to be treated as girls. They are to be addressed as Claudia and Jeannette, and I shall want to know about it at once if you catch either of them in rough play or any unladylike pursuits.'

'I will pass on what you say, Madame.' Julie stared for a moment at *Claudia* and *Jeannette*, put her hand over her mouth to stop herself from giggling, and hurried out of the room.

My mother looked in my direction and said, 'The third ballet dress was for you, Françoise. I've laid it out on your bed for you. Go and put it on, there's a good girl, and then we shall have *three* lovely little ballerinas to look at.'

I went to my room and found a white satin ballet dress on the bed. The bodice was decorated with pink and blue flowers, fine lace, and tiny glass jewels; the skirt had numerous petticoats of pink gauze, and there were white silk tights, frilled panties and dainty white satin ballet slippers to complete the ensemble. I took off my sandals, print dress and knee socks, and stood in my lace knickers, looking at the elaborate confection of satin, and gauze. I sighed, knowing I had but little choice, and carefully dressed myself in the ballet outfit. I went downstairs and my mother clapped her hands together in appreciation, on seeing me.

'Now we have our three little maids, ready for their dolls' tea party,' she exclaimed. She beckoned me over and tied my hair up in a pink ribbon, adding: 'How fine it is for you all to be *girls* together; so much nicer than horrid boys.'

Julie came in with an armful of dolls, which she had

found upstairs somewhere, and put them down on the hearth rug. Then she went out and returned a moment later, with some little porcelain cups and saucers. Giselle, who was sitting in a high-backed armchair reading a magazine, looked up and said:

'Be careful with those. They are very old, and were made in Dresden; they once belonged to your grandmother, Maria Quesnay. She probably played with them in this very room, when she was a girl.'

Claudia and Jeannette had been standing by the high mahogany bookcase, feigning to be interested in the rows of old leather-bound folios. They looked round with obvious distaste at the pile of old dolls and china tea set, uncertain what to do, and reluctant to move away from the safety of the bookcase.

'Come along girls,' said Aunt Giselle, 'I'll show you what to do.'

Aunt Giselle came over to the rug and kneeled down beside the dolls. She picked up a big doll with a white china face and poke bonnet, dressed in a lace smock and apron in the style of the last century.

'This is Bella, isn't she beautiful? She wants her tea.' Giselle fetched an oak footstool and a small Second Empire occasional table, and proceeded to lay out the porcelain cups and saucers. The boys - or rather *girls*, I should say, still hung back, although they were watching closely. At length, Jeannette came over and sat down on the rug, to be joined shortly afterwards by Claudia and I. Gradually, Giselle involved us in the play, introducing each doll by name in turn, talking to her and lifting a teacup to her lips.

'Sophie hasn't had a cup of tea yet,' said Aunt Giselle, eyeing a small black-haired doll. Claudia picked up the doll and gave her to Giselle; Jeannette passed across a teacup. The play went on for perhaps twenty minutes, until we were all joining in, handling the dolls, and giving them their tea. Then Giselle said: 'It's time for their nap now.' She took Bella and cradled her in her arms, rocking her slowly back and forth. Some of the dolls are restless,

237

I think,' she explained; 'help me get them off to sleep, girls, or they will be fractious in the morning.'

And - the miracle was - we *did* sit there with Aunt Giselle and rock the dolls to sleep. And I think we all secretly enjoyed playing with the dolls, gentle and feminine as it was.

I believe this was the turning point - at least for Claudia and Jeannette. My destiny to be female had already been decided some time before. After the dolls tea party, Claudia and Jeannette seemed to accept their fate and more or less adjusted to their new role, for the rest of the holiday at least. Aunt Giselle encouraged the three of us to take an interest in other forms of feminine pastime - she took us on country walks, taught us the names of the fragrant flowers and herbs of Provence, and showed us how to dry and preserve them. In the evenings, we would sit on the paved terrace, listening to the water from the spring tinkling and gurgling down to the lily pool where the carp glided silently, and watching the sunsets over the Rhône valley, the surface of the great river turned a myriad of spectacular colours - sometimes pinks and purples, sometimes oranges and reds - in contrast to its sluggish brown colour during the day. And while there was still sufficient light, before the sun went down below the ridge of distant hills, Aunt Giselle would show us different sewing stitches or teach us embroidery on old-fashioned frames.

On more than one occasion, at such times, I recall her looking at the three of us, then across at my mother and saying wistfully: 'If only they had been *girls* - just think what a difference it would have made. Life would be like this all the time. But I know it must end....'

To which my mother would reply, 'Not necessarily,' or 'we shall see....'

There were one or two episodes when Claudia and Jeannette forgot their new role, and began to return to their old ways, racing about the garden or up and down the stairs, but my mother soon put an end to this. She realised that they were able to run about far too freely in the ballet slippers, and so ordered some special footwear for them from Paris. This consisted of a couple of pairs each of laced and buttoned girls' boots, all of the tightest fit and with high heels. As they couldn't run - or even walk - very far in the boots, this curtailed any recidivist tendencies to lapse into their former boisterous behaviour. As a final stratagem, to put the cherry on the cake, as it were, she also ordered several pairs of white kid gloves. She insisted that they wore a pair of them during the day and forbade them to get the gloves dirty, on pain of having their corsets laced tighter.

The combination of my mother's strict discipline and Aunt Giselle's gentle coaching in all things feminine effected a marvellous change in the two children, so that after a month of the new regime, anyone visiting the villa would have taken them for *real girls*, without a second look. They were happy to play quietly with the dolls and with a beautifully crafted dolls' house which had been discovered in the attic; they sewed and embroidered, made artistic arrangements of dried and fresh flowers, and collected herbs for Cook from the hedgerows. Where formerly, as boys, they had generally met with disapproval from their mother and scolding from their Aunt Lydia, now they positively glowed in their mother's newfound interest in them and Aunt Lydia's favourable opinion.

As it drew nearer to the end of the holiday, Claudia and Jeannette were permitted to leave off the kid gloves in the mornings and were allowed to wear black leather court shoes - the ones which had come with the Fauntleroy suits - instead of the tight high-heeled boots. The court shoes had lower, square heels, were more comfortable, and looked like slightly more normal footwear for girls of their age. By this time they seemed quite to enjoy wearing the ballet dresses, and were also wearing some of the other dresses, skirts and blouses which my mother had bought at the department store in Arles.

We even went out around the town and for trips in the surrounding countryside - two young mothers and their three charming daughters. No one gave us a second glance, unless it was to look in admiration at the white Mercedes or at such a well-dressed group of young females.

We left the villa in Provence during the first week of September, and made our way by train and ferry back to England, and then north to the preparatory school in Derbyshire where my mother was to take up her first teaching appointment.

St. Saviour's School for Girls was housed in a three-storey eighteenth century mansion situated one and a half miles outside Buxton, amid the limestone hills and crags of the White Peak. The girls' dormitories were on the top floor of the main building, while the quarters for most of the staff who lived on-site were in the west wing, a Victorian addition to the house. The headmistress, Miss Leticia Simms, was a thin-faced and very upright lady in her early fifties who habitually wore a tweed twin-set and pearls under her black academic gown. We were sitting in her study, shortly after arriving from the railway station by taxi, the driver having deposited our trunks and other luggage temporarily in the hall. Miss Simms peered at me over her gold-framed spectacles and suggested that perhaps I might like to stay in one of the dormitories with the other borders, while my mother could install herself in one of the staff rooms in the west wing, if this would suit. My mother, anticipating the problems I might experience in keeping secret my true gender if I was sleeping in a dormitory, intimated that this would *not* suit, and that she would prefer for us not to be split up.

'Well, as you are a married woman with a family, perhaps the rooms in the west wing, which are mainly used by members of staff who are single, are not really suitable. I had only thought that perhaps Françoise might prefer to be with the other girls, so as not feel herself different.'

If only she knew *how* different I was from the other

240

girls, I thought.

'No, we would prefer to stay together, if possible,' answered my mother.

Miss Simms stood up and walked over to the tall Georgian window, which looked out on a broad sweep of lawn. A gravel driveway lined with ancient oaks whose leaves were turning orange and brown in the thin Autumn sunshine curved down to a pair of imposing wrought-iron gates which still bore the heraldic crest of the original owners of the old house.

'There is the gatekeeper's cottage,' said Miss Simms, indicating with a nod of her head a squat building of yellow stone which stood just to the right of the gates; 'I suppose you could have that, although it hasn't been inhabited for several months, since old Mrs Turvey, the wife of the last gatekeeper, passed on. It was a requirement of the lease that we had to let her live out her last days there, after we took over the house from the previous owners. It's probably a bit damp and dusty, but we could get Mr. Burridge, our caretaker, to help you clean it out. You're welcome to have a look at it, anyhow.'

My mother decided that the lodge would suit us very well, and after a thorough cleaning and airing, we moved in our luggage and began to unpack. We had a few days before the start of term, in which we busied ourselves settling into the lodge, and exploring the neighbourhood. My mother took me into Buxton to purchase the uniform required for pupils at St. Saviour's. This consisted of a white blouse, grey pleated skirt, grey blazer and straw boater. The blazer bore the badge of St. Saviour's on its breast pocket, as did the navy tie which was to be worn with the blouse. My mother bought me two of the blazers; several of the pleated skirts and blouses; and half a dozen pairs of navy-blue knickers which were required to be worn underneath the skirt.

'She'll also need a couple of these,' said the woman in the draper's, producing two grey cotton gymslips from a box behind the counter; 'they wear them for P.E. at St.

Saviour's.'

'No,' replied my mother, explaining to the shopkeeper that I wouldn't need the gymslips as I wouldn't be able to do P.E., due to a 'health problem.'

'What a shame,' said the shop-woman, looking down at me with sympathy, 'is it something that they can cure?'

'Yes, I believe there is a cure, and then she'll be like any other normal girl - but it'll take time.'

My mother gave me a strange look, which together with her words, filled me with a sense of foreboding.

My mother also went to Nottingham before the start of term, to visit the shop of a specialist corsetière, whom she commissioned to make a garment in my size to her own particular design, resembling a pair of panties, but with a wide front section and gusset made of a very strong, slightly elasticated fabric; she explained to the corsetière that I was suffering from a rare form of infantile inguinal hernia which could not be operated on until I was older, and that I needed extra support in the crotch area to alleviate my discomfort. The same excuse was given to Miss Simms, when my mother requested that I should be excused from P.E. and games.

The special panties were delivered from the corsetière's a couple of days later, and my mother told me to undress so that I could try them on.

'Push that nasty little worm out of the way between your legs,' she instructed, as she helped me pull up the panties. The front section and gusset were very tight-fitting and flattened my 'little worm' so firmly back between my legs that there was no sign of it at all, once I had pulled the panties fully on. My mother surveyed the gently curving mound of my crotch with evident delight and announced: 'My goodness, you really do look exactly like a girl there, now. You must wear it under your knickers at all times, from now on. I will have several pairs made up, now that we can see that it's just what you need. The corsetière refers to it as a *pantie-corselette*, but I believe it's what is known as a *cache-sexe*, when worn for the purpose for which you are wearing it. As long as you remember to do so, I don't think there's any danger of anyone discovering your little secret. I still think, however, that it would be best for you not to do P.E. and games, for the time being. Now let's see what you look like in your school uniform.'

My mother handed me a pair of the navy-blue knickers which I pulled on over the panty garment, then helped me into the pleated grey skirt and white blouse, and showed me how to do the knot of the tie. I practiced tying the knot several times, until I could do it on my own. Mother likewise showed me how to tie the bows on my shoes, which were a pair of strong black leather girl's lace-ups. Then she plonked the straw boater on my head, and stepped back to survey the finished effect.

'Umm. Not bad, but your hair's sticking out from under your hat like a hay-stack,' she said. She removed the boater and put a comb through my hair, saying, 'Your bob-cut has grown longer during the holidays; I think we need something to hold it back.' She went to the dressing table drawer and found a couple of hair slides and a pink plastic alice-band. She first tried pinning back the sides of my unruly mop with the slides, but shook her head in dissatisfaction and removed them. She then took the alice-band and eased it into my scalp, so that it held my hair back from my forehead and temples. 'Yes, that looks tidier. Now let's try the hat again.' She put the boater back on my head, arranging the elastic under my chin. 'Oh yes, what a perfect peach you look! So demure and pretty!'

Each year, before the beginning of the Autumn term, my mother would order from the Nottingham corsetière several new pairs of the pantie-corselettes, in a slightly larger size. Eventually, of course, I would have no further need of such a garment...

When term started, my mother and I both settled into the life of the school fairly easily. My mother seemed to have a natural flair for teaching, and found it easy to capture the interest of the girls, communicating her enthusiasm for whatever she taught by the force and liveliness of her personality. She soon became rather popular with the girls, although her erudition and cultured outlook did not endear her to one of two of the older members of staff, whose provincialism and lack of imagination she found stultifying. As the daughter of one of the school mistresses, I felt at first somewhat apart from the other girls, particularly from the borders, who viewed me with suspicion and envy, because I slept at the lodge rather than in the dormitory. However, I soon made friends with several of the day girls, and found that as my mother's popularity grew, most people, at least were not predisposed to dislike me.

We spent five happy years at St. Saviour's, during which time no one had the slightest inkling of my true sex. After the first few weeks, my mother decided that it would be safe even for me to do P.E. and games with the other girls, as the *cache-sexe* I always wore under my knickers concealed so effectively my 'little worm'. In my gymslip and knickers, I looked no different from the other girls, and there was no reason for me to remove my knickers while we were getting changed. Naturally on bath nights I bathed at the lodge, rather than in the bathroom at the end of the dormitory corridor, as this was the most logical thing to do.

When I was eleven years old and in my final year at St. Saviour's Preparatory School, my mother began to discuss with me how my education as a girl could be continued. She took it for granted that I would wish to continue in my current feminine gender role, and did not even ask me for my opinion on the matter. I would not in any case have demurred, as by this time I could scarcely remember my previous life as a boy, and would not have chosen to return to it. Living as a girl had become quite natural to me; I enjoyed having my hair long, wearing skirts and dresses, doing embroidery and ballet lessons, and pursuing other feminine pastimes. I enjoyed being pampered and cooed over and praised by my mother's London friends, who sometimes came up to stay with us in the holidays. Most of them were in on the secret of my gender, and were delighted to see me so girlish, pert and pretty.

Clearly, there were problems ahead, however. I could not go on to any of the local secondary schools, whether privately managed or state-run, as the effects of puberty would start to present insurmountable difficulties. After thus considering and rejecting the usual options for a girl of my age, my mother at length hit on the idea of starting *her own* school. She still had a considerable fortune from my father's estate, which could be used to purchase a suitable property; moreover, her old London friends, Linda Blakely and Julia St. John-Smythe, were prepared to invest some of their own money in the venture, and actively encouraged her to start up on her own.

Perhaps, in the early stages, my mother's plan to set up her own school was not just to provide for my continuing education, but also because she wanted the freedom it would give her to develop her own educational ideas - she had grown frustrated at St. Saviour's, with the stick-in-the-mud attitudes of most of the staff, whom she regarded as pedagogical dinosaurs. She had tried to introduce a breath of fresh air to her teaching, but could only go so far. She genuinely saw herself, I believe, as a sort of 'Miss Jean Brodie' figure, though without that lady's eccentricities.

That my mother had eccentricities of her own, her friends and acquaintances never doubted, though she was as blind to them herself as had been the unfortunate Miss Brodie. And my mother's quirks or 'kinks' led just as inevitably to her own downfall.

The first task was to find a suitable property for conversion into a private girls' secondary school. By chance, a large late-Victorian house with extensive grounds had just come onto the market that autumn of 1970 near the village of Ashton Cross, about five miles from the north Derbyshire town of Chesterfield and four miles from Matlock, on the edge the Peak District. The house had been built by a wealthy local mill-owner – Septimus Smedley - who had named the house Holloway Hall, after the old green track or 'hollow way' dating back to prehistoric times, which ran onto the moors from behind the hall.

On the top of the hill behind was a huge grit-stone slab, perhaps twelve feet across and rising to a height of about twenty-seven feet, on which had once been erected a Druidic temple or 'Fabrick', giving its name to the hill – 'Fabrick Hill'. On this alter of the ancient Celtic people who had inhabited the area it was rumoured human sacrifices had been made. Some of the locals said that the great stone was haunted by the ghosts of the sacrificial victims, and their screams could still be heard on winter evenings when the wind howled from the north.

'Poppy-cock!', announced my mother, Lydia Quesnay, on hearing the tale for the first time from the curate of the local church. 'I don't believe in such stuff and nonsense, and neither shall my girls.'

The curate, the Reverend Hodges, smiled weakly at Lydia, shrugged his shoulders, and said: 'The estate agent in Matlock will be relieved that you take no notice of such yarns. So you think you might buy it?' The Reverend Hodges had been out for a stroll on the lane that meandered beside the grounds of Holloway Hall, and had introduced himself to the striking statuesque woman and the young girl with unruly brown hair whom he met walking around the outside of the grounds.

'Holloway Hall will do very nicely for my new school.' My mother was nothing if not a woman of decision.

That afternoon a deposit was placed with the estate agents Bodkin, Bottomley and Pratt in their offices in the High Street in Matlock, and Lydia and I drove home to the Lodge at St. Saviours.

'There is no time to lose,' if we are to renovate the

246

building, recruit staff and get our first boarders by next autumn, said my mother, as we drove back towards Buxton in her venerable little red MG sports car. 'We have just under a year to complete everything.'

There was a cold bite to the air outside, where the sun was shining brightly, illuminating the rich browns and reds of the trees – it was one of those crisp, clear autumn days with wisps of mist just curling around the summits of the hills.

My mother decided to explain her plans to the headmistress of St. Saviours, Miss Leticia Simms, if possible to enlist her advice and support. Miss Simms, a horse-faced, woman of upright bearing now nearing retirement, made a useful suggestion on hearing that the name of the property to be converted into the new school was Holloway Hall:

'My dear Lydia, you can't possibly call your new venture 'Holloway School for Girls!'

'Why not,' replied my mother.

'The women's prison dear – Holloway – doesn't have quite the right associations?'

'So what shall we call it?'

Leticia Simms stared out of her study window at the steeple of a church in the distance. 'Something ecclesiastical always impresses. What is the name of the local church in the village of Ashton Cross – that's near isn't it?'

'Let me see if I can remember,' said my mother, 'we only have a brief look round the church - All Saints, I think.'

'So you could call it "All Saints Academy for Girls?'

'Maybe, but I think we should name it after a female saint.'

Miss Simms stood up and removed a book from the book shelf behind her desk.

'This lists female saints. Let me see – how about this one? Saint Hildegard. Apparently she was an author, musician, counsellor, cosmologist, artist, healer,

247

dramatist, linguist, naturalist, philosopher, poet, political consultant, prophet, visionary, and composer of music. She wrote theological, naturalistic, botanical, medicinal, and dietary texts; also letters, liturgical songs, poems, and the first surviving morality play, while supervising brilliant miniature illuminations. Seems like quite a woman.'

'Won't people think we belong to that order – that we're a Catholic school?'

'Mmmn. Possibly. If you don't claim to be an Catholic school - possibly not. I don't see how there can be a copyright on the name of a saint who lived in the 12th century in Germany.'

'Yes, I like that – Saint Hildegard's. I think I'll make the full name of the school "Saint Hildegard's High School for Girls". It has a certain ring, don't you think?' asked Lydia.

Miss Simms nodded in agreement.

" 'Saint Hildegard's High School for Girls, Ashton Cross" – I like it.'

And so it was decided. Work on converting the old buildings of Holloway Hall to "Saint Hildegard's High School for Girls" was begun before Christmas of that year, supervised by my mother's old London friends, Linda Blakely and Julia St. John-Smythe, who were investing money in the new educational project, and as women of independent means, had plenty of free time. Linda and Julia moved up into "Blossom Cottage", a small property in the grounds of Holloway Hall, to be on the spot, to deal with the everyday problems and queries regarding the renovations. Architects from Sheffield were contracted to produce designs for the conversion work, and a local builder from Chesterfield – John Furness – a round-faced man in his mid-forties with huge hands – was employed as clerk of works and supervisor of the teams of plasterers, joiners, plumbers and electricians who were brought in to do the practical work.

One late afternoon in early spring, my mother and I were up at Blossom Cottage having tea with Linda and

248

Julia. There had been a light dusting of snow the night before, which had melted that morning, leaving the ground glistening with moisture. The snowdrops were already out and the shoots of bluebells were starting to peep through the dead leaves and undergrowth in the woodlands around Holloway Hall. I was peering out the window at the darkening sky, in a sort of reverie, having stuffed myself with homemade scones and jam, when the conversation between the adults turned to the business of staffing the new school, and finding pupils.

"You need to think about advertising right now," said Julia, "if you want someone with experience who is already employed in a teaching job. They'll have to give a term's notice, which would mean giving notice at the end of this term, and working the summer term so that they are free to begin next autumn.'

'We could advertise in the "Times Educational Supplement" and in "The Guardian,"' pointed out Linda.

'Yes,' said my mother, 'but we want to get people of the right - er - background. . Why don't we try an advert in "The Lady", and perhaps "Derbyshire Life"?'

'And what about obtaining our first pupils? How on earth do we do that?' asked Julia, as she added a dash of milk to the Earl Grey tea in her china teacup. Julia St. John-Smythe was a tall, slender, blonde woman of aristocratic bearing. Her female companion Linda Blakely (in fact, her lesbian partner, as I would later come to understand), provided an almost comical contrast, as Linda was a dumpy and rather masculine woman with a shock of untidy black hair and a huge bosom. Linda was wearing a pair of scruffy blue dungarees over a lumberjack shirt of chequered pattern. Julia sat beside her in a beautiful dress of jade coloured figured silk, every inch the lady who could proudly count her ancestry back to a Breton knight who had come over with the Norman Conquest.

'We might be able to poach a few of this year's fourth year girls from St. Saviours – I know some of the parents quite well,' said my mother Lydia. 'Most of them will be hoping to get their daughters into St. Monica's in Derby, but they have a stiff entrance exam there. If they fail the exam, they might be prepared to consider a new private school, if they know I will be the first headmistress. I have built up quite a little following among my girls at St. Saviours over the five years I've been teaching there.'

Staffing the new school proved to be more of a problem. My mother intended to do some teaching herself, but decided that she still needed to recruit at least three other teachers before the school opened. The interviews were conducted in what would be the school hall and dining room at Saint Hildegard's, a long room with high windows and elaborately plastered ceilings which had previously been the picture gallery on the first floor of Holloway Hall. The interviewees were waiting nervously in the library, and were brought through one at a time to sit before my mother, Julia and Linda, who constituted the interview panel.

Eventually two women and a rather effeminate young man were selected. The young man – Stephen Tomkinson – had an awkward manner, as if in a constant state of mild embarrassment; but he was very musical and also had a First Class honours degree in Physics from the University of Oxford. He had never taught before or done a teaching qualification, but in those days in private schools these were not necessary prerequisites for a post on the staff of a private school, in contrast to state schools, where a Diploma in Education or post-graduate teaching certificate was required.

The two women were slightly older. Miss Sutherland was in her mid-twenties, a tall, slender woman with light brown hair and gold-rimmed spectacles – she had taught previously at a private school in Manchester. Her subjects were modern languages – she was fluent in French, German and Spanish. The second woman appointed was Mrs. Celia Bolter, a divorcee in her late twenties, a big-boned and rather formidable creature who wore her black frizzy hair scraped back in a tight bun. Mrs. Bolter would be in charge of Physical Education and Biology.

250

My mother would initially be responsible for teaching English and Humanities; Mr. Tomkinson, as an accomplished pianist, would take Music along with Physics and Maths; Miss Sutherland would teach Modern Languages, Needlework and Home Economics; Mrs. Bolter would take P.E. and Biology.

Julia St. John-Smythe said that as a classicist, she didn't mind teaching Latin until they could recruit someone for that. Linda Blakely had got half way through a medical degree before changing to Art History at Cambridge, but said she knew enough medicine to act as school nurse and wouldn't mind also teaching Art for the time being.

The renovations on the building were finally completed in the late summer, so miraculously St. Saint Hildegard's High School for Girls was ready to open its doors at the commencement of the autumn term, in September of 1971.

We initially had just seven new girls – including myself – starting as the first pupils of St. Hildegard's. These first students were all girls who had come from St. Saviours. In the October half-term holiday we were joined by three more pupils – BOYS! They were introduced to the school by Mrs. Bolter, who knew their mothers from a support group for recently divorced women which she had helped to run in London. Two of the boys were lads who had been expelled from other schools for bad behaviour. Patrick Kemp was an exuberant and very boisterous Irish lad with a mass of black curls and a cheeky grin, who had got into trouble for continually answering back teachers and disrupting classes. Simon Dodd had been caught smoking cannabis behind the cycle sheds of his last school. The third boy, Francis Weiner, was a rather delicate and weedy boy of diminutive size for his age, who had been bullied at all his previous schools.

Mrs. Bolter and my mother Lydia had agreed with the mothers of these boys to take them on the basis that she would have a free hand to do with them what she thought best, however unusual her methods. The mothers were all at their wits' end.

Of course you will have guessed the methods my mother chose to employ – the same training techniques she had used on my disobedient young cousins during our holiday in Provence several year ago. First of all the three boys were fitted out with corsets, velvet suits of the Fauntleroy variety, and high-heeled pumps. Patrick and Simon at first rebelled against these indignities, but my mother and Mrs Bolter prevailed with them by a combination of carrot and stick. Initially, they had to be physically held while they were laced tightly into the corsets, which were covered in black silk and decorated with frills. Their embarrassment was such at being forced to wear these undergarments, that they were soon willingly putting on the royal blue velvet Fauntleroy suits to cover them up. Under the jackets of the suits, which had nipped-in waists and lace around the collars and cuffs, they wore cream silk blouses with puffed sleeves, decorated with more exquisite and elaborate lace, and large silk bows at the blouse collars. Eventually the royal blue suits were replaced with pink figured silk suits with buckled britches to the knee, and black silk stockings underneath – and then with – well, I'll get to that in a short while. Patrick and Simon were forbidden to wear any other shoes than the patent leather high-heeled pumps, and were disciplined if they were found to have slipped off the pumps under their desks.

The third boy, Francis, did not seem to object at all to wearing the sissified clothes, and I discovered that his mother's reasons for sending him to the school were slightly different. Mrs. Weiner had agreed with my mother that as he was always being bullied and was already rather a sissy, the best thing would be to turn him into a girl as soon as possible. So Francis was put into the pink silk suit outfit immediately, and by Christmas this had been substituted for girl's school uniform – the white blouse, pleated navy skirt and blazer of St. Hildegard's, with white knee socks and low-heeled black girl's shoes. Francis's hair had already been quite long when he started at the school, and by the end of the autumn term

252

he was wearing it tied up in a bow, with hair slides at the sides to keep his bangs in order. Francis's name had been changed on the register to 'Francesca', and the six real girls and myself accepted him – or rather 'her' – as another girl without demur.

It was obvious from the outset that Francesca loved being a girl, and she settled happily into her new role, enjoying particularly the more feminine lessons such as Needlework and Home Economics.

One of the six real girls, a kind-hearted girl called Samantha Morton, whom we all liked a lot, took Francesca under her wing and became her special friend, helping her with her hair and advising her on all things girlish.

'You should have been born a girl,' said Samantha to Francesca, one morning as we were lining up for assembly, 'you look so good and natural in a skirt, and with your hair tied in a bow.'

Francesca blushed but looked rather pleased, and gave Samantha a little hug.

Patrick and Simon were standing behind in their Fauntleroy suits and scowled at Francesca. Patrick reached out has hand and gave Francesca's hair a hard tug, muttering 'you little sissy', while Simon got hold of her arm and gave her a Chinese burn. Francesca screamed, which brought Mrs. Bolter out of the hall to see what was going on.

They're picking on Francesca,' explained Samantha.

'Hmmn,' said Mrs Bolter, 'time we moved on to phase two of your training. Come with me, boys.'

The two boys were marched to my mother's study, where Mrs Bolter explained what had been going on. We didn't see Simon and Patrick for the rest of that day, but we heard later that they had been forced to dress completely in girls' clothes, with the enthusiastic help of Samantha Morton. At dinner that evening, two new 'girls' appeared in the dining room. They were not dressed in school uniform but wore outfits that would have been more appropriate for girls going to a party – frilly dresses with several layers of petticoats underneath.

Both were wearing wigs and high-heeled leather court shoes, in which they could hardly walk.

They were made to stand on the stage at the end of the hall, and were introduced by my mother as follows:

'Good evening girls. I'd like you to meet two new pupils who are joining us. This is Simone, and here is Patricia. As you can see, they are very pretty young girls, who have been given special permission to wear their party frocks rather than school uniform.' My mother gently lifted up each of their skirts to show the layers of frou-frou petticoats, the sheer silk stockings held up by suspenders, the lace-edged camisoles, and the frilly panties underneath.

'You may recall that we previously knew them as Patrick and Simon, too unpleasant boys who apparently thought it was funny to bully young Francesca and call her a sissy. Well, now you can see what happens to boys who do nasty things like that. Don't they look pretty? They thought girls and sissy boys were soppy and that it was okay to tease them. We don't agree, do we girls?' A murmur of assent went round the hall. 'Now THEY have to be girls – so they will know what it's like to be a girl. I don't know yet how long they will have to be girls for – perhaps a short time, perhaps for longer – hmmn – perhaps even for EVER! We will have to see how they behave in their new feminine roles. If they are good and obedient girls, perhaps I may relent. That is their only hope. We shall see.'

Patricia and Simone looked as if they wished the floor would open up and swallow them. Simone was actually crying a little, while Patricia was blushing profusely but looking stubborn under her wig.

'Both these new girls are wearing wigs at present because their own hair is rather short. They are forbidden to take them off – please report it immediately to me, girls, if they remove their wigs or any other item of their new girl's clothing. Of course, they are also forbidden to get their hair cut. By the spring, I hope to see their own hair will be long enough for cutting and styling in a short bob.'

The 'girl' who had once been Patrick looked up at my mother and asked:

'But surely we haven't got to stay - like this - until then? Please – no!'

'Oh yes,' replied my mother – that it the *shortest* period you can hope for. You need at least that time to discover all the delights of being a girl. Who knows? Perhaps you will like it so much you will decide you want to stay a girl!'

A giggle went round the hall as my mother said this.

Patricia and Simone were led down the steps of the stage, looking totally bewildered and abashed, and allowed to sit down at one of the dining tables.

'And be careful how you sit down, girls,' my headmistress mother exclaimed, 'you must fold your pretty dresses under you carefully and arrange the skirts so you don't crush the lovely taffeta. Keep your knees together under the skirts, girls – you must learn always to keep your legs closed when you sit down. A young lady does not sit with her legs apart – that would never do!'

*   *   *

The autumn term seemed to fly by, with the new girls and staff settling in at St. Hildegard's as the weather turned colder and brought the first covering of frost on the fields. Our timetable began each week with double Maths, a subject I had previously dreaded at my last school, but Mr. Tomkinson was so kind and such as good teacher that even I began to pick up the basics of algebra and geometry. Mr. Tomkinson was a strange young man, with a rather high-pitched voice, a slight build for a man, and beautiful long fingers with which he played the piano at morning assembly. He wore his hair in a long pony tail. He seemed not to mind being the only male member of staff and readily accepted the disciplinary measures imposed by Lydia Quesnay on Simone and Patricia.

At the Christmas concert, the teachers put on a

pantomime for us girls to enjoy, a very comical version of Cinderella, in which Miss Sutherland and Mrs. Bolter played the ugly sisters, and the part of Cinderella was taken by Mr. Tomkinson. The part of Prince Charming was played by Linda Blakely, who made a dumpy and rather masculine principal boy in black tights and leather tunic, while Julia St. John-Smythe played a tall and willowy Buttons. Mr Tomkinson made a very fetching Cinderella – in fact he was rather pretty and surprisingly convincing as a woman, with his piping voice and effeminate mannerisms. The large-boned Mrs. Bolter, on the other hand, was a formidable and quite frightening ugly sister who seemed to relish her role in bullying poor Mr. Tomkinson.

After the performance, the teachers stayed in costume and chatted to us as we had our supper of hot chocolate and oat crunchy biscuits in the dining room. A huge fire of logs blazed merrily in the great fireplace at one end of the hall; at the other end was a large Christmas tree resplendent with silver and gold glass balls, tinsel, paper streamers and other trimmings, which we girls had helped to decorate the evening before.

To complete the picture of seasonal good cheer, I noticed that it had just started snowing outside and went to a window to watch the thick flakes falling and settling on the ground. As I was coming back to my seat, I walked past the back of my mother's chair, and heard her saying to Mrs. Bolter:

'Stephen seems to be enjoying himself a little too much all dressed up as a woman. I wonder...?' Lydia raised her eyebrows questioningly at Mr. Bolter, who nodded and looked meaningfully back.

'I think a confidential chat with our Mr. Tomkinson to find out if your hunch is correct would be most appropriate,' said Mrs. Bolter. 'If you're right, it would set a very good example – an adult role model for some particular 'new' girls would be most useful...'

When school resumed after the Christmas vacation my mother introduced 'Miss Stephanie Tomkinson' as a new member of staff, who would be replacing Mr. Tomkinson for Physics, Maths and Music. The transformation was incredible – 'Miss Tomkinson' really did now look like a real female. Gone was all trace of the pantomime dame of the Christmas concert. Standing before us was a slender young woman in a smart tailored skirt suit, her face immaculately made up, her brunette hair hanging loosely to her shoulders, her ears pierced with discreet gold sleepers. Miss Stephanie Tomkinson looked every inch a beautiful young woman – for real. She seemed at ease with herself – in fact happier than she had been in her previous existence. There was no sign or trace of the awkward young man who had first come to the school. We girls were at first amazed at the transformation, but we soon grew to adore Miss Tomkinson as much as we had loved the kind school master she had replaced.

Simone and Patricia went very quiet after the appearance among us of Miss Stephanie Tomkinson; they exchanged worried glances, as if seeing a prediction of their own futures in what they had just witnessed.

With the coming of spring, their worst fears were realised. Mrs. Bolter told them to go to my mother's study one morning, as she had some important news for them. I was already sitting with my mother, as I had a bad cold and was not fit to do P.E. with Mrs. Bolter.

'You'll be pleased, girls, to hear that your mothers are coming to St. Hildegard's this afternoon to see how you are getting on. The two lads (for so they still thought of themselves at this stage) looked mortified.

'Can we get out of these party dresses now,' asked Simone hopefully.

'Of course not,' replied my mother, 'your mothers will want to see how your training is getting on.'

Patricia and Simone had to put on lace-edged navy satin panties, and Miss Sutherland helped them into training bras, padding the cups out with 'chicken fillet' silicon breast enhancers. Pale blue blouses, navy school tunics, honey-coloured tights and low-heeled black leather girls' shoes completed their outfits. Miss Sutherland showed them how to role the tights on carefully one leg at a time, so they would know how to do it in future. As their own hair by this time had grown long enough, Patricia's was tied back into two bunches held with pink bobbles, while Simone's hair was put into curlers for the first part of the morning, and then at break Miss Sutherland helped her brush it out and arrange it in soft waves. Patricia and Simone then returned to lessons, where they were made to stand out the front of the class one at a time, so we could all see how they looked in their new girls' school uniforms.

After lunch, I was again sitting with my mother in her study when the two mothers arrived, as my cold had taken a turn for the worse. I was sitting at a small desk by the window, drawing a plant on the sill, but I was able to hear everything that was said.

There was a knock on the door, and Miss Tomkinson brought the two mothers in.

Simone's mother, Mrs. Dodd, was a small, plump woman with a flustered manner. She looked closely at Miss Tomkinson as she went out of the door.

'That young woman bears a striking resemblance to Simon's Maths teacher, whom I met at parents evening last term.' Mrs. Dodd looked questioningly at my mother.

'Do take a seat, Mrs. Dodd, and you too Mrs Kemp. Yes, there have been some – er – changes. You'll notice that in a minute, when your sons come in.'

Mrs. Kemp, a red-haired Irish woman with startling green eyes and freckles across her nose, said:

'I'm so grateful to you for taking my Patrick, so I am. I could do nothin' with him at home, and his teachers at his last school just couldn't control him.'

'And my boy,' asked Mrs. Dodd, 'no more trouble with drugs?'

'Ah, here they are now,' replied my mother, as there was another knock at her study door. 'I think you will be surprised at the – changes. Please keep an open mind; my methods may be unconventional, but I think you will see that they work.'

Patricia and Simone then entered, curtseyed sweetly before their mothers, as they had been instructed to do by Mrs. Bolter, and stood either side of my mother's huge oak desk.

'Here are your mothers come to see you, girls,' said Lydia Quesnay. 'Tell them how you have been getting on.'

'Very well, thank you miss,' said Simone, blushing to the roots of her hair as her mother stared at her in amazement.

'Stop fidgeting, Patricia,' said Lydia, 'and speak to your mother.'

'Good afternoon, mother dear,' said Patricia.'

My mother beamed at Mrs. Kemp, as she sat open-mouthed before the young 'girl' who had been her troublesome son.

Good afternoon – ah – Patricia,' said Mrs Kemp, taking a tissue from her pocket and dabbing the corner of her eye.

'I see you are a little overcome by the changes we have wrought. Today the girls are in school uniform. Let me show you some pictures of their previous outfits.'

My mother produced a large leather-bound photo album and passed it to Mrs. Dodd, who turned the pages and gasped in astonishment at the photographs of her son, first in the corsets, then the Fauntleroy suits, then in the 'little girl' party dresses of taffeta and lace. In one photo, Simone was holding up her skirts to show the layers of petticoats and frilly panties beneath.

My mother rang a small bell on her desk, and Francesca Weiner entered and curtseyed demurely.

'This is Francesca,' said Lydia. 'Francesca, would you be a dear and make a cup of tea for the ladies? Bring some of the chocolate biscuits, as well.'

When Francesca had gone out, my mother smiled at Mrs. Dodd and Mrs. Kemp, and leaned back in her chair.

'Francesca,' she explained, 'is one of our great successes. Like your sons, she was also a boy when she came here. But she was a rather sissified sort of boy from the outset, and she took readily to her new gender role. She loves being a girl now, as you saw, and I have hopes that your children will similarly choose – willingly – but I am getting ahead of myself. Let me ask you first – do you like the changes that we have brought about in your sons? You approve?'

Mrs. Kemp and Mrs Dodd both nodded their heads, if a little uncertainly.

'But Miss Quesnay,' said Mrs. Kemp, 'I'm not clear how far – erm – how far this is going? Is Patrick - '

'Patricia,' interrupted my mother.

'- Is Patricia dressed as a girl all the time now?

'Of course,' replied Lydia. In order for our methods to work, we have to insist.'

Lydia then explained to the two mothers her theory and practice of corset training, sissification and petticoat punishment - how these methods for disciplining unruly boys had been used frequently and with great success in Europe during the 19th and early 20th centuries.

'Of course,' Lydia continued, 'with the great improvements in medical science, endocrinology, surgery, psychology and so fourth, we can achieve much more than the early pioneers of this sort of training. In fact, it is now possible to – to go the whole way, so to speak, if that is what the parents and the child want.'

'Go the whole way?' asked Mrs. Dodd.

'By all means,' replied my mother. 'Do you eventually want a son back – a sissified one at that – or would you prefer to have a daughter? It can be arranged, you know, if that is what you want – but naturally Patricia would have to agree to it too. We would never countenance so – irreversible and final – a change without all parties willingly consenting, including the young person herself.'

'I see,' said Mrs. Dodd. 'Well, my ex-husband would have been horrified. But – I – I can begin to see the advantages. I confess I always wanted a daughter. I often wonder what it would be like. A daughter to come shopping; a loving daughter would be such a solace as I grow older, with whom I could do all those feminine things. I've never been able to share my love of cooking and needlework, for example. But is it possible?'

'Quite possible,' replied my mother, 'and you don't have to decide now.' If you think you would like your child's development to proceed in the direction we have just been discussing, I would need you to sign a form of consent giving us permission to administer certain drugs on a regular basis to assist in physical development. Nothing needs be final at this stage. In any case, the final – changes – are surgical, and cannot be carried out until the child is 18 years old and can give her legal consent.

'So you see, there is nothing to decide now, nothing to do other than signing this.'

Lydia handed a sheet of paper to each of the mothers, and passed her pen first to Mrs. Dodd, then to Mrs. Kemp, pointing out where to sign at the bottom of the papers. Both mothers signed the forms without objection, and Lydia took them back, placed them on her desk, and stood up.

'Now ladies, I think we had better go to the dining room and see if Francesca has brought that pot of tea. I do hope it is not too stewed.'

'Girls, you may go back to your classes now.' Simone and Patricia bobbed curtseys first at Miss Quesnay, then at their mothers, and hurried out of the room.

'Amazing,' exclaimed Mrs. Dodd.

'I never would have thought it of Patrick, that I wouldn't,' said Mrs. Kemp; 'he was such a rough boy, to have made him into this – polite young girl – in so short a time. It's a miracle!'

Lydia led the two astounded ladies out to take tea in the dining room.

*   *   *

What Lydia Quesnay hadn't confided to Mrs. Kemp and Mrs. Dodd was this: Simone and Patricia had been told in no uncertain terms prior to the visit that they would *never* have even the slightest chance of being Simon and Patrick again unless they put on a good show for their mothers – convinced them that they were reformed characters who were content to be dressed as girls, curtseyed politely, and did as they were bid. *If* they cooperated in this, Lydia hinted that there might be a chance that she would allow them to be boys again. Of course, there was never any chance of this. My mother seemed to take some perverse pleasure in sissifying boys and eventually turning them completely into girls, and she had no intention of relenting in this respect regarding Patrick and Simon, anymore than in my own case.

In the first year, there were only the four of us – myself, Francesca, Simone and Patricia – who had all once been boys but were gradually being indoctrinated and brainwashed into becoming girls. The other three didn't know my true gender, and thought that I was a real girl, however – and to avoid embarrassment, I kept my true gender a secret.

My mother's predilection for changing boys into girls was apparently shared enthusiastically by her London friends, Julia St. John-Smythe and Linda Blakely. I later understood that these women were feminist radicals of the most extreme sort, who had been in at the birth of the women's liberation movement in the 1960's. They had burnt their bras and announced their loathing for the male sex along with the other women's libbers in California, where they had holidayed as students. Now they were self-proclaimed lesbians who couldn't see the point of men at all, and were very willing to assist in the complete feminisation of boys, if it meant there would be less men in the world in future.

Mrs. Bolter's support group for divorcees had likewise been a hot-bed of man-haters and assorted feminists – not surprising as some of them – including Mrs. Bolter herself – had been victims of male aggression in the past.

Of the other members of staff, Miss Stephanie – formerly Stephen Tomkinson – was now a pre-operative male to female transsexual, though I didn't know the term then. Miss Sutherland was a quiet, easily led young woman who seemed to go along with anything proposed by the more strong-minded members of staff. So there was really no one to stop what happened or ask questions about the ethics of what my mother was doing – until it was too late.

My mother ensured that as the school grew, each new member of staff was only recruited if they fitted into the prevailing orthodoxy and agreed with *all* the aims of the school.

Somehow, also – perhaps through the various women's groups and some sort of unofficial grape vine to which most the staff and parents seemed to belong or subscribe – news of the unusual and particular education provided by St. Hildegard's spread rapidly among precisely that strata of middle-class women who had the means to pay for their unruly and disobedient sons to be boarded at the school and transformed into biddable and docile young persons of the feminine gender. In most cases there were no husbands or fathers on the scene to object. Most of the mothers were either divorced and currently had no men in their lives, or had husbands who were away overseas on business or in government service; men who unwisely left the management of their families and households, including arranging the education of their children – to their wives.

More girls were also taken on as pupils, so that eventually the proportion of biological females to boys undergoing feminisation was about fifty per cent each. The real girls were sworn to secrecy by a sorority oath administered when they first arrived at the school, and lived in a separate block where they had their own dormitory. Some of the girls were sisters of boys undergoing feminisation, and so their mothers were in on the secret. These girls were mostly in favour of what was going on, liking the idea of having a sister rather than a brother, and they assisted their siblings on the path to femininity when they could. Everyone at the school attended the same lessons, which being a girls' school, meant plenty of needlework, domestic science and lessons on deportment, as well as the more academic subjects. St. Hildegard's was such a female environment that it was impossible for even the most obstreperous and boisterous boy to hold out for long.

The initial training always followed the same course – first the boy would be forced to wear a corset, which would be gradually laced more tightly until the waist was nipped in to a feminine smallness, accentuating the hips so that they looked wide and girlish. Over the top of this the boy would be forced to wear first a blue velvet Fauntleroy suit, then a pink silk one. Gradually by this process of sissification, all unruliness was suppressed and crushed out of the boy. He was then given the choice of staying in the pink Fauntleroy suit indefinitely, or undergoing full feminisation and joining the girls in normal girls' clothes. As the corset had by this time been laced so tightly as to cause constant discomfort, while the high-heeled shoes forced the boy to mince in a most sissy-like fashion, and made any running, jumping or other vigorous movement quite impossible, nearly all boys chose the latter path of complete feminisation.

One or two boys did hold out for several months at the pink Fauntleroy suit stage, but all relented finally, concluding they might as well give up and accept the inevitable. The girls in the school, by contrast with the sissified boys, wore comfortable school tunics with blouses underneath, or blouses and pleated skirts, navy cardigans and sensible low-heeled black leather shoes. They could wear white socks or flesh-coloured tights. They did P.E. and games such as hockey and netball in their gym slips, and were allowed to wear normal casual girls' clothes of the period (this was the Seventies) at weekends, including girls' slacks or even mini-skirts, to go out around the village of Ashton Cross or into the town of Matlock on the bus. Their lives seemed much more attractive to the sissified boys than their own, and so all boys eventually opted to join the girls and live fully as females.

Initially the boys who were undergoing the gender change were made to wear 'little girl' frilly dresses with petticoats, at least for a few days, before they were permitted to wear the school uniform and casual girls' clothes in the evenings and at weekends. Sometimes, if a boy's behaviour remained masculine, the petticoat training stage could go on for several weeks or even months, while the 'new girl' learnt to walk, talk and generally disport 'herself' in the feminine role. In this phase, known as 'Stage Two', the new girl was always called by her female name and referred to as 'she', 'her' etc.

Once the transition had been made from the 'petticoat training' stage to the 'normal school girl' or 'Stage Three' phase, the new girls were started on 'vitamin' pills which they took with their breakfast. These pills were in fact female hormones - tablets which were at first taken once a day, and then, as puberty progressed, twice a day, once at breakfast and once with supper. This medication was procured on private prescription through a female doctor friend of Linda Blakely's, whom she had known at medical school.

I have since looked up what these 'Progynova 2mg' pills actually are − a synthetic form of oestrogen. The effects include breast development and reduction in size and firmness of the testicles and prostate gland, some reduction and re-patterning of body hair, softening of the skin, and re-contouring of the body due to accumulating layers of feminine body fat. After about six months, 'transitioning' girls begin to notice tenderness around the nipples and budding breast growth. After a year or 18 months on these so-called 'vitamin' pills, we 'Stage Three' girls could fill at least an 'A' cup sized bra, and in some cases a 'B' cup. Of course we were all wearing bras by then, starting first with training bras and silicon breast forms, and graduating onto women's sizes as the need arose.

After the initial soreness, I enjoyed the feeling of my breasts, and couldn't help noticing and enjoying the feminine shape my body was taking on. My hips were growing wider, my skin was becoming soft and my hair, which I wore shoulder-length or in a pony-tail, was full and silky. I was becoming a young woman!

When the 'transitioning' girls were old enough, which was usually in the fourth or fifth year, at age 14 or 15, we were also given Spironolactone 100mg tablets and Provera 5mg tablets. Provera (medroxyprogesterone) is a progestin, a chemical with effects similar to progesterone – it maximizes breast development and approximates more closely the natural female hormone balance. Spironolactone is an oral anti-androgen which reduces testosterone levels. This regimen of extra female hormones and anti-androgen was 'Stage Four', and meant that in most cases we did not develop facial hair at all or grow any male-pattern body hair. In one or two instances, new girls who *were* unfortunate enough to grow a little facial hair in later puberty in spite of the female hormone treatment were taken into Sheffield once a week for electrolysis or laser sessions at a private clinic.

By the time we were in the Sixth Form, most of us Stage Four transitioning girls were indistinguishable from our genetically female friends. By this time I had a very feminine body shape, with firm rounded breasts, well-defined nipples which stuck out when I was aroused, broad hips and a tiny waist of which I was proud. My legs were long and my calves were slim and well-shaped, so that I looked great in a mini-skirt. I wore makeup and nail polish at weekends. In truth I thought of myself as a girl, and had all but forgotten that I had ever been a boy. Simone and Patricia were by this time at least reconciled to their fates, and realised they would never again be boys, while Francesca – like me – was positively enjoying being female. We were now the 'old guard', with many friends among the real girls in the school; we were also hero-worshipped by the younger Stage Two and Stage Three 'new girls' who had just begun their transitioning. We were what they were aiming for, I suppose.

Miss Stephanie Tomkinson, now head of Maths and Physics and a much loved mistress, was now a complete woman, having had a sex-change operation in Casablanca a couple of years previously. We older girls looked to her as the role-model to which *we* aspired, just as the younger girls looked up to us.

By this time the school had over 200 students, half of whom had originally been boys. There were two other post-operative transsexual women on the staff - Miss Gibson, an older woman who taught Business Studies and had been a successful businessman before her change of sex, and Miss Amanda Johnson, who had transitioned young, even before she had gone to college, with the help of a mother who had always wanted a daughter and was delighted to encourage Amanda in her change of gender. Amanda Johnson was truly beautiful – so feminine that one could not imagine how she could ever have been anything other than a real girl.

In the summer of 1975 a new swimming pool had been built in the grounds of the school, and some of us had seen Miss Johnson in her bikini, doing lengths of breast-stroke and back-stroke; we marvelled at the female curviness of her body, and we couldn't help noticing the little Lycra triangle of the bikini panties that concealed the smooth, round femaleness between her legs.

Oh, how we longed to be like her – to complete our transitioning and get rid of the shrunken dangly bits between our legs! I so much wanted to be rid of them – my residual male stigmata, to feel myself clean and uncluttered down there – to be fully and completely and finally a girl, with no going back – ever.

My mother sensed this in me, of course, and was pleased that I had now reached *Stage Five*: the last phase in my transformation to total girlhood. In the summer of my 18th year, after I had completed my 'A' levels, she took me to a private hospital in Canada, where I had my sex-change surgery.

And yes, it was painful when I came round and the anaesthetics had worn off; I had to take strong pain killers to cope with the soreness between my legs for the first few days after the operation. I also found it uncomfortable to wear the vaginal dilators or stents in the days and weeks following the operation, to dilate my new vagina and make sure it retained the depth and width I would need if I was going to function fully as a female. I used five Duratek stents of different sizes. They looked like smooth white dildos with rounded ends, which made it easier to slip them up inside me. First I used the smallest one with a diameter of 25mm; I then progressed to the 29mm stent, and worked my way up over the next weeks through 32mm and 35mm dilators, until I could wear the 38mm one without discomfort. Each of the stents was 20 cm in length, which would be enough to ensure proper sexual function, so my surgeon assured me.

I recuperated during the late summer and autumn of 1977 in our new house on the outskirts of Matlock, which Lydia had bought so that we didn't have to spend all our time 'living over the shop' as she put it, as previously we had inhabited rooms on the second floor of St. Hildegard's. As I convalesced I went out for walks in the surrounding countryside, enjoying the summer sun on my bare arms and the unencumbered feeling between my legs. After six weeks I no longer had to dilate, wash myself with salt water, or wear dressings.

One morning in November of 1977, I stood wearing just my bra and panties before the full length mirror on the door of my wardrobe, and surveyed my now completely female body with great joy. I put my hands under my breasts, feeling their weight; and then ran my fingers over my stomach and down between my legs, marvelling at how lovely and flat and rounded I was. At last I looked just right in panties, with no unsightly bulges – the way any girl should look. For I *was* a girl at last – a *real* girl.

I unclasped my bra, slid my panties down and kicked them off the end of my toes. I felt my breasts, enjoying their smooth, soft fullness; I gently massaged my nipples until they were standing erect. Then I sat down on the side of the bed and began to examine myself between the legs. Now everything was healed, and my triangle of soft hair had grown back on my mound of Venus. I ran my fingers through the hair and down to the soft nub of my clitoris, frigging it gently and massaging it until I began to feel aroused. Then I let my right hand travel down to my labia; I felt with two fingers around the lips of my new vagina and inserted them up inside – it felt already moist there, although the surgeon warned me that I would have to use lubricant when having full penetrative sex. I pushed my fingers further up, and then worked them up and down, up and down, slowly at first, and then with more vigor until – until – oh my God - I climaxed! I had just had my first orgasm as a woman! A truly wonderful and sublime feeling – like a warm wave sweeping over the lower half of my body. *Oh brave new world!* No one had prepared me for this. I lay down on the bed, and curled up on my side, with my hands between my thighs, enjoying the uncluttered sensation of freedom in my crotch, which was till tingling pleasantly.

* * *

I wasn't the only one of the 'old girls' of St. Hildegard's who had reached Stage Five and taken the final step towards femaleness during the summer just gone. I had been in touch with Fransesca by letter and telephone, and I knew that she too couldn't wait for her sex re-assignment surgery. Her mother was also keen that she should have it as soon as possible – had looked forward for many years to having a real daughter at last – and she had arranged for Francesca to spend the summer in Bangkok, where a gender re-assignment clinic had been running for some years, catering for the many Thai 'lady-boys'who required the surgery.

I didn't hear news of Simone's and Patricia's surgery

until we all got together again that Christmas at St. Hildegard's. Lydia had decided that the first crop of 'Old Hildegardians' would be invited back to perform a beauty pageant as part of the Christmas concert. There were also three other 'old girls' who had completed their transitioning and had the sex-change operation.

The six of us were invited first of all to parade in ball gowns, then to appear in bikinis, and finally in our 'usual' clothes, when we would be interviewed about our plans by Miss Tomkinson.

The bikini parade was particularly an event of note for the younger girls; a hushed gasp of astonishment went round the hall when we entered in our bikinis and high-heels, showing off our feminine curves. I knew that there were many eyes looking enviously at our well-defined breasts and the gently curving magical flatness between our legs. Two of the girls had particularly prominent busts, having had breast augmentations at the same time as their gender re-assignment surgery. One of these was Patricia, whose mother had apparently insisted that if her new daughter was going to be a proper Irish colleen, she should be as well-endowed as her three sisters. Patricia had grown into a stunningly beautiful young woman; she showed us her new breasts while we were changing, proclaiming with some pride that she was now a 36C.

The other girl who had undergone breast augmentation had not been one of our original gang, but had come to St. Hildegard's in the third year. Her name was Billie-Jolene Ogley, and she was a quiet girl from the Deep South of the U.S.A., whose parents had died in a car crash on Interstate 65, outside Franklin, when she was only nine years old. Billie-Jolene (at that time still Billy-Joe) had then gone to live with an aunt on her mother's side, an eccentric spinster who didn't like boys and had made her young nephew dress in girl's clothes from the start. Her Aunt Betty had a farm in the foothills of the Great Smoky Mountains, in Eastern Tennesse; and they had lived there among the hillbillies, her aunt educating her at home and gradually feminising her nephew more and more until to all intents and purposes she had transformed him into her niece. When, once a week, they visited the town of Gatlinburg to buy provisions, Aunt Betty made sure that he was always dressed as a girl, so relations, neighbours and friends they might meet had only ever seen Billie-Jolene as a girl.

When Billie-Jolene had reached the age of thirteen, there had been some trouble with the local public school board authority, who had tried to force Aunt Betty to send Billie-Jolene to the local Junior High School. Aunt Betty had heard by this time of St. Hildegard's, in Derbyshire, England. Billie-Jolene explained that her aunt had met Julia St. John-Smythe and Linda Blakely when she had been at college in California, in the Sixties, and had kept in touch with Julia by means of an exchange of annual letters at Christmas time.

This Christmas of 1977 was a very special one, as Aunt Betty had come over to stay with Julia and Linda for the Christmas and New Year period, so that she could see Billie-Jolene taking part in the beauty pageant. Aunt Betty, normally a rather stern woman, wept openly when she saw Billie-Jolene in her Southern Belle costume. Billie-Jolene was a slim girl with ash blonde hair and a pale complexion; after her recent breast augmentation, she was now a 38D bra size, and her ample bosoms bounced gently as she came on in a Scarlett O'Hara ball gown, complete with a wide straw hat decorated with pink ribbons, and performed the famous quotation from the book and film:

'There was a land of Cavaliers and Cotton Fields called the Old South...
Here in this pretty world Gallantry took its last bow...
Here was the last ever to be seen of Knights and their Ladies Fair,
Of Master and of Slave...
Look for it only in books,
For it is no more than a dream remembered.
A Civilization gone with the wind...'

The hall erupted in applause, as Billie-Jolene curtseyed and grinned at her aunt where she sat in the audience.

The 'What Are We Doing Next?' section of the pageant was of interest to staff and girls alike. Patricia revealed that she was returning to Ireland to take up a place on the Dental Nursing course at Trinity College, Dublin; Simone said that she was going to secretarial college in London to learn short-hand and typing; Francesca, who was another very pretty young woman, said that she hoped to get into modelling. When it was my turn, I told Miss Tomkinson that I was going to do teaching, and had got a place on the Bachelor of Education course at Nottingham University.

It was during the second year of my teaching course that the whole scandal blew up in the press and on television about St. Hildegard's. I had come back to the school to do my teaching practice in the Spring Term, so I was on the spot to witness what happened.

I suppose it was only a matter of time before it all came out. It was surprising, perhaps, that it didn't happen sooner, but for the first few years, while the school was still quite small, its secrets were guarded by both staff and students, who felt a strong and protective loyalty to St. Hildegard's and to Lydia Quesnay's management of the school. As the roll of teaching staff and pupils grew, and the number of parents who were in on the secret also increased, it became more and more likely that something would come out – it would only take one disgruntled member of staff or one doubtful parent to blow the whistle.

It was a father of one of the transitioning girls who eventually alerted the press – and it was a national rather than a local newspaper that got wind of the more unusual aspects of the education offered by St. Hildegard's.

A furtive-looking, rat-faced little man in a soiled and rumpled raincoat had been seen around the grounds of Hildegard's on several occasions, peering over the walls or hanging around behind the trees, chain smoking and apparently writing something in a notebook. When my mother and the senior members of staff first heard reports of the man, they had concluded that he was that not unusual type of voyeuristic pervert who had an unhealthy appetite directed towards watching school girls at work and play, and was hanging around to sate these proclivities. A nuisance, but usually not posing a real danger to the students, Lydia was about to report the man to the local constabulary when, one morning, he actually came into the grounds, advanced rapidly up the drive to the entrance, and presented himself to the school secretary in the office, asking if he could have an interview with the headmistress. He handed the secretary a card which revealed his identity as Mr. Dave Humble, social affairs correspondent with the Sunday tabloid newspaper, "The News of the World".

The secretary, Mrs Timms, knocked on Lydia's door, entered, and gave her the reporter's card. I was sitting with my mother discussing my lesson plans for that day's teaching practice.

My mother went white as a sheet when she read the card, and asked Mrs Timms:

'Did Mr. Humble say what it was about?'

'No, he just asked to speak to you – on a delicate and confidential matter, he said.'

'Hmmn. You'd better show him in.' I got up to go, but my mother said: 'Stay where you are, Francoise. I think I might need a witness to the conversation I am about to conduct with this Mr. Humble.'

Mr Humble was shown in by Mrs. Timms. He nodded obsequiously and sat down opposite my mother without being asked, placing a sweat-stained trilby hat on the corner of my mother's desk. He removed a notebook and a small cassette recorder from a battered attache case, placed the recorder next to the hat and switched it on. Then he took a pencil stub from an inside pocket of his tweed jacket, wet the tip of the pencil with a reptilian tongue, and said:

273

'Hope you don't mind the recorder, Miss – er – Quesnay, is it? Or is it Ms. – are you one of these women's libbers? He leered at Lydia Quesnay unpleasantly.

My mother frowned at him over her gold-rimmed spectacles and pushed a stray lock of iron-grey hair back behind her ear.

'What is this about, Mr. Humble?'

'Well, you seem to have a nice school for young ladies here, but we've had a report that suggests – all's not quite as it seems.'

'Oh yes? From where did this report emanate?' asked my mother.

'I am not at liberty at this time to reveal my sources, let's just say from someone who has good reason to be concerned.' Mr. Humble's lizard tongue flicked out again and licked his unnaturally red lips.

'What is this about, Mr. Humble?' My mother fiddled again with the stray lock of hair behind her ear, a sure sign that she was getting agitated.

'We've heard, see, that not all the girls here are *girls*. At least they don't all start out as girls. My informant says that some of your pupils are *boys* – but you force them to dress as girls – some sort of weird idea of discipling them. Is that true?'

'How have you heard this,' asked my mother.

'I told you, I'm not a liberty to say. Our informant wishes to retain his confidentiality.'

'*His* confidentiality? So your informant is a man?'

Yes, I might as well tell you this much – so you know we are on to you and it's no good making flat denials. Our informant is a father of one of the *boys* here. Yes, I said *boys*, even though this is St. Hildegard's School for Girls, I am given to understand, so I'm blessed if I can comprehend what this boy is doing here in the first place, or what *you* were doing, admitting him. I don't know what your game is, *Ms.* Quesnay, but if there is something unhealthy and perverted going on here, the public have a right to know.'

'I – I have no comment to make…' said Lydia

274

Quesnay.

'What – you have nothing to say about these accusations? This poor chap – the father of the boy – is in the oil business, see? He comes home from Saudi unexpectedly after a three year stint and his son happens to be at home – because it's the school holidays – except, it's not his *son* he finds, but -

'Apparently a young *girl* with long blonde hair pinned up in a very girlie style,' (at this point Mr. Humble referred to another page in his notebook) 'she's wearing a blue denim mini dress with a lace-edged apron, red and white puffed gingham sleeves and a lace-up front, lace petticoat and high-heeled peep-toe shoes, and she has prominent *breasts* for God' sake! Her ears are pierced and she's got dangly earrings in them, and she's even wearing nail varnish and makeup. Although Mr. – er – the gentleman in question – can barely believe his eyes, he realises that the young girl in front of him bears a slight resemblance – at least facially - to his son. He looks at his wife questioningly. She looks devastated to see him – he hadn't been expected home for months. After a very long moment of excruciating embarrassment, she wrings her hands and says, "This is Paula." The girl in the denim mini dress blushes with confusion and shame. The father says:

"Paula? Do you mean this is – *Paul?* Our *son?*"

"Paula is a *girl* now…" the mother explains.

"'I don't understand,'" says the father. And so it all comes out. The mother explains how she could no longer control their son, he was in trouble all the time and not getting on well at his previous school. She hears about St. Hildegard's and it seems the answer to her problems. She explains how *you*, Ms. Quesnay, take unruly young boys and do *this* to them. She says she didn't know what else to do, as Paul's father was away in Saudi Arabia and no help, and Paul's previous school had expelled him and she couldn't find anywhere else that would take him.

"And it's all right now," she adds, "really it is. Paula *likes* being a girl, don't you, Paula?" Paula has stopped blushing, although she cannot meet her father's eyes. She looks at her varnished nails, adjusts her skirt, and nods.

"They all do,' continues the mother, "once they've been there for a while. She wants to stay as a girl, forever – to grow up as a young woman and – you know - "

'*What?*' asks the father, a look of mounting horror on his face.

"Umm – live the rest of her life as a woman - have a sex-change operation in a couple of years, when she's old enough."

"Is this true?" asks the father.

Paula looks at her mother, and nods again.

"And I've always wanted a daughter," says the mother, "so it's all worked out fine..."

'Without saying another word, the father – our informant - walks out of the house and goes and stays in a hotel.

The following morning he phoned our news desk, and our Editor sent me to interview the man and then come out here and see what is going on.' Mr. Humble ran a hand over his balding pate, re-arranging a few strands of hair that were plastered across the top, and asked:

'So, you still have nothing to say?'

'Yes,' replied my mother, nodding slightly and holding her hands out as if to indicate she couldn't see any problem. 'Paula is well on in Stage Four of our special training. A very pretty girl.'

'That's all you're saying?'

'I'd like you to leave now,' said my mother. She walked over and opened the door. Mr Humble shrugged, collected his attaché case, hat and tape recorder, got up from his seat, and walked out.

That Sunday, "The News of the World" published a two-page exposé written by Dave Humble under the heading:

"BOYS FORCED TO CROSS-DRESS IN SEX-CHANGE SCHOOL SCANDAL"

There were photos of the school and pictures of some of the girls walking around the village of Ashton Cross. There was also a photograph of Miss Gibson, our Business Studies teacher, who although a post-operative transsexual, still looked rather masculine, under the heading:

"SEX-CHANGE STAFF FORCE BOYS TO BE GIRLS"

And so the story went on, taking a tone of moral outrage, but with a subtext of scandalised prurience. Lydia read a copy of the paper in the staff room, and threw it down with disgust. Miss Bolter picked up the paper, scanned the two-page spread about St. Hildegard's, and shook her head sadly:

'What are we going to do about this, Lydia?'

'I just don't know,' replied my mother.

We didn't have long to wait. The following Monday morning, two plain-clothes policemen arrived at the school, and asked Lydia Quesnay and Celia Bolter, (who by then was the deputy headmistress), to accompany them to the police station in order to 'help them with their enquiries.'

My mother and Miss Bolter didn't return until late in the afternoon, both looking ashen with anxiety.

The upshot of it was – the police couldn't find any way to prosecute Lydia or Celia, as nothing had been done without the written consent of at least one parent; all the transitioning girls who were interviewed by social services self-identified as early-onset transsexuals, and all said that they had willingly entered into the female gender role. So no one could prove that anything illegal had been done, but the adverse publicity ruined the school, which had to close at the end of the school year.

* * *

So, what are the main characters in my true story doing in 2007?

Well, Lydia Quesnay and Celia Bolter are retired now, and living quietly together in the West Country. I don't know what their relationship is – whether they are just companions or something closer – but I am happy that my mother has a good friend in Celia.

I am living in West Virginia, and I'll explain how it came about in a short while.

Patricia Kemp is a dental nurse in County Cork, and I visit her occasionally when I am over in Europe. She has a nice little stone-built cottage overlooking Bantry Bay, and is in a long-term relationship with the landlord of the Wolf Tone Tavern in Barrack Street, Bantry, who keeps her well supplied with Guinness. She's put on a bit of weight in recent years, and is every inch an Irish colleen; sometimes she helps out as bar maid at the Wolf Tone, and is a popular gal with the local punters and the tourists alike.

Simone finished secretarial school and for some years has been P.A. to the managing director of a London law firm. No one knows about her background. She is still single, but has a busy social life, mainly with female friends with whom she regularly goes to the West End theatres.

Francesca Weiner, as you probably know, has had a stunning career as a top fashion model; she often frequented the best cat-walks in Paris, London and Milan, and in the 1980's and 1990's her photo was never out of *Cosmopolitan* and *Vogue*. She was a Bond Girl in one of the earlier Sean Connery films. Her mother is her best friend, and she has been so thrilled to have such a successful and beautiful daughter. A few years ago Francesca was 'outed' as a post-operative transsexual, and although this ended her modelling career, she has continued to have a high public profile, has written her autobiography, and is a frequent guest on day-time television shows in the U.S., where she now lives.

Billie-Jolene Ogley returned to the States, and when her Aunt Betty died, she inherited a lot of money. Billie-Jolene invited me to stay with her in Tennesse, and I had not been staying in her Smoky Mountains retreat for long when she broached the subject with me which eventually brought me to live permanently in the U.S.A.:

'Francoise, y'all knows how them Yankee city folk think us Southerners who live down here in the mountin's is jus' hillbilly white trash?'

'I'm sure they don't all think like that,' I replied.

'Yes m'am, they surely do. They think we al' eat possum pie an' drink white lightnin' an' drive around in sum beat-up 'ole pickup truck! Well, ahm a tellin' you honey, ah aint never been on Jerry Springer an' ah don' go varmint huntin' or shoot off ma revolver in the wee small hours an' ah aint done never married ma brother Clem, neither, 'cos I aint got no brother Clem.' Billie-Jolene paused for breath.

'I been at university and ahm a' h'educated Southern lady, and ahm a fixin' to prove it.'

'Ok, you've got my full attention, Billie-Jolene.'

'Well, Franny, ah wanna open a school – a real classy school, prove we care about educa-shun, that we aint all red-necks an' poor white trash down here. I dun' inherited a big house in West Viginia from my Aunty Betty – turned out she owned a chain of hotels - and ah aint usin' the house for nuthin' yet, but I sure do plan to. I just need someone to help me. An' I thought of you – you beein' a h'educated Brit. an' all, you gone dun' qualified as a teacher, aint that right, honey?'

'Yes, that's right.'

'How 'bout this then, Franny? You be m'a headmistress – I'll be the owner, but ah wan' you to run the school for me. You talk so nice – I jus' *lurrv* - your English accent. You got real class. Whadda yer say, sweet thing, will ya do it?'

Of course, dear reader, I agreed. And so I find myself in the Appalachian Mountain Highlands of West Virginia, in a huge, venerable colonial style house built in the days of the Old South, a white stucco house with a portico and columns like something out of *Gone with the Wind*.

The grand old house has been beautifully converted into a private school for Southern young ladies, although in fact we have students from all over the world coming to us, as we advertise on the Internet. The school is in five hundred acres of its own grounds, very secluded and private. We don't get bothered much by the city folk or the authorities in Charleston. West Virginians are country people, and they know how to keep themselves to themselves.

And you've guessed, I expect? That's right! We follow our own *very special* curriculum. We take young *boys* from all over the world whose mothers are 'jest disparin'', and we turn them into good Southern young *ladies*. And at Christmas each year, we have a Southern Belles pageant...

Deborah's Decision

Deborah Carrion blushed too easily. She had auburn hair - not ginger, but she was used to hearing herself described as a red head - and she had the sort of pale complexion which freckled in the summer, and turned crimson whenever she felt embarrassed - signalling her feelings like a traffic light, for all the world to see.

Deborah felt her face burning at that moment, as Mr. Winton, one of the junior partners in the London law firm for which she worked, pointed out to her in his high-pitched voice that she had missed out a line in the letter she had typed for him. Deborah felt sure that the line had not been in the original which was lying on her desk, scrawled in Mr. Winton's spidery handwriting - but knew from past experience that it was not a good idea to point out their mistakes to junior partners.

'Yes, Mr. Winton, I'll sort that out straightaway; the letter's on the computer, so it will only take a few moments to insert the line and print it out again.'

'Thank you, Debbie. Bring it down as soon as it's ready,' replied Mr. Winton, adding unnecessarily, 'the sooner the better - Trusgrove Industries are important clients you know.'

'Yes Mr. Winton.' Deborah felt herself blushing again.

'And could you photocopy these for me? Two copies of each.' Deborah picked up the pile of papers and went back to her work station. She disliked Mr. Winton, with his whiny voice and plummy, upper-class accent. He made sure everyone was aware he'd been to Cambridge, and to public school - one of the smaller ones she'd not heard of, but he made it sound very expensive and select. Mr. Winton was shortish and overweight; he wore gold-rimmed half frame spectacles, to make him look older than he was. Although he got his suits from a good tailor's on Savile Row (he made sure everybody knew this), *he always looked slightly crumpled and dishevelled, like an over-ripe pear when its skin starts to crinkle*, thought Deborah.

After amending the letter, Deborah went to do the photocopying Mr. Winton had given her. She had to wait at the machine while a slender young man she had not seen before finished making some copies. He grinned at her in a friendly way and said:

'How're you doing?'

Deborah smiled back at him.

'Oh not too bad. I'll be glad when it's lunchtime.'

'Yeah, me too. I'm new around here, so I was wondering where to go for lunch. Where do you normally go?'

'Well, there's San Remo's - that's a coffee bar that does delicious filled rolls, just round the corner - I sometimes go there.'

'Are you going there this lunchtime?'

'I could do.'

'Mind if I tag along? What time do you normally go for lunch?'

'Half twelve,' said Deborah, wondering what she was letting herself in for. The boy was a different type altogether from most of the young men who worked in the office. He was quite small, not much taller than her, with long fair hair held back in a pony-tail. His features were rather girlish - a small nose, ridiculously long lashes fringing large brown eyes, high cheek bones, a small chin. He seemed friendly and approachable though; Deborah had liked him at once, and realised that she had not blushed or felt embarrassed at all while talking to him.

They met at the lift doors at 12:30.

'My name's Tim, by the way,' he said to her as they were getting into the lift.

'I'm Deborah - people usually call me Debbie.'

He nodded, smiling. Deborah realised that they were looking directly into each other's eyes. She looked away, watching the buttons of the lift lighting downwards for each floor. The lift stopped at the seventh floor, and a girl who had got into the lift with them moved towards the doors as they opened. No one else got into the lift;

they were alone. Deborah listened to the hum of the lift mechanism for a few moments, then looked at Tim and said:

'I haven't seen you before in the office. How long have you been working at Siddal, Platt and Rosebury's?'

'Only since last week. I'm over here for a few months.'

'Over here from Australia?'

'Yep, how did you know?'

'The accent's pretty easy to work out. I have seen *Neighbours* and *Home and Away* once or twice.

Tim groaned and said:

'Oh jeez, you can't get away from them!'

'Not your favourite viewing?'

Tim shook his head vigorously, his pony tail swishing backwards and forwards, his eyebrows arched and lips pulled back over his small white teeth in an ironic silent scream. Deborah giggled.

'I came twelve thousand miles to get away from that stuff, and you're saying it's followed me here?'

Deborah nodded.

The lift bell pinged for the ground floor. Tim followed her through the lift doors into the marble-walled vestibule, and then out into the bright spring sunshine.

San Remo's was busy as always, but they managed to get a corner table by the window after placing their orders. Deborah had ordered a tuna and salad wholemeal roll and a cappuccino; Tim was having a cottage cheese and pineapple roll and a glass of orange juice.

'Are you on a diet?' asked Debbie, looking at his spare form - there was hardly anything of him.

'I like to keep trim, but also I'm vegetarian - so that cut's down the choice of what I can order.'

Deborah noticed properly his small face, the finely arched eyebrows, the big, liquid brown eyes and soft shoulder-length ash-blonde hair, now loose around his shoulders. She thought: *he really does look like a girl - how strange.* Tim put up a hand to shade his eyes as he peered at passers-by through the blinds. She noticed his fingers

- long and narrow, tapering at the ends, with almond-shaped nails. There was altogether something so very feminine about him - he was not at all her idea of the red-blooded Aussie male, in the Mel Gibson or Crocodile Dundee mode. And yet she found she couldn't help liking him - he was so easy to be with. There was nothing threatening or predatory about him - not like some of the lads she'd been out with, pocket macho men with loud voices and roaming clammy hands.

Their food arrived. She watched Tim pick up his cottage cheese roll, delicately bite off a corner, chew it thoroughly, and then take a sip of his orange juice. *He even eats like a girl,* she thought. She watched his moist pink lips moving as he ate.

'Anything wrong?' he asked.

'Oh - no - sorry, I was miles away,' replied Deborah, suddenly aware that she was staring at him.

'What part of Australia are you from?'

'Melbourne - my parents live in a suburb called Toorak.'

'What's it like?'

'Boring, a bit like Surrey.'

Deborah took a bite of her roll:

'Hmm, delicious. They always make the rolls fresh, rather than leaving them mouldering under cling-film for half the morning, like some places,' she said, easing a piece of escaping lettuce into the corner of her mouth with the end of her finger. 'So what brings you to England?'

'I'm having a few months off before I start my law degree.

'What university will you be going to?'

'Monash - it's a university in Melbourne; my grades weren't quite good enough to get me into Melbourne University itself.'

'I wonder if I should've done something like that,' said Deborah; 'I've got some A levels.'

'Why didn't you?'

'I wanted some money in my pocket. I didn't fancy trying to get by on a grant - it's such a pittance now.'

284

Deborah took another bite of her roll and then asked: 'So how do you come to be working at Siddall, Platt and Rosebury's?'

'I'm distantly related to Anthony Tobias Platt - one of the original partners and founders of the firm; I think he's my great, great uncle, or something like that. My grandfather started the Australian offshoot of the company in Sydney, and my father opened the Melbourne office - Platt and Featherstone, where I'm hoping to work when I'm qualified. I just wanted to see Europe and live a bit before I follow in the family tradition and become a fusty old solicitor like all my forebears. The plan is that I work here for three months as a sort of office boy - some experience in a prestigious London law firm can't do me any harm, even if I'm only making the tea and photocopying - and then I'm going to spend three or four months travelling around Europe, before I go back to Australia. Maybe I'll get one of those student rail cards, or perhaps I'll just hitch. I want to see France, Greece, Italy - visit the art galleries and cathedrals, the ancient ruins and great houses. Paris, Athens, Rome, Florence - they're just magical names to me at the moment. I want to see them with my own eyes.' Deborah noticed that Tim's eyes had gone unfocused, and his delicate nostrils were quivering, as if he could already see the sights and smell the fragrances of distant European cities.

Tim's plans sounded very exciting to Deborah. She thought of her own life - the tattily furnished flat in Bromley which she shared with another girl, the boring travel on sweaty, overcrowded trains every morning and evening, with all the other grey-faced commuters. Sometimes she looked at their tired, defeated faces, as they scuttled home to their rabbit hutches in suburbia. Had they once had dreams and ambitions - and how had they sunk to this? The army of the living dead - and she had joined them: she saw her life stretching before her, forever a secretary at Sidall, Pratt and Rosebury's - or perhaps one day she would rise to the dizzying heights of P.A. to one of the senior partners, an old maid with problem hair on her top lip like Miss Armitage, whom she saw sometimes in the lift. Or she would get married to some Gary or Darren who'd she'd meet in 'The Three Tuns' in Bromley High Street. They'd be a 'courting couple' for a while, to use the old-fashioned expression still used by her Mum - and then the inevitable pompous, meaningless wedding with the reception afterwards in some dreary cold church hall with loads of relatives nobody had seen for years. No doubt in time she would have screaming brats of her own, tiring her out for a few years before she went back to work as a middle-aged dogsbody for some supercilious young legal whizz-kid at Sidall, Pratt and Rosebury's, or some other similar firm.

'Why are you looking so sad?' asked Tim, reaching across to touch her hand, where it was resting next to her plate on the table. He left his fingers on the back of her hand for a few moments. His fingers were warm and soft - and somehow a comfort to her. The gesture had been almost like a caress.

'Oh, I was just thinking about how much more exciting your life sounds than mine,' replied Deborah, looking down at the remains of her roll, and pushing the plate aside without finishing it.

She drank up her cappuccino and looked across at Tim.

'A pretty girl like you ought to have plenty of exciting things happening to her,' he said.

Deborah laughed. 'You're good for me,' she said. 'Come on, we might as well get back to the office.'

That afternoon, Mr. Winton seemed to be more techy and tedious than ever, finding fault with everything that Deborah did. She was surprised therefore when he asked if she would accompany him, the following day, to a business lunch at Rumley's of Covent Garden, which had the reputation of being one of the swishest and most sophisticated establishments in the West End.

'I'm giving lunch to Mr. Michael Trusgrove, the heir apparent at Trusgrove Industries.

'They're going public with the company - full stock

market flotation - and we're in with a chance to handle all the legal side. I need someone along to make notes, if necessary - that's where you come in.'

Deborah felt like telling Mr. Winton where he could shove his business lunch, after the way he'd been treating her, but instead smiled politely and said she'd be pleased to come to the lunch.

'Make sure you wear one of your best frocks tomorrow,' said Mr. Winton, 'we want to make a good impression on Michael Trusgrove.'

Deborah nodded, thinking that Mr. Winton was beginning to sound like a pimp.

The next morning, Deborah looked at the meagre collection of clothes in her wardrobe, and decided against wearing a dress, choosing instead a smart emerald green two-piece suit which set off to advantage her auburn hair. She took more trouble than usual with her makeup and put on her best high heeled black leather court shoes, rather than the comfortable low-heeled casuals she usually wore to work.

'Wow, what's this? We're power dressing now, are we?' exclaimed her friend Melanie, when she entered the office. Deborah gave her a snooty look without bothering to reply, and sat down at her computer.

About mid-morning, Mr. Winton passed through on his way to a meeting and asked Deborah to order a taxi for 12:15, to take them to Rumley's. Mr. Winton added:

'Miss Davison booked the table a couple of days ago, but you could just ring Rumley's to confirm the reservation, and ask them to show Mr. Trusgrove to our table, if he arrives before us.'

Michael Trusgrove in fact arrived ten minutes late. A tall, rugged-looking man in his early thirties, he made quite an entrance, first asking a waiter in a loud voice where Mr. Winton's table was, then cutting a sway vigorously through the wood panelled, deep carpeted quiet of Rumley's dining room, shaking hands with Mr. Winton, and apologising rather over-effusively for his lateness, blaming it on the traffic and the problems of finding somewhere to park.

Once seated, Michael Trusgrove smiled and nodded at Deborah, then looked expectantly at Mr. Winton and said:

'I don't think I've been introduced to your lovely colleague?'

Mr. Winton replied:

'This is my assistant, Miss Carron.'

'And what would your first name be, Miss Carron?' asked Mr. Trusgrove.

'Deborah.'

Michael Trusgrove held her gaze for a few moments; Deborah found his eyes very penetrating and had to look down, straightening her linen napkin and praying that she wouldn't do her normal school-girl trick of blushing.

'About the flotation,' began Mr. Winton in his high-pitched voice, but before he could get any further the waiter arrived and gave them the menus. Deborah looked at the bewildering list of dishes, some of which were unknown to her.

Michael Trusgrove saw her indecision and said: 'The poached salmon is very good here.'

'I'll try that, then,' replied Deborah.

The waiter wrote down their orders: poached salmon for Deborah and Michael Trusgrove, venison for Mr. Winton. Mr. Winton ordered a bottle of Bordeaux to go with his venison, and Sancerre to go with the salmon. Michael Trusgrove lit a fat cigar without asking if anyone objected to his smoking.

Soon the two men were deep in conversation about the forthcoming stock market flotation of Trusgrove Industries. Although Deborah had brought a notebook in her handbag, Mr. Winton hadn't asked her to make any notes yet, so she was able to study Michael Trusgrove as she ate. He was powerfully built - broad shouldered and muscular - Deborah thought they he looked as if worked out regularly in a gym. His hands were strong-looking although his fingers were slim and tapering. His face was healthy looking but sensitive; he had a prominent nose and permanent smile lines around the outer corners of his eyes. His greying hair was brushed straight back from a broad brow, and cut in the same sort of style as Michael Douglas's in *Wall Street*. He exuded wealth and confidence.

There's no doubt about it, he's handsome all right, and he knows it. He looks just like an older, more distinguished Gordon Gekko, thought Deborah; *he could be a Michael Douglas lookalike.*

Deborah reflected on her lunch the previous day, with Tim. How different Michael Trusgrove was from Tim! Both males, but they hardly seemed to be the same species. Tim was little more than a boy - and a very girlish boy at that, with his ponytail and delicate features. He was like one of those precious young men with their exquisite, soulful faces who look out mournfully from pre-Raphaelite paintings. Michael Trusgrove, on the hand, was a great, rangy, animated wolf of a man - a Renaissance hero. Deborah imagined him in a portrait by Michelangelo: a naked, muscular colossus, his head thrust back, his strong throat full of laughter.

Michael was laughing his deep, fruity laugh at that moment - pretending to be amused at some facile quip made by Mr. Winton.

Mr. Winton seemed to become aware that he had rather let himself go - the effect of the wine, perhaps - and in an effort to slip quickly back into his normal, boring persona as the sober city lawyer, said:

'Well now, Michael, I shall needs these figures as soon as possible.'

'I know that, I meant to bring them; I'm pretty sure I've left the folder with the papers in it back at my flat - on the hall table. I say, couldn't Miss Carron come back with me and collect them now, then I could put her in a taxi back to your office, and you'd have the papers this afternoon.'

Mr. Winton looked as if he didn't approve of the idea, but Michael Trusgrove was an important client, and he could hardly admit that he wasn't sure about trusting him with one of the firm's young secretaries.

'I suppose it's a possibility,' said Mr. Winton doubtfully, looking at Deborah; 'I do want that file as soon as possible. Would that be all right with you, Deborah?'

Deborah realised that both men were looking at her intently.

'Er - yes,' she said, shrugging her shoulders, not knowing what else to say and feeling herself starting to blush.

'That's settled then,' said Michael Trusgrove.

Michael Trusgrove car proved to be a dark green Jaguar. Deborah settled into the soft leather upholstery while Michael eased the car out into the West End traffic. Soon they were threading their way through towards the City, and then out on the Docklands road. Deborah listened to the soft hum of the car's air conditioning until Michael put on a CD of Baroque chamber music. Michael made inconsequential conversation with her, asking her how long she'd been working at Sidall's, if she liked it, etc. At length they pulled into an underground car park and Michael edged the Jaguar into a numbered parking space, then got out and went round to her side of the car to open the door for her, before she could work out how the door opened from the inside.

They entered a lift and Michael pressed the button for the sixth floor. Michael's home was a huge riverside apartment, in a warehouse conversion development.

'Would you like to have a look at my view of the river,' he asked her.

'Yes please,' Deborah replied. He took her through a succession of white walled, high ceilinged rooms, some with deep pile carpets, others with wood block floors and oriental rugs; there were abstract paintings on some of the walls, mostly vivid splodges of colour or geometric patterns. He pointed to one painting, a runny mess of dripped and flicked colour, in which Deborah thought she could make out indistinct shapes, and announced proudly:

'That's a Jackson Pollock - it cost me an arm and a leg, but I think it was worth it, don't you?'

Deborah nodded, although she wanted to say that she couldn't understand what the painting was about - or what the point of it was. It looked to her like something a three year old had done and then a cat had walked over while it was still wet.

There was a magnificent view of the river from the balcony. Deborah rested her arms on the rail and watched a pleasure boat and a couple of barges pass by. The sun came out at that moment, making the surface of the water flash in a million ripples. Deborah shivered; it was still only April and a cold breeze was blowing up the river.

Michael came out behind her and placed a camel hair coat over her shoulders:

'Wear this,' he said, 'that little jacket of yours won't keep you warm out here.'

She turned round to thank him, and found that she was looking straight up into his penetrating eyes. Before she knew what was happening, he had bent his face down close to hers and placed a kiss full on her lips. The next moment he had moved away from her and was saying, as if nothing had happened:

'Can I get you a drink or a coffee before you go?'

'No, I - I think I'd better be going; Mr. Winton will be expecting me back with the folder.'

'I'll have to phone for a taxi - it's difficult to hail one around here, without walking about a mile back to the main road. You might as well have something to drink while you're waiting.'

'Perhaps a coffee then, if it's not too much trouble.' Deborah was feeling as if she'd had too much Sancerre to drink at lunchtime. They went back into the apartment and she slipped off the camel hair coat and gave it back to him, then sat down on a low cream leather sofa while Michael went into the kitchen to make the coffee. Almost immediately he returned and asked:

'Would you like a liqueur with the coffee? Cointreau or Tia Mia maybe - or I've got a good Napoleon brandy, or Southern Comfort?'

Deborah thought for a couple of seconds, knowing that

of course she should refuse a liqueur - and then her desire to live a bit got the better of her:

'Yes please - I'd like a Southern Comfort.'

'Good girl, I'll join you. Ice?'

'Please,' Deborah nodded. What on earth was she doing? Having a liqueur in the middle of the afternoon in a rich man's penthouse flat. Was this really her? Sensible Debbie? Maybe not so sensible. 'I don't care,' she thought, 'what's the worse that can happen?'

Michael came back with two large glasses of ice balls and poured a liberal measure of Southern Comfort over the ice into each glass. He gave Deborah her drink and rested his down on a low marble-topped table while he went over to switch on an impressive stack of hi fi equipment.

'John Coltraine,' he said, as a soft saxophone riff oozed out of the speakers.

'This is it,' thought Deborah, 'make your mind up time.' Michael had picked up his drink and was coming over towards the sofa, obviously with the intention of sitting down next to her. Deborah eased herself off the sofa and said:

'I must just go to the bathroom.' Michael raised his eyebrows slightly and replied:

'It's through there, second door on the left.'

Deborah locked the door of the bathroom, took down her panties and tights, and sat on the varnished wood of the toilet seat, looking around at the gold plated taps and circular bath tub as she took a pee. Wiping herself, she stood up, reached down to her bag and took out a small tube of spermicidal cream and the white plastic container in which she kept her diaphragm. Squeezing some cream around its edges, she pinched the rubber together in her fingers and deftly inserted the cap up between her legs, then washed her hands.

In the living room, Michael was lounging back on the sofa, drink in hand.

'Come and sit down here,' he said, patting the place next to him.

Deborah picked up her drink and said to Michael:

'What about the papers for Mr. Winton? He'll be wondering where I've got to.'

'Oh don't worry about that. Let's say I couldn't find them - they weren't here after all, so I had to drive back up to my office in town and get another set printed out. You came with me to get the new papers, and then I dropped you back at you office. I will actually drive you back to your office, so it's partly true.' Michael looked at her mischievously as he said this. Deborah smiled, nodded, and sat down next to Michael on the sofa. They sipped their drinks and listened to Coltrane's saxophone - soft, sweet, silky notes rising and falling. Deborah closed her eyes and drifted with the music, thinking of smoky night clubs, cool dudes in white tuxedos and slinky ladies playing the oldest game in town.

She felt Michael nestling in close to her, touching her leg, moving his hand gently across her thigh. She turned towards him, opening her eyes and seeing his face coming nearer, then closing her eyes again and feeling him kissing her ear, her cheek - finding her lips. They gently undressed each other, caressing and kissing each other's bodies - and soon she was melting into him, until at last she felt him deep inside her.

Deborah stood in the stuffy carriage of the train on her homeward journey to Bromley that night, looking at the deadened faces of the commuters, swaying and lurching with them as the train stopped and started, but feeling she was no longer one of them; her life was now beginning to move to a different rhythm. She held on to the memory of her afternoon, glowing with her secret, wanting to shout it out to the bored faces around her, but almost afraid that it was all a dream.

When Deborah got home to her flat, she couldn't help telling Suzy, her flat mate, what had happened. Suzy was a nurse at Bromley Hospital. She prided herself on being down to earth, liking to call a spade a spade, etc. - 'It's emptying all those bed pans that make me like it, I suppose,' Suzy would say, as an excuse for her directness.

Deborah explained to Suzy how she'd met Michael Trusgrove, and what she'd had for lunch, and what a dreamy hunk of a man he was, and how he lived in a penthouse riverside flat and was so rich that he'd got a Jackson Pollock -

'A what?' asked Suzy brightly.

'A Jackson Pollock.'

'Is that something anatomical? It sounds disgusting.'

'No, on the wall.'

'What, just nailed there?'

'Jackson Pollock is an artist.'

'Oh. So he showed you his Jackson Pollock - and then what?'

Deborah was silent.

Suzy raised her eyebrows questioningly:

'Debbie, you didn't?'

Deborah nodded. 'We did.'

'You tramp!' shrieked Suzy. What if you get pregnant?'

'I had my cap.'

'Oh, you just happened to have it with you?'

'It was in my best handbag - you know, the black leather one that matches my heels I got from Saxone's. It was still in there from the last time I went out with Peter - the night we went to the NFT to see some crappy German film he was raving about, and I knew I was going back to his place afterwards to spend the night because it ended too late for me to get the last train to Bromley. But as things worked out, I didn't need it - that was the night we had the row and broke up. I got a taxi home.'

'All right, don't go on about it any more,' said Suzy; 'so you're not a tart and it was just luck that you had your cap in your bag. Not that there's anything wrong with being prepared; I always carry a condom in my bag, just in case.'

Deborah looked at Suzy, thinking of how she chose to dress when she wasn't in her prim nurse's uniform - she generally favoured skirts that were decidedly on the short side, liking to show off her legs; and tops that were usually a little too tight, accentuating her prominent breasts. Suzy was blonde, blousy and bimboesque - and that still seemed to be the type that a lot of men went for, if you could believe what she told you: Suzy was inclined to boast of her many conquests. But Deborah got on well enough with her - you could have worse flat mates.

Michael Trusgrove had asked for Deborah's home telephone number, and early Thursday evening called to ask if she would like to drive down to Kent with him at the weekend; he explained that he was looking at a few sites near the Channel Tunnel terminus where Trusgrove Industries might be able to locate a new warehouse complex to take advantage of the tunnel. Afterwards, they could go on to Canterbury and stay at a very pleasant hotel he knew of.

'Sounds like a dirty weekend, to me,' commented Suzy, when she heard about it.

'Well I'm going, anyway,' replied Deborah, thinking that it was not the sort of thing that Suzy would turn down, if she got the offer.

Michael had said that he'd stop off at her flat to pick her up, and to expect him about ten o'clock on Saturday morning. In fact he arrived a few minutes early and Deborah was not quite ready.

'I'm just finishing off my makeup,' she called through to Suzy, 'can you let Michael in for me and tell him I won't be long.'

When Deborah came through, Suzy was making coffee for Michael and they seemed to be getting on very well together. Suzy was still in her nightie and dressing gown, which was not quite done up enough, so that she was showing a lot of cleavage. Deborah was used to Suzy's mild flirtations with any males she brought home, and thought nothing more of it.

Deborah enjoyed the weekend in Kent with Michael. As they toured round, he chatted to her about some of the factories and businesses run by Trusgrove Industries - they were mainly concerned with the manufacturing of toys and plastics but were thinking of expanding into plastic recycling, importing some of the used plastic from Europe. It was clear from what Michael said that as a member of the family which owned the private companies and the obvious choice as new chief executive of the group, he personally stood to make a great deal of money from the stock market flotation, if it went through successfully. Deborah was impressed.

The hotel in Canterbury was a sumptuous timber-framed Tudor coaching inn. Michael had tactfully booked adjoining rooms, proving that he didn't take anything for granted. His room, the larger of the two, contained a beautiful four-poster bed; as soon as she saw it Deborah knew she was fated to wake up between its crisp cotton sheets on Sunday morning.

Michael was very attentive and considerate to her all weekend. In the window of an old fashioned jewellers in Canterbury she saw a delicate silver pendant, worked to look like the tracery of a medieval church window. She wondered whether the pattern was based on one of the windows in the cathedral. Michael saw how much she liked it, and despite her protestations insisted on buying it for her.

It was rather a come-down to find herself, on Monday morning, back at the photocopier, clutching some papers which Mr. Winton had asked her to copy urgently (everything was always urgent for Mr. Winton), the morning stretching before her endlessly in the usual round of routine work, without any interesting features in prospect.

Tim was ahead of her again at the photocopier, and turned round to say hello.

'Fancy a bite at San Remo's, this dinner time?' he asked.

'Why not?' she replied.

Lunchtime eventually arrived, and as before, she met Tim at the lift and they walked to the restaurant together. How different Tim was from Michael! A mere boy; his face was so smooth, it looked as if he hardly needed to shave. And yet there was something attractive about him. He was easy to talk to, almost like another girl.

When Tim asked her over lunch if she would like to go to the cinema with him after work, to see the latest American blockbuster, she couldn't see any reason why not. She hadn't arranged to do anything with Michael that evening, though she hoped he would phone later in the week. Anyway, Tim was just a friend; there was nothing between them.

After the film, Tim suggested that they get something to eat at one of the Chinese restaurants in Soho:

'I've heard there's one that does really good savoury dumplings. In Australia you can get them frozen in packets - Dim Sims they're called; of course they're not as good as the freshly made ones.'

Deborah enjoyed the dumplings, and found that she was liking Tim's company more and more; she put her arm through his as they walked back towards Charing Cross station. It was a warm, fragrant spring evening; a few wisps of cloud scudded across an otherwise clear sky, in which there was a three-quarter full moon and a tracery of stars.

They arrived at Charing Cross station, and Tim dropped a pound coin into the hand of an old homeless woman who was hunched on one of the benches.

'Why did you do that?' asked Deborah. 'It only encourages them, and then they pester people all the more.' Tim shrugged his shoulders, unable to think of an adequate response.

'Just an impulse,' he replied.

At the barrier, Tim said goodnight and kissed her on the cheek, his lips lingering for a moment. Deborah turned to look at him, surprised. Perhaps their friendship was turning into something more than platonic. She squeezed his hand and said:

'You're a kind boy, Tim. Goodnight.'

The fine early spring was followed by a drab May, day after day of dull, cloud covered skies with the sun hardly ever breaking through, and little rain to clear the air and settle the dust. London was a foetid, sticky prison, from which Deborah longed to escape. The heating system in the office was malfunctioning, so that sometimes it was much too hot and the girls' faces were soon all gleaming with perspiration, sending them scuttling into the toilets to take the shine off their noses with face powder; and then the next day there would be no heat at all, and they would all be freezing and putting on layers of cardigans to keep warm. Outside, the traffic fumes in the still air seemed worse than ever; Deborah choked, walking round the shops in her lunch hour, but could not face the prospect of returning early to her boiling hot or icy cold office. Occasionally her routine was alleviated by having lunch with Tim. She couldn't quite work him out, but he was interesting to be with - original in his views - different from most of the young men who worked in the office or whom she'd known socially in the past.

It was even harder to fathom what was going on with Michael. How serious was their relationship? During the last few weeks he'd taken her out to dinner several times, and also they'd been to the opera at Covent Garden - Michael was a great Mozart buff, and had insisted on taking her to see *The Magic Flute*, which was one of his favourite operas.

The weather finally broke at the end of May, with two days of torrential rain. On the Friday, Deborah had forgotten her umbrella, and got soaked at the start of her journey home, walking to the underground station. When she reached London Bridge, she found that her connecting train had been cancelled and she would have to wait three-quarters of an hour for the next one. When Deborah finally arrived home at the flat in Bromley, she found at least that Suzy had already cooked the tea:

'On the table in five minutes, if you're ready for it,' said Suzy.

'I'm certainly ready for it,' replied Deborah, recounting some of the low points of her day.

'Do you fancy going out somewhere different then,

this evening - cheer yourself up?' asked Suzy.

'Has Michael phoned at all?'

'No.'

Deborah looked fed up. She watched Suzy busily tucking into her chilli con carne for a moment, and then said to her:

'Where were you thinking of going?'

'It's a club a couple of streets away from Leicester Square; we could dress up a bit wacky, really go over the top - apparently everybody does who goes there, even the blokes. On the last Friday of the month, which is tonight, they have a special party there - a 'drag' night. Everybody dresses up for it.'

'Whose "everybody"?'

'It's supposed to be a really good mix; quite a few straight couples, some gay and lesbian couples, and people on their own, of every imaginable gender and sexual orientation. You see these really outrageous drag queens - some of the costumes are sensational.'

'It sounds a bit wild,' said Deborah doubtfully, 'how do you know so much about it?'

'Gloria's raved on about it to me at work. He's one of the male nurses; he's *very* gay - well and truly out of the closet, and doesn't give a damn what anybody thinks. His name is Dave, actually, but everyone calls him Gloria, even at work, and he loves it - he really enjoys camping it up. He's a good nurse, one of the best, and he's a good friend at work. He's been on at me to go to this club for some time - so why don't we give it a try?'

Deborah looked doubtful.

'How are we going to get back? I don't fancy walking around the streets of London at two or three in the morning trying to find a taxi.'

'The taxis are usually lined up outside, but you don't need to worry, Gloria said he'd run us home if we came - he only lives in Beckenham, so it's not far out of his way.'

Deborah got changed into what she thought of as

her *night-club gear* - a glittery top, her highest heels and shortest skirt - and did her makeup, putting on a bit more lippy than usual. When she came out of the bathroom she looked at Suzy's peach coloured lurex leotard, black fishnet tights, impossibly high stiletto-heeled shoes and lime green feather boa, and exclaimed:

'You can't go on the train dressed like that!'

'Why not?'

'You'll get arrested.'

'Nonsense. This is nothing. Some of the men dress much more outrageously - just wait and see.'

The Pink Seahorse Club was in a dilapidated three story red-brick building in a side street somewhere between Leicester Square and Covent Garden; it was fortunate that Suzy seemed to know where she was going, as Deborah doubted whether she would ever have found the street on her own. There was a queue of perhaps thirty weird-looking people, mostly of indeterminate gender, waiting to get in; two huge Afro-Caribbean drag queens were on the door, and their policy seemed to be to let in people in fancy dress, the more camp and outré the better, but to turn away anyone who looked too straight. While Deborah and Suzy waited in the queue, they tried to guess the gender of some of the individuals ahead of them, a game which proved even more problematic once they were in the club. The club's clientele was certainly colourful - some favoured a frenzy of frills, feathers, furbelows and frou-frou petticoats, while others had draped themselves languidly in lace, lycra, lurex or leather.

There were a few dykes with short, slicked-back hair, in three-piece suits or even white tie and tails; but the vast majority of the punters were 'girls' of one sort or another - drag queens, transvestites, transsexuals - and some of the real thing, though it was very difficult to tell who was what until you heard them speak.

Hearing anyone speak was in itself a major undertaking, as the dance music was thumping out at deafening volume from every corner, so that it was necessary to shout at the top of your voice to make yourself understood.

The club extended to all three floors, with a broad marble flight of stairs like something out of a Hollywood musical joining the ground floor to the first floor, and cast iron spiral staircases extending up from here to the floor above. There were balconies and walkways from which spectators could watch the action on one or other of the dance floors, and bars scattered throughout the premises to keep everyone well lubricated. The second floor had a quieter bar with a large video screen at one end, on which erotic movies were showing.

'Come on, let's get a drink,' said Suzy, 'what do you want?'

'I'll just have a diet Coke,' said Deborah; 'I bet the prices in this place are astronomical.'

'I don't care,' replied Suzy, 'I've worked up quite a thirst so I'm having a pint of lager. Are you sure you don't want something alcoholic?'

Deborah thought for a moment and said: 'Well I wouldn't mind a Southern Comfort; I'm getting rather a taste for it, but it'll cost an arm and a leg here. Let me give you something towards it.' She took a five pound note out of her purse and held it out towards Suzy, but a slim woman with long dark hair who was standing next to them at the bar waved Deborah's money away and said:

'I'll get you this one, seeing as I reckon this must be your first time here.'

Deborah noticed that she had an Australian accent, and turned to look at her.

She was wearing a black bustier which had no visible means of support and was held up only by her very obvious bust; a black leather miniskirt which showed off her long slender legs; and very high black stiletto boots which laced up at the back.

Deborah looked at her face - she was immaculately made up, and had not yielded to the temptation to go over the top, like most of the people in the club. She became aware that Deborah was staring at her, and turning round to face her, smiled and made eye contact. Deborah gasped.

'Tim? I don't believe it!'

The brunette nodded, still smiling.

'But you make such a convincing girl - I'd never have guessed.' Deborah thought about how Tim had seemed to her the first time they met, recalling now that she had noticed there was something very feminine about it him. Perhaps she should have guessed.

'Have you done this sort of thing before?'

'Quite a few times.'

'So you enjoy dressing as a girl?'

'Yes, I'd hardly do it otherwise, would I? Don't you enjoy dressing as a girl?'

Well yes, but *I am* a girl.'

'That's your excuse.' Deborah though about this for a moment, and then started again:

'I mean, are you - do you -'

'Yes, I am a trannie - a transvestite; although I prefer the term trangendered, and no, I haven't changed sex yet.'

Deborah was staring fixedly at her cleavage.

'But you've got -'

'Boobs?'

'Yes.'

'Hormones; I've been on them for over a year.'

'And your hair? You were a blonde before?'

'Dyed it - fancied a change.'

'How long have been doing this?'

'Well I've had the urge all my life, from the age of about four, but it's only since I've been over in England that I've come out as transgendered, although I started on the hormones while I was still in Melbourne - went to a private clinic there.'

'Look, I don't like to interrupt,' said Suzy, her tongue hanging out, 'but we still haven't got a drink.'

'Sorry, my fault,' said Tim, holding up a twenty pound note between his fingers, to signal to the barmaid (a winsome youth in a French maid's outfit) that they were waiting to be served. Deborah was staring at Tim's long

302

red fingernails, thinking that he seemed to be able to grow much better nails than she could.

'This is a friend of mine from work -' Deborah began saying to Suzy, wondering how she was going to end the sentence; it didn't seem right to introduce this feminine creature as 'Tim'.

'When I'm dressed like this, my name's Tamsin, or Tammy, if you prefer,' said Tim.

'Cheers, Tammy,' said Suzy, picking up her pint of lager from the counter. 'I think I'm going to fight my way downstairs and see if I can find Gloria; she's probably having a bop.' Suzy took a slurp of her drink and began to thread her way towards the top of the spiral staircase.

'Who's Gloria?' asked Tammy.

'Oh a friend of Suzy's. He's a *he* as well, actually. You were saying that you've only been doing this publically since you've been over here; don't they have TV's in Australia?'

'Oh yes, otherwise how would we watch *Neighbours*?'

'Very funny.'

No, actually there's quite a big trannie scene in Oz - Sydney's absolutely rife with it. But I couldn't very well get involved in the scene while I was still living at home, so I went to the clinic without my family knowing.'

'Your family don't know?'

'Not yet, though I guess they're going to find out eventually, when I get back to Australia. No one at work knows either. I'd be glad if we could keep it that way.'

'Fine.'

'Look, do you fancy getting away from here? It's so crowded and noisy it's hard to talk.'

'Okay, but I'll have to find Suzy first: I'm supposed to be getting a lift home with her and Gloria.'

'We could maybe find somewhere for a quiet drink.'

Deborah looked at her watch, and said:

'The last train's goes in twenty minutes - it doesn't give us long for a drink. If I miss that we'll have to come back here, so I can still get a lift with Gloria - or I suppose I could get a taxi, except the fare will be colossal back to

303

Bromley, unless I can share the ride.'

'You're welcome to kip down at my place; it's Saturday tomorrow anyway, so no worries, as we say in Oz. I've got a flat in Earl's Court.'

'Kangaroo Valley eh - you're a real cliché Aussie in some ways.'

'Yeah, well it was all I could get at the time - a friend found it for me. It's not much, but you can have the bed and I'll doss down on the floor. I've just bought a new sleeping bag and air mat for my trip round Europe.'

'I wouldn't dream of putting you out of your bed,' replied Deborah; 'If I agree to come back, I'll take the floor.'

'Well, we'll sort it out later.'

'When are you off to Europe, by the way?'

'Just two weeks to go - the middle of June.'

'I wish I was going too.'

'Why don't you come along?'

'What about my job?'

'Stuff it. Come round Europe with me; I could do with a travelling companion. And then you could come back to Oz - I could get you a job with my father's law firm in Melbourne; they're always on the lookout for good secretaries. You've got A levels, so you could probably do a part-time law degree as well, if you fancied it - pay your own way through - or I dare say the firm would sponsor you.'

'You've got it all worked out for me, haven't you? Don't you need a visa and a work permit?'

'Yeah, but that can be sorted out if you've got a job to go to.'

Deborah sighed, thinking about what a new life in Australia might be like. Then with a pang she remembered Michael Trusgrove. What did the pang mean? What did she feel for him? He'd certainly been very kind, and he was rich. Quite a catch, her Mum would say, certainly not the Gary or Darren they'd expect her to end up with. But did she love him? She wasn't sure; it was too early to say. Perhaps she'd grow to love him?

At that moment, a drunken drag queen, her blonde wig slightly askew, lurched into them, spattering Guinness on Tamsin's black leather skirt and on Deborah's glittery lycra top. Fortunately it beaded off the black shiny leather of Tamsin's skirt without marking it, but Deborah's top had begun to discolour where the stout was soaking into it.

'Come on Debbie,' said Tammy, 'let's try and sponge that off, and then we'll get out of here.' Tamsin took Deborah's hand and led her off in the direction of the ladies.

They sponged the sticky fabric of Deborah's lycra top with tissues at one of the sinks in the ladies. Deborah felt her nipples swell beneath the wet, flimsy material as Tammy rubbed gently at the beer stain; it was an unsettlingly erotic experience. *What is happening to me,* she thought; *am I turning into a lesbian? But then - Tamsin is really a boy. How confusing!*

They found Suzy and told her where they were going, and extricated themselves from The Pink Seahorse Club. Most of the pubs in the immediate vicinity were already shutting up. They considered trying another club, but as both of them were wearing high heels, decided against further crippling themselves by wandering around the streets on what would probably be a wild goose chase.

'Why don't we just go back to my place and have a quiet drink,' suggested Tamsin.

'Sounds okay to me,' replied Deborah.

They hailed a passing taxi and Tamsin gave the address in Earl's Court to the driver. Deborah raised her eyebrows and grinned at the way Tamsin had managed to make her voice sound softer and more feminine when speaking to the driver:

'How did you manage to do that?'

'I've been practising.'

'Incredible - I'd have no qualms at all about going out again with you as Tammy; you're really convincing as a girl.'

'Thank you; so are you.'

'Cheeky bitch!' Deborah cuddled up to Tamsin, and

then moved away from her when she noticed the driver goggling at them in the rear view mirror.

'He thinks we're dykes!'

'So what? Give him something to tell his mates.' Tamsin put her arm round Deborah's shoulder and said in a gruff voice: "'I had these couple a lesbians in the back of me cab last night, gorgeous lookers they were, too. What a waste."'

'God, you can do cockney taxi drivers as well - you *are* a talented girl.'

Tamsin's flat was small but comfortably finished. A record sleeve was pinned up on the back of the door - Transformer. Deborah got up to have a closer look.

'It's an old Lou Reed album from the early Seventies,' said Tamsin, handing her a bottle of very cold lager. 'I managed to get it in a second hand record shop off Charing Cross Road; I thought it was quite a find, then I found out you can still buy the album new, over here. It's unavailable in Australia. Do you want to hear it?'

'Why not?'

Tamsin put on the record. They talked for a while, and then Tamsin said:

'Listen to this next track - it's called *Walk on the Wildside*.

Deborah listened to the slow bass chords of the intro, and then Lou Reed's seductive New York drawl coming in:

"Holly came from Miami, FLA,
Hitchhiked her way across U.S.A.,
Plucked her eyebrows on the way,
Shaved her legs, and then he was a she,
She says, "Hey babe, take a walk on the wildside..."

When the track had finished, Deborah said:

'I've heard it before - I never listened to the lyrics though; I wonder how many people know what the song's about. I just love Lou Reed's voice; there's something

306

really decadent about it.'

After they'd finished their bottles of lager, Tamsin got out the sleeping bag and air mat, insisting that Deborah took the bed. She argued half-heartedly, then yawned and agreed, saying:

'You're a gentleman - I mean - a lady!'

Tamsin smiled, gave her a hug and a kiss, said, 'Goodnight.'

Deborah had felt Tamsin's breasts pressing against her own when they hugged; she felt confused.

Deborah curled up in Tamsin's bed, but found she couldn't drift off to sleep. She felt too excited, too aroused - thinking about Tamsin, the lovely boy-girl sleeping on the floor. She got up and tip-toed softly over to Tamsin, then shook her gently and said, 'Come into bed with me.'

'You sure?'

'I need you so much.'

Tamsin eased herself out of the sleeping bag and lay down in the bed beside Deborah; she gently kissed and carressed her, and they made love.

Deborah slept soundly until quite late on Sunday morning; when she eventually came to, Tamsin was standing over her with a steaming mug of tea:

'Thought you might need this.'

'Thanks - Tammy. That's just what I need.'

Tamsin brought her own tea over, sat down on the end of the bed and said:

'Look, why don't you stay for lunch? I'll cook you up one of my special vegetable pies.'

Deborah wondered whether Michael had been trying to contact her, then thought, *Oh blow him, he's not phoned all week*, nodded her head and said to Tamsin:

'That sounds nice. Need any help?'

'No, everything's in hand. I was hoping you'd say yes, so it's all ready to go in the oven.'

Tamsin's pie proved delicious.

'God, I can't move,' said Deborah; 'we just had to finish it up, didn't we? It was so scrumptious. Where did you learn to cook like that?'

'If you're a vegetarian, you either find out a hundred ways to cook vegetables, or you starve. My family back home all love their T-bone steaks and barbied chops.'

By the time Deborah got back to her flat in Bromley, it was already late in the afternoon. Suzy was home, sitting at the pine table in the kitchen with the Sunday paper spread out before her. She looked up as Deborah came in and said:

'Hi. Michael dropped in just before lunchtime, on the off chance of seeing you. Thought you might fancy a run out in the country for a pub lunch. Said he'd tried to phone last night but no one answered.'

'Did you say where I was?'

'I told him you were staying with a girl friend in town.'

'Thanks.'

'You seem to get on very well with Tammy.

'Yes I like her - him.'

'Confusing isn't it? I never know whether to refer to Gloria as a him or a her.'

'Is Tammy gay?'

'No - he's Tim by the way, when he's not Tammy. He's transgendered, but he definitely fancies girls. He was saying last night that most transvestites and cross-dressers are straight.'

'Weird. Personally, I prefer a real man like Michael, any day. He's rather a dish, isn't he?'

'Yes, if you like that type.'

'Don't you, then?'

'I don't know - I suppose so. What did Michael do when he found I wasn't here - go off again?'

Suzy looked suddenly rather furtive.

'Er - yes, that's right; he just shot off - said he'd give you a call next week sometime.' Suzy started turning the pages of the paper.

'I think I'll go and have a shower,' said Deborah.

Michael hadn't called by the following Wednesday. Deborah was at home on her own that evening; Suzy had said she was on a late shift at the hospital, and wouldn't be in until after eleven. Deborah decided to telephone Michael's flat. A woman's voice answered and said 'You must have the wrong number,' when Deborah asked for Michael. The voice sounded vaguely familiar, but the woman had hung up before Deborah could get her to say anything else. When she tried the second time, the telephone rang four times and then the answering machine switched on. Deborah left a brief message, saying she was sorry she had missed Michael on Sunday.

The heating continued to play up at the office, despite the efforts of the contractors to fix it. By Friday lunchtime, Deborah had a splitting headache and a dry throat. She had been feeling overheated one moment, and shivering with cold the next, but noticed that these changes in her temperature were no longer corresponding with the vagaries of the heating system. Perhaps she was getting a chill - or worse - going down with 'flu. The figures and words on her VDU screen seemed to be jumping and blurring before her eyes. She sighed, turned off the machine, and went to tell Mr. Winton that she wasn't feeling very well.

'You'd better get yourself off home then,' said Mr. Winton, looking at her over his spectacles with some concern.

Deborah was just thinking, 'Perhaps he's not so bad after all,' when Mr. Winton added:

'Oh Deborah, could you just photocopy these before you go?'

She still managed to get home a couple of hours before the start of the afternoon rush hour, which always seemed to be worse on a Friday. When she came in the door of the flat she took her coat off and went to hang it up; Suzy's furry jacket was already hanging on one of the hooks in the hall. Suzy wasn't in the kitchen so she went through into her bedroom, saying to her:

Hi, Su - are in you in here? I'm not feeling too good so I've come home early -'

Suzy was sitting up in bed, clutching the bedclothes to

cover up her naked breasts. Next to her in the bed was - Michael.

Deborah gawped at them in disbelief, then turned round and swept out of the room, without saying a word. She put her coat back on, grabbed her bag and hurried out of the flat, without any idea where she was going. She knew now who had answered the phone on Wednesday night, when she had called Michael's flat.

After walking around Bromley on autopilot for a while, Deborah found that she'd ended up back at the train station. She got on the first train to London, then got the tube to Earls Court. When Tim - or rather Tamsin - arrived home, she was sitting on the steps outside the front door of her flat:

'Hello lover,' Tamsin said to her gently, 'what are you doing here? Want to come inside?'

Deborah nodded, unable to speak. Her face had a white, pinched look about it. She felt as if there were snakes knotting themselves inside her.

When they were in the flat, she dropped on the bed and burst into tears.

'Come on, tell me all about it,' said Tammy, gathering her up and holding her tight. Gradually the sobs subsided, and Tammy gave her a tissue to wipe her eyes.

'I must look a terrible sight; I'm not feeling my best anyway. I'm sorry to inflict myself on you like this - I couldn't think of anywhere else to go. You look fantastic, by the way.'

Tamsin was wearing a short black leather mini-skirt which laced up at the side and a tight black leather bodice; her mauve eye-lids and purple lipstick gave her a goth, punky look that suited her.

'Sorry if I look like one of the living dead,' said Tamsin.

'Well that's hardly appropriate for someone who works at Siddall, Platt and Rosebury's. Your cleavage looks amazing, and I love the way the leather bodice accentuates your waist. You have a figure to die for, Tammy. And I'm glad you've reverted to sandy-blonde hair colour - it suits you better than brunette. But how did you get away with that outfit at work? '

'I haven't come straight from work; I had the afternoon off and went up to the East End to a tranny and fetish club I know.'

'You ought to go to the office like that, then you'd fit in better with all the other bloodsucking vampires there.'

'Do you reckon all the City types bloodsucking vampires?'

'Is the pope a Catholic?'

Deborah explained what had happened. Tamsin listened, frowning and shaking her head, and then gave her another hug and said:

'Well you can't go back there tonight, that's for sure. You can stay here.'

'Thanks Tammy, what a good job I've got you. I couldn't believe my eyes - I thought Suzy was my friend.'

'Some friend.'

'Yes, but it's her flat - I don't see how I can go on living there now, and I can't face going back to live with my parents. What am I going to do?'

Tamsin replied promptly:

'Go round Europe with me, and then come to Australia.'

'I'm not sure I want to be a secretary all my life, even in Australia.'

'You wouldn't have to be - you could study law part-time - and anyway, we'd be married.'

'Tim - Tammy, is this a proposal?'

'You bet.'

'Oh Tammy! You're serious aren't you?'

'Of course, if you'll have me. But the side of me you saw the other night, and how I am now - well that's part of me. I really am transgendered, Debbie; it's the way I am and always will be. I'll try and make you happy, but I can't change that about myself, and I can't promise that I won't take things further, in the future. I might want to live as a woman full-time. What would you think of that?'

' I enjoyed Tammy's company the other night.   I'd like to see her again.'

'You mean it?'

'Yes, and I don't mind if you want to be Tammy all the time.'

Tamsin hugged Deborah tightly, in relief and gratitude, and they kissed and made love.

*   *   *

Deborah gave in her notice to Mr. Winton first thing on Monday morning:

'This is very sudden, Debbie; we'll be sorry to lose you. What are you going to do?'

'I'm going to travel round Europe, and then I'm planning on going to Australia.'

'On your own?'

'No, with - a friend of mine.'

'Another girl, you mean?'

Deborah paused, then grinned and nodded.

'Something amusing?'

Deborah shook her head innocently and said:

'Just a private joke.'

Mr. Winton looked puzzled, and then commented:

It's a strange coincidence, but we have a young man in the department whose just off to do something similar to what you're planning. Tim Platt, his name is. Perhaps you'll bump into him on your travels.'

'Perhaps I will,' replied Deborah, 'you never know.'

© *2009 Kate Lesley*

THE END

Afterword

These stories were first published in illustrated serial form by FFG (Fantasy Fiction Group) in the following transgender fiction magazines:

Tales of Crossdressing Vols. 1- 8 & Vol. 10
ISSN 1353-6656

Tales of Sissy School Vols. 1 & 2
ISSN 1353-6656

Forced Femme & Girlhood Vol. 1
ISSN 1353-6656

Websites

FFG Transgender Fiction Magazines Download Website http://www.tgfiction.co.uk/
(All the above magazines are available in digital format from this website)

FFG Transgender Fiction Printed Magazines Website - http://www.tvfiction.com/
Most of the original printed editions are also still available from this website)

Follow FFG Transgender Fiction, Kate Lesley and Amber Goth on these websites:

Twitter:

FFG Tranny Fiction on Twitter - http://twitter.com/#!/trannyfiction

Amber Goth on Twitter -
http://twitter.com/#!/ambergoth

Facebook:
Transgender Fiction Facebook Site -
http://www.facebook.com/pages/FFG-Transgender-Fiction/148632725157529?ref=ts

Transgender Fiction Facebook Group -
http://www.facebook.com/mobile/?settings#!/home.php?sk=group_157755277597309

Ambergoth on Facebook -
http://www.facebook.com/ambergoth

Amber Goth on YouTube -
http://www.youtube.com/user/ambergoth -

Amber Goth's Forced Femme TG Captions -
http://amber-goth.blogspot.com/

Amber Goth's WordPress Blog -
http://ambergoth.wordpress.com/

About the Author

Kate Lesley is a writer, publisher, web designer and teacher who knew she was transgendered from the age of four. Kate never regarded it as a problem, but rather as a blessing. Married to an accepting wife who prefers her feminine side, she is the father of two children and she recently became a grandma.

Kate is the founder, editor and publisher of FFG Transgender Fiction (TGFiction.co.uk).

She started writing transgender stories in 1992, and in 1994 brought out the first edition of 'Tales of Crossdressing', which now runs to ten volumes.
Kate has also edited and written stories for 'Tales of the Maid', 'Tales of Sissy School' and 'Forced Femme and Girlhood'.

All the stories in 'How Stephen became Stephanie' were originally published in illustrated versions in these magazines between 1994 – 2009.

Kate's earliest stories appeared in 'The Beaumont Magazine' and 'Cross-Talk'.

Kate gets over to Manchester's Gay Village as often as she can, where she likes hanging out in bars; in fine weather, she enjoys sitting out on Canal Street and watching the incredible spectacle of humankind passing by in an infinite variety of sexualities and genders.

Made in the USA
Charleston, SC
09 June 2012